FUTURE GAMES

Other Books Edited by Paula Guran

Embraces
Best New Paranormal Romance
Best New Romantic Fantasy
Zombies: The Recent Dead
The Year's Best Dark Fantasy & Horror: 2010
Vampires: The Recent Undead
The Year's Best Dark Fantasy & Horror: 2011
Halloween
New Cthulhu: The Recent Weird
Brave New Love
Witches: Wicked, Wild & Wonderful
Obsession: Tales of Irresistible Desire
The Year's Best Dark Fantasy & Horror: 2012
Extreme Zombies
Ghosts: Recent Hauntings
Rock On: The Greatest Hits of Science Fiction & Fantasy
Season of Wonder

FUTURE GAMES

Edited by Paula Guran

PRIME BOOKS

Cover design by Michael King.

Prime Books
www.prime-books.com

For more information, contact Prime Books:
prime@prime-books.com

ISBN: 978-1-60701-381-5

To Andrew:
A true fan (Go Tribe!)
& determined competitor.

Contents

Preface

Paula Guran

Sports and games are an integral part of (as far as I know) every human culture. Our participation reaches back to the beginnings of humankind. Catching and throwing are utilitarian activities that could not help but rapidly evolve into games. Running, jumping, and fighting are competitive by nature. Cave paintings depicting hunting, running, and wrestling date back over seventeen thousand years. Our ancestors needed these skills to survive, but it is highly likely that individuals and groups practiced and compared their abilities as well—sport as well as survival.

Less physical, but still challenging, board games are known to have existed since the dawn of recorded history. The Egyptian game of *senet* was played before 3000 BCE and a five-thousand-year-old backgammon set with dice was discovered at the Shahr-e Sukhteh archeological site in southeastern Iran.

Competition and, consequently, winners and losers, are an important part of sport, but not its sole definition. Teams require cooperation. No quarterback can win the game alone and even if a pitcher throws a perfect game, it is due, in part, to great fielding (and someone on the team needs to get a hit to win.) But does the adage "It's not whether you win or lose but how you play the game" really apply? Only at a certain level. Winning can mean more than biochemical elation or monetary gain, it can enhance our national, ethnic, or regional pride; it can be used to support or disparage political ideology.

The element of risk also augments the playing—and perhaps the popularity—of a sport. Admittedly, the apparent physical dangers of golf and tennis do not equal those of luge or even skateboarding. Perhaps peril involving severe damage to prestige and pocketbook metaphorically equals the possibility of injury and death.

We often elevate athletes to the status of demi-gods, but we also are quick to disdain them if they do not produce the miracles we desire. And, although we may worship, we seldom see them as role models for our lives. Often considered exceptional from an early age, talented athletes are rewarded by coaches, parents, schools, and peers. If they avoid injury, make it to the professional level, and perform well, they can gain fame and fortune. But individual super-athletes—indulged for years or granted extraordinary status without the grounding to support it—often ignore society's norms for acceptable behavior. Fans tolerate bad boys (and girls) only to a certain point. They can be sex symbols, but they can't be caught with their pants too far down. They can take chances, but they can't actually gamble. They can be superhuman, but not with the help of performance-enhancing drugs. We love winners, but we expect them to play by the rules—and rules are also integral to any sport or game.

Most of us, however, participate for the fun of it, for exercise, for camaraderie, for our own personal betterment, for a challenge. We play games because, as one definition shared by both *sport* and *game* reminds us, they are *pastimes,* diversions from the humdrum and not always pleasant aspects of daily life.

For those of us who enjoy sports mostly (or only) as spectators, our appreciation can be on a number of levels: respect, awe, and admiration for fellow humans whose physical and mental skills far exceed ours; a visceral emotional connection to participants; even the intellectual challenge of statistics and odds. Perhaps it is chiefly because we want to be part of something larger than ourselves, something that makes us feel the impossible is possible, that we can be part of a triumph we could never actually achieve ourselves—even if our participation is just cheering on the real athletes . . . or sharing vanquishment with honor.

Sports bring us together and, sometimes, divide us, but whether we are couch potatoes, "fantasy" players, weekend warriors, in pursuit of better health, video gamers, rabid fans, talented amateurs, or real athletes, the thought of a future without sports and games is inconceivable. They may change—as they always have—but we can't consider a future without the thrill of victory, the agony of defeat, or just the simple pleasure of playing or watching a game.

Science fiction has long explored sports, although I feel there is far more room to do so. Some of our library of science fictional literature concerning sports and games has become dated for a variety of reasons.

And, with the fairly recent invention of video and computer gaming, real-world development often outstrips speculation. Today's "reality television" has almost caught up with earlier conjectures, as have "extreme" sports. (Although you might want to note the combination of the two in Jason Stoddard's 2011 novel *Winning Mars.*) We feel the stories selected for *Future Games*, however, remain effective and relevant.

Invented and re-imagined sports tend to be featured in film and television more than fiction (sports are far more easily portrayed visually than in text)—including rollerball (from the movies of the same name); pod racing from the Star Wars universe; and pyramid, the premier sport played in the Battlestar Galactica world—but you'll find some excellent examples in this anthology.

Nothing in science fiction literature has yet matched fantasy's quidditch (created by J. K. Rowling in her Harry Potter series) as far as a fully-realized, albeit derivative, sport unless you count Suzanne Collins' Hunger Games, which is really only a dystopic combination of reality games, human hunting, and gladiatorial combat. Interestingly, in both, females compete with males and both were invented by women. One hopes we are beginning to see more stories by and/or about women in sports and games. *Future Games* offers some fine stories by women or featuring female protagonists, but I would love to see more in the genre.

In the following pages there's a great diversity of fictional explorations of future games and sports. You'll find baseball used as a means of communication with beings from other worlds, football played against remarkably well-suited aliens, ice hockey that defies our meager scope, games that serve as war substitutes or war itself, virtual games more meaningful than mere leisure play, game shows with far too real risks, sports invented by the technologies or the environments of tomorrow, athletes with minds more powerful than their bodies, players whose uniqueness is used against them . . . and much, much more from sixteen world-champion-level writers.

Let the games begin!

Paula Guran
September 2012

Few of us can truly envision what being a great athlete is like. But try to imagine you are involved in a planet-hurling competition which requires that, with your right hand, you throw a discus with Olympic skill, while your legs are performing an elaborate ballet movement and with your left hand you are playing a world tennis champion (and winning), and in between racquet strokes you must move a piece to attack a champion chessmaster effectively on a three-dimensional chessboard. If you can imagine doing all that in near simultaneity, then you know something *of what it is to be a waverider . . .*

Will the Chill

John Shirley

"I refuse to speak to him," declared Tondius Will.

"If you don't, there will be no more sponsor," replied Great Senses.

The biocyber computer paused, its wall of lights changed from considering-yellow to assertion-blue; the programming room's shadows fled before the brighter blue so that the oval chamber resembled the interior of a great turquoise egg.

The ship's computer asserted: "Sports-eyes is serious. No interview, no sponsorship."

"Very well. Let there be an end to it."

"Nonsense. You cannot live without Contest. Mina's death proved that."

Great Senses said, its fifty-by-fifty-meter panel of honeycomb-crystal glowing red for regret amid the blue of assertion. "You cannot live without Contest and you cannot Contest without a contestship. And this starship is owned by Sports-eyes. And there is the immense cost of the planet-pushcoils to consider . . . "

"I'll find a way to sponsor it myself." But even as he said it, Tondius Will knew it was impossible.

"Sports-eyes has legal access to this ship. If you refuse to speak with the reporter, you'll have to talk to the show's director. And he'll come here *personally.* And you know how they like to touch you in greeting—on the lips. Latest homeworld fad."

Will the Chill spat in disgust. The self-cleaning walls of the ship absorbed the spittle.

"All right," said Will. "I'll speak to the reporter. But only on the screen. Should I dress? What is the present custom?"

"No need. Nudity is sanctioned."

Will turned and strode to the lift, rode the compression tube to tertiary level, communications. He glimpsed his reflection in the glass of the communication room's inactive screen. He was golden-skinned, compact but muscular, utterly hairless, his bald scalp gleaming with metal hookup panels—for his physical guidance-rapport with Great Senses and the contestship—set flush with his cranium. His dark-eyed, pensive features, already cold, intensified as he approached the screen. His full lips hardened to thin lines; his hairless brows creased.

A nulgrav cushion darted from a wall niche to uphold him as he sat. The screen flickered alive. The Sports-eyes communications emblem, a spaceship shaped like an eye, flashed onto the screen. The sign faded, and Will faced a spindly, nude, gray-haired man with tiny, restive blue eyes and lips that seemed permanently puckered.

The stranger ceremoniously blew Will a kiss. Will merely nodded. The man moved uneasily in his seat; his shoulders bobbed, his thin cheeks ticked, his prominent Adam's apple bounced. "Eric Blue here." He spoke rapidly. "They call me Blue the Glue. This is a guh-reat honor for me, Tondius Will. A very great honor."

Will shrugged.

Blue the Glue pounced on Will the Chill. "Will, it's my understanding that you didn't want to give this interview. Correct?"

Will nodded slightly.

"Well, uh, Will—heh—why is that? Can you be frank? I mean, you're Titleholder for four Contests, you've been a planet-hurlin' waverider for many longuns now. Twice my lifetime. You've earned two replenishings, so you'll live another century at least. Is this the last interview for another century? As far as I know only one other SprtZ NewZ holorag has spoken to you in your entire—"

"What is the pertinence of this?" Will asked sharply. Blue's voice was abundant with hidden meanings. His face was not his face. Will wished he were back on Five, listening to those who spoke with no faces at all.

"It's relevant to your image. And your image is important to your audience-draw. And your audience-draw is dropping off, Will. Though some say you're the best damn planet-hurler since Fiessar in 2270. Still, you don't—?"

"I don't caper and jape for the cameras like Svoboda? I don't brag endlessly on my prowess and gossip about lovers like Browning? I don't soak up publicity like Munger? Is that your complaint?"

"Look, Will, there's a difference between, uh, maintaining *dignity*—and being cold. And you're *cold*, man. That's why they call you Will the—"

"There's a difference between being emotive and artistic, Blue."

"Look here, let me put it to you in the plainest terms. I'm a Sports-eyes reporter, my job is public relations—*you've* failed to give me anything to relate to that public, Will. Sports-eyes stars need *audience appeal.* They have to be likable characters. They have to be likable—ah—*folks.* They have to be fellows people can identify with. Not cold and distant automatons—"

"All waveriders are cold and distant, as you put it, Blue," said Will, coldly and distantly. "But most of them pretend they're not, in order to maintain themselves in the public eye. But it is not coldness, not really. Not inside. It is the aura of unflinching and unremitting dedication."

Blue the Glue looked startled. "Well. Now we're making progress. The Philosophical Waverider? Image BoyZ might be able to do something with that."

Will snorted.

"Will, I wonder if you'll be kind enough to examine a holovid I have with me and give me your analysis of it. I'll feed it into your screen, with your permission." Without waiting for permission, Blue punched a button and the screen was filled with a simplified holoimage of the final weeks (time-lapsed, sped-up to twenty minutes condensed action) of Will's Contest with Opponent Brigg in system GV5498. Two planets approached one another, one brown-black, crescent-edged with silver, its atmosphere swirling turmoil; the other, Will's masspiece, shining, chrome-blue like the shield of Perseus. Both were approximately Earth-sized and devoid of life, as was customary. Relative to the viewer's plane of perspective, the planets closed obliquely, Brigg's from the lower left-hand corner and Will's from the upper right-hand corner of the rectangular screen.

How diluted the public impression of Contest! Will thought.

The right-hand planet, GV5498 Number Four, showed white pushcoil flares at its equator and southern pole. Atmospheric disturbances and volcanic explosions roiled the contiguous faces of the planets as gravitational fields meshed and struggled.

Involuntarily, Will twitched and flexed his arms as if he were in hookup again, adjusting pushcoils, controlling the tilt, impetus, spin, momentum, and mass resistance of his masspiece.

Seconds before impact, as dead seas boiled and ice caps fractured, as continents buckled, the pushcoil on the south polar face toward Will's Opponent flared and forced the pole to swing back, tilting the axis, lobbing the north polar bulge forward, precipitating collision before Opponent expected it.

Opponent's planet took the worst of the collision forces. And after the impact, the orgasmic rending of two worlds: more of Will's masspiece remained intact than remained of Opponent's. So Tondius Will won the Contest. And took Title from Brigg.

The two Sports-eyes contestships, Will's and Brigg's, were glimpsed speeding to safety from the still-exploding bodies—

The image vanished, the face of Blue the Glue returned. "Now," said Blue, "why did you fire that pushcoil on your south pole, the face toward Opponent, during the last stage's final—"

"It should be obvious," Will interrupted wearily. "You must have noticed that my masspiece had a more irregular spherism than Brigg's. There was more mass in the north polar hemispheres. I applied torque in order to use the club-end of the planet with the greatest force of momentum—this can be useful only in rare instances, and Brigg probably hadn't seen it before. Most impacts are initiated along the equatorial swell."

"I see. Beautiful. Uh, such niceties are too often lost on the Sports-eyes viewer who sees—"

"Niceties! It was the most obvious ploy of the game. Brigg perceived it instantly but too late; he couldn't compensate in time. Niceties! The most important plays of the game are the early stages when masspieces are moved into place for the final approach to designated impact zone. What is this whole affair to you, Blue? What can you know of the exquisite visions of hookup? You see only very limited aspects of Contest. You observe composite images, you see them in timelapse and you see only brief flashes of the months of preparation. There is no comprehension of the internal artistry requisite—we spend weeks at a time in hookup, assessing and tasting and physically experiencing every known factor in hundreds of millions of cubic kilometers of space!" Will was not aware that he was shouting. "*What is it to you?* A contest between two waveriders hovering off dead planets which they seem to—to shove about by remote control, kicking—*kicking!*—the planets out of orbit and tossing them at one another—and the piece surviving impact with the greatest mass determines Winner. That's all it is, to you. You *huzzah* at the 'flight' of planets, their gargantuan turnings; they seem like colossal bowling balls in the hands of mites riding tiny specks and you swill your drink and clap your hands when you see the wracking and cracking of impact. You enjoy the sight of planets cracked like eggshells! Idiots! What do you know of the possession of men by worlds? Can you even for an instant imagine—"

Will stopped. He swallowed, sat back, untensing. Specks of black swarmed his vision.

Blue was grinning.

"I suppose," said Tondius Will ruefully, "that you're proud of yourself now, eh, Blue? You recorded my little tirade, no doubt. You'll crow about it at the SprtZwrtrZ Club. How you got a rise out of Will the Chill." Will's tone was bitter ice.

"It's good to see passion in you, Will! Though I have to admit I don't entirely get your meaning. But why are you so tight with your enthusiasm, Will? We can build your ratings if you'll give me more of that. And, really, can't you leak us just a little of your love life?"

"I have no lover: male, female, or bimale. None."

"No? None? Except your masspieces and playing fields, perhaps. But you had a lover once, didn't you, Tondius?"

Will felt his face growing hard and dark with anger.

Blue spoke rapidly. "Just for the sake of accurate historical perspective, listen, please, and answer my question—a yes or no will do. I have a document here I'd like to read to you. I want to know if what it states is true or false. Is this true? 'In 2649 CE Tondius Will's fourth confrontation with Enphon brought him at last into the public eye and put him in the running for Title. It was said he had prepared for this Contest for eight years; Enphon's reputation doubtless warranted this, but eight years is unprecedented even for a waverider.

"It is known that at this time Will's lover, Mina Threeface, was not permitted to visit the waverider—he avoided all distractions. For eight years he refused to screen to her for more than a period of ten minutes once a month. The lover of a waverider is best advised to understand his need for utter concentration. Apparently, Mina did not understand. She hovered just out of scanrange in her father's yacht and, minutes before impact, she dove on a sure course for the impact zone between masspieces, dispatching an emergency transmission to Tondius Will: *I've gone to Impact Zone. Avert your masspiece, lose Contest because you love me. Or I die.* His Great Senses dutifully relayed this message to Will. Tondius Will's thoughts can only be conjectured. He had to measure the scope of two loves. He found he could not permit himself to surrender or even stalemate Contest simply to save Mina. She was trapped between impacting planets, she died there and, though Will won Contest, it was this victory that also won him the cognomen Will the Chill—"

"Yes," Will said softly, though inwardly he shook with the effort at self-control. "It's all true. It's true." And he added: "Your heart, Blue—your heart is far more *chill* than mine will ever be."

Will broke contact and strode to the hookup chambers.

Hookup flushed Will's circulation, winnowing fatigue poisons from his blood, unclouding his brain. Refreshed, he adjusted hookup from *yoga* to *extern*. The cushions at his back, the cups gripping his shaven pate, the crowded instrument panel—all seemed to vanish. He closed his eyes and saw the universe.

The senses (but not the mind) of Great Senses were his, now. He scanned first through visible light. He had been orbiting Roche Five for two months; the alien constellations overwheeling the Roche system seemed almost natively familiar. Dominating the right-hand scope of his vision: Five, fifth planet from Roche's Star, bulking half in golden-red light, half in shadow. Five was Will's Contest masspiece. And patching into a drifting Sports-eyes camera satellite's signal, he could see himself: his contestship soaring above the twilight border, north-south over the face of the Earth-sized planet. The contestship, with its outspread solar panels and the beaked globe at its forward end, resembled a metallic vulture scanning the barren planet face beneath.

Not quite barren, thought Will the Chill. The survey crew was wrong—there's more than desert and ruins down there.

He looked up from Five, and sought for Opponent. Focusing away from visible light, he worked his way down ("down") through infrared's multifarious blaze, down through the longer wavelengths. He sorted through the transmissions of the star itself, discarded background sources, letting frequencies riffle by like an endless deck of cards, each card with its wave-length-identifying signet. He was looking for a Queen of Diamonds. She wasn't transmitting. He worked his way up ("up"), toward shorter wavelengths, and ten thousand hairs split themselves ten thousand times apiece. He skimmed X-rays, and, through hookup's multifaceted neutrino-focused eyes, spotted her, traced her spoor of nuclear radiation—she was using a hydrogen-scoop, fusing, traveling overspace, so Will's Great Senses (constantly monitoring gravwave ripplings) wouldn't notice her change of position. She was far from Three, her own masspiece.

What was she doing? Then—Will shuddered. A strong probe signal had bounced from his contestship. He felt it again, and again. He waited. It came no more. He traced the signals and found that the source was Opponent's contestship, fusing to travel unnoticed in ordinary space. Will tied in with Great Senses. "Did you feel that?"

"Someone tasted our defense screens with a probe signal," Great Senses replied, voice particularly mechanical coming through hookup channels. "Who was it?"

"It was Opponent! She's traveling through upper space so we wouldn't be likely to think the probe came from her . . . no reason for her to assess us from that direction, surreptitiously. She knew in this stage we'd expect to find her waveriding. What do you think? Is she testing our reflexes or trying to kill us?"

"Three sleeps gone there was a disguised Opponent drone—I recognized it for what it was because it was maneuvering in a pattern for which a Sports-eyes vehicle would have no use. It was probing our defense systems."

"You didn't tell me."

"I was waiting for confirmation of my suspicions. We have it now."

"She plans to kill me."

"That's within the scope of Contest rules. She has the right to kill you. Under certain conditions."

"It's accepted technically, but it's not considered sporting. No one's killed an Opponent for half a thousand Contests."

"Shall we kill her first?"

"No. I shall Contest, and I'll defend myself. She's inexperienced. Luck brought her this far. She's too impulsive to take the Title."

"But she has innersight. Admittedly she's injudicious, little precision as yet. Her Opponent second to last died in deep space . . . She admitted nothing. They said it was a leak."

"I didn't know." Will snorted. "So, she's a killer. Let her kill if she can. That's all—I'm going back to scanning—"

"One moment. Do you want me to maintain ship's gravity?"

"Yes. I'll be going planetside. After hookup. I've got to go down to—ah—" He hesitated. Why lie to Great Senses? But he couldn't bring himself to voice the truth. So he said: "I'm going down to inspect the fusion scoops. All that dust—there may be corrosion on the pushcoils. And we'll keep the planet in this orbit for another sleep. Until then, maintain gravity. I want to be gray-adjusted—I might be going planetside fairly often." He broke contact with Great Senses.

But in the programming room the lights of Great Senses went from questioning-green to doubting-orange.

The atmosphere of Five was breathable, but too rarefied to nourish him long. So he wore a respirator. Also, a thermalsuit against the bitter cold, cutting winds. That was all. Unweaponed (against the advice of Great Senses: Opponent skulked nearer), he leaped from the airlock of the lander. He stretched, getting the wieldiness of planetside back into his limbs. He walked a few meters to a large boulder, clambered atop it, and looked about him.

Just below, the double-domed lander squatted on spidery limbs. Beyond the lander, many kilometers across the battered yellow plain, rose the shining column of the nearest pushcoil, the planetmover.

Anemic sunlight glanced from its argent hide, light streaks chasing the shadows of striated dust clouds skating low in the bluegray sky. It was afternoon, but overhead a few stars guttered, visible in thin atmosphere.

The pushcoil column towered, broad and austere, into the clouds and beyond. Its lower end widened into a compression skirt that uniformly clamped the ground; steam and fumes trailed from vents in the conical skirt: the column was converting minerals into energy, building power for conversion into magnetic push. There were ten such columns placed at regular intervals about the planet. Put there by the Sports-eyes Corporation for Will the Chill's exclusive use.

Made from metals extracted from Five's core, the columns were powered geothermally. Sports-eyes had built hundreds on hundreds of worlds. Worlds now asteroid belts and clouds of dust; crushed and dispersed for the amusement of jaded millions on the homeworld.

The Sports-eyes crew had departed months before; Will was glad that they were gone. He hadn't spoken to another human being, except on screen, since Mina's death, years before.

Will turned and gazed west. Roche's Star was low, opposite the column. Long shadows reached from the endless scatter of boulders and crater rims. The meteorite-scored hills to the north stretched to him like the pitted, skeletal fingers of a dead giant.

Will strode into the grasp of those peninsular fingers.

In those hills were the ruins, and the sunharp, and the voices. Will began to climb, anticipation growing.

In the ship. In the hookup chamber. In the hookup seat. In hookup.

Time to re-examine the playing field. He tested the solar wind, noted its slant and strength.

Then he immersed himself in somatic-eidetic impressions of gravitational energy. An exquisitely fine and resiliently powerful fabric flexed between star systems. On this skein a star and ten planets moved like monstrous spiders, electromagnetic grips adhering them to the field, bending the webwork. The gravitational field was the playing field, and Will examined each component's interaction with the whole.

Will needed no numerical calculation. No holotrigonometry. He had never got beyond the multiplication tables. All he needed was hookup and Great Senses and the skill, the innersight. Great Senses was navigator, astrogator, life-systems watch. Hookup was Will's cerebral connection with the ship's electronic nerves, a binding of synthetic and biological neural systems. Will's was the instinct, the athleticism, the determination. Determiner of destinations.

He knew the ship physically.

The ship's cognizance of (and interaction with) visible light, cosmic rays, gamma rays, nuclear forces—these he felt in his loins. Physically.

De hipbone is connected to de backbone; the electro is connected to the magnetic. The seat of his magnetic sensorium was his spine. This chakra he experienced in the region of his heart. Electricity in the heart. Physically.

He comprehended the gravitational field through shoulders, legs, arms. Very physically.

In loins, light-packets. In heart, electromagnetism. In limbs, gravity.

In hookup they integrated as variations on the wave-particle theme: in his brain. Sometimes, Tondius Will remembered a poem, one of many the ship's library had recited to him. It was Blake.

> *Energy is the only life and is from the body:*
> *and Reason is the bound or outward*
> *circumference of Energy.*
> *Energy is Eternal Delight.*

Innersight hookup. On one level he knew the vast gravitational field in term of mass and weight, gross proportions.

Take it down, another and broader condition of unity.

He penetrated the vacillation of gravitrons, the endless alternation between wave and particle forms, slipped the knife edge of his innersight into the transitory sequence between wave into particle and particle into wave; waves, here, revealed as particles and particles ex- posed: packets of waves.

His brain took a Picture, recorded and filed it. He had memorized the playing field.

And that was enough for now. He willed internalization. Hookup shut down his connection with Great Senses. He sat up and yawned. But his eyes glittered.

He was hungry, and there was no hookup here to feed and refresh him. He was weary, but the hills drew him on. There was only the sighing wind, hiss of breath in respirator, clink of small air tanks on his belt, crunch of his boot steps in sand. And the wide-open, the empty. He trudged the rim of a crater, admiring the crystalline glitter streaking its slopes, the red nipple of iron oxides in the impact basin. On the far side of this crater were the ruins, upthrusting along the broken ridges like exposed spinal segments. Light splashed off the sunharp, still half a kilometer away.

The sun was westering behind the mesas, the jet sky overhead spread shadow wings to enfold the bluer horizons.

Will slid down the embankment, enjoying the earthy heft of hillside resisting his boots. He reached the floor of the gully and picked his way over rough shin-high boulders to the base of the hill whose crown exposed the first stretch of ragged ruins, uneven walls like battlements above.

The hills were not simple hills—they were barrows, grave mounds cloaking the remains of a once-city. Here, an earthslide triggered by a meteorite strike had exposed a portion of the city's skeleton. The walls of rusted metal and cracked glass and tired plastics, throwing jagged shadows in the fading daylight, were notched and scored with age, erosion.

But there were no signs of war on the ruins. These were not broken battlements . . . Genetic Manipulation experiments had released an unstoppable plague, robbing the world of most of its life and all its fertility. No offspring were born to lower life forms, or to the world's people. People they were, of a sort, with tendrils instead of boned fingers and large golden whiteless eyes like polished stones. The plants withered, the air thinned, the land died. Those who survived, one hundred thousand living on chemically synthesized food, were so long-lived they were nearly immortal. Childless, living without societal evolution in an endlessly bleak landscape, they surrendered to a growing collective sense of futility. A new religion arose, preaching fulfillment beyond the veil of death, advocating mass suicide. A vote was taken, its tally unanimous. The remaining one hundred thousand decided to die. To die by poison, together, and all at once . . .

For so Will had been told. The voices in the sunharp told him this.

He passed through the maze of roofless ruins, coming to the broad square at their radial center. He beheld the sunharp. Everything here had decayed but the sunharp. It had been built at the end, as a monument. Built to endure a nova.

The diamond-shaped sunharp's frame was constructed of light silvery tubing. A coppery netting was woven densely between the frames, for sifting and carrying light impulses.

The final rays of sunset, veering lances of red, broke the thin dust cloud and struck the coppery sunharp wires. Till now it had been singing in the subsonic. Struck full by crepuscular rays, its netting vibrated visibly, resonated internally, interpreted the sun shiver. Translated into sound waves, photons sang out. Choirs of alien races, chorus of human voices, subhuman voices, wolves baying and birds singing: all in concert. The wind sounds of thousands of landscapes (each landscape altering the wind song as Bach's inventions vary the hymnal theme) combining into a single voice. The nature of rippling endlessly defined in song.

Will listened, and more than listening: he heeded. And if Blue the Glue had seen Will's face just then, he might not have recognized him; he did not associate joy with Will the Chill.

Royal purple gathered in the ground hollows, dusty darkness collected in the dead windows of the ruins, the stars shone more fiercely, the mesas at the horizon swallowed the sun. The sunharp's call dwindled to lower frequencies, softly moaning to starlight and occasionally pinging to cosmic rays. Other sighs came to replace the sunharp's voice. Will shuddered and, for an instant, dread enfolded his heart. But the fear left him abruptly, as it always did before they spoke to him. He smiled. "Hello," he said aloud.

There came a reply, one hundred thousand voices speaking the same word at once, a mighty susurration in an alien tongue. A greeting.

Then they spoke subvocally, in his own tongue, echoes within the skull.

For the fifth time you have returned to us (said the voices). But the first time and the three thereafter you came alone. Why have you now brought a companion?

"I have no companions," said Tondius Will.

We see now that you do not know about the one who follows you. It is a lurking *he* who does the bidding of a distant *she*. The *he* comes to destroy you.

"Then he is an assassin," said Will sadly, "sent by my Opponent. She becomes reckless. She has breached the rules of Contest. Death-dealing must be done by Opponent or by her machines only. Still, I will not protest. Let him come."

The time is not yet, Tondius Will.

"Will the time be soon?"

You doubt us. You wonder if you are the One prophesied by the Gatekeeper. You are he. Ten thousand times in ten thousand millennia we have attempted transit to the fuller spheres. Ten thousand times we have been denied. *One hundred thousand cannot enter as one*, said the Gatekeeper, *unless they become onemind, or unless they are guided by a sailor of inner seeing*. We were bound together by a united death. Simultaneity. We plunged together into that tenuous Place, this between. We need a guide to lead us out. Do not doubt us. You are He. The Gatekeeper whose seven stony visages exhale blacklight said to us: *One who wields spheres below can guide you through spheres above* . . . You are He. We know your history, Tondius Will.

"My father . . ."

Was an orbitglider, a great athlete of space race.

"My mother . . ."

Was a freefall ballerina for a space-station ballet company.

"My paternal grandfather . . ."

Was an Earthborn snow skier of Earth who journeyed to the ultimate ski course on mountainous Reginald IV, and died on Thornslope.

"His father, my great-grandfather . . . "

Was a Terran trapeze artist.

"One of my great-grandmothers . . . "

Was a surfer on the vast seas of terraformed Venus, and once rode a wave for seven days.

"And I came to waveriding . . . "

When your mother killed herself en route to Earth from your father's doom on Reginald IV, and the captain of the transport adopted you; he was himself a retired waverider.

"And I know your history, and how you came to die, one hundred thousand at a single stroke, trapped by imperfect unity . . . "

We are as one hundred thousand waves . . .

"On a single sea."

The understanding forged anew, the voices hushed. The air about him began to course and whirl, a dust-devil rose up and the spirit host—seen in the dark of his closed eyes as endless banners of unfurling white—enclosed Tondius Will. He wept in unbridled joy and relief as they entered him, and swept him up . . . He could not abide the touch of flesh on flesh, not since he had crushed Mina between two worlds. They took him with them, for a while, and let him incorporeally ride, like a surfer on a sea constituted of the ectoplasm of one hundred thousand souls. For this time of merging, loneliness was beyond conception. For this time of—

But it ended.

Returned to his body, he felt like an infant coughed from the womb into a snowdrift.

He screamed. He begged. "Please!"

No longer (the voices said), for now. If we kept you from your body any longer, you'd wither and pass on to us. It would be too soon. You're not quite ready to lead us yet, though you have the innersight of energies, particles, and planes. You are a born sailor of upper spheres. But not quite yet. Next time. Soon.

"Wait! One thing! You said you would search for her. Have you found her? Was she too far away?"

Linear distances don't impede our call. We have found her. She was very much alone. She is coming. Next time. Soon. (The voices faded.)

They were gone. Will was alone in the dark.

The sunharp moaned faintly. Distant whispers; starlight rumors stirred its webwork.

He shivered in sudden awareness of the night's cold. Stretching, he fought numbness from his limbs. He turned up the heat in his thermalsuit, checked his air tanks' reading. Best get back to the landing pod, and soon.

He turned and began to descend the hillside. At the outermost finger of the ragged walls, he stopped and listened. He nodded to himself.

He took a light from his belt, flicked it alive, and set the small beacon on a ledge of the crumbling wall. "Come out and face me as you shoot me!" he called.

Silence, except for the echo of his shout.

Then, a squeak of boot steps on gravel. A broad, dark figure in a gray thermalsuit stepped warily from a murky doorway. He was two meters from Will. Most of the assassin's face was concealed by goggles and respirator mask. "You are one of the guild," Tondius Will observed. The assassin nodded. He held a small silver tube lightly in his right hand. The tube's muzzle was directed at Will's chest. Will said, "It is a tenet of your guild that if your quarry discovers you and challenges you then you are compelled to face him. Yes?"

The assassin nodded.

"Well then, come into the light of my lamp. I want to see some of your face as you kill me. You can't begrudge me that, surely."

The assassin took two strides forward, stepping into the ring of light. His lips were compressed, his eyes were gray as the ice a thousand meters beneath the ice cap. His thick legs were well apart and braced.

Will the Chill fastened his eyes on those of the assassin. The stranger frowned.

Tondius Will spoke in a voice compelling; it was compelling because his voice was the raiment of his will power, and his will was backed by the unspeakable mass of all the planets he had hurled. He said: "I am going to move my arm quickly in order to show you something. Do not fire the weapon, I am not going to reach for you. I'm going to reach into this wall . . . The guild of assassins esteems its members greatly skilled in martial arts . . . "

To his left was a high wall of transparent bricks backed by old metal. Ancient but solid. Will had explored these ruins thoroughly. He knew there was a metal urn on the other side of the wall, lying on a shelf; he knew just where it was. He moved, visualizing his left hand passing through the obstruction as if through a cloud, fingers closing about the small urn; he pitted perfect form against the mass resistance of the wall.

There was a *crack!* and a small explosion in the wall side; dust billowed, chips of glass rained. The assassin twitched but did not fire. Will withdrew his arm from the hole he'd made. He held something in his bare hand. A stoppered urn of age-dulled gold. "Waveriders learn that masses are merely electron-bounded fields of space-influence," he remarked casually, examining the urn in the dim light, "and all fields have a weak point, where that which seems impenetrable may be penetrated." He paused, glanced up, murmuring, "That's the principle behind the traversing of space between stars: knowledge of secret passages through the fabric of spacestuff. And it's the principle behind what you've just seen, assassin." Will reached out with his right hand, poised it over the urn, and, with a motion outspeeding the eye, he stabbed a rigid thumb at the metal casing held in his other hand. The urn split neatly in two; half of it dropped to the ground. The assassin took a step backward; his eyes dancing with wonder, he held his fire.

Tondius Will reached into the half of the urn in his left hand and extracted something that had lain there for ten thousand millennia. A tiny skeleton to which a thin shroud of skin clung; a miniature mummy. "It's an infant who died at birth," Will muttered. "The urn was his sarcophagus. A shame to disturb it. So . . . " He bent, retrieved the fallen half, replaced it over the mummy. Clamping the two halves snug with his left hand, with the thumb of his right he pressed the seams of the urn, all the way around, fusing it shut. Moving slowly and easily, he replaced the urn in the hole he had made in the wall. Then he returned his gaze to the eyes of the assassin. "Now: can you match what I have just done?"

The assassin slowly shook his head.

"Then, you know that I could kill you," said Will lightly, taking a cautious step forward so that he was within striking distance. "I could kill you even before you pressed the fire stud of your charge gun." Will smiled. "Yes?"

Looking stooped and weary, the assassin nodded.

"Therefore, your mission is useless. Depart now, in peace."

The assassin shook his head . . . The tenets of the assassin's guild.

Will saw the man's eyes narrow. Will knew, a split-second realization, that the assassin was depressing the stud of his charge gun.

Will struck, doubly. One hand struck aside the charge gun, the other dipped into the assassin's chest. Just as that hand had penetrated the wall.

Will took something from the man's chest and held it up for him to see.

Spurting blood from the gaping crater in his chest, the assassin took two seconds to collapse, two more to die.

In 1976 CE the physicist-philosopher Denis Postle said: "Mass-energy tells space-time how to curve and curved space-time tells mass-energy how to move."

Imagine you are involved in a competition which requires that, with your right hand, you throw a discus with Olympic skill, while your legs are performing an elaborate ballet movement and with your left hand you are playing the world tennis champion (and winning), and in between racquet strokes you must move a piece to attack a champion chessmaster effectively on a three-dimensional chessboard. If you can imagine doing all that in near simultaneity, then you know something of what it is to be a waverider.

Externally. In hookup, Will's eyes were closed, his hands were clamped rigidly on armrests, his legs flexed and poised; except for his heaving chest, he seemed inert—about to fly to activity like a drawn bowstring.

Internally. He saw himself, in his mind's eye, floating naked in space; outside him were luminous matrices, the energy fields, flickering in and out of ken as he looked up and down the spectrum. He approached a pulsing sphere—to innersight, the sphere seemed only ten meters across. It traveled in preordained paths through the matrix. Paths *he* had ordained. He had set this globe on the road it was taking by manipulating pushcoils situated about the vast surface of its genuine counterpart, Roche Five.

He felt the presence of Opponent, though he could not yet see her.

He sensed her position as a man with closed eyes knows the whereabouts of the sun by the feel of its glare on his eyelids. She had not yet moved Roche Three from tertiary-stage orbit. But she was there, satelliting Three elliptically, just within pushcoil-control range. She was waiting for Will to serve.

Will served. He reached out, mentally, for the imaged sphere. He placed his hand near the eastcenter south polar pushcoil, poised over the pushcoil column in a hand posture that told Great Senses exactly how much push should be exerted by the coil, and for how long, and at what intervals.

Through hookup, Great Senses drank Will's muscular expressions, translated them into mathematical formulas. Great Senses knew Will's flesh, though Will denied that flesh to humanity.

Except for autonomic functions, breathing and blood moving, Will's every movement (as visualized on the noumenon plane, hookup) represented, to Great Senses, a signal to be transmitted to the pushcoil control units on Five.

Externally. He was rippling like an eel, rippling purposefully, sending three dozen signals in one dozen seconds. Sometimes several pushcoils were activated simultaneously, sometimes one at a time; on each occasion the activation signal carried a precisely quantified regulation of the thrust applied.

Roche Five moved out of orbit.

A man about 1.8 meters high and weighing 170 pounds moved a mass of about six billion trillion tons, some 11,000 kilometers in diameter. And he did this (apparently) by rotating his hips and flexing shoulder muscles.

Internally. Swimming through space after the sphere, waving his hands about it in intricate patterns like a wizard invoking visions from a crystal ball, he swept it easily (but not effortlessly) in a wide arc, ninety degrees from the solar system's orbital plane, right angles from its former path.

This was stage three-fifty in Contest. Six months since stage one.

The greater the scope entailed in implementing an activity, the greater the need for strict attention to small details.

Each split-second decision taking into account all that Will read of gravitational fields, electromagnetic and heat-energy factors, gravdrag on nearby asteroids, influence of solar wind—the consequences of interaction with these factors.

Will struggled with ecstasy. Each aspect of the celestial field had its own music, in Will's mind, and its own fireworks, exquisite and hypnotic: a threat of distraction.

Opponent drew Roche Three in ever-widening spirals, never quite breaking free of the gravitational field of the sun. She used the pull of the sun, increasing her speed as she neared it. She expended weeks in each strategic repositioning, always moving with strict reference to the ploys of Will the Chill . . .

Concentration opaqued time; Will's fixation on Contest never faltered. The weeks collapsed upon themselves; Three and Five spun nearer, and nearer.

Hookup fed and cleansed him. In place of sleep it washed his unconscious and hung it to dry in the winds of dreaming. Weeks melted into minutes. Sports-eyes recorded all. Sports-eyes staring from a thousand angles, a thousand droneships with camera snouts preparing the composite timelapse vid reducing Contest to the relative simplicity of a bullfight.

They entered the specified ninety thousand cubic kilometers of space agreed upon as Impact Zone.

Like macrocosmic sumo wrestlers, the planets closed, bulk upon bulk.

The masspieces were ten thousand kilometers apart.

She was closing fast, impulsively, driving straight as a billiard ball, utilizing the equatorial bulge as impending impact point. She was over-confident, perhaps, because Will had not been performing as well as in the past; his mind was troubled, divided. He had to struggle to keep from thinking of the ruins, the sunharp, the voices, and Mina.

This was his final Contest, and his heart pleaded with him to play it to denouement.

But as the two planets engaged for impact—each making minute split-second adjustments in trajectory, rate of spin, and lean of axis—Will rose up from hookup, thinking: Sports-eyes, this time you're cheated. Crack your own eggshells.

Great Senses was not capable of surprise. But it was capable of alarm.

Alarmed by Will's withdrawal from hookup, the computer spoke to him through ship's intercom. "What's wrong? Impact is in—"

"I know. Less than two hours. So it is scheduled, and so Opponent expects. But there will be no impact. We are stalemating; no one wins. I'll back out of the approach pattern as if I'm preparing another. But Five will never collide with Three."

"Because of the voices in the ruins?"

Will was capable of surprise. "You aren't supposed to read my mind."

"I read only what hookup leaks to me. I know you want to preserve the planet for the voices. The dead one hundred thousand. Why? They're already dead. Do you want to preserve Five intact as a monument to them?"

"In a way, it will be a monument. But—do you know what they require of me?"

"They want you to guide them upspectrum. Beyond the shortest known wavelengths, the highest frequencies. Into the fuller spheres."

"I want to go. I want to see upspectrum. And I want Mina . . . We have to depart from an intact planet; it's like a door into the Farther Place. If the game were consummated, most of Five would be destroyed . . . The only reason—beyond my love of Contest—that I've played this far was to be near Five. I had to Contest to stay near, since this is sponsor's Ship."

"Within an hour the quakes on Five will begin. If you want to preserve the ruins—"

"I've programmed the backup navigator. You won't have to do a thing. In forty-five minutes the pushcoil will veer Five. Opponent's momentum will prevent her from coming about to strike. As soon as we're out of impact zone, on that instant, transmit a message to her, tell her, as is my right at this point, I declare stalemate, by right of points accrued. That will infuriate her."

"And you'll go to the surface of Five."

"Yes . . . and you'll go to serve another waverider."

"And on Five you'll die and go with the unseen multitude."

"Yes."

"How? Will you crash the lander?"

"No. I've got to be in sunharp rapport with them when I die."

"Then—you'll remove your respirator? An ugly death."

"I don't think that will be necessary. She's proved herself to be vindictive. When she discovers the stalemate she'll come after me. She'll find me in rapport."

That was where she found him.

The sudden change in orbital trajectory had riven the surface of Five. The sky was mordant with volcanic smog. Some of the ruins crumbled. The sunharp survived.

Roche Five was moving into a wide, cold, permanent orbit. The pushcoil column, in the waning light like a colossal mailed fist and forearm, flared for the last time.

He stood before the sunharp, tranced by its distant hum. The voices whispered, sang louder, a cry touched by exultation.

"Hello," he said.

Again you have not come alone (said the voices). A *she* comes in a small, armed ship. Just out of sight, in the clouds. She approaches.

"I know. She will be the instrument of our union."

Tondius . . .

"Mina!" shouted Will the Chill warmly.

I'm here.

The planet was rotating into darkness. Light diminished, night engulfed Five. But Tondius Will had no lack of light: "Mina!" he breathed.

She touched him before the others, a chill breath, a kiss of ether. Then the others came and he was borne up, the surfer deliquesced; a sea of one hundred thousand and two waves. His body, still standing, remained alive and for a few moments it tethered him to that plane.

Something metallic broke from the clouds. A chip of light glittered low in the black sky, growing. It was a contestship, diving like a vulture. It spat a beam of harsh red light; the laser passed through Will's chest and through his heart—but before his body crumpled his ears resounded with a joyous cry, the song of the sunharp: struck by the laser passed through his flesh.

One wavelength, infinitely divisible.

Freed of his body Will had no need of hookup. He showed them the way. In a moment, the one hundred thousand and two had gone.

Far over the surface of Five, Great Senses surveyed the planet. Its face of honeycombed crystal was a mixture of three colors: red for regret, blue for considering, green for triumph.

Great Senses veered from Five and departed the system.

Opponent's ship departed as well.

Now, Roche Five, icing over, a frigid forever monument to a transcended race, was utterly empty. Except for the lonely ghost of a forgotten assassin.

Football players keep getting bigger and stronger. In 2011, of the 1,948 active NFL players, the average weight was 247 pounds; 426 players weighed over three hundred pounds, five players tipped the scales at over 350. The introduction of Nautilus machines in the mid-1970s allowed wider use of slow-resistance weights; development of the science of timing weightlifting routines made the machines even more effective. The result was stronger athletes. Future football players will probably be even bigger and stronger . . . but not stronger than beings from a heavy-gravity planet. Although not swift, a team of such aliens would still easily dominate a human team. Or would they?

Run to Starlight

George R. R. Martin

Hill stared dourly at the latest free-fall football results from the Belt as they danced across the face of his desk console, but his mind was elsewhere. For the seventeenth time that week, he was silently cursing the stupidity and shortsightedness of the members of the Starport City Council.

The damn councilmen persisted in cutting the allocation for an artificial gravity grid out of the departmental budget every time Hill put it in. They had the nerve to tell him to stick to "traditional" sports in planning his recreational program for the year.

The old fools had no idea of the way free-fall football was catching on throughout the system, although he'd tried to explain it to them God knows how many times. The Belt sport should be an integral part of any self-respecting recreational program. And, on Earth, that meant you had to have a gravity grid. He'd planned on installing it beneath the stadium, but now—

The door to his office slid open with a soft hum. Hill looked up and frowned, snapping off the console. An agitated Jack De Angelis stepped through.

"What is it now?" Hill snapped.

"Uh, Rog, there's a guy here I think you better talk to," De Angelis replied. "He wants to enter a team in the City Football League."

"Registration closed on Tuesday," Hill said. "We've already got twelve teams. No room for any more. And why the hell can't you handle this? You're in charge of the football program."

"This is a special case," De Angelis said.

"Then make an exception and let the team in if you want to," Hill interrupted. "Or don't let them in. It's your program. It's your decision. Must I be bothered with every bit of trivia in this whole damned department?"

"Hey, take it easy, Rog," De Angelis protested. "I don't know what you're so steamed up about. Look, I—hell, I'll show you the problem." He turned and went to the door. "Sir, would you step in here a minute," he said to someone outside.

Hill started to rise from his seat, but sank slowly back into the chair when the visitor appeared in the doorway.

De Angelis was smiling. "This is Roger Hill, the director of the Starport Department of Recreation," he said smoothly. "Rog, let me introduce Remjhard-nei, the head of the Brish'diri trade mission to Earth."

Hill rose again, and offered his hand numbly to the visitor. The Brish'dir was squat and grotesquely broad. He was a good foot shorter than Hill, who stood six four, but he still gave the impression of dwarfing the director somehow. A hairless, bullet-shaped head was set squarely atop the alien's massive shoulders. His eyes were glittering green marbles sunk in the slick, leathery gray skin. There were no external ears, only small holes on either side of the skull. The mouth was a lipless slash.

Diplomatically ignoring Hill's openmouthed stare, Remjhard bared his teeth in a quick smile and crushed the director's hand in his own. "I am most pleased to meet you, sir," he said in fluent English, his voice a deep bass growl. "I have come to enter a football team in the fine league your city so graciously runs."

Hill gestured for the alien to take a seat, and sat down himself. De Angelis, still smiling at his boss's stricken look, pulled another chair up to the desk for himself.

"Well, I—" Hill began, uncertainly. "This team, is it a—a Brish'diri team?"

Remjhard smiled again. "Yes," he answered. "Your football, it is a fine game. We of the mission have many times watched it being played on the 3-V wallscreens your people were so kind as to install. It has fascinated us. And now some of the half-men of our mission desire to try to play it." He reached slowly into the pocket of the black-and-silver uniform he wore, and pulled out a folded sheet of paper.

"This is a roster of our players," he said, handing it to Hill. "I believe the newsfax said such a list is required to enter your league."

Hill took the paper and glanced down at it uncertainly. It was a list of some fifteen Brish'diri names, neatly spelled out. Everything seemed to be in order, but still—

"You'll forgive me, I hope," Hill said, "but I'm somewhat unfamiliar with the expressions of your people. You said—*half-men*? Do you mean children?"

Remjhard nodded, a quick inclination of his bulletlike head. "Yes. Male children, the sons of mission personnel. All are aged either eight or nine Earth seasons."

Hill silently sighed with relief. "I'm afraid it's out of the question, then," he said. "Mr. De Angelis said you were interested in the City League, but that league is for boys aged eighteen and up. Occasionally we'll admit a younger boy with exceptional talent and experience, but never anyone this young." He paused briefly. "We do have several leagues for younger boys, but they've already begun play. It's much too late to add another team at this point."

"Pardon, Director Hill, but I think you misunderstand," Remjhard said. "A Brish'diri male is fully mature at fourteen Earth years. In our culture, such a person is regarded as a full adult. A nine-year-old Brish'dir is roughly equivalent to an eighteen-year-old Terran male in terms of physical and intellectual development. That is why our half-men wish to register for this league and not one of the others, you see."

"He's correct, Rog," De Angelis said. "I've read a little about the Brish'diri, and I'm sure of it. In terms of maturity, these youngsters are eligible for the City League."

Hill threw De Angelis a withering glance. If there was one thing he didn't need at the moment, it was a Brish'diri football team in one of his leagues, and Remjhard was arguing convincingly enough without Jack's help.

"Well, all right," Hill said. "Your team may well be of age, but there are still problems. The Rec Department sports program is for local residents only. We simply don't have room to accommodate everyone who wants to participate. And your home planet is, as I understand, several hundred light-years beyond the Starport city limits." He smiled.

"True," Remjhard said. "But our trade mission has been in Starport for six years. An ideal location due to your city's proximity to Grissom Interstellar Spaceport, from which most of the Brish'diri traders operate while on Earth. All of the current members of the mission have been here for two Earth years, at least. We are Starport residents, Director Hill. I fail to understand how the location of Brishun enters into the matter at hand."

Hill squirmed uncomfortably in his seat, and glared at De Angelis, who was grinning. "Yes, you're probably right again," he said. "But I'm still afraid we won't be able to help you. Our junior leagues are touch football, but the City League, as you might know, is tackle. It can get quite rough at times. State safety regulations require the use of special equipment. To make sure no one is injured seriously. I'm sure you understand. And the Brish'diri . . . "

He groped for words, anxious not to offend. "The—uh—physical construction of the Brish'diri is so different from the Terran that our equipment couldn't possibly fit. Chances of injury would be too great, and the department would be liable. No. I'm sure it couldn't be allowed. Too much risk."

"We would provide special protective equipment," Remjhard said quietly. "We would never risk our own offspring if we did not feel it was safe."

Hill started to say something, stopped, and looked to De Angelis for help. He had run out of good reasons why the Brish'diri couldn't enter the league.

Jack smiled. "One problem remains, however," he said, coming to the director's rescue. "A bureaucratic snag, but a difficult one. Registration for the league closed on Tuesday. We've already had to turn away several teams, and if we make an exception in your case, well—" De Angelis shrugged. "Trouble. Complaints. I'm sorry, but we must apply the same rule to all."

Remjhard rose slowly from his seat, and picked up the roster from where it lay on the desk. "Of course," he said gravely. "All must follow the regulations. Perhaps next year we will be on time." He made a formal half-bow to Hill, turned, and walked from the office.

When he was sure the Brish'dir was out of earshot, Hill gave a heartfelt sigh and swiveled to face De Angelis. "That was close," he said. "Christ, a Baldy football team. Half the people in this town lost sons in the Brish'diri War, and they still hate them. I can imagine the complaints." Hill frowned. "And you! Why couldn't you just get rid of him right away instead of putting me through that?"

De Angelis grinned. "Too much fun to pass up," he said. "I wondered if you'd figure out the right way to discourage him. The Brish'diri have an almost religious respect for laws, rules, and regulations. They wouldn't think of doing anything that would force someone to break a rule. In their culture, that's just as bad as breaking a rule yourself."

Hill nodded. "I would have remembered that myself if I hadn't been so paralyzed at the thought of a Brish'diri team in one of our leagues," he said limply. "And now that that's over with, I want to talk to you about that gravity grid. Do you think there's any way we could rent one instead of buying it outright? The Council might go for that. And I was thinking . . ."

A little over three hours later, Hill was signing some equipment requisitions when the office door slid open to admit a brawny, dark-haired man in a nondescript gray suit.

"Yes?" the director said, a trifle impatiently. "Can I help you?"

The dark-haired man flashed a government ID as he took a seat. "Maybe you can. But you certainly haven't so far, I'll tell you that much. My name's Tomkins. Mac Tomkins. I'm from the Federal E. T. Relations Board."

Hill groaned. "I suppose it's about that Brish'diri mess this morning," he said, shaking his head in resignation.

"Yes," Tomkins cut in at once. "We understand that the Brish'diri wanted to register some of their youngsters for a local football league. You forbade it on a technicality. We want to know why."

"Why?" said Hill incredulously, staring at the government man. "Why? For God's sakes, the Brish'diri War was only over seven years ago. Half of those boys on our football teams had brothers killed by the Bulletbrains. Now you want me to tell them to play football with the subhuman monsters of seven years back? They'd run me out of town."

Tomkins grimaced, and looked around the room. "Can that door be locked?" he asked, pointing to the door he had come in by.

"Of course," Hill replied, puzzled.

"Lock it then," Tomkins said. Hill adjusted the appropriate control on his desk.

"What I'm going to tell you should not go beyond this room," Tomkins began.

Hill cut him off with a snort. "Oh, come now, Mr. Tomkins. I may be only a small-time sports official, but I'm not stupid. You're hardly about to impart some galaxy-shattering top secret to a man you met a few seconds ago."

Tomkins smiled. "True. The information's not secret, but it is a little ticklish. We would prefer that every Joe in the street doesn't know about it."

"All right, I'll buy that for now. Now what's this all about? I'm sorry if I've got no patience with subtlety, but the most difficult problem I've handled in the last year was the protest in the championship game in the Class B Soccer League. Diplomacy just isn't my forte."

"I'll be brief," Tomkins said. "We—E. T. Relations, that is—we want you to admit the Brish'diri team into your football league."

"You realize the furor it would cause?" Hill asked.

"We have some idea. In spite of that, we want them admitted."

"Why, may I ask?"

"Because of the furor if they aren't admitted." Tomkins paused to stare at Hill for a second, then apparently reached a decision of some sort and continued. "The Earth-Brishun War was a ghastly, bloody deadlock, although our propaganda men insist on pretending it was a great victory. No sane man on either side wants it resumed. But not everyone is sane."

The agent frowned in distaste. "There are elements among us who regard the Brish'diri—or the Bulletbrains, or Baldies, or whatever you want to call them—as monsters, even now, seven years after the killing has ended."

"And you think a Brish'diri football team would help to overcome the leftover hates?" Hill interrupted.

"Partially. But that's not the important part. You see, there is also an element among the Brish'diri that regards humans as subhuman-vermin to be wiped from the galaxy. They are a very virile, competitive race. Their whole culture stresses combat. The dissident element I mentioned will seize on your refusal to admit a Brish'diri team as a sign of fear, an admission of human inferiority. They'll use it to agitate for a resumption of the war. We don't want to risk giving them a propaganda victory like that. Relations are too strained as it is."

"But the Brish'dir I spoke to—" Hill objected. "I explained it all to him. A rule. Surely their respect for law—"

"Remjhard-nei is a leader of the Brish'diri peace faction. He personally will defend your position. But he and his son were disappointed by the refusal. They will talk. They already have been talking. And that means that eventually the war faction will get hold of the story and turn it against us."

"I see. But what can I do at this point? I've already told Remjhard that registration closed Tuesday. If I understand correctly, his own morality would never permit him to take advantage of an exception now."

Tomkins nodded. "True. You can't make an exception. Just change the rule. Let in all the teams you refused. Expand the league."

Hill shook his head, wincing. "But our budget—it couldn't take it. We'd have more games. We'd need more time, more referees, more equipment."

Tomkins dismissed the problem with a wave of his hand. "The government is already buying the Brish'diri special football uniforms. We'd be happy to cover all your extra costs. You'd get a better recreational program for all concerned."

Hill still looked doubtful. "Well . . . "

"Moreover," Tomkins said, "we might be able to arrange a government grant or two to bolster other improvements in your program. Now how about it?"

Hill's eyes sparkled with sudden interest. "A grant? How big a grant? Could you swing a gravity grid?"

"No problem," said Tomkins. A slow grin spread across his face.

Hill returned the grin. "Then, mister, Starport's got itself a Brish'diri football team. But oh, are they going to scream!" He flicked on the desk intercom. "Get Jack De Angelis in here," he ordered. "I've got a little surprise for him."

The sky above Starport Municipal Stadium was bleak and dreary on a windy Saturday morning a week later, but Hill didn't mind it at all. The stadium force bubble kept out the thin, wet drizzle that had soaked him to the bones on the way to the game, and the weather fitted his mood beautifully.

Normally, Hill was far too busy to attend any of his department's sporting events. Normally *everyone* was too busy to attend the department's sporting events. The Rec Department leagues got fairly good coverage in the local newspaper, but they seldom drew many spectators. The record was something like four hundred people for a championship game a few years ago.

Or rather, that *was* the record, Hill reminded himself. No more. The stadium was packed today, in spite of the hour, the rain, and everything else. Municipal Stadium was never packed except for the traditional Thanksgiving Day football game between Starport High and its archrival, Grissom City Prep. But today it was packed.

Hill knew why. It had been drilled into him the hard way after he had made the damn-fool decision to let the Brish'diri into the league. The whole city was up in arms. Six local teams had withdrawn from the City League rather than play with the "inhuman monsters." The office switchboard had been flooded with calls daily, the vast majority of them angry denunciations of Hill. A city council member had called for his resignation.

And that, Hill reflected glumly, was probably what it would come to in the end. The local newspaper, which had always been hard-line conservative on foreign affairs, was backing the drive to force Hill out of office. One of its editorials had reminded him gleefully that Starport Municipal Stadium was dedicated to those who had given their lives in the Brish'diri War, and had screamed about "desecration." Meanwhile, on its sports pages, the paper had taken to calling the Brish'diri team "the Baldy Eagles."

Hill squirmed uncomfortably in his seat on the fifty-yard line, and prayed silently that the game would begin. He could feel the angry stares on the back of his neck, and he had the uneasy impression that he was going to be hit with a rock any second now.

Across the field, he could see the camera installation of one of the big 3-V networks. All five of them were here, of course; the game had gotten planetwide publicity. The newsfax wires had also sent reporters, although they had seemed a little confused about what kind of a story this was. One had sent a political reporter, the other a sportswriter.

Out on the stadium's artificial grass, the human team was running through a few plays and warming up. Their bright-red uniforms were emblazoned with KEN'S COMPUTER REPAIR in white lettering, and they wore matching white helmets. They looked pretty good, Hill decided from watching them practice, although they were far from championship caliber. Still, against a team that had never played football before, they should mop up.

De Angelis, wearing a pained expression and a ref's striped shirt, was out on the field talking to his officials. Hill was taking no chances with bad calls in this game. He'd made sure the department's best men were on hand to officiate.

Tomkins was also there, sitting in the stands a few sections away from Hill. But the Brish'diri were not. Remjhard wanted to attend, but E. T. Relations, on Hill's advice, had told him to stay at the mission. Instead, the game was being piped to him over closed circuit 3-V.

Hill suddenly straightened in his seat. The Brish'diri team, which called itself the Kosg-Anjehn after a flying carnivore native to Brishun, had arrived, and the players were walking slowly out onto the field.

There was a brief instant of silence, and then someone in the crowd started booing. Others picked it up. Then others. The stadium was filled with the boos. Although, Hill noted with relief, not everyone was joining in. Maybe there were some people who saw things his way.

The Brish'diri ignored the catcalls. Or seemed to, at any rate. Hill had never seen an angry Brish'dir, and was unsure how one would go about showing his anger.

The Kosg-Anjehn wore tight-fitting black uniforms, with odd-looking elongated silver helmets to cover their bullet-shaped heads. They looked like no football team Hill had ever seen. Only a handful of them stood over five feet, but they were all as squat and broad as a tackle for the Packers. Their arms and legs were thick and stumpy, but rippled with muscles that bulged in the wrong places. The helmeted heads, however, gave an impression of frailty, like eggshells ready to shatter at the slightest impact.

Two of the Brish'diri detached themselves from the group and walked over to De Angelis. Evidently they felt they didn't need a warm-up, and wanted to start immediately. De Angelis talked to them for an instant, then turned and beckoned to the captain of the human team.

"How do you think it'll go?"

Hill turned. It was Tomkins. The E. T. agent had struggled through the crowd to his side.

"Hard to say," the director replied. "The Brish'diri have never really played football before, so the odds are they'll lose. Being from a heavy-gravity planet, they'll be stronger than the humans, so that might give them an edge. But they're also a lot slower, from what I hear."

"I'll have to root them home," Tomkins said with a smile. "Bolster the cause of interstellar relations and all that."

Hill scowled. "You root them home if you like. I'm pulling for the humans. Thanks to you, I'm in enough trouble already. If they catch me rooting for the Brish'diri they'll tear me to shreds."

He turned his attention back to the field. The Computermen had won the toss, and elected to receive. One of the taller Brish'diri was going back to kick off.

"Tuhgayh-dei," Tomkins provided helpfully. "The son of the mission's chief linguist." Hill nodded.

Tuhgayh-dei ran forward with a ponderous, lumbering gallop, nearly stopped when he finally reached the football, and slammed his foot into it awkwardly but hard. The ball landed in the upper tier of the stands, and a murmur went through the crowd.

"Pretty good," Tomkins said. "Don't you think?"

"Too good," replied Hill. He did not elaborate.

The humans took the ball on their twenty. The Computermen went into a huddle, broke it with a loud clap, and ran to their positions. A ragged cheer went up from the stands.

The humans went down into the three-point stance. Their Brish'diri opponents did not. The alien linemen just stood there, hands dangling at their sides, crouching a little.

"They don't know much about football," Hill said. "But after that kickoff, I wonder if they have to."

The ball was snapped, and the quarterback for Ken's Computer Repair, a rangy ex-high-school star named Sullivan, faded back to pass. The Brish'diri rushed forward in a crude blitz, and crashed into the human linemen.

An instant later, Sullivan was lying face down in the grass, buried under three Brish'diri. The aliens had blown through the offensive line as if it didn't exist.

That made it second-and-fifteen. The humans huddled again, came out to another cheer, not quite so loud as the first one. The ball was snapped. Sullivan handed off to a beefy fullback, who crashed straight ahead.

One of the Brish'diri brought him down before he went half a yard. It was a clumsy tackle, around the shoulders. But the force of the contact knocked the fullback several yards in the wrong direction.

When the humans broke from their huddle for the third time the cheer could scarcely be heard. Again Sullivan tried to pass. Again the Brish'diri blasted through the line en masse. Again Sullivan went down for a loss.

Hill groaned. "This looks worse every minute," he said.

Tomkins didn't agree. "I don't think so. They're doing fine. What difference does it make who wins?"

Hill didn't bother to answer that.

There was no cheering when the humans came out in punt formation. Once more the Brish'diri put on a strong rush, but the punter got the ball away before they reached him.

It was a good, deep kick. The Kosg-Anjehn took over on their own twenty-five yard line. Marhdain-nei, Remjhard's son, was the Brish'diri quarterback. On the first play from scrimmage, he handed off to a halfback, a runt built like a tank.

The Brish'diri blockers flattened their human opponents almost effortlessly, and the runt plowed through the gaping hole, ran over two would-be tacklers, and burst into the clear. He was horribly slow, however, and the defenders finally brought him down from behind after a modest thirty-yard gain. But it took three people to stop him.

On the next play, Marhdain tried to pass. He got excellent protection, but his receivers, trudging along at top speed, had defensemen all over them. And the ball, when thrown, went sizzling over the heads of Brish'diri and humans alike.

Marhdain returned to the ground again after that, and handed off to a runt halfback once more. This time he tried to sweep around end, but was hauled to the ground after a gain of only five yards by a quartet of human tacklers.

That made it third-and-five. Marhdain kept to the ground. He gave the ball to his other halfback, and the brawny Brish'dir smashed up the middle. He was a little bit faster than the runt. When he got in the clear, only one man managed to catch him from behind. And one wasn't enough. The alien shrugged off the tackle and lumbered on across the goal line.

The extra point try went under the crossbar instead of over it. But it still nearly killed the poor guy in the stands who tried to catch the ball.

Tomkins was grinning. Hill shook his head in disgust. "This isn't the way it's supposed to go," he said. "They'll kill us if the Brish'diri win."

The kickoff went out of the stadium entirely this time. On the first play from the twenty, a Brish'diri lineman roared through the line and hit Sullivan just as he was handing off. Sullivan fumbled.

Another Brish'dir picked up the loose ball and carried it into the end zone while most of the humans were still lying on the ground.

"My God," said Hill, feeling a bit numb. "They're too strong. They're too damn strong. The humans can't cope with their strength. Can't stop them."

"Cheer up," said Tomkins. "It can't get much worse for your side."

But it did. It got a lot worse.

On offense, the Brish'diri were well-nigh unstoppable. Their runners were all short on speed, but made up for it with muscle. On play after play, they smashed straight up the middle behind a wall of blockers, flicking tacklers aside like bothersome insects.

And then Marhdain began to hit on his passes. Short passes, of course. The Brish'diri lacked the speed to cover much ground. But they could outjump any human, and they snared pass after pass in the air. There was no need to worry about interceptions. The humans simply couldn't hang on to Marhdain's smoking pitches.

On defense, things were every bit as bad. The Computermen couldn't run against the Brish'diri line. And Sullivan seldom had time to complete a pass, for the alien rushers were unstoppable. The few passes he did hit on went for touchdowns; no Brish'diri could catch a human from behind. But those were few and far between.

When Hill fled the stadium in despair at the half, the score was Kosg-Anjehn 37, Ken's Computer Repair 7.

The final score was 57 to 14. The Brish'diri had emptied their bench in the second half.

Hill didn't have the courage to attend the next Brish'diri game later in the week. But nearly everyone else in the city showed up to see if the Kosg-Anjehn could do it again.

They did. In fact, they did even better. They beat Anderson's Drugs by a lopsided 61 to 9 score.

After the Brish'diri won their third contest, 43 to 17, the huge crowds began tapering off. The Starport Municipal Stadium was only three-quarters full when the Kosg-Anjehn rolled over the Stardusters, 38 to 0, and a mere handful showed up on a rainy Thursday afternoon to see the aliens punish the United Veterans Association 51 to 6. And no one came after that.

For Hill, the Brish'diri win over the UVA-sponsored team was the final straw. The local paper made a heyday out of that, going on and on about the "ironic injustice" of having the UVA slaughtered by the Brish'diri in a stadium dedicated to the dead veterans of the Brish'diri 'War. And Hill, of course, was the main villain in the piece.

The phone calls had finally let up by that point. But the mail had been flowing into his office steadily, and most of it was not very comforting. The harassed Rec director got a few letters of commendation and support, but the bulk of the flood speculated crudely about his ancestry or threatened his life and property.

Two more city councilmen had come out publicly in favor of Hill's dismissal after the Brish'diri defeated UVA. Several others on the council were wavering, while Hill's supporters, who backed him strongly in private, were afraid to say anything for the record. The municipal elections were simply too close, and none were willing to risk their political skins.

And of course the assistant director of recreation, next in line for Hill's job, had wasted no time in saying *he* would certainly never have done such an unpatriotic thing.

With disaster piling upon disaster, it was only natural that Hill reacted with something less than enthusiasm when he walked into his office a few days after the fifth Kosg-Anjehn victory and found Tomkins sitting at his desk waiting for him.

"And what in the hell do you want now?" Hill roared at the E. T. Relations man.

Tomkins looked slightly abashed, and got up from the director's chair. He had been watching the latest free-fall football results on the desk console while waiting for Hill to arrive.

"I've got to talk to you," Tomkins said. "We've got a problem."

"We've got lots of problems," Hill replied. He strode angrily to his desk, sat down, flicked off the console, and pulled a sheaf of papers from a drawer.

"This is the latest of them," he continued, waving the papers at Tomkins. "One of the kids broke his leg in the Starduster game. It happens all the time. Football's a rough game. You can't do anything to prevent it. On a normal case, the department would send a letter of apology to the parents, our insurance would pay for it, and everything would be forgotten.

"But not in this case. Oh, no. This injury was inflicted while the kid was playing against the Brish'diri. So his parents are charging negligence on our part and suing the city. So our insurance company refuses to pay up. It claims the policy doesn't cover damage by inhuman, superstrong, alien monsters. Bah! How's that for a problem, Mr. Tomkins? Plenty more where that came from."

Tomkins frowned. "Very unfortunate. But my problem is a lot more serious than that." Hill started to interrupt, but the E. T. Relations man waved him down. "No, please, hear me out. This is very important."

He looked around for a seat, grabbed the nearest chair, and pulled it up to the desk. "Our plans have backfired badly," he began. "There has been a serious miscalculation—our fault entirely, I'm afraid. E. T. Relations failed to consider all the ramifications of this Brish'diri football team."

Hill fixed him with an iron stare. "What's wrong now?"

"Well," Tomkins said awkwardly, "we knew that refusal to admit the Kosg-Anjehn into your league would be a sign of human weakness and fear to the Brish'diri war faction. But once you admitted them, we thought the problem was solved.

"It wasn't. We went wrong when we assumed that winning or losing would make no difference to the Brish'diri. To us, it was just a game. Didn't matter who won. After all, Brish'diri and Terrans would be getting to know each other, competing harmlessly on even terms. Nothing but good could come from it, we felt."

"So?" Hill interrupted. "Get to the point."

Tomkins shook his head sadly. "The point is, we didn't know the Brish'diri would win so *big*. And so *regularly*." He paused. "We—uh—we got a transmission late last night from one of our men on Brishun. It seems the Brish'diri war faction is using the one-sided football scores as propaganda to prove the racial inferiority of humans. They seem to be getting a lot of mileage out of it."

Hill winced. "So it was all for nothing. So I've subjected myself to all this abuse and endangered my career for absolutely nothing. Great! That was all I needed, I tell you."

"We still might be able to salvage something," Tomkins said. "That's why I came to see you. If you can arrange it for the Brish'diri to *lose*, it would knock holes in that superiority yarn and make the war faction look like fools. It would discredit them for quite a while."

"And just how am I supposed to arrange for them to lose, as you so nicely put it? What do you think I'm running here anyway, professional wrestling?"

Tomkins just shrugged lamely. "I was hoping you'd have some ideas," he said.

Hill leaned forward, and flicked on his intercom. "Is Jack out there?" he asked. "Good. Send him in."

The lanky sports official appeared less than a minute later. "You're on top of this City football mess," Hill said. "What's the chances the Kosg-Anjehn will lose?"

De Angelis looked puzzled. "Not all that good, offhand," he replied. "They've got a damn fine team."

He reached into his back pocket and pulled out a notebook. "Let me check their schedule," he continued, thumbing through the pages. He stopped when he found the place.

"Well, the league's got a round-robin schedule, as you know. Every team plays every other team once, best record is champion. Now the Brish'diri are currently five to zero, and they've beaten a few of the better teams. We've got ten teams left in the league, so they've got four games left to play. Only, two of those are with the weakest teams in the league, and the third opponent is only mediocre."

"And the fourth?" Hill said hopefully.

"That's your only chance. An outfit sponsored by a local tavern, the Blastoff Inn. Good team. Fast, strong. Plenty of talent. They're also five to zero, and should give the Brish'diri some trouble." De Angelis frowned. "But, to be frank, I've seen both teams, and I'd still pick the Brish'diri. That ground game of theirs is just too much." He snapped the notebook shut and pocketed it again.

"Would a close game be good enough?" Hill said, turning to Tomkins again.

The E. T. Relations man shook his head. "No. They have to be beaten. If they lose, the whole season's meaningless. Proves nothing but that the two races can compete on roughly equal terms. But if they win, it looks like they're invincible, and our stature in Brish'diri eyes takes a nose dive."

"Then they'll have to lose, I guess," Hill said. His gaze shifted back to De Angelis. "Jack, you and me are going to have to do some hard thinking about how the Kosg-Anjehn can be beaten. And then we're going to call up the manager of the Blastoff Inn team and give him a few tips. You have any ideas?"

De Angelis scratched his head thoughtfully. "Well—" he began. "Maybe we—"

During the weeks that followed, De Angelis met with the Blastoff Inn coach regularly to discuss plans and strategy, and supervised a few practice sessions. Hill, meanwhile, was fighting desperately to keep his job, and jotting down ideas on how to beat the Brish'diri during every spare moment

Untouched by the furor, the Kosg-Anjehn won its sixth game handily, 40 to 7, and then rolled to devastating victories over the circuit's two cellar-dwellers. The margins were 73 to 0 and 62 to 7. That gave them an unblemished 8 to 0 ledger, with one game left to play.

But the Blastoff Inn team was also winning regularly, although never as decisively. It too would enter the last game of the season undefeated.

The local news heralded the showdown with a sports-section streamer on the day before the game. The lead opened, "The stakes will be high for the entire human race tomorrow at Municipal Stadium, when Blastoff Inn meets the Brish'diri Baldy Eagles for the championship of the Department of Recreation City Football League."

The reporter who wrote the story never dreamed how close to the truth he actually was.

The crowds returned to the stadium for the championship game, although they fell far short of a packed house. The local reporter was there too. But the 3-V networks and the newsfax wires were long gone. The novelty of the story had worn off quickly.

Hill arrived late, just before game time, and joined Tomkins on the fifty-yard line. The E. T. agent seemed to have cheered up somewhat. "Our guys looked pretty good during the warm-up," he told the director. "I think we've got a chance."

His enthusiasm was not catching, however. "Blastoff Inn might have a chance, but I sure don't," Hill said glumly. "The city council is meeting tonight to consider a motion for calling for my dismissal. I have a strong suspicion that it's going to pass, no matter who wins this afternoon."

"Hmmmm," said Tomkins, for want of anything better to say. "Just ignore the old fools. Look, the game's starting."

Hill muttered something under his breath and turned his attention back to the field. The Brish'diri had lost the toss once more, and the kickoff had once again soared out of the stadium. It was first-and-ten for Blastoff Inn on its own twenty.

And at that point the script suddenly changed.

The humans lined up for their first play of the game but with a difference. Instead of playing immediately in back of the center, the Blastoff quarterback was several yards deep, in a shotgun formation.

The idea, Hill recalled, was to take maximum advantage of human speed, and mount a strong passing offense. Running against the Brish'diri was all but impossible, he and De Angelis had concluded after careful consideration. That meant an aerial attack, and the only way to provide that was to give the Blastoff quarterback time to pass. Ergo, the shotgun formation.

The hike from center was dead on target and the Blastoff receivers shot off downfield, easily outpacing the ponderous Brish'diri defensemen. As usual, the Kosg-Anjehn crashed through the line en masse, but they had covered only half the distance to the quarterback before he got off the pass.

It was a long bomb, a psychological gambit to shake up the Brish'diri by scoring on the first play of the game. Unfortunately, the pass was slightly overthrown.

Hill swore.

It was now second-and-ten. Again the humans lined up in a shotgun offense, and again the Blastoff quarterback got off the pass in time. It was a short, quick pitch to the sideline, complete for a nine-yard gain. The crowd cheered lustily.

Hill wasn't sure what the Brish'diri would expect on third-and-one. But whatever it was, they didn't get it. With the aliens still slightly off balance, Blastoff went for the bomb again.

This time it was complete. All alone in the open, the fleet human receiver snagged the pass neatly and went all the way in for the score. The Brish'diri never laid a hand on him.

The crowd sat in stunned silence for a moment when the pass was caught. Then, when it became clear that there was no way to prevent the score, the cheering began, and peaked slowly to an ear-splitting roar. The stadium rose to its feet as one, screaming wildly.

For the first time all season, the Kosg-Anjehn trailed. A picture-perfect place kick made the score 7 to 0 in favor of Blastoff Inn.

Tomkins was on his feet, cheering loudly. Hill, who had remained seated, regarded him dourly. "Sit down," he said. "The game's not over yet."

The Brish'diri soon underlined that point. No sooner did they take over the ball than they came pounding back upfield, smashing into the line again and again. The humans alternated between a dozen different defensive formations. None of them seemed to do any good. The Brish'diri steamroller ground ahead inexorably.

The touchdown was an anticlimax. Luckily, however, the extra point try failed. Tuhgayh-dei lost a lot of footballs, but he had still not developed a knack for putting his kicks between the crossbars.

The Blastoff offense took the field again. They looked determined.

The first play from scrimmage was a short pass over the middle, complete for fifteen yards. Next came a tricky double pass. Complete for twelve yards.

On the following play, the Blastoff fullback tried to go up the middle. He got creamed for a five-yard loss.

"If they stop our passing, we're dead," Hill said to Tomkins, without taking his eyes off the field.

Luckily, the Blastoff quarterback quickly gave up on the idea of establishing a running game. A prompt return to the air gave the humans another first down. Three plays later, they scored. Again the crowd roared.

Trailing now 14 to 6, the Brish'diri once more began to pound their way upfield. But the humans, elated by their lead, were a little tougher now. Reading the Brish'diri offense with confident precision, the defensemen began gang-tackling the alien runners.

The Kosg-Anjehn drive slowed down, then stalled. They were forced to surrender the ball near the fifty-yard line.

Tomkins started pounding Hill on the back. "You did it," he said. "We stopped them on offense too. We're going to win."

"Take it easy," Hill replied. "That was a fluke. Several of our men just happened to be in the right place at the right time. It's happened before. No one ever said the Brish'diri scored every time they got the ball. Only most of the time."

Back on the field, the Blastoff passing attack was still humming smoothly. A few accurate throws put the humans on the Kosg-Anjehn's thirty.

And then the aliens changed formations. They took several men off the rush, and put them on pass defense. They started double-teaming the Blastoff receivers. Except it wasn't normal double-teaming. The second defender was playing far back of the line of scrimmage. By the time the human had outrun the first Brish'dir, the second would be right on top of him.

"I was afraid of something like this," Hill said. "We're not the only ones who can react to circumstances."

The Blastoff quarterback ignored the shift in the alien defense, and stuck to his aerial game plan. But his first pass from the thirty, dead on target, was batted away by a Brish'dir defender who happened to be right on top of the play.

The same thing happened on second down. That made it third-and-ten. The humans called time out. There was a hurried conference on the sidelines.

When action resumed, the Blastoff offense abandoned the shotgun formation. Without the awesome Brish'diri blitz to worry about, the quarterback was relatively safe in his usual position.

There was a quick snap, and the quarterback got rid of the ball equally quickly, an instant before a charging Brish'dir bore him to the ground. The halfback who got the handoff streaked to the left in an end run.

The other Brish'diri defenders lumbered towards him en masse to seal shut the sideline. But just as he reached the sideline, still behind the line of scrimmage, the Blastoff halfback handed off to a teammate streaking right.

A wide grin spread across Hill's face. A reverse!

The Brish'diri were painfully slow to change directions. The human swept around right end with ridiculous ease and shot upfield, surrounded by blockers. The remaining Brish'diri closed in. One or two were taken out by team blocks. The rest found it impossible to lay their hands on the swift, darting runner. Dodging this way and that, he wove a path neatly between them and loped into the end zone.

Once more the stadium rose to its feet. This time Hill stood up too.

Tomkins was beaming again. "Ha!" he said. "I thought you were the one who said we couldn't run against them."

"Normally we can't," the director replied. "There's no way to run over or through them, so runs up the middle are out. End runs are better, but if they're in their formal formation, that too is a dreary prospect. There is no way a human runner can get past a wall of charging Brish'diri.

"However, when they spread out like they just did, they give us an open field to work with. We can't go over or through them, no, but we sure as hell can go *between* them when they're scattered all over the field. And Blastoff Inn has several excellent open-field runners."

The crowd interrupted him with another roar to herald a successful extra-point conversion. It was now 21 to 6.

The game was far from over, however. The human defense was not nearly as successful on the next series of downs. Instead of relying exclusively on the running game, Marhdain-nei kept his opponents guessing with some of his patented short, hard pop passes.

To put on a more effective rush, the Blastoff defense spread out at wide intervals. The offensive line thus opened up, and several humans managed to fake out slower Brish'diri blockers and get past them to the quarterback. Marhdain was even thrown for a loss once.

But the Blastoff success was short-lived. Marhdain adjusted quickly. The widely spread human defense, highly effective against the pass, was a total failure against the run. The humans were too far apart to gang-tackle. And there was no way short of mass assault to stop a Brish'dir in full stride.

After that there was no stopping the Kosg-Anjehn, as Marhdain alternated between the pass and the run according to the human defensive formation. The aliens marched upfield quickly for their second touchdown.

This time, even the extra point was on target.

The Brish'diri score had taken some of the steam out of the crowd, but the Blastoff Inn offense showed no signs of being disheartened when they took the field again. With the aliens back in their original blitz defense, the human quarterback fell back on the shotgun once more.

His first pass was overthrown, but the next three in a row were dead on target and moved Blastoff to the Kosg-Anjehn forty. A running play, inserted to break the monotony, ended in a six-yard loss. Then came another incomplete pass. The toss was perfect, but the receiver dropped the ball.

That made it third-and-ten, and a tremor of apprehension went through the crowd. Nearly everyone in the stadium realized that the humans had to keep scoring to stay in the game.

The snap from center was quick and clean. The Blastoff quarterback snagged the ball, took a few unhurried steps backward to keep at a safe distance from the oncoming Brish'diri rushers, and tried to pick out a receiver. He scanned the field carefully. Then he reared back and unleashed a bomb.

It looked like another touchdown. The human had his alien defender beaten by a good five yards and was still gaining ground. The pass was a beauty.

But then, as the ball began to spiral downward, the Brish'diri defender stopped suddenly in midstride. Giving up his hopeless chase, he craned his head around to look for the ball, spotted it, braced himself—and jumped.

Brish'diri leg muscles, evolved for the heavy gravity of Brishun, were far more powerful than their human counterparts. Despite their heavier bodies, the Brish'diri could easily outjump any human. But so far they had only taken advantage of that fact to snare Marhdain's pop passes.

But now, as Hill blinked in disbelief, the Kosg-Anjehn defenseman leaped at least five feet into the air to meet the descending ball in midair and knock it aside with a vicious backhand slap.

The stadium moaned.

Forced into a punting situation, Blastoff Inn suddenly seemed to go limp. The punter fumbled the snap from center, and kicked the ball away when he tried to pick it up. The Brish'dir who picked it up got twenty yards before he was brought down.

The human defense this time put up only token resistance as Marhdain led his team downfield on a series of short passes and devastating runs.

It took the Brish'diri exactly six plays to narrow the gap to 21 to 19. Luckily, Tuhgayh missed another extra point.

There was a loud cheer when the Blastoff offense took the field again. But right from the first play after the kickoff, it was obvious that something had gone out of them.

The human quarterback, who had been giving a brilliant performance, suddenly became erratic. To add to his problems, the Brish'diri were suddenly jumping all over the field.

The alien kangaroo-pass defense had several severe limitations. It demanded precise timing and excellent reflexes on the part of the jumpers, neither of which was a Brish'diri forte. But it was a disconcerting tactic that the Blastoff quarterback had never come up against before. He didn't know quite how to cope with it.

The humans drove to their own forty, bogged down, and were forced to punt. The Kosg-Anjehn promptly marched the ball back the other way and scored. For the first time in the game, they led.

The next Blastoff drive was a bit more successful, and reached the Brish'diri twenty before it ground to a halt. The humans salvaged the situation with a field goal.

The Kosg-Anjehn rolled up another score, driving over the goal line just seconds before the half ended.

The score stood at 31 to 24 in favor of the Brish'diri.

And there was no secret about the way the tide was running.

■ ■ ■

It had grown very quiet in the stands.

Tomkins, wearing a worried expression, turned to Hill with a sigh. "Well, maybe we'll make a comeback in the second half. We're only down seven. That's not so bad."

"Maybe," Hill said doubtfully. "But I don't think so. They've got all the momentum. I hate to say so, but I think we're going to get run out of the stadium in the second half."

Tomkins frowned. "I certainly hope not. I'd hate to see what the Brish'diri war faction would do with a really lopsided score. Why, they'd—" He stopped, suddenly aware that Hill wasn't paying the slightest bit of attention. The director's eyes had wandered back to the field.

"Look," Hill said, pointing. "By the gate. Do you see what I see?"

"It looks like a car from the trade mission," the E. T. agent said, squinting to make it out.

"And who's that getting out?"

Tomkins hesitated. "Remjhard-nei," he said at last.

The Brish'dir climbed smoothly from the low-slung black vehicle, walked a short distance across the stadium grass, and vanished through the door leading to one of the dressing rooms.

"What's he doing here?" Hill asked. "Wasn't he supposed to stay away from the games?"

Tomkins scratched his head uneasily. "Well, that's what we advised. Especially at first, when hostility was at its highest. But he's not a *prisoner*, you know. There's no way we could force him to stay away from the games if he wants to attend."

Hill was frowning. "Why should he take your advice all season and suddenly disregard it now?"

Tomkins shrugged. "Maybe he wanted to see his son win a championship."

"Maybe. But I don't think so. There's something funny going on here."

By the time the second half was ready to begin, Hill was feeling even more apprehensive. The Kosg-Anjehn had taken the field a few minutes earlier, but Remjhard had not reappeared. He was still down in the alien locker room.

Moreover, there was something subtly different about the Brish'diri as they lined up to receive the kickoff. Nothing drastic. Nothing obvious. But somehow the atmosphere was changed. The aliens appeared more carefree, more relaxed. Almost as if they had stopped taking their opponents seriously.

Hill could sense the difference. He'd seen other teams with the same sort of attitude before, in dozens of other contests. It was the attitude of a team that already knows how the game is going to come out. The attitude of a team that knows it is sure to win—or doomed to lose.

The kickoff was poor and wobbly. A squat Brish'dir took it near the thirty and headed upfield. Two Blastoff tacklers met him at the thirty-five.

He fumbled.

The crowd roared. For a second the ball rolled loose on the stadium grass. A dozen hands reached for it, knocking it this way and that. Finally, a brawny Blastoff lineman landed squarely on top of it and trapped it beneath him.

And suddenly the game turned around again.

"I don't believe it," Hill said. "That was it. The break we needed. After that touchdown pass was knocked aside, our team just lost heart. But now, after this, look at them. We're back in this game."

The Blastoff offense raced onto the field, broke the huddle with an enthusiastic shout, and lined up. It was first-and-ten from the Brish'diri twenty-eight.

The first pass was deflected off a bounding Brish'dir. The second, however, went for a touchdown.

The score was tied.

The Kosg-Anjehn held on to the kickoff this time. They put the ball in play near the twenty-five.

Marhdain opened the series of downs with a pass. No one, human or Brish'dir, was within ten yards of where it came down. The next play was a run. But the Kosg-Anjehn halfback hesitated oddly after he took the hand-off. Given time to react, four humans smashed into him at the line of scrimmage. Marhdain went back to the air. The pass was incomplete again.

The Brish'diri were forced to punt.

Up in the stands, Tomkins was laughing wildly. He began slapping Hill on the back again. "Look at that! Not even a first down. We held them. And you said they were going to run us out of the stadium."

A strange half-smile danced across the director's face. "Ummm," he said. "So I did." The smile faded.

It was a good, solid punt, but Blastoff's deep man fielded it superbly and ran it back to the fifty. From there, it took only seven plays for the human quarterback, suddenly looking cool and confident again, to put the ball in the end zone.

Bouncing Brish'diri had evidently ceased to disturb him. He simply threw the ball through spots where they did not happen to be bouncing.

This time the humans missed the extra point. But no one cared. The score was 37 to 31. Blastoff Inn was ahead again.

And they were ahead to stay. No sooner had the Kosg-Anjehn taken over again than Marhdain threw an interception. It was the first interception he had thrown all season.

Naturally, it was run back for a touchdown.

After that, the Brish'diri seemed to revive a little. They drove three quarters of the way down the field, but then they bogged down as soon as they got within the shadow of the goal posts. On fourth-and-one from the twelve-yard line, the top Brish'diri runner slipped and fell behind the line of scrimmage.

Blastoff took over. And scored.

From then on, it was more of the same.

The final score was 56 to 31. The wrong team had been run out of the stadium.

Tomkins, of course, was in ecstasy. "We did it. I knew we could do it. This is perfect, just perfect. We humiliated them. The war faction will be totally discredited now. They'll never be able to stand up under the ridicule." He grinned and slapped Hill soundly on the back once again.

Hill winced under the blow, and eyed the E. T. man dourly. "There's something funny going on here. If the Brish'diri had played all season the way they played in the second half, they never would have gotten this far. Something happened in that locker room during half-time."

Nothing could dent Tomkins' grin, however. "No, no," he said. "It was the fumble. That was what did it. It demoralized them, and they fell apart. They just clutched, that's all. It happens all the time."

"Not to teams this good it doesn't," Hill replied. But Tomkins wasn't around to hear. The E. T. agent had turned abruptly and was weaving his way through the crowd, shouting something about being right back.

Hill frowned and turned back to the field. The stadium was emptying quickly. The Rec director stood there for a second, still looking puzzled.

Then suddenly he vaulted the low fence around the field, and set off across the grass.

He walked briskly across the stadium and down into the visitors' locker room. The Brish'diri were changing clothes in sullen silence, and filing out of the room slowly to the airbus that would carry them back to the trade mission.

Remjhard-nei was sitting in a corner of the room.

The Brish'dir greeted him with a slight nod. "Director Hill. Did you enjoy the game? It was a pity our half-men failed in their final test. But they still performed creditably, do you not think?"

Hill ignored the question. "Don't give me the bit about failing, Remjhard. I'm not as stupid as I look. Maybe no one else in the stadium realized what was going on out there this afternoon, but I did. You didn't lose that game. You threw it. Deliberately. And I want to know why!"

Remjhard stared at Hill for a long minute. Then, very slowly, he rose from the bench on which he was seated. His face was blank and expressionless, but his eyes glittered in the dim light.

Hill suddenly realized that they were alone in the locker room. Then he remembered the awesome Brish'diri strength, and took a hasty step backwards away from the alien.

"You realize," Remjhard said gravely, "that it is a grave insult to accuse a Brish'dir of dishonorable conduct?"

The emissary took another careful look around the locker room to make sure the two of them were alone. Then he took another step towards Hill.

And broke into a wide smile when the director, edging backwards, almost tripped over a locker.

"But, of course, there is no question of dishonor here," the alien continued. "Honor is too big for a half-man's play. And, to be sure, in the rules that you furnished us, there was no provisions requiring participants to—" He paused. "—to play at their best, shall we say?"

Hill, untangling himself from the locker, sputtered. "But there are unwritten rules, traditions. This sort of thing simply is not sporting."

Remjhard was still smiling. "To a Brish'dir, there is nothing as meaningless as an unwritten rule. It is a contradiction in terms, as you say."

"But why?" said Hill. "That's what I can't understand. Everyone keeps telling me that your culture is virile, competitive, proud. Why should you throw the game? Why should you make yourself look bad? Why?"

Remjhard made an odd gurgling noise. Had he been a human, Hill would have thought he was choking. Instead, he assumed he was laughing.

"Humans amuse me," the Brish'dir said at last. "You attach a few catch phrases to a culture, and you think you understand it. And, if something disagrees with your picture, you are shocked.

"I am sorry, Director Hill. Cultures are not that simple. They are very complex mechanisms. A word like 'pride' does not describe everything about the Brish'diri.

"Oh, we are proud. Yes. And competitive. Yes. But we are also intelligent. And our values are flexible enough to adjust to the situation at hand."

Remjhard paused again, and looked Hill over carefully. Then he decided to continue. "This football of yours is a fine game, Director Hill. I told you that once before. I mean it. It is very enjoyable, a good exercise of mind and body.

"But it is only a game. Competing in games is important, of course. But there are larger competitions. More important ones. And I am intelligent enough to know which one gets our first priority.

"I received word from Brishun this afternoon about the use to which the Kosg-Anjehn victories were being put. Your friend from Extraterrestrial Relations must have told you that I rank among the leaders of the Brish'diri Peace Party. I would not be here on Earth otherwise. None of our opponents is willing to work with humans, whom they consider animals.

"Naturally I came at once to the stadium and informed our half-men that they must lose. And they, of course, complied. They too realize that some competitions are more important than others.

"For in losing, we have won. Our opponents on Brishun will not survive this humiliation. In the next Great Choosing many will turn against them. And I, and others at the mission, will profit. And the Brish'diri will profit.

"Yes, Director Hill," Remjhard concluded, still smiling. "We are a competitive race. But competition for control of a world takes precedence over a football game."

Hill was smiling himself by now. Then he began to laugh. "Of course," he said. "And when I think of the ways we pounded our heads out to think of strategies to beat you. When all we had to do was tell you what was going on." He laughed again.

Remjhard was about to add something when suddenly the locker-room door swung open and Tomkins stalked in. The E. T. agent was still beaming.

"Thought I'd find you here, Hill," he began. "Still trying to investigate those conspiracy theories of yours, eh?" He chuckled and winked at Remjhard.

"Not really," Hill replied. "It was a harebrained theory. Obviously it was the fumble that did it."

"Of course," Tomkins said. "Glad to hear it. Anyway, I've got good news for you."

"Oh? What's that? That the world is saved? Fine. But I'm still out of a job come tonight."

"Not at all," Tomkins replied. "That's what my call was about. We've got a job for you. We want you to join E. T. Relations."

Hill looked dubious. "Come, now," he said. "Me an E. T. agent? I don't know the first thing about it. I'm a small-time local bureaucrat and sports official. How am I supposed to fit into E. T. Relations?"

"As a sports director," Tomkins replied. "Ever since this Brish'diri thing broke, we've been getting dozens of requests from other alien trade missions and diplomatic stations on Earth. They all want a crack at it too. So, to promote goodwill and all that, we're going to set up a program. And we want you to run it. At double your present salary, of course."

Hill thought about the difficulties of running a sports program for two dozen wildly different types of extraterrestrials.

Then he thought about the money he'd get for doing it.

Then he thought about the Starport City Council.

"Sounds like a fine idea," he said. "But tell me. That gravity grid you were going to give to Starport—is that transferable too?"

"Of course," Tomkins said.

"Then I accept." He glanced over at Remjhard. "Although I may live to regret it when I see what the Brish'diri can do on a basketball court."

The origins of Japanese sumo wrestling date back more than a thousand years; it began as a Shinto ritual used to predict the success of crops or to divine the gods' intentions. Sumo as a spectator sport developed during the Edo period (between 1603 to 1868). The basic rules are simple: win by knocking your opponent out of the ring (dohyō), *or forcing any portion of his body but the soles of his feet to touch the ground. Professional sumo wrestling is practiced only in Japan, where it is the national sport. (Wrestlers of other nationalities are allowed to participate, however only one foreigner per training stable—*heya*—is currently allowed.) Amateur sumo wrestling is practiced in scores of countries. Other than its expansion into an international sport and the development of telekinetic abilities, Howard Waldrop's future* zen-sumo *and its rituals are quite similar to today's sumo—or sumo two centuries ago.*

Man-Mountain Gentian

Howard Waldrop

> Just after the beginning of the present century it was realized that some of the wrestlers were throwing their opponents from the ring without touching them.
>
> —Ichinaga Naya, *Zen-Suomo: Sport and Ritual*
> (All-Japan Zen-Sumo Association Books, Kyoto, 2024)

It was the fourteenth day of the January Tokyo tournament. Sitting with the other wrestlers, Man-Mountain Gentian watched as the next match began.

Ground Sloth Ikimoto was taking on Killer Kudzu. They entered the tamped-earth ring and began their *shikiri*. Ground Sloth, a *sumotori* of the old school, had changed over from traditional to *zen-sumo* four years before. He weighed 180 kilos in his *mawashi.* He entered at the white tassel salt corner. He clapped his huge hands, rinsed his mouth, threw salt, rubbed his body with tissue paper, then began his high leg lifts, stamping his feet, his hands gripping far down his calves. The ring shook with each stamp. All the muscles rippled on his big frame. His stomach, a flesh-colored boulder, shook and vibrated.

Killer Kudzu was small, and thin, weighing barely over ninety kilos. On his forehead was the tattoo of his homeland, the PRC, one large star and five smaller stars blazing in a constellation. He also went into his ritual *shikiri*, but as he clapped he held in one hand a small box, ten centimeters on a side, showing his intention to bring it into the match. Sometimes these were objects for meditation, sometimes favors from male or female lovers, sometimes no one knew what. The only rule was that they could not be used as weapons.

The wrestlers were separated from the onlookers by four clear walls and a roof of plastic. Over this hung the traditional canopy and tassels, symbolizing heaven and the four winds. Through the plastic walls ran a mesh of fine wiring, connected to a six-volt battery next to the north-side judge.

A large number of 600X slow motion video cameras were placed around the auditorium to be used by the judges if necessary.

Killer Kudzu placed the box on his side of the line. He returned to his corner and threw more salt.

Ground Sloth Ikimoto stamped once more, twice, went to his line, settled into position like a football lineman, legs apart, knuckles to the ground. His nearly-bare buttocks looked like giant rocks. Killer Kudzu finished his *shikiri*, squatted at his line, where he settled his hand near his votive box, and glared at his opponent.

The referee, in his ceremonial robes, had been standing to one side during the preliminaries. Now he came to a position halfway between the wrestlers, his war fan down. He leaned away from the two men, left leg back to one side as if ready to run. He stared at the midpoint between the two and flipped his fan downward.

Instantly sweat sprang to their foreheads and shoulders, their bodies rippled as if pushing against great unmoving weights, their toes curled into the clay of the ring. They stayed immobile on their respective marks.

Killer Kudzu's neck muscles strained. With his left hand he reached and quickly opened the votive box.

Man-Mountain Gentian and the other wrestlers on the east side drew in their breaths.

Ground Sloth Ikimoto was a vegetarian and always had been. In training for traditional sumo, he had shunned the *chunko-nabe*, the communal stew of fish, chicken, meat, eggs, onions, cabbage, carrots, turnips, sugar, and soy sauce. Traditional *sumotori* ate as much as they could hold twice a day, and weight gain was tremendous.

Ikimoto had instead trained twice as hard, eating only vegetables, starches, and sugars. Meat and eggs had never touched his lips.

What Killer Kudzu brought out of the box was a cheeseburger. With one swift movement he bit into it only half a meter from Ground Sloth's face.

Ikimoto blanched and started to scream. As he did, he lifted into the air as if chopped in the chest with an ax, arms and legs flailing, a Dopplering wail of revulsion coming from his emptied lungs. He passed the bales marking the edge of the ring, one foot dragging the ground, upending a boundary bale, and smashed to the ground between the ring and the square bales at the plastic walls.

The referee signaled Killer Kudzu the winner. As he squatted the *gyoji* offered him a small envelope signifying a cash prize from his sponsors. Kudzu, left hand on his knee, with his right hand made three chopping gestures from the left, right, and above, thanking man, earth, and heaven. Kudzu took the envelope, then stepped through the doorway of the plastic enclosure and left the arena to rejoin the other west-side wrestlers.

The audience of eleven thousand was on its feet cheering. Across Japan and the world, two hundred million viewers watched.

Ground Sloth Ikimoto had risen to his feet, bowed and left by the other door. Attendants rushed in to repair the damaged ring.

Man-Mountain Gentian looked up at the scoring clock. The match had taken 4.1324 seconds. It was 3:30 in the afternoon on the fourteenth day of the Tokyo tournament.

The next match would pit Cast Iron Pekowski of Poland against Typhoon Takanaka.

After that would be Gentian's bout with the South African veldt wrestler Knockdown Krugerand.

Man-Mountain Gentian stood at 13-0 in the tournament, having defeated an opponent each day so far. He wanted to retire as the first Grand Champion to win six tournaments in a row, undefeated. He was not very worried about his contest later this afternoon.

Tomorrow, though, the last day of the January tournament, he would face Killer Kudzu, who, after this match, also stood undefeated at 14-0.

Man-Mountain Gentian was 1.976 meters tall and weighed exactly two hundred kilos. He had been a *sumotori* for six years, had been *yokozuna* for the last two of those. He was twice holder of the Emperor's Cup. He was the highest paid, the most famous *zen-sumotori* in the world.

He was twenty-three years old.

He and Knockdown Krugerand finished their shikiri. They got on their marks. The gyoji flipped his fan.

The match was over in 3.1916 seconds. He helped Krugerand to his feet, accepted the envelope and the thunderous applause of the crowd, and left the reverberating plastic enclosure.

"You are the wife of Man-Mountain Gentian?" asked a voice next to her.

Melissa put on her public smile and turned to the voice. Her nephew, on the other side, leaned around to look.

The man talking to her had five stars tattooed to his forehead. She knew he was a famous *sumotori*, though he was very slim and his *chonmage* had been combed out and washed and his hair was now a fluffy explosion above his head.

"I am Killer Kudzu," he said. "I'm surprised you aren't at the tournament."

"I am here with my nephew, Hari. Hari, this is Mr. Killer Kudzu." The nephew, dressed in his winter Little League outfit, shook hands firmly. "His team, the Mitsubishi Zeroes, play the Kawasaki Claudes next game."

They paused while a foul ball caused great excitement three rows down the bleachers. Hari leapt for it but some construction foreman of a father came up grinning with the ball.

"And what do you play?" asked Killer Kudzu.

"Utility outfield. When I play," said Hari, averting his eyes and sitting back down.

"Oh. How's your batting?"

"Pretty bad—.123 for the year," said Hari.

"Well, maybe this will be the night you shine," said Kudzu.

"I hope so," said Hari. "Half our team has the American flu."

"Just the reason I'm here," said Kudzu. "I was to meet a businessman whose son was to play this game. I find him not to be here, as his son has the influenza also."

It was hot in the domed stadium and Kudzu insisted they let him buy them Sno-cones. Just as the vendor got to them, Hari's coach signaled and the nephew ran down the bleachers and followed the rest of his teammates into the warmup area under the stadium.

Soon the other lackluster game was over and Hari's team took the field.

The first batter for the Claudes, a twelve-year-old built like an orangutan, got up and smashed a line drive off the Mitsubishi third baseman's chest. The third baseman had been waving to his mother. They carried him into the dugout. Melissa soon saw him up yelling again.

So it went through three innings. The Claudes had the Zeroes down by three runs, 6-3. In the fourth inning, Hari took the right field, injuries having whittled the flu-ridden team down to the third-stringers.

One of the Claudes hit a high looping fly straight to right field. Hari started in after it, but something happened with his feet; he fell and the ball dropped a meter from his outstretched glove. The center fielder chased it down and made the relay and by a miracle they got the runner sliding into home plate. He took out the Zeroes catcher doing it.

"It doesn't look good for the Zeroes," said Melissa.

"Oh, things might get better," said Killer Kudzu. "The opera's not over till the fat lady sings."

"A *diva* couldn't do much worse out there," said Melissa.

"They still don't like baseball in my country," he said. "Decadent. Bourgeois, they say. As if anything could be more decadent and middle-class than China."

"Yet you wear the flag?" She pointed toward his head.

"Call it a gesture to former greatness," he said.

Bottom of the sixth, last inning in Little League. The Zeroes had the bases loaded but they had two outs in the process. Hari came up to bat.

Things were tense. The outfielders were nearly falling down from tension.

The pitcher threw a blistering curve that got the outside. Hari was caught looking.

From the dugout the manager's voice saying unkind things carried to the crowd.

Eight thousand people were on their feet.

The pitcher wound up and threw.

Hari started a swing that should have ended in a grounder or a pop-up.

Halfway through, it looked like someone had speeded up a projector. The leisurely swing blurred. Hari literally threw himself to the ground. The bat cracked and broke in two at his feet.

The ball, a frozen white streak, cometed through the air and hit the scoreboard 110 meters away with a terrific crash, putting the inning indicator out of commission.

Everyone was stock-still. Hari was staring. Every player was turned toward the scoreboard.

"It's a home run, kid," the umpire reminded Hari. Slowly, unbelieving, Hari began to trot toward first base.

The place exploded, fans jumping to their feet. Hari's teammates on the bases headed for home. The dugout emptied, waiting for him to round third.

The Claudes stood fuming. The Zeroes climbed all over Hari.

"I didn't know you could do that more than once a day," said Melissa, her eyes narrowed.

"Who, me?" asked Kudzu.

"You're perverting your talent," she said.

"We're *not* supposed to be able to do that more than once every twenty-four hours," said Killer Kudzu, flashing a smile.

"I know that's not true, at least, not really," said Melissa.

"Oh, yes. You are *married* to a *sumotori*, aren't you?"

Melissa blushed.

"The kid seemed to feel bad enough about the dropped fly. Besides, it's just a game."

At home plate, Hari's teammates climbed over him, slapping him on the back.

The game was over, the scoreboard said 7-6, and the technicians were already climbing over the inning indicator.

Melissa rose. "I have to go pick up Hari. I suppose I will see you at the tournament tomorrow?"

"How are you getting home?" asked Killer Kudzu.

"We walk. Hari lives near."

"It's snowing."

"Oh."

"Let me give you a ride. My electric vehicle is outside."

"That would be nice. I live several kilometers away from—"

"I know where you live, of course."

"Fine, then."

Hari ran up. "Aunt Melissa! Did you see?! I don't know what happened! I just felt, I don't know, I just *hit* it!"

"That was wonderful." She smiled at him. Killer Kudzu was looking up, very interested in the stadium support structure.

The stable in which Man-Mountain Gentian trained was being entertained that night. That meant that the wrestlers would have to do all the entertaining.

Even at the top of his sport, Man-Mountain had never gotten used to the fans. Their kingly prizes, their raucous behavior at matches, their donations of gifts, clothing, vehicles, and in some cases houses and land to their favorite wrestlers. It was all appalling.

It was a carryover from traditional sumo, he knew. But *zen-sumo* had become a worldwide, not just a national sport. Many saved for years to come to Japan to watch the January or May tournaments. People here in Japan sometimes sacrificed at home to be able to contribute toward a new *kesho-mawashi* apron for a wrestler entering the ring. Money, in this business, flowed like water, appearing in small envelopes in the mail, in the locker room, after feasts such as the one tonight.

Once a month, Man-Mountain Gentian gathered them all up and took them to his accountant, who had instructions to give it all, above a certain princely level, away to charity. Other wrestlers had more, or less, or none of the same arrangements. The tax men never seemed surprised by whatever amount wrestlers reported.

He entered the club. Things were already rocking. One of the hostesses took his shoes and coat. She had to put the overcoat over her shoulders to carry it into the cloakroom.

The party was a haze of blue smoke, dishes, bottles, businessmen, wrestlers, and funny paper hats. Waitresses came in and out with more food. Three musicians played unheard on a raised dais at one side of the room. Someone was telling a snappy story. The room exploded with laughter.

"Ah!" said someone. "Yokozuna Gentian has arrived."

Man-Mountain bowed deeply. They made two or three places for him at the low table. He saw that several of the host-party were Americans. Probably one or more were from the CIA.

They and the Russians were still trying to perfect *zen-sumo* as an assassination weapon. They offered active and retired *sumotori* large amounts of money in an effort to get them to develop their powers in some nominally destructive form. So far, no one he knew of had. There were rumors about the Brazilians, however.

He could see it now, a future with premiers, millionaires, presidents, and paranoids in all walks of life wearing wire-mesh clothing and checking their Eveready batteries before going out each morning.

He had been approached twice, by each side. He was sometimes followed. They all were. People in governments simply did *not* understand.

He began to talk, while saki flowed, with Cast Iron Pekowski. Pekowski, now 12-2 for the tournament, had graciously lost his match with Typhoon Takanaka. (There was an old saying: In a tournament, no one who won more than nine matches ever beat an opponent who has lost seven. Which had been the case with Takanaka. Eight was the number of wins needed to retain current ranking.)

"I could feel him going," said Pekowski in Polish. "I think we should talk to him about the May tournament."

"Have you mentioned this to his stablemaster?"

"I thought of doing so after the tournament. I was hoping you could come with me to see him."

"I'll be just another retired *sekitori* by then."

"Takanaka respects you above all the others. Besides, your *dampatsu-shiki* ceremony won't be for another two weeks. You'll still have your hair. And while we're at it, I still wish you would change your mind."

"Perhaps I could be Takanaka's dew-sweeper, if he decides."

"Good! You'll come with me then, Friday morning?"

"Yes."

The hosts were very much drunker than the wrestlers. Nayakano the stablemaster was feeling no pain but still remained upright. Mounds of food were being consumed. A businessman tried to grab-ass a waitress. This was going to become every bit as nasty as all such parties.

"A song! A song!" yelled the head of the fan club, a businessman in his sixties. "Who will favor us with a song?"

Man-Mountain Gentian got to his feet, went over to the musicians. He talked with the samisen player. Then he stood facing his drunk, attentive audience.

How many of these parties had he been to in his career? Two, three hundred? Always the same, drunkenness, discord, braggadocio on the part of the host-clubs. Some fans really loved the sport, some lived vicariously through it. He would not miss the parties. But as the player began the tune he realized this might be the last party he would have to face.

He began to sing:

> *I met my lover by still Lake Biwa*
> *just before Taira war banners flew . . .*

And so on through all six verses, in a clear pure voice belonging to a man half his size.

They stood and applauded him, some of the wrestlers in the stable looking away, as only they, not even the stablemaster, knew of his retirement plans and what this party probably meant.

He went to the stablemaster, who took him to the club host, made apologies concerning the tournament and a slight cold, shook hands, bowed and went out into the lobby, where the hostess valiantly brought him his shoes and overcoat. He wanted to help her, but she reshouldered the coat grimly and brought it to him. He handed her a tip and signed the autograph she asked for.

It had begun to snow outside. The neon made the sky a swirling multicolored smudge. Man-Mountain Gentian walked through the quickly-emptying streets. Even the ever-present taxis scurried from the snow like roaches from a light. His home was only two kilometers away. He liked the stillness of the falling snow, the quietness of the city in times such as this.

"Shelter for a stormy night?" asked a ragged old man on a corner. Man-Mountain Gentian stopped.

"Change for shelter for an old man?" asked the beggar again, looking very far up at Gentian's face.

Man-Mountain Gentian reached in his pocket, took out three or four small ornate paper envelopes which had been thrust on him as he left the club.

The old man took them, opened one. Then another and another.

"There must be more than eight hundred thousand yen here . . . " he said, very quietly and very slowly.

"I suggest the Imperial or the Hilton," said Man-Mountain Gentian. Then the wrestler turned and walked away.

The old man laughed, then straightened himself with dignity, stepped to the curb and imperiously summoned an approaching pedicab.

■ ■ ■

Melissa was not home.

He turned on the entry light as he took off his shoes. He passed through the spartanly furnished low living room, turned off the light at the other switch.

He went to the bathroom, put depilatory gel on his face, wiped it off. He went to the kitchen, pick up half a ham and ate it, washing it down with three liters of milk. He returned to the bathroom, brushed his teeth, went to the bedroom, unrolled his futon and placed his cinderblock at the head of it.

He punched on the hidden tape deck and an old recording of Kimio Eto playing "Rukodan" on the koto quietly filled the house.

The only decoration in the sleeping room was Shuncho's print, "The Strongest and the Most Fair," showing a theater-district beauty and a *sumotori* three times her size, hanging on the far wall.

He turned off the light. Instantly the silhouettes of falling snowflakes showed through the paper walls of the house, cast by the strong streetlight outside. He watched the snowflakes fall, listening to the music, and was filled with *mono no aware* for the transience of beauty in the world.

Man-Mountain Gentian pulled up the puffed cotton covers, put his head on the building block and drifted off to sleep.

They had let Hari off at his house. The interior of the runabout was warm. They were drinking coffee in the near-empty parking lot of Tokyo Sonic #113.

"I read somewhere you were an architect," said Killer Kudzu.

"Barely," said Melissa.

"Would you like to see Kudzu House?" he asked.

For an architect, it was like being asked to one of Frank Lloyd Wright's vacation homes, or one of the birdlike buildings designed by Eino Saarinen in the later twentieth century. Melissa considered.

"I should call home first," she said after a moment.

"I think your husband will still be at the Nue Vue Club, whooping it up with the money-men."

"You're probably right. I'll call him later. I'd love to see your house."

The old man lay dying on his bed.

"I see you finally heard," he said. His voice was tired.

Man-Mountain Gentian had not seen him in seven years. He had always been old, but he had never looked this old, this weak.

Dr. Wu had been his mentor. He had started him on the path toward *zen-sumo* (though he did not know it at the time). Dr. Wu had not been one of those cryptic koan-spouting quiet men. He had been boisterous, laughing, playing with his pupils, yelling at them, whatever was needed to get them *to see.*

There had been the occasional letter from him. Now, for the first time, there was a call in the middle of the night.

"I'm sorry," said Man-Mountain Gentian. "It's snowing outside."

"At your house, too?" asked Dr. Wu.

Wu's attendant was dressed in Buddhist robes and seemingly paid no attention to either of them.

"Is there anything I can do for you?" asked Man-Mountain Gentian.

"Physically, no. This is nothing a pain shift can help. Emotionally, there is."

"What?"

"You can win tomorrow, though I won't be around to share it."

Man-Mountain Gentian was quiet a moment. "I'm not sure I can promise you that."

"I didn't think so. You are forgetting the kitten and the bowl of milk."

"No. Not at all. I think I've finally come up against something new and strong in the world. I will either win or lose. Either way, I will retire."

"If it did not mean anything to you, you could have lost by now," said Dr. Wu.

Man-Mountain Gentian was quiet again.

Wu shifted uneasily on his pillows. "Well, there is not much time. Lean close. Listen to what I have to say.

"The novice Itsu went to the Master and asked him: 'Master, what is the key to all enlightenment?'

" 'You must teach yourself never to think of the white horse,' said the Master.

"Itsu applied himself with all his being. One day while raking gravel he achieved insight.

" 'Master! Master!' yelled Itsu, running to his quarters. 'Master! I have made myself not think about the white horse!'

" 'Quick!' said the Master. 'When you were not thinking of the white horse, where was Itsu?'

"The novice could make no answer.

"The Master dealt Itsu a smart blow with his staff.

"At this, Itsu was enlightened."

Then Dr. Wu let his head back down on his bed.

"Good-bye," he said.

In his bed in the lamasery in Tibet, Dr. Wu let out a ragged breath and died.

Man-Mountain Gentian, standing on his futon in his bedroom in Tokyo, began to cry.

Kudzu House took up a city block in the middle of Tokyo. The taxes alone must have been enormous.

Through the decreasing snow, Melissa saw the lights. Their beams stabbed up into the night. All she could see from a block away was the tangled kudzu.

Kudzu was a vine, originally transplanted from China, raised in Japan for centuries. Its crushed root was used as a starch base in cooking; its leaves were used for teas and medicines, its fibers to make cloth and paper. What kudzu was most famous for was its ability to grow over and cover anything that didn't move out of its way.

In the Depression thirties of the last century, it had been planted on road cuts in the southeastern United States to stop erosion. Kudzu had almost stopped progress there. In those ideal conditions it grew runners more than twenty meters long in a single summer, several to a root. Its vines climbed utility poles, hills, trees. It completely covered other vegetation, cutting off its sunlight.

Many places in the American South were covered three kilometers wide to each side of the highways with kudzu vines. The Great Kudzu Forest of central Georgia was a U.S. National Park.

In the bleaker conditions of Japan the weed could be kept under control. Except that this owner didn't want to. The lights playing into the snowy sky were part of the heating and watering system which kept vines growing year-round. All this Melissa had read before. Seeing it was something again. The entire block was a green tangle of vines and lights.

"Do you ever trim it?" she asked.

"The traffic keeps it back," said Killer Kudzu, and laughed. "I have gardeners who come in and fight it once a week. They're losing."

They went into the green tunnel of a driveway. Melissa saw the edge of the house, cast concrete, as they dropped into the sunken vehicle area.

There were three boats, four road vehicles, a hovercraft, and a small sport flyer parked there. Lights shone up into a dense green roof from which hundreds of vines grew downward toward the light sources.

"We have to move the spotlights every week," he said.

A butler met them at the door. "Just a tour, Mord," said Killer Kudzu. "We'll have drinks in the sitting room in thirty minutes."

"Very good, sir."

"This way."

Melissa went to a railing. The living area was the size of a bowling alley, or the lobby of a terrible old hotel. The balcony on the second level jutted out from the east wall. Killer Kudzu went to a console, punched buttons.

Moe and the Meanies boomed from dozens of speakers.

Killer Kudzu stood snapping his fingers for a moment. "O, send me! Honorable cats!" he said. "That's from Spike Jones, an irreverent American musician of the last century. He died of cancer," he added.

Melissa followed him, noticing the things everyone noticed—the Chrome Room, the Supercharger Inhalorium, the archery range ("the object is *not* to hit the targets," said Kudzu), the Mosasaur Pool with the fossils embedded in the sides and bottom.

She was more affected by the house and its tawdriness than she thought she would be.

"You've done very well for yourself."

"Some manage it, some give it away, some save it. I *spend* it."

They were drinking kudzu tea highballs in the sitting room, which was one of the most comfortable rooms Melissa had ever been in.

"Tasteless, isn't it?" asked Killer Kudzu.

"Not quite," said Melissa. "Well worth the trip."

"You could stay, you know?" said Kudzu.

"I thought I could." She sighed. "It would only give me one more excuse not to finish the dishes at home." She gave him a long look. "Besides, it wouldn't give you an advantage in the match."

"That never really crossed my mind."

"I'm quite sure."

"You are a beautiful woman."

"You have a nice house."

"Hmmm. Time to get you home."

"I'm sure."

They sat outside her house in the cold. The snow had stopped. Stars peeped through the low scud.

"I'm going to win tomorrow," said Killer Kudzu.

"You might," said Melissa.

"It is sometimes possible to do more than win," he said.

"I'll tell my husband."

"My offer is always open," he said. He reached over and opened her door on the runabout. "Life won't be the same after he's lost. Or after he retires."

She climbed out, shaking from more than the cold. He closed the door, whipped the vehicle in a circle and was gone down the crunching street. He blinked his lights once before he drove out of sight.

She found her husband in the kitchen. His eyes were red; he was as pale as she had ever seen him.

"Dr. Wu is dead," he said, and wrapped his huge arms around her, covering her like an upright sofa.

He began to cry again. She talked to him quietly.

"Come, let's try to get some sleep," she said.

"No, I couldn't rest. I wanted to see you first. I'm going down to the stable." She helped him dress in his warmest clothing. He kissed her and left, walking the few blocks through the snowy sidewalks to the training building.

The junior wrestlers were awakened at 4:00 a.m. They were to begin the day's work of sweeping, cleaning, cooking, bathing, feeding, and catering to the senior wrestlers. When they came in they found him, stripped to his *mawashi*, at the 300-kilo push bag, pushing, pushing, straining, crying all the while, not saying a word. The floor of the arena was torn and grooved. They cleaned up the area for the morning workouts, one following him around with the sand-trowel.

At 7:00 a.m. he slumped exhausted on a bench. Two of the *juryo* covered him with quilts and set an alarm clock beside him for 1:00 p.m.

"Your opponent was at the ball game last night," said Nayakano the stablemaster. Man-Mountain Gentian sat in the dressing rooms while the barber combed and greased his elaborate *chonmage*. "Your wife asked me to give you this."

It was a note in a plain envelope, addressed in her beautiful calligraphy.

He opened and read it. She warned him of what Kudzu said about "more than winning" the night before, and wished him luck.

He turned to the stablemaster.

"Has Killer Kudzu injured any opponent before he became *yokozuna* last tournament?"

Nayakano's answer was immediate. "No. That's unheard of. Let me see that note." He reached out.

Man-Mountain Gentian put it back in the envelope, tucked it in his *mawashi*.

"Should I alert the judges?"

"Sorry I mentioned it," said Man-Mountain Gentian.

"I don't like this," said the stablemaster.

Three hefty junior wrestlers ran in carrying Gentian's *kenzo-mawashi* between them.

The last day of the January tournament always packed them in. Even the *maegashira* and *komusubi* matches, in which young boys threw each other, or tried to, drew enough of an audience to make the novices feel good.

The call for the Ozeki class wrestlers came, and they went through the grandiose ring-entering ceremony, wearing their great *kenzo-mawashi* aprons of brocade, silk, and gold while their dew-sweepers and sword bearers squatted to the sides. Then they retired to their benches, east or west, to await the call by the falsetto-voiced *yobidashi*.

Man-Mountain Gentian watched as the assistants helped Killer Kudzu out of his ceremonial apron, gold with silk kudzu leaves, purple flowers, yellow stars. His forehead blazed with the PRC flag. He looked directly at Gentian's place and smiled a broad smile.

There was a great match between Gorilla Tsunami and Typhoon Takanaka which went on for more than thirty seconds by the clock, both men straining, groaning, sweating until the *gyoji* made them stop, and rise, and then get on their marks again.

Those were the worst kinds of matches for the wrestlers, each opponent alternately straining, then bending with the other, neither getting advantage. There was a legendary match five years ago which took six thirty-second tries before one wrestler bested the other.

The referee flipped his fan. Gorilla Tsunami fell flat on his face in a heap, then wriggled backwards out of the ring.

The crowd screamed and applauded Takanaka.

Then the *yobidashi* said, "East—Man-Mountain Gentian. West—Killer Kudzu."

They hurried their *shikiri*. Each threw salt twice, rinsing once. Then Man-Mountain Gentian, moving with the grace of a dancer, lifted his right leg and stamped it, then his left, and the sound was like the double echo of a cannon throughout the stadium.

He went immediately to his mark.

Killer Kudzu jumped down to his mark, glaring across the meter that separated them.

The *gyoji*, off guard, took a few seconds to turn sideways to them and bring his fan into position.

In that time, Man-Mountain Gentian could hear the quiet hum of the electrical grid, hear muffled intake of breath from the other wrestlers, hear a whistle in the nostril of the north-side judge.

"Huuu!" said the referee and his fan jerked.

Man-Mountain Gentian felt like two freight trains had collided in his head. There was a snap as his muscles went tense all over and the momentum of the explosion in his brain began to push at him, lifting, threatening to make him give or tear through the back of his head. His feet were on a slippery sandy bottom, neck-high wave crests smashed into him, a rip tide was pushing at his shoulder, at one side, pulling his legs up, twisting his muscles. He could feel his eyes pushed back in their sockets as if by iron thumbs, ready to pop them like ripe plums. His ligaments were iron wires stretched tight on the turnbuckles of his bones. His arms ended in strands of noodles, his face was soft cheese.

The sand under him was soft, so soft, and he knew that all he had to do was to sink in it, let go, cease to resist.

And through all that haze and blindness he knew what he was not supposed to think about.

Everything quit: He reached out one mental hand, as big as the sun, as fast as light, as long as time, and he pushed against his opponent's chest.

The lights were back, he was in the stadium, in the arena, and the dull pounding was applause, screams.

Killer Kudzu lay blinking among the ring-bales.

"Hooves?" Man-Mountain Gentian heard him ask in bewilderment before he picked himself up.

Man-Mountain Gentian took the envelope from the referee with the three quick chopping motions, then made a fourth to the audience, and they knew then and only then that they would never see him in the ring again.

The official clock said .9981 seconds.

"How did you do it, Man-Mountain?" asked the Tokyo paparazzi as he showered out his chonmage and put on his clothes. He said nothing.

He met his wife outside the stadium. A lone newsman was with her, "Scoop" Hakimoto.

"For old times' sake," begged Hakimoto. "How did you do it?"

Man-Mountain Gentian turned to Melissa. "Tell him how I did it," he said.

"He didn't think about the white horse," she said. They left the newsman standing, staring.

Killer Kudzu, tired and pale, was getting in his vehicle. Hakimoto came running up. "What's all this I hear about Gentian and a white horse?" he asked.

Kudzu's eyes widened, then narrowed.

"No comment," he said.

That night, to celebrate, Man-Mountain Gentian took Melissa to the Beef Bowl.

He had seventeen orders and helped Melissa finish her second one.

They went back home, climbed onto their futons and turned on the TV.

Gilligan was on his island. All was right with the world.

He had been trained in nothing but the game all his life, but now the game began to consume him . . . *Ender Wiggins is one of the best-known young characters in science fiction and with the major motion picture,* Ender's Game, *to be released later this year, he may well become* the *best known. This is the story in which young Ender was* first *introduced. It earned Orson Scott Card the John W. Campbell Award for Best New Writer before being expanded into the Nebula and Hugo Award-winning novel of the same title. As for the relevance of "Ender's Game": "Militainment" video games are now used to recruit and train U.S. soldiers. We already use weapons that are controlled remotely by pilots who are on the other side of the world.*

Ender's Game

Orson Scott Card

"Whatever your gravity is when you get to the door, remember—the enemy's gate is down. If you step through your own door like you're out for a stroll, you're a big target and you deserve to get hit. With more than a flasher." Ender Wiggins paused and looked over the group. Most were just watching him nervously. A few understanding. A few sullen and resisting.

First day with this army, all fresh from the teacher squads, and Ender had forgotten how young new kids could be. He'd been in it for three years, they'd had six months—nobody over nine years old in the whole bunch. But they were his. At eleven, he was half a year early to be a commander. He'd had a toon of his own and knew a few tricks, but there were forty in his new army. Green. All marksmen with a flasher, all in top shape, or they wouldn't be here—but they were all just as likely as not to get wiped out first time into battle.

"Remember," he went on, "they can't see you till you get through that door. But the second you're out, they'll be on you. So hit that door the way you want to be when they shoot at you. Legs up under you, going straight *down*." He pointed at a sullen kid who looked like he was only seven, the smallest of them all. "Which way is down, greenoh!"

"Toward the enemy door." The answer was quick. It was also surly, as if to say, Yeah, yeah, now get on with the important stuff.

"Name, kid?"

"Bean."

"Get that for size or for brains?"

Bean didn't answer. The rest laughed a little. Ender had chosen right. This kid *was* younger than the rest, must have been advanced because he was sharp. The others didn't like him much, they were happy to see him taken down a little. Like Ender's first commander had taken him down.

"Well, Bean, you're right onto things. Now I tell you this, nobody's gonna get through that door without a good chance of getting hit. A lot of you are going to be turned into cement somewhere. Make sure it's your legs. Right? If only your legs get hit, then only your legs get frozen, and in nullo that's no sweat." Ender turned to one of the dazed ones. "What're legs for? Hmmm?"

Blank stare. Confusion. Stammer.

"Forget it. Guess I'll have to ask Bean here."

"Legs are for pushing off walls." Still bored.

"Thanks, Bean. Get that, everybody?" They all got it, and didn't like getting it from Bean. "Right. You can't see with legs, you can't *shoot* with legs, and most of the time they just get in the way. If they get frozen sticking straight out you've turned yourself into a blimp. No way to hide. So how do legs go?"

A few answered this time, to prove that Bean wasn't the only one who knew anything. "Under you. Tucked up under."

"Right. A shield. You're kneeling on a shield, and the shield is your own legs. And there's a trick to the suits. Even when your legs are flashed you can *still* kick off. I've never seen anybody do it but me—but you're all gonna learn it."

Ender Wiggins turned on his flasher. It glowed faintly green in his hand. Then he let himself rise in the weightless workout room, pulled his legs under him as though he were kneeling, and flashed both of them. Immediately his suit stiffened at the knees and ankles, so that he couldn't bend at all.

"Okay, I'm frozen, see?"

He was floating a meter above them. They all looked up at him, puzzled.

He leaned back and caught one of the handholds on the wall behind him, and pulled himself flush against the wall.

"I'm stuck at a wall. If I had legs, I'd use legs, and string myself out like a string *bean*, right?"

They laughed.

"But I don't have legs, and that's *better*, got it? Because of this." Ender jackknifed at the waist, then straightened out violently, He was across the workout room in only a moment. From the other side he called to them. "Got that? I didn't use hands, so I still had use of my flasher. *And* I didn't have my legs floating five feet behind me. Now watch it again."

He repeated the jackknife, and caught a handhold on the wall near them. "Now, I don't just want you to do that when they've flashed your legs. I want you to do that when you've still got legs, because it's better. And because they'll never be expecting it. All right now, everybody up in the air and kneeling."

Most were up in a few seconds. Ender flashed the stragglers, and they dangled, helplessly frozen, while the others laughed. "When I give an order, you move. Got it? When we're at the door and they clear it, I'll be giving you orders in two seconds, as soon as I see the setup. And when I give the order you better be out there, because whoever's out there first is going to win, unless he's a fool. I'm not. And you better not be, or I'll have you back in the teacher squads." He saw more than a few of them gulp, and the frozen ones looked at him with fear. "You guys who are hanging there. You watch. You'll thaw out in about fifteen minutes, and let's see if you can catch up to the others."

For the next half hour Ender had them jackknifing off walls. He called a stop when he saw that they all had the basic idea. They were a good group, maybe. They'd get better.

"Now you're warmed up," he said to them, "we'll start working."

Ender was the last one out after practice, since he stayed to help some of the slower ones improve on technique. They'd had good teachers, but like all armies they were uneven, and some of them could be a real drawback in battle. Their first battle might be weeks away. It might be tomorrow. A schedule was never posted. The commander just woke up and found a note by his bunk, giving him the time of his battle and the name of his opponent. So for the first while he was going to drive his boys until they were in top shape—all of them. Ready for anything, at any time. Strategy was nice, but it was worth nothing if the soldiers couldn't hold up under the strain.

He turned the corner into the residence wing and found himself face to face with Bean, the seven-year-old he had picked on all through practice that day. Problems. Ender didn't want problems right now.

"Ho, Bean."

"Ho, Ender."

Pause.

"Sir," Ender said softly.

"We're not on duty."

"In my army, Bean, we're always on duty." Ender brushed past him.

Bean's high voice piped up behind him. "I know what you're doing, Ender, sir, and I'm warning you."

Ender turned slowly and looked at him. "Warning me?"

"I'm the best man you've got. But I'd better be treated like it."

"Or what?" Ender smiled menacingly.

"Or I'll be the worst man you've got. One or the other."

"And what do you want? Love and kisses?" Ender was getting angry now.

Bean was unworried. "I want a toon."

Ender walked back to him and stood looking down into his eyes. "I'll give a toon," he said, "to the boys who prove they're worth something. They've got to be good soldiers, they've got to know how to take orders, they've got to be able to think for themselves in a pinch, and they've got to be able to keep respect. That's how I got to be a commander. That's how you'll get to be a toon leader. Got it?"

Bean smiled. "That's fair. *If* you actually work that way, I'll be a toon leader in a month."

Ender reached down and grabbed the front of his uniform and shoved him into the wall. "When I say I work a certain way, Bean, then that's the way I work."

Bean just smiled. Ender let go of him and walked away, and didn't look back. He was sure, without looking, that Bean was still watching, still smiling, still just a little contemptuous. He might make a good toon leader at that. Ender would keep an eye on him.

Captain Graff, six foot two and a little chubby, stroked his belly as he leaned back in his chair. Across his desk sat Lieutenant Anderson, who was earnestly pointing out high points on a chart.

"Here it is, Captain," Anderson said. "Ender's already got them doing a tactic that's going to throw off everyone who meets it. Doubled their speed."

Graff nodded.

"And you know his test scores. He thinks well, too."

Graff smiled. "All true, all true, Anderson, he's a fine student, shows real promise."

They waited.

Graff sighed. "So what do you want me to do?"

"Ender's the one. He's got to be."

"He'll never be ready in time, Lieutenant. He's eleven, for heaven's sake, man, what do you want, a miracle?"

"I want him into battles, every day starting tomorrow. I want him to have a year's worth of battles in a month."

Graff shook his head. "That would be his army in the hospital."

"No, sir. He's getting them into form. And we need Ender."

"Correction, Lieutenant. We need somebody. You think it's Ender."

"All right, I think it's Ender. Which of the commanders if it isn't him?"

"I don't know, Lieutenant." Graff ran his hands over his slightly fuzzy bald head. "These are children, Anderson. Do you realize that? Ender's army is nine years old. Are we going to put them against the older kids? Are we going to put them through hell for a month like that?"

Lieutenant Anderson leaned even farther over Graff's desk.

"Ender's test scores, Captain!"

"I've seen his bloody test scores! I've watched him in battle, I've listened to tapes of his training sessions, I've watched his sleep patterns, I've heard tapes of his conversations in the corridors and in the bathrooms, I'm more aware of Ender Wiggins that you could possibly imagine! And against all the arguments, against his obvious qualities, I'm weighing one thing. I have this picture of Ender a year from now, if you have your way. I see him completely useless, worn down, a failure, because he was pushed farther than he or any living person could go. But it doesn't weigh enough, does it, Lieutenant, because there's a war on, and our best talent is gone, and the biggest battles are ahead. So give Ender a battle every day this week. And then bring me a report."

Anderson stood and saluted. "Thank you, sir."

He had almost reached the door when Graff called his name. He turned and faced the captain.

"Anderson," Captain Graff said. "Have you been outside, lately I mean?"

"Not since last leave, six months ago."

"I didn't think so. Not that it makes any difference. But have you ever been to Beaman Park, there in the city? Hmm? Beautiful park. Trees. Grass. No mallo, no battles, no worries. Do you know what else there is in Beaman Park?"

"What, sir?" Lieutenant Anderson asked.

"Children," Graff answered.

"Of course children," said Anderson.

"I mean children. I mean kids who get up in the morning when their mothers call them and they go to school and then in the afternoons they go to Beaman Park and play. They're happy, they smile a lot, they laugh, they have fun. Hmmm?"

"I'm sure they do, sir."

"Is that all you can say, Anderson?"

Anderson cleared his throat. "It's good for children to have fun, I think, sir. I know I did when I was a boy. But right now the world needs soldiers. And this is the way to get them."

Graff nodded and closed his eyes. "Oh, indeed, you're right, by statistical proof and by all the important theories, and dammit they work and the system is right but all the same Ender's older than I am. He's not a child. He's barely a person."

"If that's true, sir, then at least we all know that Ender is making it possible for the others of his age to be playing in the park."

"And Jesus died to save all men, of course." Graff sat up and looked at Anderson almost sadly. "But we're the ones," Graff said, "we're the ones who are driving in the nails."

Ender Wiggins lay on his bed staring at the ceiling. He never slept more than five hours a night—but the lights went off at 2200 and didn't come on again until 0600. So he stared at the ceiling and thought.

He'd had his army for three and a half weeks. Dragon Army. The name was assigned, and it wasn't a lucky one. Oh, the charts said that about nine years ago a Dragon Army had done fairly well. But for the next six years the name had been attached to inferior armies, and finally, because of the superstition that was beginning to play about the name, Dragon Army was retired. Until now. And now, Ender thought, smiling, Dragon Army was going to take them by surprise.

The door opened quietly. Ender did not turn his head. Someone stepped softly into his room, then left with the sound of the door shutting. When soft steps died away Ender rolled over and saw a white slip of paper lying on the floor. He reached down and picked it up.

"Dragon Army against Rabbit Army, Ender Wiggins and Carn Carby, 0700."

The first battle. Ender got out of bed and quickly dressed. He went rapidly to the rooms of each of the toon leaders and told them to rouse their boys. In five minutes they were all gathered in the corridor, sleepy and slow. Ender spoke softly.

"First battle, 0700 against Rabbit Army. I've fought them twice before but they've got a new commander. Never heard of him. They're an older group, though, and I knew a few of their olds tricks. Now wake up. Run, doublefast, warmup in workroom three."

For an hour and a half they worked out, with three mock battles and calisthenics in the corridor out of the nullo. Then for fifteen minutes they all lay up in the air, totally relaxing in the weightlessness. At 0650 Ender roused them and they hurried into the corridor. Ender led them down the corridor, running again, and occasionally leaping to touch a light panel on the ceiling. The boys all touched the same light panel. And at 0658 they reached their gate to the battleroom.

The members of toons C and D grabbed the first eight handholds in the ceiling of the corridor. Toons A, B, and E crouched on the floor. Ender hooked his feet into two handholds in the middle of the ceiling, so he was out of everyone's way.

"Which way is the enemy's door?" he hissed.

"Down!" they whispered back, and laughed.

"Flashers on." The boxes in their hands glowed green. They waited for a few seconds more, and then the gray wall in front of them disappeared and the battleroom was visible.

Ender sized it up immediately. The familiar open grid of most early games, like the monkey bars at the park, with seven or eight boxes scattered through the grid. They called the boxes *stars*. There were enough of them, and in forward enough positions, that they were worth going for. Ender decided this in a second, and he hissed, "Spread to near stars. E hold!"

The four groups in the corners plunged through the forcefield at the doorway and fell down into the battleroom. Before the enemy even appeared through the opposite gate Ender's army had spread from the door to the nearest stars.

Then the enemy soldiers came through the door. From their stance Ender knew they had been in a different gravity, and didn't know enough to disorient themselves from it. They came through standing up, their entire bodies spread and defenseless.

"Kill 'em, E!" Ender hissed, and threw himself out the door knees first, with his flasher between his legs and firing. While Ender's group flew across the room the rest of Dragon Army lay down a protecting fire, so that E group reached a forward position with only one boy frozen completely, though they had all lost the use of their legs—which didn't impair them in the least. There was a lull as Ender and his opponent, Carn Carby, assessed their positions. Aside from Rabbit Army's losses at the gate, there had been few casualties, and both armies were near full strength. But Carn had no originality—he was in the four-corner spread that any five-year-old in the teacher squads might have thought of. And Ender knew how to defeat it.

He called out, loudly, "E covers A, C down. B, D angle east wall." Under E toon's cover, B and D toons lunged away from their stars. While they were still exposed, A and C toons left their stars and drifted toward the near wall. They reached it together, and together jackknifed off the wall. At double the normal speed they appeared behind the enemy's stars, and opened fire. In a few seconds the battle was over, with the enemy almost entirely frozen, including the commander, and the rest scattered to the corners. For the next five minutes, in squads of four, Dragon Army cleaned out the dark corners of the battleroom and shepherded the enemy into the center, where their bodies, frozen at impossible angles, jostled each other. Then Ender took three of his boys to the enemy gate and went through the formality of reversing the one-way field by simultaneously touching a Dragon Army helmet at each corner. Then Ender assembled his army in vertical files near the knot of frozen Rabbit Army soldiers.

Only three of Dragon Army's soldiers were immobile. Their victory margin—38 to 0—was ridiculously high, and Ender began to laugh. Dragon Army joined him, laughing long and loud. They were still laughing when Lieutenant Anderson and Lieutenant Morris came in from the teachergate at the south end of the battleroom.

Lieutenant Anderson kept his face stiff and unsmiling, but Ender saw him wink as he held out his hand and offered the stiff, formal congratulations that were ritually given to the victor in the game.

Morris found Carn Carby and unfroze him, and the thirteen-year-old came and presented himself to Ender, who laughed without malice and held out his hand. Carn graciously took Ender's hand and bowed his head over it. It was that or be flashed again.

Lieutenant Anderson dismissed Dragon Army, and they silently left the battleroom through the enemy's door—again part of the ritual. A light was blinking on the north side of the square door, indicating where the gravity was in that corridor. Ender, leading his soldiers, changed his orientation and went through the forcefield and into gravity on his feet. His army followed him at a brisk run back to the workroom. When they got there they formed up into squads, and Ender hung in the air, watching them.

"Good first battle," he said, which was excuse enough for a cheer, which he quieted. "Dragon Army did all right against Rabbits. But the enemy isn't always going to be that bad. And if that had been a good army we would have been smashed. We still would have won, but we would have been smashed. Now let me see B and D toons out here. Your takeoff from the stars was way too slow. If Rabbit Army knew how to aim a flasher, you all would have been frozen solid before A and C even got to the wall."

They worked out for the rest of the day.

That night Ender went for the first time to the commanders' mess hall. No one was allowed there until he had won at least one battle, and Ender was the youngest commander ever to make it. There was no great stir when he came in. But when some of the other boys saw the Dragon on his breast pocket, they stared at him openly, and by the time he got his tray and sat at an empty table, the entire room was silent, with the other commanders watching him. Intensely self-conscious, Ender wondered how they all knew, and why they all looked so hostile.

Then he looked above the door he had just come through. There was a huge scoreboard across the entire wall. It showed the win/loss record for the commander of every army; that day's battles were lit in red. Only four of them. The other three winners had barely made it—the best of them had only two men whole and eleven mobile at the end of the game. Dragon Army's score of thirty-eight mobile was embarrassingly better.

Other new commanders had been admitted to the commanders' mess hall with cheers and congratulations. Other new commanders hadn't won thirty-eight to zero.

Ender looked for Rabbit Army on the scoreboard. He was surprised to find that Carn Carby's score to date was eight wins and three losses. Was he that good? Or had he only fought against inferior armies? Whichever, there was still a zero in Carn's mobile and whole columns, and Ender looked down from the scoreboard grinning. No one smiled back, and Ender knew that they were afraid of him, which meant that they would hate him, which meant that anyone who went into battle against Dragon Army would be scared and angry and less competent. Ender looked for Carn Carby in the crowd, and found him not too far away. He stared at Carby until one of the other boys nudged the Rabbit commander and pointed to Ender. Ender smiled again and waved slightly. Carby turned red, and Ender, satisfied, leaned over his dinner and began to eat.

At the end of the week Dragon Army had fought seven battles in seven days. The score stood 7 wins and 0 losses. Ender had never had more than five boys frozen in any game. It was no longer possible for the other commanders to ignore Ender. A few of them sat with him and quietly conversed about game strategies that Ender's opponents had used. Other much larger groups were talking with the commanders that Ender had defeated, trying to find out what Ender had done to beat them.

In the middle of the meal the teacher door opened and the groups fell silent as Lieutenant Anderson stepped in and looked over the group. When he located Ender he strode quickly across the room and whispered in Ender's ear. Ender nodded, finished his glass of water, and left with the lieutenant. On the way out, Anderson handed a slip of paper to one of the older boys. The room became very noisy with conversation as Anderson and Ender left.

Ender was escorted down corridors he had never seen before. They didn't have the blue glow of the soldier corridors. Most were wood paneled, and the floors were carpeted. The doors were wood, with nameplates on them, and they stopped at one that said "Captain Graff, supervisor." Anderson knocked softly, and a low voice said, "Come in."

They went in. Captain Graff was seated behind a desk, his hands folded across his potbelly. He nodded, and Anderson sat. Ender also sat down. Graff cleared his throat and spoke.

"Seven days since your first battle, Ender."

Ender did not reply.

"Won seven battles, one every day."

Ender nodded.

"Scores unusually high, too."

Ender blinked.

"Why?" Graff asked him.

Ender glanced at Anderson, and then spoke to the captain behind the desk. "Two new tactics, sir. Legs doubled up as a shield, so that a flash doesn't immobilize. Jackknife takeoffs from the walls. Superior strategy, as Lieutenant Anderson taught, think places, not spaces. Five toons of eight instead of four of ten. Incompetent opponents. Excellent toon leaders, good soldiers."

Graff looked at Ender without expression. Waiting for what, Ender wondered. Lieutenant Anderson spoke up.

"Ender, what's the condition of your army?"

Do they want me to ask for relief? Not a chance, he decided. "A little tired, in peak condition, morale high, learning fast. Anxious for the next battle."

Anderson looked at Graff. Graff shrugged slightly and turned to Ender.

"Is there anything you want to know/"

Ender held his hands loosely in his lap. "When are you going to put us up against a good army?"

Graff's laughter rang in the room, and when it stopped, Graff handed a piece of paper to Ender. "Now," the captain said, and Ender read the paper. "Dragon Army against Leopard Army, Ender Wiggins and Pol Slattery, 2000."

Ender looked up at Captain Graff. "That's ten minutes from now, sir."

Graff smiled. "Better hurry, then, boy."

As Ender left he realized Pol Slattery was the boy who had been handed his orders as Ender left the mess hall.

He got to his army five minutes later. Three toon leaders were already undressed and lying naked on their beds. He sent them all flying down the corridors to rouse their toons, and gathered up their suits himself. When all his boys were assembled in the corridor, most of them still getting dressed, Ender spoke to them.

"This one's hot and there's no time. We'll be late to the door, and the enemy'll be deployed right outside our gate. Ambush, and I've never heard of it happening before. So we'll take our time at the door. A and B toons, keep your belts loose, and give your flashers to the leaders and seconds of the other toons."

Puzzled, his soldiers complied. By then all were dressed, and Ender led them at a trot to the gate. When they reached it the forcefield was already on one-way, and some of his soldiers were panting. They had had one battle that day and a full workout. They were tired.

Ender stopped at the entrance and looked at the placements of the enemy soldiers. Some of them were grouped not more than twenty feet out from the gate. There was no grid, there were no stars. A big empty space. Where were most of the enemy soldiers? There should have been thirty more.

"They're flat against this wall," Ender said, "where we can't see them."

He took A and B toons and made them kneel, their hands on their hips. Then he flashed them, so that their bodies were frozen rigid.

"You're shields," Ender said, and then had boys from C and D kneel on their legs and hook both arms under the frozen boys' belts. Each boy was holding two flashers. Then Ender and the members of E toon picked up the duos, three at a time, and threw them out the door.

Of course, the enemy opened fire immediately. But they mainly hit the boys who were already flashed, and in a few moments pandemonium broke out in the battleroom. All the soldiers of Leopard Army were easy targets as they lay pressed flat against the wall or floated, unprotected, in the middle of the battleroom; and Ender's soldiers, armed with two flashers each, carved them up easily. Pol Slattery reacted quickly, ordering his men away from the wall, but not quickly enough—only a few were able to move, and they were flashed before they could get a quarter of the way across the battleroom.

When the battle was over Dragon Army had only twelve boys whole, the lowest score they had ever had. But Ender was satisfied. And during the ritual of surrender Pol Slattery broke form by shaking hands and asking, "Why did you wait so long getting out of the gate?"

Ender glanced at Anderson, who was floating nearby. "I was informed late," he said. "It was an ambush."

Slattery grinned, and gripped Ender's hand again. "Good game."

Ender didn't smile at Anderson this time. He knew that now the games would be arranged against him, to even up the odds. He didn't like it.

It was 2150, nearly time for lights out, when Ender knocked at the door of the room shared by Bean and three other soldiers. One of the others opened the door, then stepped back and held it wide. Ender stood for a moment, then asked if he could come in. They answered, of course, of course, come in, and he walked to the upper bunk, where Bean had set down his book and was leaning on one elbow to look at Ender.

"Bean, can you give me twenty minutes?"

"Near lights out," Bean answered.

"My room," Ender answered. "I'll cover for you."

Bean sat up and slid off his bed. Together he and Ender padded silently down the corridor to Ender's room. Ender entered first, and Bean closed the door behind them.

"Sit down," Ender said, and they both sat on the edge of the bed, looking at each other.

"Remember four weeks ago, Bean? When you told me to make you a toon leader?"

"Yeah."

"I've made five toon leaders since then, haven't I? And none of them was you."

Bean look at him calmly.

"Was I right?" Ender asked.

"Yes, sir," Bean answered.

Ender nodded. "How have you done in these battles?"

Bean cocked his head to one side. "I've never been immobilized, sir, and I've immobilized forty-three of the enemy. I've obeyed orders quickly, and I've commanded a squad in mop-up and never lost a soldier."

"Then you'll understand this." Ender paused, then decided to back up and say something else first.

"You know you're early, Bean, by a good half year. I was, too, and I've been made a commander six months early. Now they've put me into battles after only three weeks of training with my army. They've given me eight battles in seven days. I've already had more battles than boys who were made commander four months ago. I've won more battles than many who've been commanders for a year. And then tonight. You know what happened tonight."

Bean nodded. "They told you late."

"I don't know what the teachers are doing. But my army is getting tired, and I'm getting tired, and now they're changing the rules of the game. You see, Bean, I've looked in the old charts. No one has ever destroyed so many enemies and kept so many of his own soldiers whole in the history of the game. I'm unique—and I'm getting unique treatment."

Bean smiled. "You're the best, Ender."

Ender shook his head. "Maybe. But it was no accident that I got the soldiers I got. My worst soldier could be a toon leader in another army. I've got the best. They've loaded things my way—but now they're loading it all against me. I don't know why. But I know I have to be ready for it. I need your help."

"Why mine?"

"Because even though there are some better soldiers than you in Dragon Army—not many, but some—there's nobody who can think better and faster than you." Bean said nothing. They both knew it was true.

Ender continued. "I need to be ready, but I can't retrain the whole army. So I'm going to cut every toon down by one, including you. With four others you'll be a special squad under me. And you'll learn to do some new things. Most of the time you'll be in the regular toons just like you are now. But when I need you. See?"

Bean smiled and nodded. "That's right, that's good, can I pick them myself?"

"One from each toon except your own, and you can't take any toon leaders."

"What do you want us to do?"

"Bean, I don't know. I don't know what they'll throw at us. What would you do if suddenly our flashers didn't work, and the enemy's did? What would you do if we had to face two armies at once? The only thing I know is—there may be a game where we don't even try for score. Where we just go for the enemy's gate. I want you ready to do that any time I call for it. Got it? You take them for two hours a day during regular workout. Then you and I and your soldiers, we'll work at night after dinner."

"We'll get tired."

"I have a feeling we don't know what tired is." Ender reached out and took Bean's hand, and gripped it. "Even when it's rigged against us, Bean. We'll win."

Bean left in silence and padded down the corridor.

Dragon Army wasn't the only army working out after hours now. The other commanders had finally realized they had some catching up to do. From early morning to lights out soldiers all over Training and Command Center, none of them over fourteen years old, were learning to jackknife off walls and use each other as shields.

But while other commanders mastered the techniques that Ender had used to defeat them, Ender and Bean worked on solutions to problems that had never come up.

There were still battles every day, but for a while they were normal, with grids and stars and sudden plunges through the gate. And after the battles, Ender and Bean and four other soldiers would leave the main group and practice strange maneuvers. Attacks without flashers, using feet to physically disarm or disorient an enemy. Using four frozen soldiers to reverse the enemy's gate in less than two seconds. And one day Bean came in workout with a 30-meter cord.

"What's that for?"

"I don't know yet." Absently Bean spun one end of the cord. It wasn't more than an eighth of an inch thick, but it would have lifted ten adults without breaking.

"Where did you get it?"

"Commissary. They asked what for. I said to practice tying knots."

Bean tied a loop in the end of the rope and slid it over his shoulders.

"Here, you two, hang on to the wall here. Now don't let go of the rope. Give me about twenty meters of slack." They complied, and Bean moved about ten feet from them along the wall. As soon as he was sure they were ready, he jackknifed off the wall and flew straight out, twenty meters. Then the rope snapped taut. It was so fine that it was virtually invisible, but it was strong enough to force Bean to veer off at almost a right angle. It happened so suddenly that he had inscribed a perfect arc and hit the wall hard before most of the other soldiers knew what had happened. Bean did a perfect rebound and drifted quickly back to where Ender and the others waited for him.

Many of the soldiers in the five regular squads hadn't noticed the rope, and were demanding to know how it was done. It was impossible to change direction that abruptly in nullo. Bean just laughed.

"Wait till the next game without a grid! They'll never know what hit them."

They never did. The next game was only two hours later, but Bean and two others had become pretty good at aiming and shooting while they flew at ridiculous speeds at the end of the rope. The slip of paper was delivered, and Dragon Army trotted off to the gate, to battle with Griffin Army. Bean coiled the rope all the way.

When the gate opened, all they could see was a large brown star only fifteen feet away, completely blocking their view of the enemy's gate.

Ender didn't pause. "Bean, give yourself fifty feet of rope and go around the star." Bean and his four soldiers dropped through the gate and in a moment Bean was launched sideways away from the star. The rope snapped taut, and Bean flew forward. As the rope was stopped by each edge of the star in turn, his arc became tighter and his speed greater, until when he hit the wall only a few feet away from the gate he was barely able to control his rebound to end up behind the star. But he immediately moved all his arms and legs so that those waiting inside the gate would know that the enemy hadn't flashed him anywhere.

Ender dropped through the gate, and Bean quickly told him how Griffin Army was situated. "They'vc got two squares of stars, all the away around the gate. All their soldiers are under cover, and there's no way to hit any of them until we're clear to the bottom wall. Even with shields, we'd get there at half strength and we wouldn't have a chance."

"They moving?" Ender asked.

"Do they need to?"

"I would." Ender thought for a moment. "This one's tough. We'll go for the gate, Bean."

Griffin Army began to call out to them.

"Hey, is anybody there?"

"Wake up, there's a war on!"

"We wanna join the picnic!"

They were still calling when Ender's army came out from behind their star with a shield of fourteen frozen soldiers. William Bee, Griffin Army's commander, waited patiently as the screen approached, his men waiting at the fringes of their stars for the moment when whatever was behind the screen became visible. About ten yards away the screen suddenly exploded as the soldiers behind it shoved the screen north. The momentum carried them south twice as fast, and at the same moment the rest of Dragon Army burst from behind their star at the opposite end of the room, firing rapidly.

William Bee's boys joined battle immediately, of course, but William Bee was far more interested in what had been left behind when the shield disappeared. A formation of four frozen Dragon Army soldiers were moving headfirst toward the Griffin Army gate, held together by another frozen soldier whose feet and hands were hooked through their belts. A sixth soldier hung to the waist and trailed like the tail of a kite. Griffin Army was winning the battle easily, and William Bee concentrated on the formation as it approached the gate. Suddenly the soldier trailing in back moved—he wasn't frozen at all! And even though William Bee flashed him immediately, the damage was done. The format drifted in the Griffin Army gate, and their helmets touched all four corners simultaneously. A buzzer sounded, the gate reversed, and the frozen soldiers in the middle were carried by momentum right through the gate. All the flashers stopped working, and the game was over.

The teachergate opened and Lieutenant Anderson came in. Anderson stopped himself with a slight movement of his hands when he reached the center of the battleroom. "Ender," he called, breaking protocol. One of the frozen Dragon soldiers near the south wall tried to call through jaws that were clamped shut by the suit. Anderson drifted to him and unfroze him.

Ender was smiling.

"I beat you again, sir," Ender said.

Anderson didn't smile. "That's nonsense, Ender," Anderson said softly. "Your battle was with William Bee of Griffin Army."

Ender raised an eyebrow.

"After that maneuver," Anderson said, "the rules are being revised to require that all of the enemy's soldiers must be immobilized before the gate can be reversed."

"That's all right," Ender said. "It could only work once anyway." Anderson nodded, and was turning away when Ender added, "Is there going to be a new rule that armies be given equal positions to fight from?"

Anderson turned back around. "If you're in one of the positions, Ender, you can hardly call them equal, whatever they are."

William Bee counted carefully and wondered how in the world he had lost when not one of his soldiers had been flashed and only four of Ender's soldiers were even mobile.

And that night as Ender came into the commanders' mess hall, he was greeted with applause and cheers, and his table was crowded with respectful commanders, many of them two or three years older than he was. He was friendly, but while he ate he wondered what the teachers would do to him in his next battle. He didn't need to worry. His next two battles were easy victories, and after that he never saw the battleroom again.

It was 2100 and Ender was a little irritated to hear someone knock at his door. His army was exhausted, and he had ordered them all to be in bed after 2030. The last two days had been regular battles, and Ender was expecting the worst in the morning.

It was Bean. He came in sheepishly, and saluted.

Ender returned his salute and snapped, "Bean, I wanted everybody in bed."

Bean nodded but didn't leave. Ender considered ordering him out. But as he looked at Bean, it occurred to him for the first time in weeks just how young Bean was. He had turned eight a week before, and he was still small and—no, Ender thought, he wasn't young. Nobody was young. Bean had been in battle, and with a whole army depending on him he had come through and won. And even though he was small, Ender could never think of him as young again.

Ender shrugged and Bean came over and sat on the edge of the bed. The younger boy looked at his hands for a while, and finally Ender grew impatient and asked, "Well, what is it?"

"I'm transferred. Got orders just a few minutes ago."

Ender closed his eyes for a moment. "I knew they'd pull something new. Now they're taking—where are you going?"

"Rabbit Army."

"How can they put you under an idiot like Carn Carby!"

"Carn was graduated. Support squad."

Ender looked up. "Well, who's commanding Rabbit then?"

Bean held his hands out helplessly.

"Me," he said.

Ender nodded, and the smiled. "Of course. After all, you're only four years younger than the regular age."

"It isn't funny," Bean said. "I don't know what's going on here. First all the changes in the game. And now this. I wasn't the only one transferred, either, Ender. Ren, Peder, Brian, Wins, Younger. All commanders now."

Ender stood up angrily and strode to the wall. "Every damn toon leader I've got!" he said, and whirled to face Bean. "If they're going to break up my army, Bean, why did they bother making me a commander at all?"

Bean shook his head. "I don't know. You're the best, Ender. Nobody's ever done what you've done. Nineteen battles in fifteen days, sir, and you won every one of them, no matter what they did to you."

"And now you and the other are commanders. You know every trick I've got, I trained you, and who am I supposed to replace you with? Are they going to stick me with six greenohs?"

"It stinks, Ender, but you know that if they gave you five crippled midgets and armed you with a roll of toilet paper you'd win."

They both laughed, and then they noticed that the door was open.

Lieutenant Anderson stepped in. He was followed by Captain Graff.

"Ender Wiggins," Graff said, holding his hands across his stomach.

"Yes, sir." Ender answered.

"Orders."

Anderson extended a slip of paper. Ender read it quickly, then crumpled it, still looking at the air where the paper had been. After a few minutes he asked, "Can I tell my army?"

"They'll find out," Graff answered. "It's better not to talk to them after orders. It makes it easier."

"For you or for me?" Ender asked. He didn't wait for an answer. He turned quickly to Bean, took his hand for a moment, and then headed for the door.

"Wait," Bean said. "Where are you going? Tactical or Support School?"

"Command School," Ender answered, and then he was gone and Anderson closed the door.

Command School, Bean thought. Nobody went to Command School until they had gone through three years of Tactical. But then, nobody went to Tactical until they had been through at least five years of Battle School. Ender had only had three.

The system was breaking up. No doubt about it, Bean thought. Either somebody at the top was going crazy, or something was going wrong with the war—the real war, the one they were training to fight in. Why else would they break down the training system, advance somebody—even somebody as good as Ender—straight to Command School? Why else would they ever have an eight-year-old greenoh like Bean command an army?

Bean wondered about it for a long time, and then he finally lay down on Ender's bed and realized that he'd never see Ender again, probably. For some reason that made him want to cry. But he didn't cry, of course. Training in the preschools had taught him how to force down emotions like that. He remembered how his first teacher, when he was three, would have been upset to see his lip quivering and his eyes full of tears.

Bean went through the relaxing routine until he didn't feel like crying anymore. Then he drifted off to sleep. His hand was near his mouth. It lay on his pillow hesitantly, as if Bean couldn't decide whether to bite his nails or suck on his fingertips. His forehead was creased and furrowed. His breathing was quick and light. He was a soldier, and if anyone had asked him what he wanted to be when he grew up, he wouldn't have known what they meant.

There's a war on, they said, and that was excuse enough for all the hurry in the world. They said it like a password and flashed a little card at every ticket counter and customs check and guard station. It got them to the head of every line.

Ender Wiggins was rushed from place to place so quickly he had no time to examine anything. But he did see trees for the first time. He saw men who were not in uniform. He saw women. He saw strange animals that didn't speak, but that followed docilely behind women and small children. He saw suitcases and conveyor belts and signs that said words he had never heard of. He would have asked someone what the words meant, except that purpose and authority surrounded him in the persons of four very high officers who never spoke to each other and never spoke to him.

Ender Wiggins was a stranger to the world he was being trained to save. He did not remember ever leaving Battle School before. His earliest memories were of childish war games under the direction of a teacher, of meals with other boys in the gray and green uniforms of the armed forces of his world. He did not know that the gray represented the sky and the green represented the great forests of his planet. All he knew of the world was from vague references to "outside."

And before he could make any sense of the strange world he was seeing for the first time, they enclosed him again within the shell of the military, where nobody had to say *There's a war on* anymore because no one within the shell of the military forgot it for a single instant of a single day.

They put him in a spaceship and launched him to a large artificial satellite that circled the world.

This space station was called Command School. It held the ansible.

On his first day Ender Wiggins was taught about the ansible and what it meant to warfare. It meant that even though the starships of today's battles were launched a hundred years ago, the commanders of the starships were men of today, who used the ansible to send messages to the computers and the few men on each ship. The ansible sent words as they were spoken, orders as they were made. Battleplans as they were fought. Light was a pedestrian.

For two months Ender Wiggins didn't meet a single person. They came to him namelessly, taught him what they knew, and left him to other teachers. He had no time to miss his friends at Battle School. He only had time to learn how to operate the simulator, which flashed battle patterns around him as if he were in a starship at the center of the battle. How to command mock ships in mock battles by manipulating the keys on the simulator and speaking words into the ansible. How to recognize instantly every enemy ship and the weapons it carried by the pattern that the simulator showed. How to transfer all that he learned in the nullo battles at Battle School to the starship battles at Command School.

He had thought the game was taken seriously before. Here they hurried him through every step, were angry and worried beyond reason every time he forgot something or made a mistake. But he worked as he had always worked, and learned as he had always learned. After a while he didn't make any more mistakes. He used the simulator as if it were a part of himself. Then they stopped being worried and gave him a teacher.

Maezr Rackham was sitting cross-legged on the floor when Ender awoke. He said nothing as Ender got up and showered and dressed, and Ender did not bother to ask him anything. He had long since learned that when something unusual was going on, he would often find out more information faster by waiting than by asking.

Maezr still hadn't spoken when Ender was ready and went to the door to leave the room. The door didn't open. Ender turned to face the man sitting on the floor. Maezr was at least forty, which made him the oldest man Ender had ever seen close up. He had a day's growth of black and white whiskers that grizzled his face only slightly less than his close-cut hair. His face sagged a little and his eyes were surrounded by creases and lines. He looked at Ender without interest.

Ender turned back to the door and tried again to open it.

"All right," he said, giving up. "Why's the door locked?"

Maezr continued to look at him blankly.

Ender became impatient. "I'm going to be late. If I'm not supposed to be there until later, then tell me so I can go back to bed." No answer. "Is it a guessing game?" Ender asked. No answer. Ender decided that maybe the man was trying to make him angry, so he went through a relaxing exercise as he leaned on the door, and soon he was calm again. Maezr didn't take his eyes off Ender.

For the next two hours the silence endured. Maezr watching Ender constantly, Ender trying to pretend he didn't notice the old man. The boy became more and more nervous, and finally ended up walking from one end of the room to the other in a sporadic pattern.

He walked by Maezr as he had several times before, and Maezr's hand shot out and pushed Ender's left leg into his right in the middle of a step. Ender fell flat on the floor.

He leaped to his feet immediately, furious. He found Maezr sitting calmly, cross-legged, as if he had never moved. Ender stood poised to fight. But the man's immobility made it impossible for Ender to attack, and he found himself wondering if he had only imagined the old man's hand tripping him up.

The pacing continued for another hour, with Ender Wiggins trying the door every now and then. At last he gave up and took off his uniform and walked to his bed.

As he leaned over to pull the covers back, he felt a hand jab roughly between his thighs and another hand grab his hair. In a moment he had been turned upside down. His face and shoulders were being pressed into the floor by the old man's knee, while his back was excruciatingly bent and his legs were pinioned by Maezr's arm. Ender was helpless to use his arms, and he couldn't bend his back to gain slack so he could use his legs. In less than two seconds the old man had completely defeated Ender Wiggins.

"All right," Ender gasped. "You win."

Maezr's knee thrust painfully downward.

"Since when," Maezr asked in a soft, rasping voice, "do you have to tell the enemy when he has won?"

Ender remained silent.

"I surprised you once, Ender Wiggins. Why didn't you destroy me immediately? Just because I looked peaceful? You turned your back on me. Stupid. You have learned nothing. You have never had a teacher."

Ender was angry now. "I've had too many damned teachers, how was I supposed to know you'd turn out to be a—" Ender hunted for the word. Maezr supplied one.

"An enemy, Ender Wiggins," Maezr whispered. "I am your enemy, the first one you've ever had who was smarter than you. There is no teacher but the enemy, Ender Wiggins. No one but the enemy will ever tell you what the enemy is going to do. No one but the enemy will ever teach you how to destroy and conquer. I am your enemy, from now on. From now on I am your teacher."

Then Maezr let Ender's legs fall to the floor. Because the old man still held Ender's head to the floor, the boy couldn't use his arms to compensate, and his legs hit the plastic surface with a loud crack and a sickening pain that made Ender wince. Then Maezr stood and let Ender rise.

Slowly the boy pulled his legs under him, with a faint groan of pain, and he knelt on all fours for a moment, recovering. Then his right arm flashed out. Maezr quickly danced back and Ender's hand closed on air as his teacher's foot shot forward to catch Ender on the chin.

Ender's chin wasn't there. He was lying flat on his back, spinning on the floor, and during the moment that Maezr was off balance from his kick Ender's feet smashed into Maezr's other leg. The old man fell on the ground in a heap.

What seemed to be a heap was really a hornet's nest. Ender couldn't find an arm or a leg that held still long enough to be grabbed, and in the meantime blows were landing on his back and arms. Ender was smaller—he couldn't reach past the old man's flailing limbs.

So he leaped back out of the way and stood poised near the door.

The old man stopped thrashing about and sat up, cross-legged again, laughing. "Better, this time, boy. But slow. You will have to be better with a fleet than you are with your body or no one will be safe with you in command. Lesson learned?"

Ender nodded slowly.

Maezr smiled. "Good. Then we'll never have such a battle again. All the rest with the simulator. I will program your battles, I will devise the strategy of your enemy, and you will learn to be quick and discover what tricks the enemy has for you. Remember, boy. From now on the enemy is more clever than you. From now on the enemy is stronger than you. From now on you are always about to lose."

Then Maezr's face became serious again. "You will be about to lose, Ender, but you will win. You will learn to defeat the enemy. He will teach you how."

Maezr got up and walked to the door. Ender stepped out of the way. As the old man touched the handle of the door, Ender leaped into the air and kicked Maezr in the small of the back with both feet. He hit hard enough that he rebounded onto his feet, as Maezr cried out and collapsed on the floor.

Maezr got up slowly, holding on to the door handle, his face contorted with pain. He seemed disabled, but Ender didn't trust him. He waited warily. And yet in spite of his suspicion he was caught off guard by Maezr's speed. In a moment he found himself on the floor near the opposite wall, his nose and lip bleeding where his face had hit the bed. He was able to turn enough to see Maezr open the door and leave. The old man was limping and walking slowly.

Ender smiled in spite of the pain, then rolled over onto his back and laughed until his mouth filled with blood and he started to gag. Then he got up and painfully made his way to his bed. He lay down and in a few minutes a medic came and took care of his injuries.

As the drug had its effect and Ender drifted off to sleep he remembered the way Maezr limped out of his room and laughed again. He was still laughing softly as his mind went blank and the medic pulled the blanket over him and snapped off the light. He slept until pain woke him in the morning. He dreamed of defeating Maezr.

The next day Ender went to the simulator room with his nose bandaged and his lip still puffy. Maezr was not there. Instead, a captain who had worked with him before showed him an addition that had been made. The captain pointed to a tube with a loop at one end. "Radio. Primitive, I know, but it loops over your ear and we tuck the other end into your mouth like this."

"Watch it," Ender said as the captain pushed the end of the tube into his swollen lip.

"Sorry. Now you just talk."

"Good. Who to?"

The captain smiled. "Ask and see."

Ender shrugged and turned to the simulator. As he did a voice reverberated through his skull. It was too loud for him to understand, and he ripped the radio off his year.

"What are you trying to do, make me deaf?"

The captain shook his head and turned a dial on a small box on a nearby table. Ender put the radio back on.

"Commander," the radio said in a familiar voice.

Ender answered, "Yes."

"Instructions, sir?"

The voice was definitely familiar. "Bean?" Ender asked.

"Yes, sir."

"Bean, this is Ender."

Silence. And then a burst of laughter from the other side. Then six or seven more voices laughing, and Ender waited for silence to return. When it did, he asked, "Who else?"

A few voices spoke at once, but Bean drowned them out. "Me, I'm Bean, and Peder, Wins, Younger, Lee, and Vlad."

Ender thought for a moment. Then he asked what the hell was going on. They laughed again.

"They can't break up the group," Bean said. "We were commanders for maybe two weeks, and here we are at Command School, training with the simulator, and all of a sudden they told us we were going to form a fleet with a new commander. And that's you."

Ender smiled. "Are you boys any good?"

"If we aren't, you'll let us know."

Ender chuckled a little. "Might work out. A fleet."

For the next ten days Ender trained his toon leaders until they could maneuver their ships like precision dancers. It was like being back in the battleroom again, except that now Ender could always see everything, and could speak to his toon leaders and change their orders at any time.

One day as Ender sat down at the control board and switched on the simulator, harsh green lights appeared in the space—the enemy.

"This is it," Ender said. "X, Y, bullet, C, D, reserve screen, E, south loop, Bean, angle north."

The enemy was grouped in a globe, and outnumbered Ender two to one. Half of Ender's force was grouped in a tight, bulletlike formation, with the rest in a flat circular screen—except for a tiny force under Bean that moved off the simulator, heading behind the enemy's formation. Ender quickly learned the enemy's strategy: whenever Ender's bullet formation came close, the enemy would give way, hoping to draw Ender inside the globe where he would be surrounded. So Ender obligingly fell into the trap, bringing his bullet to the center of the globe.

The enemy began to contract slowly, not wanting to come within range until all their weapons could be brought to bear at once. Then Ender began to work in earnest. His reserve screen approached the outside of the globe, and the enemy began to concentrate his forces there. Then Bean's force appeared on the opposite side, and the enemy again deployed ships on that side.

Which left most of the globe only thinly defended. Ender's bullet attacked, and since at the point of attack it outnumbered the enemy overwhelmingly, he tore a hole in the formation. The enemy reacted to try to plug the gap, but in the confusion the reserve force and Bean's small force attacked simultaneously, while the bullet moved to another part of the globe. In a few more minutes the formation was shattered, most of the enemy ships destroyed, and the few survivors rushing away as fast as they could go.

Ender switched the simulator off. All the lights faded. Maezr was standing beside Ender, his hands in his pockets, his body tense. Ender looked up at him.

"I thought you said the enemy would be smart," Ender said.

Maezr's face remained expressionless. "What did you learn?"

"I lcarned that a sphere only works if your enemy's a fool. He had his forces so spread out that I outnumbered him whenever I engaged him."

"And?"

"And," Ender said, "you can't stay committed to one pattern. It makes you too easy to predict."

"Is that all?" Maezr asked quietly.

Ender took off his radio. "The enemy could have defeated me by breaking the sphere earlier."

Maezr nodded. "You had an unfair advantage."

Ender looked up at him coldly. "I was outnumbered two to one."

Maezr shook his head. "You have the ansible. The enemy doesn't. We include that in the mock battles. Their messages travel at the speed of light."

Ender glanced toward the simulator. "Is there enough space to make a difference?"

"Don't you know?" Maezr asked. "None of the ships was ever closer than thirty thousand kilometers to any other."

Ender tried to figure the size of the enemy's sphere. Astronomy was beyond him. But now his curiously was stirred.

"What kind of weapons are on those ships? To be able to strike so fast?"

Maezr shook his head. "The science is too much for you. You'd have to study many more years than you've lived to understand even the basics. All you need to know is that the weapons work."

"Why do we have to come so close to be in range?"

"The ships are all protected by forcefields. A certain distance away the weapons are weaker and can't get through. Closer in the weapons are stronger than the shields. But the computers take care of all that. They're constantly firing in any direction that won't hurt one of our ships. The computers pick targets, aim; they do all the detail work. You just tell them when and get them in a position to win. All right?"

"No," Ender twisted the tube of the radio around his fingers. "I have to know how the weapons work."

"I told you, it would take—"

"I can't command a fleet—not even on the simulator—unless I know." Ender waited a moment, then added, "Just the rough idea."

Maezr stood up and walked a few steps away. "All right, Ender. It won't make any sense, but I'll try. As simply as I can." He shoved his hands into his pockets. "It's this way, Ender. Everything is made up of atoms, little particles so small you can't see them with your eyes. These atoms, there are only a few different types, and they're all made up of even smaller particles that are pretty much the same. These atoms can be broken, so that they stop being atoms. So that this metal doesn't hold together anymore. Or the plastic floor. Or your body. Or even the air. They just seem to disappear, if you break the atoms. All that's left is the pieces. And they fly around and break more atoms. The weapons on the ships set up an area where it's impossible for atoms of anything to stay together. They all break down. So things in that area—they disappear."

Ender nodded. "You're right, I don't understand it. Can it be blocked?"

"No. But it gets wider and weaker the farther it goes from the ship, so that after a while a forcefield will block it. Okay? And to make it strong at all, it has to be focused so that a ship can only fire effectively in maybe three or four directions at once."

Ender nodded again, but he didn't really understand, not well enough. "If the pieces of the broken atoms go breaking more atoms, why doesn't it just make everything disappear?"

"Space. Those thousands of kilometers between the ships, they're empty. Almost no atoms. The pieces don't hit anything, and when they finally do hit something, they're so spread out they can't do any harm." Maezr cocked his head quizzically. "Anything else you need to know?"

"Do the weapons on the ships—do they work against anything besides ships?"

Maezr moved in close to Ender and said firmly, "We only use them against ships. Never anything else. If we used them against anything else, the enemy would use them against us. Got it?"

Maezr walked away, and was nearly out the door when Ender called to him.

"I don't know your name yet," Ender said blandly.

"Maezr Rackham."

"Maezr Rackham," Ender said, "I defeated you."

Maezr laughed.

"Ender, you weren't fighting me today," he said. "You were fighting the stupidest computer in the Command School, set on a ten-year-old program. You don't think I'd use a sphere, do you?" He shook his head. "Ender, my dear little fellow, when you fight me, you'll know it. Because you'll lose." And Maezr left the room.

Ender still practiced ten hours a day with his toon leaders. He never saw them, though, only heard their voices on the radio. Battles came every two or three days. The enemy had something new every time, something harder—but Ender coped with it. And won every time. And after every battle Maezr would point out mistakes and show Ender that he had really lost. Maezr only let Ender finish so that he would learn to handle the end of the game.

Until finally Maezr came in and solemnly shook Ender's hand and said, "That, boy, was a good battle."

Because the praise was so long in coming, it pleased Ender more than praise had ever pleased him before. And because it was so condescending, he resented it.

"So from now on." Maezr said, "we can give you hard ones."

From then on Ender's life was a slow nervous breakdown.

He began fighting two battles a day, with problems that steadily grew more difficult. He had been trained in nothing but the game all his life, but now the game began to consume him. He woke in the morning with new strategies for the simulator and went fitfully to sleep at night with the mistakes of the day preying on him. Sometimes he would wake up in the middle of the night crying for a reason he didn't remember. Sometimes he woke up with his knuckles bloody from biting them. But every day he went impassively to the simulator and drilled his toon leaders until the battles, and drilled his toon leaders after the battles, and endured and studied the harsh criticism that Rackham piled on him. He noted that Rackham perversely criticized him more after his hardest battles. He noted that every time he thought of a new strategy the enemy was using it within a few days. And he noted that while his fleet always stayed the same size, the enemy increased in numbers every day.

He asked his teacher.

"We are showing you what it will be like when you really command. The ratios of enemy to us."

"Why does the enemy always outnumber us?"

Maezr bowed his gray head for a moment, as if deciding whether to answer. Finally he looked up and reached out his hand and touched Ender on the shoulder. "I will tell you, even though the information is secret. You see, the enemy attacked us first. He had good reason to attack us, but that is a matter for politicians, and whether the fault was ours or his, we could not let him win. So when the enemy came to our worlds, we fought back, hard, and spent the finest of our young men in the fleets. But we won, and the enemy retreated."

Maezr smiled ruefully. "But the enemy was not through, boy. The enemy would never be through. They came again, with more numbers, and it was harder to beat them. And another generation of young men was spent. Only a few survived. So we came up with a plan—the big men came up with the plan. We knew that we had to destroy the enemy once and for all, totally, eliminate his ability to make war against us. To do that we had to go to his home worlds—his home world, really, since the enemy's empire is all tied to his capital world."

"And so?" Ender asked.

"And so we made a fleet. We made more ships than the enemy ever had. We made a hundred ships for every ship he had sent against us. And we launched them against his twenty-eight worlds. They started leaving a hundred years ago. And they carried on them the ansible, and only a few men. So that someday a commander could sit on a planet somewhere far from the battle and command the fleet. So that our best minds would not be destroyed by the enemy."

Ender's questions had still not been answered. "Why do they outnumber us?"

Maezr laughed. "Because it took a hundred years for our ships to get there. They've had a hundred years to prepare for us. They'd be fools, don't you think, boy, if they waited in old tugboats to defend their harbors. They have new ships, great ships, hundreds of ships. All we have is the ansible, that and the fact that they have to put a commander with every fleet, and when they lose—and they will lose—they lose one of their best minds every time."

Ender started to ask another question.

"No more, Ender Wiggins. I've told you more than you ought to know as it is."

Ender stood angrily and turned away. "I have a right to know. Do you think this can go on forever, pushing me through one school and another and never telling me what my life is for? You use me and the others as a tool, someday we'll command your ships, someday maybe we'll save your lives, but I'm not a computer, and I have to *know*!"

"Ask me a question, then, boy," Maezr said, "and if I can answer, I will."

"If you use your best minds to command the fleets, and you never lose any, then what do you need me for? Who am I replacing, if they're all still there?"

Maezr shook his head. "I can't tell you the answer to that, Ender. Be content that we will need you, soon. It's late. Go to bed. You have a battle in the morning."

Ender walked out of the simulator room. But when Maezr left by the same door a few moments later, the boy was waiting in the hall.

"All right, boy," Maezr said impatiently, "what is it? I don't have all night and you need to sleep."

Ender wasn't sure what his question was, but Maezr waited. Finally Ender asked softly, "Do they live?"

"Do who live?"

"The other commanders. The ones now. And before me."

Maezr snorted. "Live. Of course they live. He wonders if they live." Still chuckling, the old man walked off down the hall. Ender stood in the corridor for a while, but at last he was tired and he went off to bed. They live, he thought. They live, but he can't tell me what happens to them.

That night Ender didn't wake up crying. But he did wake up with blood on his hands.

Months wore on with battles every day, until at last Ender settled into the routine of the destruction of himself. He slept less every night, dreamed more, and he began to have terrible pains in his stomach. They put him on a very bland diet, but soon he didn't even have an appetite for that. "Eat," Maezr said, and Ender would mechanically put food in his mouth. But if nobody told him to eat he didn't eat.

One day as he was drilling his toon leaders the room went black and he woke up on the floor with his face bloody where he had hit the controls.

They put him to bed then, and for three days he was very ill. He remembered seeing faces in his dreams, but they weren't real faces, and he knew it even while he thought he saw them. He thought he saw Bean sometimes, and sometimes he thought he saw Lieutenant Anderson and Captain Graff. And then he woke up and it was only his enemy, Maezr Rackham.

"I'm awake," he said to Maezr Rackham.

"So I see," Maezr answered. "Took you long enough. You have a battle today."

So Ender got up and fought the battle and he won it. But there was no second battle that day, and they let him go to bed earlier. His hands were shaking as he undressed.

During the night he thought he felt hands touching him gently, and he dreamed he heard voices saying, "How long can he go on?"

"Long enough."

"So soon?"

"In a few days, then he's through."

"How will he do?"

"Fine. Even today, he was better than ever."

Ender recognized the last voice as Maezr Rackham's. He resented Rackham's intruding even in his sleep.

He woke up and fought another battle and won.

Then he went to bed.

He woke up and won again.

And the next day was his last day in Command School, though he didn't know it. He got up and went to the simulator for the battle.

Maezr was waiting for him. Ender walked slowly into the simulator room. His step was slightly shuffling, and he seemed tired and dull. Maezr frowned.

"Are you awake, boy?" If Ender had been alert, he would have cared more about the concern in his teacher's voice. Instead, he simply went to the controls and sat down. Maezr spoke to him.

"Today's game needs a little explanation, Ender Wiggins. Please turn around and pay strict attention."

Ender turned around, and for the first time he noticed that there were people at the back of the room. He recognized Graff and Anderson from Battle School, and vaguely remembered a few of the men from Command School—teachers for a few hours at some time or another. But most of the people he didn't know at all.

"Who are they?"

Maezr shook his head and answered, "Observers. Every now and then we let observers come in to watch the battle. If you don't want them, we'll send them out."

Ender shrugged. Maezr began his explanation. "Today's game, boy, has a new element. We're staging this battle around a planet. This will complicate things in two ways. The planet isn't large, on the scale we're using, but the ansible can't detect anything on the other side of it—so there's a blind spot. Also, it's against the rules to use weapons against the planet itself. All right?"

"Why, don't the weapons work against planets?"

Maezr answered coldly, "There are rules of war, Ender, that apply even in training games."

Ender shook his head slowly. "Can the planet attack?"

Maezr looked nonplussed for a moment, then smiled. "I guess you'll have to find that one out, boy. And one more thing. Today, Ender, your opponent isn't the computer. I am your enemy today, and today I won't be letting you off so easily. Today is a battle to the end. And I'll use any means I can to defeat you."

Then Maezr was gone, and Ender expressionlessly led his toon leaders through maneuvers. Ender was doing well, of course, but several of the observers shook their heads, and Graff kept clasping and unclasping his hands, crossing and uncrossing his legs. Ender would be slow today, and today Ender couldn't afford to be slow.

A warning buzzer sounded, and Ender cleared the simulator board, waiting for today's game to appear. He felt muddled today, and wondered why people were there watching. Were they going to judge him today? Decide if he was good enough for something else? For another two years of grueling training, another two years of struggling to exceed his best? Ender was twelve. He felt very old. And as he waited for the game to appear, he wished he could simply lose it, lose the battle badly and completely so that they would remove him from the program, punish him however they wanted, he didn't care, just so he could sleep.

Then the enemy formation appeared, and Ender's weariness turned to desperation.

The enemy outnumbered them a thousand to one, the simulator glowed green with them, and Ender knew that he couldn't win.

And the enemy was not stupid. There was no formation that Ender could study and attack. Instead the vast swarms of ships were constantly moving, constantly shifting from one momentary formation to another, so that a space that for one moment was empty was immediately filled with a formidable enemy force. And even though Ender's fleet was the largest he had ever had, there was no place he could deploy it where he would outnumber the enemy long enough to accomplish anything.

And behind the enemy was the planet. The planet, which Maezr had warned him about. What difference did a planet make, when Ender couldn't hope to get near it? Ender waited, waited for the flash of insight that would tell him what to do, how to destroy the enemy. And as he waited, he heard the observers behind him begin to shift in their seats, wondering what Ender was doing, what plan he would follow. And finally it was obvious to everyone that Ender didn't know what to do, that there was nothing to do, and a few of the men at the back of the room made quiet little sounds in their throats.

Then Ender heard Bean's voice in his ear. Bean chuckled and said, "Remember, the enemy's gate is *down*." A few of the other toon leaders laughed, and Ender thought back to the simple games he had played and won in Battle School. They had put him against hopeless odds there, too. And he had beaten them. And he'd be damned if he'd let Maezr Rackham beat him with a cheap trick like outnumbering him a thousand to one. He had won a game in Battle School by going for something the enemy didn't expect, something against the rules—he had won by going against the enemy's gate.

And the enemy's gate was down.

Ender smiled, and realized that if he broke this rule they'd probably kick him out of school, and that way he'd win for sure. He would never have to play a game again.

He whispered into the microphone. His six commanders each took a part of the fleet and launched themselves against the enemy. They pursued erratic courses, darting off in one direction and then another. The enemy immediately stopped his aimless maneuvering and began to group around Ender's six fleets.

Ender took off his microphone, leaned back in his chair, and watched. The observers murmured out loud, now. Ender was doing nothing—he had thrown the game away.

But a pattern began to emerge from the quick confrontations with the enemy. Ender's six groups lost ships constantly as they brushed with each enemy force—but they never stopped for a fight, even when for a moment they could have won a small tactical victory. Instead they continued on their erratic course that led, eventually, down. Toward the enemy planet.

And because of their seemingly random course the enemy didn't realize it until the same time that the observers did. By then it was too late, just as it had been too late for William Bee to stop Ender's soldiers from activating the gate. More of Ender's ships could be hit and destroyed, so that of the six fleets only two were able to get to the planet, and those were decimated. But those tiny groups *did* get through, and they opened fire on the planet.

Ender leaned forward now, anxious to see if his guess would pay off. He half expected a buzzer to sound and the game to be stopped, because he had broken the rule. But he was betting on the accuracy of the simulator. If it could simulate a planet, it could simulate what would happen to a planet under attack.

It did.

The weapons that blew up little ships didn't blow up the entire planet at first. But they did cause terrible explosions. And on the planet there was no space to dissipate the chain reaction. On the planet the chain reaction found more and more fuel to feed it.

The planet's surface seemed to be moving back and forth, but soon the surface gave way to an immense explosion that sent light flashing in all directions. It swallowed up Ender's entire fleet. And then it reached the enemy ships.

The first simply vanished in the explosion. Then, as the explosion spread and became less bright, it was clear what happened to each ship. As the light reached them they flashed brightly for a moment and disappeared. They were all fuel for the fire of the planet.

It took more than three minutes for the explosion to reach the limits of the simulator, and by then it was much fainter. All the ships were gone, and if any had escaped before the explosion reached them, they were few and not worth worrying about. Where the planet had been there was nothing. The simulator was empty.

Ender had destroyed the enemy by sacrificing his entire fleet and breaking the rule against destroying the enemy planet. He wasn't sure whether to feel triumphant at his victory or defiant at the rebuke he was certain would come. So instead he felt nothing. He was tired. He wanted to go to bed and sleep.

He switched off the simulator, and finally heard the noise behind him.

There were no longer two rows of dignified military observers. Instead there was chaos. Some of them were slapping each other on the back, some of them were bowed, head in hands, others were openly weeping. Captain Graff detached himself from the group and came to Ender. Tears streamed down his face, but he was smiling. He reached out his arms, and to Ender's surprise he embraced the boy, held him tightly, and whispered, "Thank you, thank you, thank you, Ender."

Soon all the observers were gathered around the bewildered child, thanking him and cheering him and patting him on the shoulder and shaking his hand. Ender tried to make sense of what they were saying. Had he passed the test after all? Why did it matter so much to them?

Then the crowd parted and Maezr Rackham walked through. He came straight up to Ender Wiggins and held out his hand.

"You made the hard choice, boy. But heaven knows there was no other way you could have done it. Congratulations. You beat them, and it's all over."

All over. Beat them. "I beat *you*, Maezr Rackham."

Maezr laughed, a loud laugh that filled the room. "Ender Wiggins, you never played me. You never played a *game* since I was your teacher."

Ender didn't get the joke. He had played a great many games, at a terrible cost to himself. He began to get angry.

Maezr reached out and touched his shoulder. Ender shrugged him off. Maezr then grew serious and said, "Ender Wiggins, for the last months you have been the commander of our fleets. There were no games. The battles were real. Your only enemy was *the* enemy. You won every battle. And finally today you fought them at their home world, and you destroyed their world, their fleet, you destroyed them completely, and they'll never come against us again. You did it. You."

Real. Not a game. Ender's mind was too tired to cope with it all. He walked away from Maezr, walked silently through the crowd that still whispered thanks and congratulations by the boy, walked out of the simulator room and finally arrived in his bedroom and closed the door.

He was asleep when Graff and Maezr Rackham found him. They came in quietly and roused him. He awoke slowly, and when he recognized them he turned away to go back to sleep.

"Ender," Graff said. "We need to talk to you."

Ender rolled back to face them. He said nothing.

Graff smiled. "It was a shock to you yesterday, I know. But it must make you feel good to know you won the war."

Ender nodded slowly.

"Maezr Rackham here, he never played against you. He only analyzed your battles to find out your weak spots, to help you improve. It worked, didn't it?"

Ender closed his eyes tightly. They waited. He said, "Why didn't you tell me?"

Maezr smiled. "A hundred years ago, Ender, we found out some things. That when a commander's life is in danger he becomes afraid, and fear slows down his thinking. When a commander knows that he's killing people, he becomes cautious or insane, and neither of those help him do well. And when he's mature, when he has responsibilities and an understanding of the world, he becomes cautious and sluggish and can't do his job. So we trained children, who didn't know anything but the game, and never knew when it would become real. That was the theory, and you proved that the theory worked."

Graff reached out and touched Ender's shoulder. "We launched the ships so that they would all arrive at their destination during these few months. We knew that we'd probably have only one good commander, if we were lucky. In history it's been very rare to have more than one genius in a war. So we planned on having a genius. We were gambling. And you came along and we won."

Ender opened his eyes again and they realized that he was angry. "Yes, you won."

Graff and Maezr Rackham looked at each other. "He doesn't understand," Graff whispered.

"I understand," Ender said. "You needed a weapon, and you got it, and it was me."

"That's right," Maezr answered.

"So tell me," Ender went on, "how many people lived on that planet that I destroyed."

They didn't answer him. They waited awhile in silence, and then Graff spoke. "Weapons don't need to understand what they're pointed at, Ender. We did the pointing, and so we're responsible. You just did your job."

Maezr smiled. "Of course, Ender, you'll be taken care of. The government will never forget you. You served us all very well."

Ender rolled over and faced the wall, and even though they tried to talk to him, he didn't answer them. Finally they left.

Ender lay in his bed for a long time before anyone disturbed him again. The door opened softly. Ender didn't turn to see who it was. Then a hand touched him softly.

"Ender, it's me, Bean."

Ender turned over and looked at the little boy who was standing by his bed.

"Sit down," Ender said.

Bean sat. "That last battle, Ender. I didn't know how you'd get us out of it."

Ender smiled. "I didn't. I cheated. I thought they'd kick me out."

"Can you believe it! We won the war. The whole war's over, and we thought we'd have to wait till we grew up to fight in it, and it was us fighting it all the time. I mean, Ender, we're little kids. I'm a little kid, anyway." Bean laughed and Ender smiled. Then they were silent for a little while, Bean sitting on the edge of the bed, Ender watching him out of half-closed eyes.

Finally Bean thought of something else to say.

"What will we do now that the war's over?" he said.

Ender closed his eyes and said, "I need some sleep, Bean."

Bean got up and left and Ender slept.

Graff and Anderson walked through the gates into the park. There was a breeze, but the sun was hot on their shoulders.

"Abba Technics? In the capital?" Graff asked.

"No, in Biggock County. Training division," Anderson replied. "They think my work with children is good preparation. And you?"

Graff smiled and shook his head. "No plans. I'll be here for a few more months. Reports, winding down. I've had offers. Personnel development for DCIA, executive vice-president for U and P, but I said no. Publisher wants me to do memoirs of the war. I don't know."

They sat on a bench and watched leaves shivering in the breeze. Children on the monkey bars were laughing and yelling, but the wind and the distance swallowed their words. "Look," Graff said, pointing. A little boy jumped from the bars and ran near the bench where the two men sat. Another boy followed him, and holding his hands like a gun he made an explosive sound. The child he was shooting at didn't stop. He fired again.

"I got you! Come back here!"

The other little boy ran on out of sight.

"Don't you know when you're dead?" The boy shoved his hands in his pockets and kicked a rock back to the monkey bars.

Anderson smiled and shook his head. "Kids," he said. Then he and Graff stood up and walked on out of the park.

If you've ever been a fan of Cleveland teams—the Indians, the Browns, the Cavs—this story is a great comfort as it explains so many *things. It also may account for otherwise normal people owning seventy-three-inch flat-screen TVs and the invention of smartphones. One cannot help but feel, however, that the arcane initiation rite referred to herein has expanded to include at least* some *women and now exempts* some *men . . .*

The Fate of Nations

James Morrow

Pushing aside the knotted pairs of running socks, I lift the journal from my dresser drawer. I unfasten the delicate lock, turn to a fresh page, and ready my ballpoint pen. Click.

Dear Diary, let me say at the outset that I once counted myself among the luckiest of women. Dennis had a lucrative job as a software engineer at Micromega. Our daughter, Angela, loved school and always brought home top grades. Thanks to the saltwater fish fad, my little pet shop—Carlotta's Critturs in Copley Square—was turning a tidy profit.

The first signs of trouble were subtle. I'm thinking especially of Dennis's decision to become a Boston Bruins fan and a Philadelphia Flyers fan simultaneously, an allegiance that served no evident purpose beyond allowing him to watch twice as much hockey as before. I also recall his insistence on replacing our coffee cups and drink tumblers with ceramic mugs bearing the New England Patriots logo. Then there was Dennis's baseball-card collection, featuring the 1986 Red Sox starting lineup. Wasn't that a hobby more suited to a ten-year-old?

It soon became clear that Dennis was battling a full-blown addiction. The instant he got home from work, he plunked himself in front of the tube and started watching ESPN, ESPN2, or ESPN3. Dozens of teams enlisted his loyalty, not merely the Boston franchises. He followed the NFL, the NHL, the NBA, and Major League Baseball. Our erotic encounters were short and perfunctory, bounded by the seventh inning stretch. Whenever we went on vacation, Dennis brought his portable Sony along. Our trips to Martha's Vineyard were keyed to the All-Star Game. Our winter sojourns in Florida centered around the Stanley Cup.

"What do you *get* out of it?" I asked. The edge in my voice could nick a hockey puck.

"A great deal," he replied.

"What does it *matter*?" I wailed.

"I can't explain."

After much pleading, hectoring, and finagling, I convinced Dennis that we needed a marriage counselor. He insisted that we employ Dr. Robert Lezzer in Framingham. I acquiesced. A male therapist was better than none.

The instant I entered Dr. Lezzer's presence, I began feeling better. He was a small, perky, beaming gnome in a white cotton shirt and a red bow-tie. He said to call him Bob.

It took me half an hour to make my case. The lonely dinners. The one-way conversations. The chronic vacancy in our bed. As far as I was concerned, ESPN stood for Expect Sex Practically Never.

No sooner had I offered my story than Dennis and Bob traded significant glances, exchanged semantically freighted winks, and favored each other with identical nods.

"Should I tell her?" asked Dennis.

"Depends on whether you trust her," Bob replied.

"I do."

"Then let her in. It's the only way to save your marriage."

Dennis bent back his left ear to reveal a miniscule radio receiver, no bigger than a pinhead, embedded in the fleshy lobe. The implantation had occurred on his eighteenth birthday, he explained, as part of an arcane initiation rite. Every adult male in North America had one.

"Throughout the long history of Western civilization," said Dennis, "no secret has been better kept."

"But what is it *for*?" I asked.

"If he gave you the short answer, you wouldn't believe him," said Bob, bending close so I could see his transceiver.

"Luckily, we're only four hours from New York City," said Dennis, stroking me affectionately on the knee.

Bob recommended that we leave as soon as possible. We arranged for Angela to spend the night at a friend's house, then took off at two o'clock. By dinnertime we were zooming south down the West Side Highway, heading toward the heart of Manhattan.

We left our Volvo in the Park & Lock on 42nd Street near Tenth Avenue, hiked four blocks east, and entered the subway system. Although I'd often walked through the Times Square station during my undergraduate days at NYU, this was the first time I'd noticed a narrow steel door beside the stairwell leading to the N and R trains. Dennis retrieved his wallet, pulled out a black plastic card, and swiped it though a nearby magnetic reader, thereby causing the portal to open. An elevator car awaited us. We entered. The car descended for a full five minutes, carrying us a thousand feet into the bedrock.

Disembarking, we entered a small foyer decorated with two dozen full-figure portraits of men dressed in baseball uniforms. I recognized Ty Cobb and Pete Rose. Dennis guided me into an immense steel cavern dominated by a sparkling three-dimensional map that, according to the caption, depicted our spiral arm of the Milky Way. Five thousand tiny red lights pulsed amid the flashing white stars. Five thousand planets boasting intelligent life, Dennis explained. Five thousand advanced civilizations.

So: we were not alone in the galaxy—nor were we alone in the cavern. A dozen men wearing lime-green jumpsuits and walkie-talkie headsets paced in nervous circles before the great map, evidently receiving information from distant locales and relaying it to a hidden but eager audience.

I must admit, dear Diary, I'd never been more confused in my life.

Four other couples occupied the cavern. Each wife wore an expression identical to my own: exasperation leavened by perplexity. The husbands' faces all betrayed a peculiar mixture of fearfulness and relief.

"The Milky Way is a strange place," said Dennis. "Stranger than any of us can imagine. Some of its underlying laws may remain forevermore obscure."

"It's chilly down here," I said, rubbing each shoulder with the opposite hand.

"For reasons that scientists are just beginning to fathom," Dennis continued, "political events on these five thousand worlds are intimately connected to particular athletic contests on Earth. Before each such game, these dispatchers in the jumpsuits switch on their mikes and inform us exactly what's at stake."

"I don't understand."

"Women have difficulty with this. Bear with me. Here's how the universe works. Because the Dallas Cowboys won Super Bowl XII, the slave trade on 16 Cygni Beta ended after ten centuries of misery and oppression. By contrast, it's unfortunate that the Saint Louis Cardinals took home the National League Pennant in 1987, for this sparked the revocation of the Homosexual Toleration Act on 70 Virginis Kappa. Physicists call it PROSPOCAP—the Professional Sports Causality Principle. With me, darling?"

"I guess." I was so flabbergasted that my breath came only with great effort, although the cavern's poor ventilation was also to blame.

"Thanks to PROSPOCAP, we know that the advent of women's suffrage on 14 Herculis Gamma traced directly to the Oakland Raiders' emergence as the AFC Wild Card Team in 1980. We also realize that the end of theocratic dictatorship throughout 79 Ceti Delta followed directly upon the New York Yankees' trouncing of the Atlanta Braves in the 1999 World Series. On a darker note, the most devastating nuclear war ever to occur on Gliese 86 Omicron had its roots in the Boston Celtics' domination of the 1963 NBA Playoffs, Eastern Conference."

I decided to ask the obvious question. "How could a sports fan possibly cheer for his home team knowing that victory means nuclear war on another planet?"

"A fan learns the implication of any given win or loss only *ex post facto*. Until the moment of revelation, it makes sense to assume that your team is on the side of the angels. After all, even the most morally reprehensible outcome is preferable to oblivion."

"Oblivion?"

"The instant any team's supporters stop caring sufficiently, all the creatures on the affected planet become comatose."

I looked into Dennis's eyes. For the first time in our marriage, I understood my husband. "You care, don't you, darling? You really *care*."

"I really care."

"If only I'd *known*—I never would've harassed you for watching the Pro Bowl on my birthday. Do you forgive me?"

"Yes, Carlotta, I forgive you."

"Comatose? All of them?"

"Comatose. All of them. Death by dehydration follows in a matter of days."

Dennis went on to disclose an equally well-established fact. When it came to awareness of PROSPOCAP, a radical numerical disparity between males and females was an ontological necessity. Should the ratio ever exceed one knowledgeable woman for every two hundred knowledgeable men, the entire galaxy would implode, sucking all sentient lifeforms into the resultant maelstrom.

So you see why I picked up my pen today, dear Diary. I simply had to tell *someone* about this vast, astonishing, and apparently benign conspiracy.

Earlier tonight Dennis and I watched the Denver Broncos face the San Diego Chargers on Monday Night Football. The Broncos won, 21 to 14. As a result, an airplane manufacturer on Epsilon Eridani Prime managed to recall four hundred defective jetliners before any fatal crashes occurred.

"I'm curious about something," I told Dennis as we trod the stairs to our bedroom. "Do they have athletic events on other planets?"

"Ball sports are a constant throughout the galaxy."

"And do these sports also have . . . consequences?"

"In Terran Year 1863 CE, the Pegasi Secundus Juggernauts beat the Tau Bootes Berserkers in the Pangalactic Plasmacock Playoffs. A few hours later, three generals named Heth, Pender, and Pickett led the disastrous Confederate charge at Gettysburg."

"I see."

"In the subsequent century, the Iota Horologii Leviathans scored an upset over the Rho Cancri Demons in the Third Annual Ursa Majoris Lava Hockey Tournament, whereupon Communism began its rapid collapse in Eastern Europe. Need I go on?"

"No, my sweet. You needn't."

As Dennis said when he first showed me the great map beneath Manhattan, the Milky Way is a strange place—stranger than any of us can imagine. But I am obligated to keep my awareness of PROSPOCAP a secret, lest the galaxy evaporate.

Next Monday evening the Patriots will play the Pittsburgh Steelers. I'll be there, oh yes, cheering my team on. You see, dear Diary, I've finally learned to care.

According to Robert W. Henderson, the origins of ball games date back to religious rites in ancient Egypt, where the ball represented a fertility symbol and opposing teams' mock combat symbolized the fight between good and evil. As a character in "Unsportsmanlike Conduct" puts it, only one animal—the human—organizes play-fighting into complex contests of skill. The conflict in sport, the victory and vanquishment, is carefully hidden under dozens of rules and accommodations. But when humans on an alien planet discover the indigenous beings want to play "their" sport, an extremely interesting series of events follow.

Unsportsmanlike Conduct

Scott Westerfeld

Part One

There's a lot you can fit into a 851-gram teleport.

Lean beef is about two-thirds water, so more than two-and-a-half kilos of ground chuck can be reconstituted from a transport that size. Enough for twenty-nine decent hamburgers, one for every human being on the planet. For fixings we had lettuce and plenty of soybread, and our tomatoes were bigger than golf balls that second year on Tau.

Alternatively, each member of the colony could have received a seven-page letter. Not text or camfeeds, but actual pieces of paper touched by our loved ones, marked with tactile incisions of the pen. (And try spraying perfume on a textfile.)

With 851 grams of hops pellets, we could have produced about 2,000 liters of homebrew. We had our own sugar and malt, but they'd never given us seed crop for hops, to make sure we couldn't drink more beer than Houston decreed.

Or, for a truly exotic experience, three medium-sized oranges would have massed about the same. Not dehydrated, pre-juiced, or even peeled. Just the real things smelling of an earthly summer's hard sunlight. We had a tiny anti-scurvy orchard, of course. But our starship had brought only fast-growing limes, our oldest trees four feet tall and delivering a small, bitter fruit.

None of these items were in the transport, however. We had voted. With one annoyed abstention, the choice had been made.

The tube glowed, scattering its weird light through the shed. The familiar room turned eerie around us, bent like the colors of an Oklahoma landscape just before a tornado folds into shape overhead. Seven light-years away in the packed suburbs of Houston, lights dimmed and air-conditioning faltered as a grid serving fourteen million was poached. This torrent of power crowded its way into some unthinkably long and narrow channel of the quantum that led to us, 851 grams of matter riding the wave.

When the tube light faded, we all stood blinking.

I popped the clean-seal, which hissed at me as vacuum equalized, but waited a moment before opening it. My instincts insisted that the transport would still be hot to the touch inside, however ridiculous that notion was. And worse, if the squirt had blown, we'd all wasted weeks of mass allowance on a pile of splinters.

But the transport had come in clean. I lifted it up for Alex and Yoshi to admire.

"Beautiful," Yoshi said.

"Much better than my old one." Alex was right. The thirty-ounce Louisville Slugger felt much sweeter than our broken bat. The long, wide grain of the wood showed the considerable age of the ash tree from which it had been hewn. The finish lent it an emerald gleam in the antiseptic lights of the clean shed, and it hefted like a feather in my hand.

Of course, our pals back on Earth wouldn't have sent us anything but the best. The price of a solid-gold bat wouldn't approach the energy costs of a 851-gram transport.

Still, this Slugger was a beauty.

Yoshi took it gingerly from my hands, a look of relief on his face. It had been his wild swing that had cracked the first one two weeks before, reducing it to the two most expensive pieces of firewood in human history, leaving us without the game.

Alex patted him on the shoulder, all forgiven now. The old bat, nine gloves, and six baseballs had comprised her entire personal mass allowance on the starship out, and had proven the most popular contribution to the public good. (With the possible exception of Iain Claymore's micro-still.)

Alex took the bat from Yoshi, stepped back, and took a practice swing. She grinned like a kid on her birthday.

"Let's play some ball."

Half an hour later, we had two teams out on the field.

Our baseball field was a medium-age impact crater full of sheetgrass, basically flat if you ignored the low, concentric ripples emanating from the natural pitcher's mound in its exact center. The home-run "fence" was a ring of chalky two-meter cliffs at the crater's edge, reachable even by amateurs like us thanks to Tau's nine-five gravity. The sheetgrass surface was impeccable, tractable, soft in a fall, quick-drying after the heavy Coriolis rains which swept across us every afternoon; the best of astroturf and earthly grass combined.

Of course, sheetgrass wasn't grass in any botanical sense, but a genetically identical colony of cilia that acted as water filtration system for the composite organism that filled the crater. In a way, we owed our presence here on Tau to the rain-catch organisms. They accounted for most of the biomass of the planet, and thus most of the rich oil field below our feet had once been sheetgrass or some ancient relative.

It had been two weeks (six Tau-day microlunar months, actually, a bit over a hundred hours each) since Yoshi's swing had snapped our old bat and brought baseball on the planet to a halt. It hadn't taken much arm-twisting to get two enthusiastic teams of nine onto the field. We even had a few human spectators in addition to the usual audience of Taus.

"Looks like pretty good attendance today, Doctor."

"I count sixty-seven." Dr. Helene Chirac lifted her tablet and peered at the screen. "That beats the previous record by five."

"Think they missed it, Doc?"

"It seems likely they noticed our absence on the field."

As always, Dr. Chirac was our umpire. (With seventeen PhDs and three MDs between us, that title was usually ignored, but something about the gray-haired, imperiously formal Dr. Chirac made it unavoidable.) As head of the xeno team, she had attended every game since the Taus had started watching, hoping that her elusive linguistic breakthrough might be found here on the field.

Other than becoming baseball fans, the Taus didn't have much to do with us. No Tau had ever set foot on the land we'd developed, steering well clear of the camp, solar array, drill site, and farmland. Whether it was out of respect for our claims or fear of contagion, we didn't know. Like good spectators, they stayed at the edge of the baseball field. And when the odd home run came their way, they always scattered to let one of us retrieve the ball.

The rest of the xeno team were biologists and could work with other life-forms or long-distance observations. But Dr. Chirac, a linguist, needed face-to-face contact with the dominant species. Umping baseball was as close as she got.

Our Tau fans were definitely learning the game. They knew when to cheer now. They showed no favoritism, making their characteristic stuck-pig squeals on tough catches as well as long drives, and a few were clapping as my team took the field for the top of the first inning. They were finally starting to get some sound out of those big, soft hands. I waved to them as I took the mound.

My opposing captain was at the plate. Two full ranks my junior, Alex really was a captain, as well as our pilot for the landing two years before, company meteorologist, and a damn fine cajun cook.

"Seven innings?" she shouted, swinging the bat with pleasure. She didn't usually lead off the order, but rank hath its privileges.

I looked at the angle of the reddish sun. Plenty of afternoon left. We were taking off an extra half-day in honor of our new bat, and to celebrate our latest pipeline milestone, which we'd reached ahead of schedule. Probably a longer game would tire everyone out for a good night's sleep. Morale needed a boost, I figured.

"Let's go for nine," I called.

Alex gave me a questioning look.

I nodded. "That's right. Cancel the late shift. It's a beer night."

"You got it, Colonel." She stepped into the batter's box. "Doctor?"

Dr. Chirac completed a sweep with her tablet, with which she'd been snapping pictures of our alien audience, and nodded curtly. "Play ball."

I took a deep breath, slapping our best baseball into the worn pocket of my glove. The ritual begun, I cracked my neck on both sides with a dip of each shoulder, squinted at Yoshi on first and McGill at third, tugged aside my filter mask and spat, then licked my lips once from right to left.

Wound up.

And threw. A bit low and to the left.

"Ball one!" Dr. Chirac shouted in her familiar way, loud enough to carry to the alien observers. The xenos weren't quite sure of the Taus' hearing range yet, but Chirac called the game at high volume, introducing minimal variation in baseball's signs and signifiers. The more consistent she was, the easier it would be for the Tau to learn the patterns of the game. She stepped back, folding her arms to gaze at the audience as she did between each pitch.

Hunter returned the ball to me. I cracked my neck again, checked the bases, and licked my lips. He gave me two fingers down, to which I nodded. Alex couldn't stand up to my fastball.

I wound up, pitched it in hard. Swing and a crack, straight up or just about. I ran a few steps forward, but Hunter sprang up and waved me off, taking the catch.

The humans in the field raised a ragged cheer, echoed by the high-pitched hooting of the Taus.

"How'd she feel?" I yelled to Alex as she trudged back from halfway to first base.

She laughed. "What, are baseball bats feminine now?"

"That one is."

Alex picked it up from where it had flown from her grasp and ran her fingers down its length. "Maybe you're right. She's pretty sweet."

"Don't ask, don't tell, Captain." I smiled, mentally moving myself to the top of my team's order, and returned to the mound.

The game went long, and our shadows lengthened, then doubled as Antipodes rose, full as it was every weekend. Like most small-town baseball games, ours was a dramatic affair, the score padded by overthrows, dropped catches, and stolen bases. By the bottom of the ninth, the teams were tied at twelve runs apiece.

"Come on guys, extra innings," Alex shouted as her team took the field.

"No way. Let's wrap this up," I exhorted my own troops.

The Taus seemed to have caught the growing tension. They'd been agitated since the end of the seventh. I wondered if they'd noticed we were playing a couple of more innings than usual.

No one knew how smart the Taus were. They were definitely tool-users well into the agricultural revolution, planting their ferny staple plants with stick hoes and fending off large predators collectively, using spears and slings and a lot of hooting. According to some of our Earthbound theorists, their social rituals were about as advanced as humans at the beginning of language development, although Dr. Chirac always warned me about making comparisons. Their repertoire of vocal noises sounded awfully sophisticated to me, and fully half of it was too high for human hearing.

My job had little to do with contact, of course. Our mission priority was getting the pipeline up, never mind the local environment and culture, intelligent or not. With a global population of about a hundred thousand Taus, we weren't exactly crowding them. And they had no use for the oil we were stealing, anyway. Maybe twenty thousand years from now they'd miss it. But I figured we were doing them a favor. We'd leave them enough accessible oil for a short run at internal combustion, but not enough to fuck their planet as thoroughly as we had ours.

In the meantime, Earth's billions needed oil for plastics, our ancestors having apparently forgotten that petroleum is useful for things other than burning. And of course the U.S. needed another few decades of cheap gas and big cars to complete our conversion.

Hunter went in and hit a single, and got a big cheer from the Taus. I wondered for a moment if our alien audience knew the score was tied.

"The natives are restless," a voice behind me observed.

"I didn't know you were watching, Ashley. Thought you didn't approve."

Ashley Newkirk shrugged. "A base imitation of the mother game, without subtlety or grace."

"Aye, but at least it doesnae take five days." Iain Claymore was another abstainer from baseball, and physical activity in general, but was happy to take any side against Ashley. The two Brits were on the xeno team, like all of the non-Americans in the colony, but were strictly horticulturists. They had little to do with the dominant species, too busy observing how our invader species were affecting the local flora.

"One day you must tell me the rules again," I said, praying he would ignore the offer. Ashley had once tried to reveal the mysteries of cricket to me, but his explanation turned to apoplexy every time I made an analogy to baseball. In his mind, any query that compared the two was like asking of Rembrandt's painting: "Interior or exterior?"

Jenny Flagg was up next. She had once been a reliable single, specializing in Texas-leaguers that landed just behind the shortstop. The problem was, after two years everybody knew her one trick. The outfield moved in.

The first pitch flew past her wild swing. She was looking to hit it hard, trying to force the fielders deep. They didn't buy it.

"Strike one!" Dr. Chirac declaimed. If nothing else, the Taus would probably learn to count to three.

"Jenny!" I made a calming gesture with my hands. With the score tied, all we needed was her usual single.

She nodded, took a less aggressive stance.

But she slashed again at the next pitch, a drive that flew high over second base, clearing the center fielder's outstretched glove by centimeters. Jenny ran a leisurely double while Hunter pounded home.

"That's the ball game!" Dr. Chirac shouted. The Taus cheered.

The field jogged desultorily in. Our team gathered around Hunter and Jenny, providing the Taus a textbook example of a human victory celebration.

"The beer's on me," I announced, then turned to Jenny. "But I should have you up on insubordination charges, Sergeant Flagg."

She shrugged as we headed back toward camp. "I thought you and I were engaged in a subtle deception, Colonel."

I laughed. "At least now you'll get a little respect for your long ball—"

"Colonel!"

I turned at the shout. Dr. Chirac still stood at home plate, transfixed and staring into the outfield.

A small party of Taus was approaching.

I signaled for everyone to stop where they were and walked with quick, even steps to Chirac's side.

"Sweet Jesus," I said. They were armed, as always, slings at the ready around their necks. Over the last two years, we'd cleared the field of rocks pretty thoroughly, but the Tau could be deadly with improvised projectiles. I was more awed than worried, though. This was the first time they'd entered the human colony.

"They look friendly, I guess."

"Don't you see it?" Chirac was breathing hard, her tablet making the small reminder beep that indicated high-memory motion capture.

"See what?"

"There are nine of them."

They didn't want gloves.

That made sense, at least. Their big hands were already baseball glove-sized. It had crossed my mind to wonder once or twice if that's why they watched the game. We must have looked a bit more Tau-like with brown leather webbing our fingers.

As Dr. Chirac quickly briefed me, I realized that she was in command for the next couple of hours. At long last, we were in a contact situation.

"Keep the winning team playing, in the same positions for consistency. Play nine innings, no matter how dark it gets. Go along with any call I make, however strange."

"Thinking of cheating, Doc?"

"Absolutely not, but I may have to adapt the rules a bit. With their body structure, it's going to be a small strike zone. Go easy on them, but play to win. And for god's sake don't hurt one. Any questions?"

"Just one."

"What?"

"Are we the visitors or the home team?"

She nodded. "Interesting. It's our field, but their planet. Still, they won't be aware of the distinction, given that we haven't had any visiting teams lately. Let them bat first."

I was glad Dr. Chirac had chosen who would play. Everyone wanted to be in the first interspecies baseball game.

Contact had been one of our mission parameters from the beginning, but after the excitement of finding Tau inhabited, two years of being snubbed by the natives had left those of us in the military and construction side feeling left out of the explorers' club. But the old excitement came back quickly. The news spread through handcom calls, and before the game had started the entire human population of Tau was in attendance. Yoshi and the rest of the xeno team frantically mounted fixed cameras to record the game.

"Play ball!" Dr. Chirac shouted as I took the mound.

I faced the Tau at bat, preparing myself to throw the first interspecies pitch in baseball history.

She (a ninety-percent chance with Taus) was gripping the Slugger with her two sling hands, shifting her weight on the other four like a restive batter. The two mid-hands popped up occasionally to scratch her thorax and stroke the bat.

They had been watching us closely. One of the Tau's sling hands let go of the bat for a moment to touch its brow, as if adjusting an invisible cap.

I dipped my shoulders one by one, getting a pair of good cracks from my neck, hoping my arm would stay in the game for nine more innings. Checked first and third, spat, and licked my lips.

The creature in front of me didn't look ready for a fastball. For a first-time batter, she didn't seem utterly clueless, but she held the bat a bit too far back, as if stuck in the wind-up of a swing.

I threw at a nice, easy speed.

Like many first balls of new seasons, it was not a great pitch, dipping low enough that Hunter had to scoop it up from the dirt. But the Tau gamely swung, missing by a country mile. (Or, as Chirac's tablet recorded, a good forty centimeters.)

I saw Dr. Chirac hesitate before she called, "Strike one!" Her eyes narrowed a bit above her filter mask, as if thinking I'd thrown an unhittable ball on purpose.

I shrugged as it flew back to me.

My second pitch tightened up and went in right at thorax level, where the Tau's first swing had passed over the plate. She swung and missed again, low this time, but closer.

"Strike two!"

The ball came back from Hunter, who yelled his usual, "You got her now, Colonel!"

I smiled at Hunter's attitude. It wasn't like the Tau were going to walk in here and win a game off us. We had to assume this was as much about contact for them as it was for us. They might as well get a real baseball experience.

Hunter flashed me two fingers down, and I nodded.

After nine innings, my fastball isn't exactly scorching, but it ain't bad for an old man's. I laid the ball straight into Hunter's glove, and the Tau batter swung late by a solid second.

"Strike three!" Chirac called, and cocked her thumb for the Tau to go.

There was dead silence for a moment. Did she know she was out? Had my fastball constituted humanity's first interstellar diplomatic blunder?

The batter hung its head, rested the Slugger on its abdomen, and trudged back toward the other Taus clustered to the right of home plate.

Hunter started the cheer. "Way to go, Colonel!" He clapped and whistled. The remaining humans and the Taus around the field joined in. When the batter got back to her teammates, they put up their sling hands to pat her head softly, almost like a team high-fiving each other.

I looked at Dr. Chirac, who was recording the display. They apparently knew the rules, at least the basics. Over a year or so of watching the game, the Tau had learned some baseball.

It occurred to me that of everything we had accomplished here—prospecting for oil, building a solar array to power the tube, planting the farm, drinking and fighting with (and screwing) each other—this game was our only real collective ritual.

Our colony had no common religion. The small group that had once held Mass had dwindled due to a schism: Some wanted to observe every seven Tau days, some every lunar week, others to match Earth Sundays. As a result, any prayers nowadays were pretty much done in private. After a few weeks on-planet, I'd let the military protocol loosen. There were only seven of us who were U.S. Army, so I saw little point in raising the flag every morning. Even our work schedules were erratic. Everyone adapted differently to the eighteen-hour day, and McGill and I let our people change their shifts when Tau-lag left them sleepless in the planet's long twilit night.

To the Tau, we must have seemed an unruly lot, chaotic and unpredictable. But in baseball we had found ritual and ceremony, a focus that brought us—the twenty Americans, four Japanese, two Cubans, and our French umpire, at least—together.

So perhaps it didn't matter if the Tau never got a hit.

It's not whether you win or lose, but how you play the game.

Three up, three down.

The top of the Tau order only got the bat on the ball once, producing a foul tip that went over Hunter's head. For a moment, I wondered if the batter would mistakenly run, but she knew it had gone foul and just eased onto her back four, waiting as Hunter chased it down. Then she struck out swinging on the next pitch.

We were up.

"Jenny," I called as we came off the field. "You go in first."

"And do what, Colonel?"

I shrugged. "Chirac says play to win. But no dangerous line drives. And don't argue with the doctor's calls."

"Can they even pitch?"

"I guess we'll find out. They're pretty good with those slings, though."

I could see Jenny's lips purse even through her filter mask. "Deadly, actually." We'd seen them take down the local predators at a hundred meters with a fusillade of rocks the size of human fists.

"Relax, Jenny. So far they seem to know the rules. I don't think they're suddenly going to throw beanballs at us."

"Wish I had a batter's helmet, just in case the pitcher pulls out her sling."

I looked back at the Taus. They were throwing the ball to each other, warming up like humans taking the field. They had adapted their sling technique to a throw, like an underarm pitch tilted forty-five degrees.

"You'll be okay." I patted Jenny's shoulder and jogged over to join Yoshi by one of the cameras.

"They're throwing pretty good."

He nodded, following the ball with the camera headsup, a zoomed-in view on a translucent layer over his face.

"I've seen the kids toss rocks like this," he said. "My guess is that it's the original behavior that the sling was adapted to augment."

"They used to hunt barehanded?"

"They're built for it." Yoshi sent me a headsup. He had some software running that interpolated Tau skeletal structure. (Conveniently, the Tau practiced ritual exposure after death. Given that carrion-eaters usually dragged away the corpse, we figured an autopsy or two wouldn't stretch the bounds of cultural sensitivity.) As the Tau with the ball wound up, I watched the compound socket that allowed her arm smooth 360-degree rotation. She was far more fluid than a human throwing underarm. Faster, too.

I wondered if Jenny was really safe. These guys were built to throw.

The Tau team had managed a pretty fair imitation of our field placings, and when the alien on the mound raised a hand, another slung the ball to her.

Jenny hefted the bat and walked up to the plate, and my jaw dropped.

"Did you see that, Yoshi?"

"Well, I guess they can tell us apart," he said quietly.

The outfielders had moved in, covering the ground where Jenny's Texas-leaguers tended to land.

"The question is," Yoshi said, "do they really understand Jenny's hitting style, or are they just imitating our strategy?"

"Good point. Remember, she got a hit by going deep last game."

"Barely," Yoshi muttered. Then I remembered that he'd been the one in center field for Jenny's last at-bat.

She knocked the dust from her shoes and stood at the ready, glancing at the Tau playing catcher. It was the closest any of us had actually gotten to the dominant life form before today. Just behind the catcher, Dr. Chirac looked ecstatic.

"Play ball!" she shouted.

The Tau started to jitter on the mound, some sort of pre-pitch dance. She finished with jerk of the head accompanied by a little coughing noise. I heard a giggle from my team, which spread throughout the humans.

"Well, Colonel," said Yoshi, "she's got you cold."

I blinked, then saw it: the little dance had been an imitation of my wind-up ritual. She'd bobbed her shoulders one by one, checked the bases, then spat on the ground. No doubt she would have licked her lips if she'd had a tongue.

Of course, as far as the Tau knew, it was in the *rules* that you had to spit before you pitched. All four humans who regularly spent time on the mound had a tendency to do so. As observers, the Tau had the classic problem of a small sample size: They couldn't distinguish between the explicit laws of the game, its long-held traditions, and the personal habits of the few players they'd seen.

Jenny readied herself, and the first pitch came at her. It was low and outside, but she stepped back nervously. The pitch had looked tentative to me, slower than they'd been throwing in the outfield. Hopefully, that meant the Tau were trying not to hurt us.

The catcher scooped it in effortlessly and tossed it back with a high, arcing throw, an imitation of Hunter's returns.

"Ball one!" Chirac called, focused on her tablet as the pitcher warmed up again. The humans around me tittered again as the alien performed its little pantomime of me.

"Can't wait to get a sample of that fresh saliva," Yoshi said.

"Well, at least I've made one contribution to science," I said.

The second pitch got a little closer to the plate; I reckoned it was between knees and chest, but still outside. Chirac called another ball.

Jenny looked more confident now. The outside pitches seemed cautious to a fault, and when the third came almost within reach, she leaned forward across home plate and took a swing at it.

The ball smacked off down the first-base line. Jenny started to run, but checked herself as it drifted foul. The Tau playing first base managed to get in front of the ball, but didn't get her hands low enough. It bounced off the hard abdominal carapace and rolled toward Yoshi and me.

I scooped it up.

"Is she okay?" I said softly.

"Sure," Yoshi said. "They're tough. As long as we don't hit one in the head."

I tossed the ball softly to the first baseman, then looked down at my hand. I'd touched a ball that had been touched by an alien. Not since my boots had first planted themselves on Tau soil had I felt such an otherworldly thrill.

"Strike one!" called Chirac, nodding approvingly.

From then on, Jenny gamely tried to get a hit, managing to strike out chasing the errant pitches. The Tau on the mound was getting better, but she still was about as accurate as a drunk little-leaguer. At least she was throwing faster, apparently confident that she wouldn't kill anyone.

"Sorry, Coach," Jenny said, "but I didn't want to get walked, you know?"

"That was fine, Sergeant. We're all playing it by ear."

The other human batters followed Jenny's lead, swinging at whatever the Tau pitcher could get to them. But she was too fast and wild. For the next few innings, strike-out followed strike-out for both teams.

"I wonder if we're teaching them bad baseball," Yoshi said. "I mean, shouldn't we take a walk at some point?"

I shrugged. "All in good time. Maybe she'll throw some strikes one of these days."

In the fourth inning, with two down, Hunter got a hit. He connected off a low, straight fastball that popped into short left field. A human probably would have caught it, but the Tau aren't very fast on their feet. The alien fielder collected it on one bounce and slung it toward first base, where Hunter was already camped out.

After the frustrations of the early innings, we cheered him loudly, joined by the Taus in the audience, who apparently weren't taking sides.

"Very cricket of them," Ashley Newkirk said approvingly.

"We'll have to teach them the Bronx cheer," I said.

The pitcher had found her range, and the next two humans managed what looked like genuine little-league at-bats: not great pitching, and some over-enthusiastic swings to be sure, but both made it onto base. The Taus were not good fielders. Their six-legged body design didn't allow for much backward or sideways motion. They had to turn their whole body around to chase balls that flew long.

Still, Yoshi was one happy xenozoologist. He'd captured more unique movements in four innings than in two years of field work.

With the bases loaded, I was up again.

As I approached the plate, I glanced at Dr. Chirac, remembering what she'd said. Play to win.

The first pitch came in high, and I pulled back.

"Ball one!"

The second looked good, and I took a shot at it. But I hadn't expected a good pitch, and my swing was late.

"Strike one!"

The third pitch was low, and I let it go. The fourth was inside, and I left that, too. I snuck a look at Chirac, who nodded subtly.

The next pitch was way outside.

"Ball four—take your base."

I jogged to first, and Hunter walked in to score. The Tau audience squealed with appreciation. A few of my teammates remembered to high-five Hunter, but they looked embarrassed. We'd scored on a walk, against a pitcher who'd never held a baseball before today.

The rest of the game went scoreless. Hunter got another hit, a couple of us managed tepid grounders and were thrown out at first. As my arm started to go, a couple of Taus got walked as well. But when nine innings were over, the first interplanetary baseball game had been won by humanity, one to zero.

The last Tau batter trotted over to his teammates, and they all touched his head softly with their big hands. A cheer rose up from them, echoing the squeals of the Taus out beyond the fence, and the visiting team made its way across the field and out of sight.

"Shouldn't we have let them win?" McGill asked. McGill looked like what he was: an aging rig worker, his skin leathery from summers off the Louisiana and California coasts, black half-moons of crude apparently tattooed under his fingernails. He was also the Halihunt rep here on Tau and head of the construction team. Halihunt were our corporate sponsors, who had put up some of the funding and all of the political bribes necessary to make the mission happen, and would reap the lion's share of benefits. His eyes had the bright sheen they'd shown a year before when we'd had our one fatality, Peter Hernandez lost to a drilling cave-in. Bad PR scared the hell out of McGill.

Dr. Chirac shrugged. "We don't even know if they understand that they lost the game. They knew it was over, because we'd played nine innings and the score was uneven. But do they know actually what winning means?"

We all looked at each other, clueless.

While the rest of the colony celebrated a new bat, the end of a day off, and a new era in human interplanetary contact, the xeno staff and the military had taken our homebrews into the command tent. We had to get our story straight before our various reports went back to Earth via the tube.

"I just feel bad about the way we won," Alex said.

I took a deep breath. "I know, Alex, taking that walk seemed like a lame way to score, but the game's the game."

Dr. Chirac jumped in. "I think the colonel is correct. We want to test their understanding in as many ways as possible. How much of what they are doing is sheer imitation? How much is pattern recognition? And how much is creative thinking—real strategy? Are they actually trying to win?"

"They've seen us react when we win and lose," Jenny said. "They must know we like winning better."

"They have no way of understanding human body language, sergeant," Dr. Chirac said. "Our cheers may sound like moans of pain to them. And perhaps they have no concept of mock conquest, which is what winning a game is. The desirability of winning might be a difficult concept for them to come to."

"I'm no linguist," Ashley Newkirk said, puffing at his empty pipe. "But lots of animals play-fight and engage in submission rituals."

Dr. Chirac nodded her head slowly. "But only one animal organizes play-fighting into complex contests of skill. The conflict in sport, the victory and vanquishment, is carefully hidden under dozens of rules and accommodations. We cannot assume the Tau understand that this is a fight. It doesn't look like one on the surface. We must discover if they know what it is to win. How far they'll go to avoid losing. If they'd ever cheat."

"Cheating?" Ashley Newkirk protested. "I think we should assume they're trying to play fair."

"A noble assumption, and a proper one so far," Dr. Chirac said. "I merely point out that we should let them push the parameters of the game as far as they can. We have been handed the tool we need to make real contact."

Chirac's words were measured and intense, the look in her eyes one of a lifelong dream coming true before her. When the xeno contact team had been equipped ten years ago, we'd had only the vaguest idea there was intelligent life on Tau. Evidence of cultivation had been glimpsed from space, but the locals had stayed clear of the ground probes. On landing, we had discovered the Tau's reticence. To make things still harder, their speech and hearing stretched into much higher frequencies than human, higher even than we could analyze with the dolphin gear we'd brought in through the tube. Without specialized devices, of the sort that only a larger xeno team and bigger industrial base could supply, we didn't have the technical capacity to learn their language. Except for a few spy cams, we could hardly even study their physical culture.

But now they were playing baseball with us.

Chirac continued. "This game is clearly our best hope for communication. In baseball, everything happens within a relatively simple framework, visible to the naked human eye. A framework which we understand, and hopefully they have come to learn. We shouldn't be caught up with notions of chivalry, Mr. Newkirk. We should try to win these games—that's the best way to test their understanding of rules and strategy."

"Personally," I said, "I doubt they can tell rules from habits. Like when they imitated my warm-up ritual. Do they think you *have* to spit before you pitch?"

"Ach, from watching you lot, I had assumed it was a rule myself," Iain Claymore said.

"And sliding into home plate," Alex said. "Do they know you do it to avoid being tagged, or do they think it's just a decorative flourish?"

"That's what we'll be finding out over the next few weeks," Dr. Chirac said.

"Maybe, maybe not," Jenny Flagg said. "Our big problem right now is their physical limitation. I mean, *can* the Taus slide? At the moment, they can't even get a hit. Maybe they'll never be able to. It'll be hard to explore their strategic thinking if their skills aren't up to it."

We all looked at Yoshi. An evolutionary biologist who doubled as one of our MDs, he had the best understanding of Tau physical abilities.

"Look, they've got plenty of physical skills. They're deadly with those slings. Literally. And they have a number of sling-related behaviors that look game-like. Adolescents throw rocks to each other; adults stage mock sling attacks. Some of those behaviors might, in fact, be rule-governed sports rather than unstructured play."

"Wait a second," I interrupted. "We're the ones with the spy cams and the PhDs. How come they learned how to play baseball before we figured out how any of their games work?"

He shrugged. "Because there's more of them than us. We've only got three people working full-time on dominant species behavior. Dozens of Taus have been watching baseball for over a year. But I'll be prioritizing gameplay from now on, I assure you."

"But can they hit a ball?" Jenny asked.

Yoshi nodded. "There's no mechanical reason they can't. They use spears to fend off projectiles in pre-hunt play. They have superhuman vision and great hand-to-eye. They may not run very fast, but neither did Babe Ruth."

Ashley Newkirk looked quizzical at the name, but no one bothered to explain.

"I think their pitching will come along first. Like I said, it's already in the culture. Probably the only reason they've thrown poorly so far is that we've been playing adults, who generally use slings. As far as fielding goes, they're not used to the dynamics of a perfect sphere, but they should pick that up easy enough. Tau adolescent play includes catching rocks on the fly, but not on the bounce."

"So they'll have more trouble with grounders."

"Probably. But once the ball's in hand, the throw to first base should be fast and accurate. As for batting . . . " He shrugged. "It's anyone's guess. But it's a difficult skill even for humans to learn. They're pretty good with spears. Let's give them a chance to develop before we start intentionally walking them."

"Intentional walking?" Ashley said. "What does that mean?"

"When you throw wide on purpose, letting someone get on base without a hit," Alex explained. "For tactical reasons."

Ashley raised his eyebrows and muttered, "Bloody odd game."

I cleared my throat. "Okay, for the moment we play regular ball, the same as we would against a bunch of kids. Take it easy, but play real baseball. Show them the ropes. At least, that's what we'll suggest to NASA."

"You think you'll get permission?" Iain Claymore asked. "Playing games with wee beasties may take valuable time away from stealing their oil. We've got a whole planet to exploit here."

McGill spoke up, ignoring the Scotsman's tone. "Contact is our second mission priority. In my report, I'll point out that we're ahead of schedule on the pipeline. I'm sure Halihunt won't have any objections to pursuing scientific aims here."

I nodded. "And we won't have any trouble finding volunteers to play, even if they have to use free time. But at some point we may not be so far ahead of schedule, and we'll need support to keep playing. When xeno writes its report, you've got to sell this project. Make it big: baseball as Rosetta stone."

Dr. Chirac offered us a rare chuckle. "I may steal that line."

"Please do. Any questions?"

"Just one," Ashley said, a smile visible behind his pipe. "What if today they decided they don't like baseball and never show up again?"

Yoshi laughed aloud. "Don't worry about that, Newkirk. Everyone likes baseball."

NASA and Halihunt, of course, decided to play ball.

Our request couldn't have come at a better time. The current powers in Washington were not those who had originally funded the mission, and the space agency, as always, was looking for ways to improve its image. Within the U.S., the idea of exporting the national pastime to Tau was a natural. The Halihunt public relations wing immediately annexed half our discretionary data bandwidth, demanding video of aliens at play. The mission had been a Halihunt loss leader for a decade now, tough to swallow for corporate execs used to thinking about the next quarter, not eight-year space journeys. But here was good PR with its own revenue stream. They wanted to license images and find sponsors for equipment teleports. There were even plans to send us uniforms through the tube. With snazzy corporate logos, of course.

On the international front, a breakthrough in the mission's scientific side was a godsend. Outside the reach of the U.S. media, the Tau expedition was pretty much seen for what it was: an attempt to restore the U.S. to unquestioned superpower status. Seventy years of unilateralism on global warming, oil dependence, and off-and-on military occupation of the Middle East had pissed off pretty much the whole world. Despite the fact that every other economic bloc had converted to renewable, Earth's fossil fuel supply was finally drying up. America's decision to open up whole new worlds to drilling was going down like day-old fried eggs.

After two years of hard work, I'd started to get nervous, wondering if the economics of our primary mission would prove viable. Our oil wells were useless unless the hundred-square-kilometer solar array could keep transport cheap: The energy costs went down geometrically when power was available at both ends of the tube. And the longer you kept a single tube open, the cheaper and more stable it became. Thus, the London-New York-Bejing tube was very efficient, and long-haul aircraft a thing of the past, but you still had to drive to the local store. The math said that a perpetual tube carrying a thousand barrels a minute of crude from Tau to Earth was profitable in the extreme and would give the U.S. economy another hundred years to switch over. But the technology had never been tested in industrial quantities on an interplanetary scale.

If Tau's frequent Coriolis rains interrupted input to the solar array, if the planet's petroleum reserves varied unusably in composition, if the transport math didn't hold up over interstellar distances . . . I had lived daily with the possibility that all our work here might be pointless.

Until now.

As of that first game, we had done something no other human beings had ever done. After two years of being snubbed by the locals, as if they knew what we were up to and didn't approve, we had finally made contact with them. They had walked into our camp, held our tools in their big hands, tried to communicate on our terms.

They even wanted to play with us.

That night after the first game, having drunk six beers and sent off my report, I went to bed happy, feeling as if my little colony finally belonged here on Tau.

Part Two

Yoshi was right; they mastered the pitching first.

Their fast balls were wicked, slapping hard into the catcher's soft, bare hands. They introduced their first game adaptation as a result, rotating catchers every inning, just behind the line-up, so that the next few batters up would have unbruised hands. And they developed a selection of deadly curve balls.

They seemed to understand the battle of the count very well. You never knew whether they were going to throw a hittable fast ball or a slicing curve. Of course, as Dr. Chirac pointed out, a random number generator could provide the same challenge. But when you swung through empty air, it sure felt like there was guile behind those mean, fast pitches.

Hunter and Alex loved batting against real pitching for a change, but for old guys like me, it became seriously difficult to get a hit. I took to bunting, putting the ball onto the ground to take advantage of their shaky fielding. This engendered their second big adaptation, moving the infield in whenever slow swingers were at the plate. For three straight games, I couldn't buy a base.

Then one day, standing ready to get out again, I noticed something that I'd missed. Before the pitch, the catcher pointed two of his fat, short fingers at the ground. I reacted instinctively, swinging hard as the pitcher let go. One of our brand new Sluggers (Louisville Sportscraft was one of our official sponsors now) connected with the ball, electrifying my hands with the bright shiver of the sweet spot. The ball soared over the insultingly contracted outfield, and I rounded second before the sheetgrass brought the ball to a stop, three Tau fielders in shambolic pursuit.

I pulled up at third, out of breath and not wanting to risk the awesome Tau throw-in. Alex came out to coach.

"Nice hit, Colonel. Looks like you're out of your slump."

"There's been a new development." She waited patiently as my breath came back. "I read their signs."

"You what? They're flashing signs?" She looked at the third baseman a few meters from us. Her slightly spicy scent drifted over to us in the light breeze.

I nodded. "*Our* signs, that Hunter and I always used."

"You guys had signs?"

"Yeah. Hunter's idea. No one ever figured it out. Except the Tau, apparently."

"You think they saw you flash all the way from the fence?"

"Too far. They must have picked them up since they started playing us. Still learning."

"And they're consistent?"

"Let's find out."

Honorio, our Cuban military attaché, stepped up to the plate. I squinted at the catcher. As quick as Hunter's agile fingers, she flashed three to the side.

"Change-up."

The pitcher started her usual fastball wind up, but the ball came out of the whirlwind moving a hair slow. Honorio swung early, missing everything.

"Good eye," Alex said quietly.

I called the next two pitches. Honorio did not, and found himself headed to the bench.

"Superb, Colonel," Alex said. "They've adopted our symbolic behavior. Learned our language."

"Chirac's going to eat this up. But I wonder if the Tau know they're supposed to be secret."

"That'll be easy enough to find out, Colonel. Just make it clear we recognize your old signs and we're getting hits because of it. Maybe then they'll make up their own."

"Good idea, but let's talk to Chirac first. And not a word about this to anyone until after the game."

"Sir?"

"Right now I'm going to get me some hits."

"Wittgenstein speaks of a 'language game' in which two workers are building a wall. Worker A says 'block,' 'pillar,' 'slab,' or 'beam.' Worker B hands him the appropriate piece of rock or wood, and the wall gets built."

"So, Doctor," Jenny Flagg spoke up, "exactly where was, uh . . . Wittgenstein going with this?"

Dr. Chirac smiled. "His point was that the worker delivering the components doesn't need to know how the slabs and beams are used. Worker B doesn't even need to know that it's a wall they're building. All he has to do is respond to each word with the appropriate action. In this language game, as in most cases when we use natural language, what matters is not understanding, but the appropriate response."

"Sort of like our pitching signs," Alex said. "The pitcher doesn't have to know why the catcher wants a slider or a fastball, as long as the catcher's done her homework."

"And as long as the signs are interpreted correctly, and the right pitch delivered, yes. The pitcher, like Worker B, doesn't actually have to understand the task beyond appropriate responses."

"The pitcher's like a robot," Hunter said, winking at me.

I ignored him, saying, "But in this case, the catcher, Worker A, is also a Tau. She must have some kind of a clue what she wants the pitcher to throw, which means she's got to have some objective in mind."

Dr. Chirac opened her hands to the heavens. "Or possibly Worker A is herself following a learned response. A certain sequence of pitches for a certain batter. Or perhaps they're simply repeating all our pitches since they began their observation, in the same order."

"How come we never just assume they're playing baseball?" Jenny Flagg asked.

"Oh, I assure you, Sergeant," Dr. Chirac said, "they *are* playing baseball. Wittgenstein's point is that Worker B is still building a wall, whether or not he understands the exact purpose of each piece in it. When we teach children how to use language, we start with just such an absence of background knowledge."

Jenny spoke for all of us. "Huh?"

"Ask a young girl how old she is. She'll say 'three' and hold up three fingers. But this three-year-old cannot accurately define for you what a year is or even know that each finger represents one year in some abstract sense. She has simply been taught to make a certain gesture and sound in response to a certain question."

She turned to Hunter. "But children are not robots, of course. They are simply people with incomplete language development. These simple language games are how they learn the language, like a puzzle falling into place from meaningless pieces."

"So you're saying it doesn't matter whether they're just imitating us or whether they actually understand the game," I said.

"It *does* matter. With good reason, teachers and parents want to know when the child actually comprehends what a year is. That understanding is the goal of the developmental language game. But in the meantime, what we are doing is not useless. We are teaching them the imitative responses around which real comprehension is built."

I decided to bring it back to my original question. "So we shouldn't let them win?"

She shook her head. "I don't think so. The appropriate response in any game is to try to win. We should be upset when we walk a Tau player, not walk several in a row to give up runs. And we should clap and cheer when we win. That's what winning means: It's the thing you want to happen. We must continue to demonstrate that and strive to keep our reactions consistent."

Jenny Flagg shook her head. "But humans don't always try to win every game. Sometimes you let kids win. And you always pitch a little bit easier to them."

"Perhaps my analogy is straining. These are not children. We must assume that these Tau are researchers, scientists even. They may not have PhDs as we understand them, but they have been selected to make contact and learn what they can about us. Right now, that means playing baseball properly."

McGill, who'd read the last transmission from Halihunt and NASA, looked at me.

"Well, I got to say, Houston isn't going to be happy with that," I said. "The PR angle was great, until they realized that the Taus still haven't got so much as a single, and that we clobber them every game. Kind of takes the shine off it."

"We're ambassadors here," McGill chimed in. "We've come in the spirit of friendship. Would it kill us to let them win a couple?"

"Frankly, I think the problem is in your attitude. You're being very American, I must say." We all looked at Ashley Newkirk, who continued. "This isn't about winning, but playing the game properly, which means doing your best. You Americans seem transfixed by the idea that a game that can't be won isn't worth playing. One example: I was in the States once for your so-called 'World Series,' to which no other countries are invited, I might add."

"Except Canada," Jenny said.

"And Havana is in the league now, excuse me," Honorio added.

"Very well, but what happened was this: I understood this 'World Series' was to be seven games long. But when one of the sides won the first four, they simply stopped playing!"

No one else said a word, so I offered, "And . . . ?"

Ashley shook his head. "So typical. Can't win, go home. In cricket, a five-test series always is played to the end, even when one of the sides can no longer possibly win."

"But why?" Jenny cried.

"Because a test series has five matches," Ashley said, not too helpfully. "Why get so caught up with winning? As long as the Tau are willing to play, why not play?"

"Well, we are American, and this is baseball," I said. "And it *is* a problem."

What I didn't explain was the other part of NASA's concern: how the imbalance in our interplanetary league was playing to the rest of the world. A fundamentally American team was beating a bunch of untrained beginners at our own national game, relentlessly, day in and day out. The perfect sports metaphor for the way we'd been dealing with the rest of the world for the last century.

"It's not quite the morale builder it used to be, either," Jenny added. "With their pitching so good, at least it's fun to try to get hits off them. But three-up, three-down from them nine innings every game is getting tedious. It's not good sport."

Alex gestured to Yoshi. "Any chance of that changing?"

He looked dubious. "Here's the problem."

The wallscreen lit, showing a Tau at bat with skeleton superimposed. It moved slowly through a swing, and red highlights appeared at its upper elbow joints.

"When humans swing a bat, most of the rotation doesn't come from our shoulders; it comes from the elbow and wrist. Taus don't have much mobility there; their two elbows bend less than our one, and they have relatively little wrist action. That's why they throw straight-arm."

"So they'll never get much force?"

"Not enough for a solid hit. And if we pitch slower, like Jenny suggested, it'll just make it worse. They need to connect with a fastball to get any power. As far as I can see, they'll only ever be really good at bunting. For them to score consistently, we'd have to fake some seriously bad fielding."

Alex sighed. "And they're so damn observant, they'd know what we were up to."

"Or worse, interpret it as part of the game," Dr. Chirac said.

"Well, we're damned if we do and damned if we don't," I said. "Any ideas?"

"What about mixed teams?" Jenny said. "Some Tau and some humans on each side."

We looked at Chirac.

"A fascinating idea, but how would we ask?"

A week later, everything changed.

I was warming up for another desultory first inning of striking out three hapless Tau when a new batter came up to the plate.

We knew the usual Tau team by now. They rotated among about a dozen regulars, distinguishable by thorax markings, the gray and yellow speckled across what I thought of as their chests. This Tau had a distinct cluster of reddish dots near her right shoulder that I'd never seen before.

She also had a strange stance, the bat held out low, almost over the plate, as if she wasn't quite ready yet.

I decided to go easy on her, waving off Hunter's signal for a fastball. (We had changed our signs, given that the Tau were reading them, but our opponents, disappointingly, had yet to alter theirs.) Hunter glanced at the new player, nodded understanding, and signaled a slow ball, a new pitch we'd invented without telling Dr. Chirac. She'd probably noticed the easy throws we were sneaking in, but hadn't complained. The Tau had managed to get a piece of one or two, but never out of the infield. Yoshi was right: If you threw slow, their puny swings couldn't generate any power. If you threw fast, they missed completely.

I did my usual wind-up ritual, spitting with a little extra distance to make the newcomer feel at home, and threw.

The Tau did not swing.

"Strike one!" Chirac called.

I shrugged to Hunter and sent in another meat pitch.

Again, it ignored the ball.

"Strike two!"

"Mighty Casey at the bat," I muttered.

On my third slow pitch, the Tau feebly lifted her bat to meet the ball. It connected, and tipped over Hunter's head. He ran after it, gathered it up, and threw it back to me.

My fourth pitch got the same treatment.

As did my fifth.

Hunter, running back with an annoyed look on his face, signaled for a fastball.

I nodded and wound up, then let a hard one fly.

The Tau's knees bent, the bat rising to again meet the ball. This time the hit angled away from home plate at ninety degrees, rolling toward Yoshi within his forest of new tubed-in cameras.

Yoshi threw it back to me with a puzzled expression.

I shook off Hunter until he gave me a slider, then threw the meanest pitch I could, which broke to the outside just before it reached the Tau.

She didn't swing.

"Ball one!" Chirac cried.

I stretched to loosen up my shoulder, which had twinged a bit on delivery. The Tau didn't swing at bad pitches much anymore. Their incredible eyesight and observational skills were pretty hard to beat. But this was a new player. She was awfully cool for a creature who'd never held a baseball bat before.

Were they reading our signs again?

When Hunter signaled for a fastball, I nodded.

And threw a change-up.

Hunter may have been fooled, but the batter reached out with impeccable timing and tapped the ball backward at about forty-five degrees. One of the xeno team assisting Yoshi was already there, and threw it back to Hunter.

I swallowed. The Taus, or one of them anyway, had come up with a strategy.

Hunter must have realized I wasn't sure about our signs, and his fingers flashed gobbledygook.

I nodded, and threw a curve ball. The Tau left it alone again, and it zoomed past an unprepared Hunter.

"Ball two!"

I tried three more fast balls in succession. The Tau tapped the first two away effortlessly, but by the third my arm was wearing, and she remained motionless as the ball carried low and outside.

"Ball three!"

I threw one into the dirt, aiming for the Tau's bat.

It stepped back, and the ball bounced off Hunter's glove, rolling back toward me across the sheetgrass.

"Ball four. Take your base!" Dr. Chirac cried.

I tugged on my cap and looked around at the fielders. They stared back at me a bit befuddled. We had walked Tau batters before, but none had ever *deserved* it like this batter. She'd worked the ball like a pro, and frustrated me into giving her the base.

I stretched my arm, hoping there weren't going to be any more at-bats like that one.

There were.

The next batter, a regular player with broad gray stripes that faded in the middle of her thorax, also sat out the first two pitches. But once she had two strikes on her, she consistently tipped the ball over Hunter's head, defending the strike zone with effortless precision. I didn't throw her any intentional balls, but she finally walked when my arm faltered after twelve hard pitches.

"Take your base!"

For the first time ever, a Tau was in scoring position.

I tried deception next. Hunter and I rotated through my selection of curve balls, knuckleballs, and sliders. I did my best to stay on the periphery of the strike zone, trying to give Dr. Chirac some tricky calls.

This Tau also proved too smooth for me, though. She took a stab at anything even approaching a strike, only leaving the obvious wild pitches alone. Since she didn't need a solid hit, she could swing and connect with everything that wasn't garbage. The balls eventually came.

The bases were loaded.

With the next Tau I went inside, hoping the thin end of the bat might pop one up for Hunter to catch. But that extra elbow came in handy; she pulled back easily and used the top of the sweet spot, sending every ball fast and high over Hunter's head. He was getting exhausted from chasing balls.

The first Tau, that new one, walked into home. The Tau had scored their first run.

The usual cheer came from the alien audience, with what sounded to my untrained ear like a little something extra. A few of the humans managed to find their voices as well.

I called Hunter to the mound, and Alex jogged over from third base.

"You need relief, Colonel?"

I rubbed my arm, which was screaming. "Not yet. Let's try one more thing. Hunter, how about you stand up?"

"What?"

"It'll put you in better position to catch the high tips."

"Yeah, with my face." Although we had a catcher's mask, Hunter didn't have a proper chest protector. I made a mental note to request one.

"I'll send some slow ones in. See if we can't get a foul out."

"Okay?" He sounded dubious.

"What are you smiling about?"

Alex shrugged. "This is great. They've found a way to score. Talk about strategic thinking. A whole new way to play baseball."

"Yeah. I guess. If you can call it baseball."

The rest of the inning went much the same way. I got one actual out, managing to squeeze a pop fly from the bottom of their order, the pitcher. After that, they scored five more runs to make it an even ten, walking all the way. Then the next two stood impassively and let me strike them out, which took some doing at that point, my arm on fire from shoulder to fingertips.

Across the rest of the game, we put up a mighty struggle, posting eleven runs of our own, more than we had in ages. We subbed through five different pitchers (I was done after that first inning), but no one managed to get more than one out per inning. It was always the Tau who decided when their ups were over. They scored exactly ten runs per inning, and when the game was done they had walked into home an even ninety times.

For the first time in history, humanity had lost a baseball game.

By seventy-nine runs.

The usual xeno team was there, all on time for once, along with the military and McGill. I sat down and turned to Yoshi.

"So what the hell happened?"

"They got a new strategy, I guess."

"No kidding. But how did it happen so fast? From zero runs to ninety in one game."

He nodded. "It surprised me, too. But now that I've thought about it, the real question is: Why didn't they do it all along?"

He queued a field recording, a Tau frozen in the pixelated grayscale of a fly-sized spycam. The creature held a spear out before itself like a sword.

Yoshi eye-moused, and the screen jumped into motion. The Tau wove and dodged, hitting at flying objects with the spear.

"This is one of their pre-hunting rituals, or games, or punishments. I've been focusing on it since our first game with the Tau. The other adults in the hunt are slinging rocks at her, and she's fending them off with her spear."

"Looks dangerous," Jenny said.

"Not for a Tau. Their hand-to-eye is too good, and with those double elbows they can cover their whole body efficiently. The Tau may not swing with any power, but they're good at blocking an object that's coming toward them."

I frowned. "So they've always been capable of the batting they showed today?"

"Sure. Those slings can get a projectile up to two hundred K. And they don't hold back. Any adult Tau could fend off balls thrown by humans. Add a little understanding of the strike zone, and they can get a walk pretty much at will."

"Two hundred kilometers per hour?" I repeated.

He nodded. "Yep. Much faster than any pitch you're going to manage, Colonel."

I opened my mouth, then closed it again.

"So why did they wait until now to kick our asses?" Alex asked.

Yoshi shrugged. "'Cause they didn't think of it?"

Dr. Chirac spoke up. "It wasn't part of the grammar of baseball as they understood it. Human players generally try to get a hit. Look at your terminology: You think of the tipped ball as 'foul,' or bad. You count the first two as strikes. But for a player with the Taus' skill set, the foul ball ultimately puts the batter in control." She nodded to herself. "It seems probable that until now they were imitating us, trying to play the way we do. They were probably more interested in experiencing the game's normal rituals than in beating us."

"But that new player," I said, "the one who led off today, had a different idea."

"She wanted to win," Alex said.

Dr. Chirac lowered her voice. "This is the conceptual breakthrough we have been hoping for."

"And the PR save we needed," McGill said happily. "The Tau finally got a game off us, and they did it by figuring out a totally new way to play baseball."

"Not exactly, Mr. McGill."

We all looked at Alex.

"The way they were playing reminded me of something I read about when I was a kid. While you guys on the field were getting mopped up by aliens, I burned most of my data allowance doing some historical research."

A headsup limned her face, dense fields of scrolling stats. "It turns out this is not a new way to play baseball. In 1887, there was a St. Louis Browns player named James Edward O'Neill. He was known generally as 'Tip' O'Neill, because of his expertise at foul tips. He could keep any ball in play, never striking out, wearing down pitchers until he could get on base. Back then, walks were part of your batting average, so he didn't care if he walked or hit his way on. His average was .485 that year."

"Almost *five hundred*?" Yoshi shook his head. "That's pretty damn good."

"Yeah, but our six-legged friends are about twice that good."

"They should be," Yoshi said. "They're designed for it."

"So someone must have found a way to stop this O'Neill guy," I said. "I mean, I've never heard of him."

"They didn't stop him," Alex said. "They changed the rules. Since that year, walks don't count in your average. So these days, collecting four balls earns you about as much glory as getting hit by a pitch."

"Yeah," Yoshi said, "except that the Tau don't know about batting averages. We don't even know if they can conceive of averages."

"Hell," I muttered. "We don't even know if they can *count*. I mean, they beat us like a rented mule. Seventy-nine runs!"

"They clearly can count," Chirac said. "They were quite exact in scoring ten runs each inning."

"Do you think that's significant?" Alex asked. "Is it some kind of SETI thing, like they're trying to establish a base-ten rubric for future communication?"

"Perhaps they were declaring," Ashley Newkirk said. "In the mother game, a far better side doesn't keep relentlessly thrashing an opponent once they've beat them. Wouldn't be cricket."

"But ninety runs?" I said. "That's one hell of a safety margin."

Yoshi grunted. "It's nothing to the score they could have racked up. They let us off the hook after ten runs an inning. Our pitching only ever got their pitcher out, and then only about every other at-bat."

"Thank god they don't know about designated hitters," Jenny muttered.

Alex still had her headsup on, and her fingers moved. "So we manage only one out every eighteen ups, which is three outs every fifty-four. That's fifty-one runs an inning. Which is . . . four hundred fifty-nine runs a game."

"Good god," Ashley said, "that sounds rather like a—" He stopped without saying another word.

"Like a royal ass-kicking," Jenny Flagg said.

There's only one thing worse than always winning, and that's always losing.

The games went incredibly long now. The Tau innings were torturous. Each lasted thirteen at-bats, and every one of those went at least ten pitches. The Tau went through relief pitchers like potato chips on Super Bowl Sunday, leaving half the human inhabitants of the planet walking around with their arms in a sling. Late in the game, we had to intentionally walk to save our arms for the gimme outs. Otherwise, there'd be no one left who could throw a strike at all.

Playing the Tau was so depressing that it became hard to motivate nine players onto the field. Chirac and the rest of the xenos were merciless, however. They weren't about to give up their close contact just because a bunch of whining soldiers and construction workers didn't want to get their butts kicked every day. And Chirac refused to give us a bigger strike zone. Just as she had when the Taus were losing, she insisted on sticking with Alexander Cartwright's rules.

Halihunt and NASA didn't like the way things were going any more than we did. The U.S. media took less than a week to go into crisis mode, with long essays about how the country's ascendancy was clearly over. Beaten at our own game by the first aliens we'd run into. My team's inability to get an out became the current metaphor for America's outdated infrastructure, our dependence on old paradigms and fossil fuels, our preference for force over finesse. Halihunt's sponsorship schemes crumbled like a cheap taco in a Texas tornado, and their stock price took a beating. How was our little colony supposed to save the American economy if we couldn't throw a strike?

Needless to say, the rest of the world just ate it up with a spoon. Finally, the little guys were kicking our ass. But we were forbidden from giving up the game. The last thing Houston, or Washington for that matter, could abide was for us to look like bad losers.

We were still damned if we did and damned if we didn't.

And boy, was my right arm sore.

Other than our troubles on the field, everything was going swell. Work on the array was still on schedule. The solar collection elements were finally propagating in the mica-rich soil, turning a huge mountainside into a shimmering mirror. It was beautiful at sunrise, and generated enough power to contribute significantly to the tube. Our transport rations tripled, then tripled again, and we even got to the point where we could reverse the usual flow, sending a few specks of Tau dust back to Houston for analysis. As our power increased and the math held up, morale recovered quickly from our perpetual losing streak. Once the tube got wider and more stable, humans could pass through safely. The nagging question of when and if we were all getting back to Earth had been answered.

We had a long dry spell, the Coriolis rains not interrupting our power supply for long enough to fully charge our batteries, and managed to keep the tube open for fifteen straight days. Finally we had the stability to make every teleport a smooth one, and that's when some genius in Houston got the idea . . .

It was Alex and Yoshi and me again. This time in secret.

We kept the transport shed unlit, using the night vision on our headsups. It was local midnight, when the fewest humans would be awake to notice our little brownout. If something went wrong—a one-in-forty chance at our current power levels—we didn't want anyone to know what had happened, here on Tau or back in the rest of humanity. I would have kept Yoshi out of it, but he was the only MD who I could imagine being sympathetic to our little plan.

Alex stepped up to the tube controls, checking the connection strength, and nodded to me. I could see her fingers crossed in the grainy green of my headsup.

"Night vision off, unless you want to go blind," I said. My accomplices, the tube, and shed disappeared into blackness.

"Three, two . . . " Alex said softly.

The tube glowed, and suddenly everything was as white as a fresh snowfall at noon. I heard a shout of surprise somewhere else in the camp as we leeched every drop of juice. On Earth, whole cities must have flickered.

The light sputtered, then dropped off into blackness again.

I switched my headsup back on and blinked until the green shapes became recognizable.

"Alex, you don't have to look."

"Not a problem, sir."

"Do I?" Yoshi asked.

"That's why you're here."

I saw Yoshi's headsup flicker to life as he stepped forward toward the transport. I popped the clean-seals and was surprised by the absence of a vacuum hiss. Of course, they'd spent the extra power to send air along this time.

No point in waiting. I pulled the lid up hard.

"Madre!"

That was a good sign.

"Madre de dios!"

"Mr. Rodriguez?" Yoshi asked. "How do you feel?"

"Like someone put mescal in my cornflakes, man. Do you guys do this all the time?"

Alex and I looked at each other. This was our first hint that Sammy "La Bamba" Rodriguez had not been fully briefed on the situation.

But at least he was alive.

The Tau human team had a new ringer.

After two years and four months (Earth time) in a community of twenty-nine people isolated from the rest of the species by light-years, walking into a mess tent with a brand new human being creates something of a stir. Some don't notice him, almost don't *see* the newcomer, as if the stranger recognition centers of their brains have atrophied. Some react as they would to an invader when encountering the first unfamiliar face in years. A few immediately want to screw the guy. Most simply think they've lost their minds.

Only Jenny Flagg immediately saw what was up.

"New talent?"

I nodded. "Get a team together, a good one. The best eight we can field, for a game at the usual time."

"But not the usual game, I see, sir."

I nodded. "And pull Hunter off whatever he's doing right now. We'll need an hour of warm-up to acclimate La Bamba's arm to point-nine-five gees."

"You got it, sir." She stood, scanning the mess tent for the best players, a happy smile on her face. Jenny had never stopped trying to win.

"She's cute," Rodriguez said.

I blinked. It had a been a couple of years since I'd heard a typical male response to a new female face. "Let's talk about baseball, Mr. Rodriguez."

"I am here to play."

"You know our problem."

"I've seen video. You have trouble getting a strike-out. They keep tipping until you walk them."

"Right. They'll give you the first two strikes, but after that it's impossible."

"Not for La Bamba."

"We'll see. Just make sure you throw soft for the first two balls. Nice, easy strikes. Might as well not give them any warning."

"Don't worry, Colonel. I will win your game for you. For America. For humanity."

Sammy Rodriguez was a man in purgatory. Early in his brilliant career, it was thought he'd be one of the great pitchers in the history of the game. He'd been a rare unanimous selection for the Cy Young Award. Over his first three playoff series he'd managed an ERA of less than one, and was one of the few modern pitchers who regularly went nine innings. He'd come within a walk of a perfect game three times. The guy could even swing a bat. He had an average of .274, the best of any pitcher in the National League. On a planet of amateurs, he was Babe Ruth squared.

He also had an addiction. The man liked to gamble. If only he'd kept it to the horses, the slots, the Super Bowl—hell, *anything* but baseball—he'd be in Tampa right now instead of seven light-years from the nearest beach. But for the moment, he was banned for life from the game he loved, an exile odious enough that he had risked a quite possibly fatal ride down a quantum tube to get one more crack at immortality. And, of course, redemption of a very lucrative kind.

NASA and Halihunt loved this narrative. Immigrant laborer embraced and enriched by his new country, falls from grace due to tragic character flaw, and rebuilds his life on the new frontier. The story was all set up and ready to go. They had been working the U.S. media around to the angle that *we* were the underdogs now, playing to win against a superhuman foe whose idea of baseball was pernicious and un-American and, frankly, not baseball at all. But La Bamba had come here to save us—in secret even, wanting no credit (and in case he'd turned to mush in the tube)—and to save baseball itself.

If the Taus realized we had a newcomer, they didn't show it.

Sammy bounded out to the mound with that walk we'd all had two years before, not quite toned down for the low gravity yet. NASA had been training him with a specially designed, taxpayer-funded, ninety-five-percent-weight ball for a couple of weeks, so after a few perfect deliveries to Hunter, I'd decided to save his arm for the game. The two of them had spent the rest of the morning on a new set of signs. I wanted every advantage in this first encounter. It was possible the Tau would adapt to his pitching after a few games and prove once and for all that they could beat any team of humans, professional or amateur, at any time. But at least we'd have this one win after our string of fifty-three losses.

I was pleased when the first Tau stepped up to the plate, the one with reddish dots who'd started our losing streak in the first place. She would be the one to suffer maximum shock when La Bamba opened up his big guns.

"Play ball," Chirac yelled, and even the humans in the never-reached outfield looked ready to go.

Rodriguez followed my advice and sent the first two in soft and easy. The Tau let them by, giving up the strikes.

La Bamba, it must be said, had a sense of drama. He allowed himself a long warm-up for the third pitch, checking the bases as if they were loaded, squinting at Hunter's sign although we'd already agreed on a screwball for this pitch.

When he let fly, it was spectacular. I'd never watched a major-league pitcher from dugout range before. The ball screamed toward the plate, looking to go inside. The Tau had picked up its hind feet, ready to step back for a ball, when it broke back to the right and down, smacking into Hunter's glove in the middle of the strike zone.

"Strike three, you're out!" Chirac cried.

The Tau had struck out looking.

Maybe it was my imagination, but the creature seemed a bit stunned as it headed back toward the alien dugout. Except for when the Taus declared after ten runs, that particular player had never gotten out in her career.

"Builds character," I said to myself.

La Bamba worked his magic on the next two aliens in short order. They managed a couple of pokes to send the ball foul, but they weren't ready for his speed and breadth of repertoire. After years as the best pitcher on the planet, I had forgotten how mediocre I really was. Probably, that was for the best. I'd done very little to prepare our alien friends for what a real human pitcher could do.

For our ups, we led off with Rodriguez, and he managed a credible double off the third pitch. From second, he caught my eye and nodded his head, showing some respect. The Tau were fine pitchers; they simply were no more prepared for a pro batter than they had been for a pro pitcher.

The rest of the human team rose to the occasion, lifting their offensive game so that La Bamba, then Hunter and Alex could score in the first. Rodriguez ploughed through the Tau order for the next two innings without breaking a sweat, and by the time the fourth rolled around, we were up eight to zero.

And the reddish-spotted Tau was back.

After the first two strikes, she shifted her stance, adjusting the bat to bring it higher. He threw her a standard curve next, which she managed to glance past Hunter. She fended off the next two pitches as well.

An epic battle ensued. Rodriguez worked her from every conceivable angle, attacking the strike zone with knuckle balls and screws and straight-up speed. But she deftly kept her at-bat alive.

I was so mesmerized by the contest that I almost missed Alex waving at me from third. She was making our sign for intentional walk.

I passed it to Hunter, who signaled La Bamba. The man waved it off at first, but after a few more foul tips he relented, letting the Tau on base. As long as it was just this one, we could afford it, and we had to keep Rodriguez's arm in the game.

We got out of that inning okay, but the Taus were gradually adapting.

They scored their first run in the seventh. Our ringer had intentionally walked a couple of Taus who were proving troublesome, and had been whittled down by a third. With two outs, they were back at the top of the order, and Redspots managed to force in a run before Rodriguez sealed the inning.

By that time, the human team had scored twenty-three, the most runs our dispirited crew had put together in ages. But it was clear the Taus were getting better with every inning, analyzing the new pitches coming their way, and full counts were the norm as they wore down La Bamba's arm with long and exhausting at-bats.

I sighed. If only this had been a seven-inning game. But the geniuses at NASA had demanded a regulation nine.

In the eighth, the Tau really started to score. The effortless look had returned to their batting, and Hunter was panting from chasing the foul tips that soared over his head. La Bamba pitched heroically, pain distorting his face with every throw, but they chipped away at our lead. With the bases loaded he dispatched their pitcher, battled through the order for one more out, then got the pitcher again. Seven runs, for a total of eight.

Rodriguez came back to our dugout, all the low-gravity bounce gone from his step, and clutched an ice pack to his right arm.

"How're you doing?"

He looked at me sullenly. "We will win, Coach. Don't worry."

Alex trotted over from third. "Colonel, we've got twenty-three runs, so we've got to get seven more."

"How do you figure?"

"If Sammy keeps fighting every batter, he's going to lose his arm for good. But he can still get their pitcher. Hell, even *you* get her every once in a while."

I let that pass. Yesterday I'd been the best pitcher on the planet. How quickly they forget.

Alex continued. "If Rodriguez walks the other eight players, that's three times through the full order. Twenty-four batters on base, minus three to load: twenty-one runs. That'll give them twenty-nine total. If we can haul thirty runs, we win. And we've got two more ups. We can do it!"

I nodded, but seven runs in two innings was a tall order.

"Let's see how this one goes."

We almost sealed it in the bottom of the eighth. Alex passed the word that we needed more runs, and we managed to load the bases. La Bamba, gritting his teeth in pain, drove in all three of them, then Alex sent him home. After a couple of strike-outs, we had the bases loaded again.

But Jenny Flagg let us down. The Tau sent her a meat pitch, and she dropped her usual Texas-leaguer into the close outfield. The Tau were already in motion, though, coming in to make the catch.

She staggered to a stop on the way to first, hands over her face.

I shook my head. You had to admit the Tau had learned a lot from us.

"Don't worry, Jenny," I shouted. "We've got one more inning."

I told Rodriguez the plan.

"Eight intentional walks in a row? *Madre!*"

"Don't fight them, Sammy. Save your arm for the pitcher. She's the weak link."

He shook his head, pulled down his filter mask and spat. "That is no way to win." He walked to the mound without another word.

He fought the first batter in the order, but the red-spotted Tau took him apart, whacking his fastball around like a piñata on a short string. Sammy's arm was faltering, weakening with every pitch, and the pain finally convinced him that Alex's plan was the only way. For the next seven batters, Hunter stood off to the side to catch underhanded throws, and we watched the Taus' score climb to thirteen. Then La Bamba plugged away at the pitcher, taking her down with four exquisite pitches. Eight walks later, they had twenty-one. For a second out, Rodriguez's third pitch caught the pitcher looking with a crafty knuckle ball that dropped like a rock into the strike zone.

He walked eight more, until they had twenty-nine, then motioned Hunter back to the plate.

It was a fierce battle, fifteen pitches of trench warfare with a full count and bases loaded, eight more runs looming if La Bamba let the pitcher on base, but he finally managed to find that third strike. She went swinging.

Bottom of the ninth, and we were two runs behind. And we did *not* want to go into extra innings.

Yoshi batted first. He took a vicious swing at the first pitch and sent a pop fly soaring into the red sky. Three Taus converged beneath it between second and third, squeaking at each other as if telling jokes while they waited to make thc catch.

Then came Hunter. He fouled off the first, then let a strike go past, then missed a fast ball that Joe Dimaggio couldn't have connected with.

Two up, two down.

La Bamba was next, and we all relaxed for the moment. He would at least keep us alive. At a National League game, you usually take a piss-break when the pitcher's up, not realizing that most of them are in the top percentile of humanity. Against the still-amateur Taus, he was batting a thousand so far.

Alex went on deck, warming up with two extra bats. I remembered with some nostalgia the days when we'd had only one Slugger, worn electrical tape around its neck to replace the grip, and nothing at stake.

The first pitch came in, and Sammy ignored it.

"Strike one!" Chirac proclaimed.

He stepped back on the second pitch, scratching his ear disdainfully.

"Strike two!"

He moved into a bunter's crouch. When the next pitch came in, he glanced it off toward third base, well foul. He foul tipped the next one as well.

Alex jogged over and hissed, "Is he doing what I think he's doing?"

I nodded. "He's getting them back. Playing their own game against them."

"Why doesn't he just *wail* on it?"

He bunted another pitch foul.

"Could be his arm. Could be his ego."

He stepped back from the next pitch, a ball. One-fourth of a walk.

But La Bamba's plans were subtler than we knew. Two pitches later, he hauled off and swung for real, hoping to catch us all by surprise. But the bat cracked like a rifle shot, scattering splinters from home plate to the mound. The ball bounced tepidly to first, where the baseman picked it up and stepped on the bag.

Humanity had lost again.

"Maybe a team entirely of pro pitchers. One for every inning."

"No, all-star swingers to rack up a big score, with lots of relief at the end."

"Better hope they never hear about the designated hitter rule."

We were sitting in the mess tent—defeated players, the military, the xeno team—trying to figure what to do next. Somehow, the discussion had got around to whether *any* team of humans could ever beat the Taus.

La Bamba sat with his head on the table, three ice packs strapped to his pitching arm. He kept saying, "Everything, everything."

Alex rubbed his shoulders. "Cheer up, Sammy. You'll still be a hero for trying."

He turned his head from side to side without lifting it from the table, as if rolling out pie crust with his face.

"No, I lose everything! House . . . car . . . "

I shared a look with Alex. "Rodriguez? You didn't *bet* on this game, did you?"

He was silent.

Then I remembered that some London bookie had offered twenty-to-one that humans wouldn't beat the Tau on their own planet anytime this year. Rodriguez must have figured that his secret call-up was the fix of the century.

"Swimming pool," he whimpered.

"You win for humanity, huh?" I said.

Alex shrugged and continued to rub his shoulders.

McGill groaned, his eyes rolling up in his head. "This is a PR disaster! We bring in a pro to beat the poor defenseless aliens, and we *still* lose. Then it turns out our ringer was betting on the game."

"Maybe you should just sneak me home. Like you snuck me here," Rodriguez said. "Forget this game ever happened."

"That would be nice," I said. "But not everyone on this planet is U.S. military. We can only control the story for so long."

Alex stopped her massage. "Wait a second, Sammy. Did you say send you home?"

"Yes. I want to go home now. My arm is broken."

I swallowed. La Bamba had not in fact been fully briefed. "Rodriguez, you *do* know that the tube isn't up to two-way teleport yet, right? We don't have enough power for a push from this end. Nothing bigger than a speck of dust, anyway."

"Speck of dust? What?"

Alex leaned closer, her hands still on his shoulders. "You can't go back for six months at least, Sammy."

"Madre!"

Late that night, Ashley Newkirk showed up at my tent.

"Any brilliant solutions to your sporting dilemma yet, Colonel?"

I looked up at him through a haze of Iain Claymore's whisky.

"Not much of a dilemma. Don't see that I have any choice one way or the other. Lose or lose does not constitute a dilemma."

"And you were so close. Poor Mr. Rodriguez doesn't have another game in him?"

"He's on strike. Breach of contract."

"Ah, labor disputes. Always a messy business in sport. But surely there are choices. You could give up the game."

I shook my head. "Make us look even worse. Besides, there's glory in losing. Must soldier on. Every country remembers the battles they lost: Bunker Hill, Pearl Harbor, Gallipoli, Damascus. 'Remember the Alamo,' we still say in Texas. No survivors that fine day, Ashley. Not a one."

"Do you really think that today's game was a sublime and memorable defeat?"

"Not particularly." I poured myself another drink, not offering. "All I hope is that once the oil starts flowing, everyone'll forget all about baseball. Until then, we'll just have to look bad."

He nodded, and took a seat uninvited.

"What if I said there was an alternative?"

I looked up at him.

"A way to take some of the sting out of losing. Maybe even win a few for humanity."

I emptied the glass down my throat, then slapped it to the table. "Talk."

He handed over a piece of paper. I took it carefully. Real paper was still something precious here on Tau. If you've ever moved a box of books, you know how heavy it can get. But we all had a notebook or two: the only place to store our private thoughts.

On the sheet was a list of equipment. I skimmed to the bottom and cried out at the total mass.

"Christ, Ashley, fifty kilos? La Bamba just about blew NASA's budget for the year."

"All very necessary. And I'm sure Halihunt still has some money socked away."

I sighed, nodding. Whole political parties had disappeared by underestimating the wealth of oil companies. And Ashley's idea had one unmistakable advantage: It got me off the hook. I imagined long, luxurious days of worrying about solar arrays and oil drills instead of batting orders.

"Have you talked to Dr. Chirac about this?"

He nodded vigorously. "She's thrilled with the idea. Wants to do a comparative study and all that. But I leave convincing Mr. McGill to you."

"And you think we can win?"

He sighed. "If you insist on putting it in those narrow terms, yes. There are certain tactical advantages which I would be glad to explain."

"Spare me." I took a deep breath and nodded. "If NASA and Halihunt are game, I am. Just one thing: Do you really need the uniforms? We've got some already."

"But we have *baseball* uniforms, my dear colonel. They have *colors* on them, for God's sake. If we want the Tau to have a genuine cultural experience, we simply can't take the field in anything other than all white."

"Because . . . ?"

He sighed, rolling his eyes. "It just wouldn't be cricket."

Four days later, I visited Ashley in the field.

"No, you're supposed to be at third man!" he was yelling at Jenny Flagg. "Third man, I said! You're at fine leg! Get over to third man! Good heavens. Look, just move over to bloody *left field*!"

She finally nodded and jogged across the outfield.

Or perhaps it was the infield. Backfield? It was hard to tell. The two wickets were placed about twenty meters apart in the middle of the field, and there were *two* Taus batting. I seem to remember that cricket switched directions every half-dozen pitches or so. There were fielders dotted all around me, dressed in the fresh new white uniforms that had cost Pasadena its air-conditioning for three long summer nights.

As Ashley Newkirk continued his battle with field placements, I found Alex standing close to one of the batters, just to one side of the newly rolled rectangle of dirt between the wickets. She took off her helmet as I approached.

"How's it going, Captain?"

"Pretty well so far. We got their first batter—sorry, *batsman*—on a deflection. The one with red spots, and we got her for only twenty runs."

"*Only* twenty?"

"It's okay; they're chasing our score of three ninety, and that's just our first innings."

I shook my head.

"Bit funny playing without gloves, though," she added.

I looked around. "Hunter's got some."

"He's the wicket-keeper."

"Ah. And how come you're the only one with a helmet?"

"Because I'm at silly mid-off."

"I recognize all those words, Alex, but not in that order."

She cleared her throat. "I'm standing right next to the batsman, in case she tips it short. But it's a bit dangerous if she hits it hard, which is what 'silly' means. Yoshi's at short leg on the other side. And take a look at that slips cordon."

I followed her gesture to the row of five fielders strung out behind one of the Tau batters. If only we'd thought of that for baseball: just put the fielders *behind* the batter. Any foul tip would go straight into their hands.

Of course, you can't put your fielders in foul territory. Wouldn't be baseball.

"How do the Taus like it?"

"They love it. The attendance is bigger, at least. It's the perfect sport for the Taus. You can hit the ball in any direction and score."

"So how come they aren't beating us yet?"

"Because you can't get a walk in cricket. Simple as that. And we can put fielders in position all three hundred and sixty degrees around them. The field placements are totally up to the captain, um, to Ashley. We have a chance of catching any deflection they make."

I nodded. Simple as that.

"What if they come up with something unexpected? Like their foul tipping in baseball?"

She shrugged. "Ashley says the game's been played for eight hundred years. Seems like it'd be hard to come up with any new tricks."

"Yeah, we'll see."

"Colonel, please?" Ashley had set his field, and waved me off.

I retreated to the edge of the impact crater. Alex was right. There were at least two hundred Taus around the field, raptly watching the new game. According to Dr. Chirac's first report, the aliens had decided to learn this new set of rules by more usual methods: sign language and direct example rather than passive observation. The xeno team was having its first face-to-face conversations with the Taus, pointing and miming to explain wickets and bowling and whatever the hell silly mid-off was.

A breakthrough of cosmic proportions.

Ashley had backed up to a spot about thirty meters from one wicket. He ran toward it, charging all the way up to the little wooden triptych and releasing the ball straight toward the Tau at the other wicket. The ball bounced short, flying up from the diveted ground at an unexpected angle. The Tau swung the broad, flat bat and got a piece of it. It soared over her right shoulder, just above the cordon of fielders behind her. She started running as Jenny, placed deeper, ran it down and threw it in.

The two Taus held up their run, having changed positions once.

"Not a bad stroke, eh, Colonel?"

Iain Claymore had appeared next to me. He held one of Yoshi's cameras and a small flask.

"You understand this game?"

He looked around and lowered his voice. "My mother's from Manchester. Tell no one."

"Your secret is safe with me."

We watched another delivery. The batter clipped it, angling it away at ninety degrees, just over Alex's reach and almost to the edge. The Taus ran again, switching places twice.

"Two runs, I presume?"

"Aye. They're learning to play cricket even faster than they did that daft American game."

I nodded, smiling to myself. "I just hope Ashley knows what he's in for."

"How do you mean?"

"It's not much fun to have your national game taken away from you."

Claymore lifted his head and laughed. "You Americans crack me up. Cricket, taken away from the English? Those poor bastards havenae won a cricket series in decades. The Indians, the Sri Lankans, the South Africans all kick the crap out of them on a regular basis. Christ, they were put out of the Cup by bloody *Yemen* last year."

I shook my head. "But what are they going to do when the tube opens for good, and *aliens* show up and beat them at their own game?"

"Ach, that happened about two hundred years ago. Only they were called Australians."

I swallowed. "It's not the same."

"Don't be daft, Colonel. The English are wankers, but at least they gave up their empire gracefully. You lot could learn something from that. They don't mind losing a friendly game against the old possessions. They don't need to win. They're just happy that two billion people on the Indian subcontinent drive on the left side of the road. It may not be much of a legacy, but it's a damn sight better than the mess that you Yanks are going to leave behind in the Middle East."

I turned to Iain with surprise. I'd never heard him say anything remotely political before, unless his relentless attacks on Ashley Newkirk's cooking counted.

"But enough of that," he said. "Let's watch the game."

Of course, these days everyone on Earth has a opinion about Iain Claymore.

All those years, as we all know now, our charming half-Scot had been brewing up more than whisky in his still. Slowly and surely, he had engineered a bacterium distantly related to the ones that eat oil slicks off the ocean surface, but adapted for Tau's deep underground reserves.

For a Greenpeace radical, he was quite an interventionist. By the time we started pumping, he had infected every oil reserve within a thousand clicks of our facility. Like metal spikes driven into old-growth trees, Iain's creation made Tau crude useless for earthly consumption. No amount of retooling at our refineries back at home could save the tainted oil.

But not everyone knows what really became of him. Contrary to the official story, "St. Iain" was not executed. As a United European subject, I didn't consider him a traitor, whatever my commanders said. Besides, after all our labor and heartache on that planet, killing was too good for him.

Instead, I exiled him on Tau after it was clear that the oil was useless, the array not worth maintaining, the tube closing forever on Earth's first contact era after the last of us had stepped back through. And I made sure that Claymore had all the equipment and supplies necessary for a long, lonely life on an alien planet, surrounded by a hundred thousand inhuman creatures who wanted nothing to do with him except to play a very English game.

Of course, to give him a fighting chance of staying sane, I let him keep his still.

After all the whisky I'd drunk from it, I thought that only cricket.

This unnerving story was first published in 1976, long before the format for the reality show Survivor *was created in 1992. But Kate Wilhelm is still, so far, in the realm of science fiction with her version of a real-time survival "game" and the technology it takes for the masses to immerse themselves in a life-and-death competition—but not by much. As for an addiction to reality shows, "Ladies and Gentlemen, This Is Your Crisis!" may already be, well, reality . . .*

Ladies and Gentlemen, This Is Your Crisis!

Kate Wilhelm

4:00 p.m. Friday

Lottie's factory closed early on Friday, as most of them did now. It was four when she got home, after stopping for frozen dinners, bread, sandwich meats, beer. She switched on the wall TV screen before she put her bag down. In the kitchen she turned on another set, a portable, and watched it as she put the food away. She had missed four hours.

They were in the mountains. That was good. Lottie liked it when they chose mountains. A stocky man was sliding down a slope, feet out before him, legs stiff—too conscious of the camera, though. Lottie couldn't tell if he had meant to slide, but he did not look happy. She turned her attention to the others.

A young woman was walking slowly, waist high in ferns, so apparently unconscious of the camera that it could only be a pose this early in the game. She looked vaguely familiar. Her blond hair was loose, like a girl in a shampoo commercial, Lottie decided. She narrowed her eyes, trying to remember where she had seen the girl. A model, probably, wanting to be a star. She would wander aimlessly, not even trying for the prize, content with the publicity she was getting.

The other woman was another sort altogether. A bit overweight, her thighs bulged in the heavy trousers the contestants wore; her hair was dyed black and fastened with a rubber band in a no-nonsense manner. She was examining a tree intently. Lottie nodded at her. Everything about her spoke of purpose, of concentration, of planning. She'd do.

The final contestant was a tall black man, in his forties probably. He wore old-fashioned eyeglasses—a mistake. He'd lose them and be seriously handicapped. He kept glancing about with a lopsided grin.

Lottie had finished putting the groceries away; she returned to the living room to sit before the large unit that gave her a better view of the map above the sectioned screen. The Andes, she had decided, and was surprised and pleased to find she was wrong. Alaska! There were bears and wolves in Alaska still, and elk and moose.

The picture shifted, and a thrill of anticipation raised the hairs on Lottie's arms and scalp. Now the main screen was evenly divided; one half showed the man who had been sliding. He was huddled against the cliff, breathing very hard. On the other half of the screen was an enlarged aerial view. Lottie gasped. Needle-like snow-capped peaks, cliffs, precipices, a raging stream . . . The yellow dot of light that represented the man was on the edge of a steep hill covered with boulders and loose gravel. If he got on that, Lottie thought, he'd be lost. From where he was, there was no way he could know what lay ahead. She leaned forward, examining him for signs that he understood, that he was afraid, anything. His face was empty; all he needed now was more air than he could get with his labored breathing.

Andy Stevens stepped in front of the aerial map; it was three feet taller than he. "As you can see, ladies and gentlemen, there is only this scrub growth to Dr. Burnside's left. Those roots might be strong enough to hold, but I'd guess they are shallowly rooted, wouldn't you? And if he chooses this direction, he'll need something to grasp, won't he?"

Andy had his tape measure and a pointer. He looked worried. He touched the yellow dot of light. "Here he is. As you can see, he is resting, for the moment, on a narrow ledge after his slide down sixty-five feet of loose dirt and gravel. He doesn't appear to be hurt. Our own Dr. Leder man is watching him along with the rest of us, and he assures me that Dr. Burnside is not injured."

Andy pointed out the hazards of Dr. Burnside's precarious position, and the dangers involved in moving. Lottie nodded, her lips tight and grim. It was off to a good start.

6:00 p.m. Friday

Butcher got home, as usual, at six. Lottie heard him at the door but didn't get up to open it for him. Dr. Burnside was still sitting there. He had to move. Move, you bastard! Do something!

"Whyn't you unlock the door?" Butcher yelled, yanking off his jacket.

Lottie paid no attention. Butcher always came home mad, resentful because she had got off early, mad at his boss because the warehouse didn't close down early, mad at traffic, mad at everything.

"They say anything about them yet?" Butcher asked, sitting in his recliner.

Lottie shook her head. Move, you bastard! Move!

The man began to inch his way to the left and Lottie's heart thumped, her hands clenched.

"What's the deal?" Butcher asked hoarsely, already responding to Lottie's tension.

"Dead end that way," Lottie muttered, her gaze on the screen. "Slide with boulders and junk if he tries to go down. He's gotta go right."

The man moved cautiously, never lifting his feet from the ground but sliding them along, testing each step. He paused again, this time with less room than before. He looked desperate. He was perspiring heavily. Now he could see the way he had chosen offered little hope of getting down. More slowly than before, he began to back up; dirt and gravel shifted constantly.

The amplifiers picked up the noise of the stuff rushing downward, like a waterfall heard from a distance, and now and then a muttered unintelligible word from the man. The volume came up: he was cursing. Again and again he stopped. He was pale and sweat ran down his face. He didn't move his hands from the cliff to wipe it away.

Lottie was sweating too. Her lips moved occasionally with a faint curse or prayer. Her hands gripped the sofa.

7:30 p.m. Friday

Lottie fell back onto the sofa with a grunt, weak from sustained tension. They were safe. It had taken over an hour to work his way to this place where the cliff and steep slope gave way to a gentle hill. The man was sprawled out face down, his back heaving.

Butcher abruptly got up and went to the bathroom. Lottie couldn't move yet. The screen shifted and the aerial view filled the larger part. Andy pointed out the contestants' lights and finally began the recap.

Lottie watched on the portable set as she got out their frozen dinners and heated the oven. Dr. Lederman was talking about Angie Dawes, the young aspiring actress whose problem was that of having been overprotected all her life. He said she was a potential suicide, and the panel of examining physicians had agreed Crisis Therapy would be helpful.

The next contestant was Mildred Ormsby, a chemist, divorced, no children. She had started on a self-destructive course through drugs, said Dr. Lederman, and would be benefited by Crisis Therapy.

The tall black man, Clyde Williams, was an economist; he taught at Harvard and had tried to murder his wife and their three children by burning down their house with them in it. Crisis Therapy had been indicated.

Finally Dr. Edward Burnside, the man who had started the show with such drama, was shown being interviewed. Forty-one, unmarried, living with a woman, he was a statistician for a major firm. Recently he had started to feed the wrong data into the computer, aware but unable to stop himself.

Dr. Lederman's desk was superimposed on the aerial view and he started his taped explanation of what Crisis Therapy was. Lottie made coffee. When she looked again Eddie was still lying on the ground, exhausted, maybe even crying. She wished he would roll over so she could see if he was crying.

Andy returned to explain how the game was played: the winner received one million dollars, after taxes, and all the contestants were undergoing Crisis Therapy that would enrich their lives beyond measure. Andy explained the automatic, air-cushioned, five-day cameras focused electronically on the contestants, the orbiting satellite that made it possible to keep them under observation at all times, the light amplification, infrared system that would keep them visible all night. This part made Lottie's head ache.

Next came the full-screen commercial for the wall units. Only those who had them could see the entire show. Down the left side of the screen were the four contestants, each in a separate panel, and over them a topographical map that showed the entire region, where the exit points were, the nearest roads, towns. Center screen could be divided any way the director chose. Above this picture was the show's slogan: "This Is Your Crisis!" and a constantly running commercial. In the far right corner there was an aerial view of the selected site, with the colored dots of light. Mildred's was red, Angie's was green. Eddie's yellow, Clyde's blue. Anything else larger than a rabbit or squirrel that moved into the viewing area would be white.

The contestants were shown being taken to the site, first by airplane, then helicopter. They were left there on noon Friday and had until midnight Sunday to reach one of the dozen trucks that ringed the area. The first one to report in at one of the trucks was the winner.

10:00 p.m. Friday

Lottie made up her bed on the couch while Butcher opened his recliner full length and brought out a blanket and pillow from the bedroom. He had another beer and Lottie drank milk and ate cookies, and presently they turned off the light and there was only the glow from the screen in the room.

The contestants were settled down for the night, each in a sleeping bag, campfires burning low, the long northern twilight still not faded. Andy began to explain the contents of the backpacks.

Lottie closed her eyes, opened them several times, just to check, and finally fell asleep.

1:00 a.m. Saturday

Lottie sat up suddenly, wide awake, her heart thumping. The red beeper had come on. On center screen the girl was sitting up, staring into darkness, obviously frightened. She must have heard something. Only her dot showed on her screen, but there was no way for her to know that. Lottie lay down again, watching, and became aware of Butcher's heavy snoring. She shook his leg and he shifted and for a few moments breathed deeply, without the snore, then began again.

Francine Dumont was the night M.C.; now she stepped to one side of the screen. "If she panics," Francine said in a hushed voice, "it could be the end of the game for her." She pointed out the hazards in the area—boulders, a steep drop-off, the thickening trees on two sides. "Let's watch," she whispered and stepped back out of the way.

The volume was turned up; there were rustlings in the undergrowth. Lottie closed her eyes and tried to hear them through the girl's ears, and felt only contempt for her. The girl was stiff with fear. She began to build up her campfire. Lottie nodded. She'd stay awake all night, and by late tomorrow she'd be finished. She would be lifted out, the end of Miss Smarty Pants Dawes.

Lottie sniffed and closed her eyes, but now Butcher's snores were louder. If only he didn't sound like a dying man, she thought—sucking in air, holding it, holding it, then suddenly erupting into a loud snort that turned into a gurgle. She pressed her hands over her ears and finally slept again.

2:00 p.m. Saturday

There were beer cans on the table, on the floor around it. There was half a loaf of bread and a knife with dried mustard and the mustard jar without a top. The salami was drying out, hard, and there were onion skins and bits of brown lettuce and an open jar of pickles. The butter had melted in its dish, and the butter knife was on the floor, spreading a dark stain on the rug.

Nothing was happening on the screen now. Angie Dawes hadn't left the fern patch. She was brushing her hair.

Mildred was following the stream, but it became a waterfall ahead and she would have to think of something else.

The stout man was still making his way downward as directly as possible, obviously convinced it was the fastest way and no more dangerous than any other.

The black man was being logical, like Mildred, Lottie admitted. He watched the shadows and continued in a southeasterly direction, tackling the hurdles as he came to them, methodically, without haste. Ahead of him, invisible to him, but clearly visible to the floating cameras and the audience, were a mother bear and two cubs in a field of blueberries.

Things would pick up again in an hour or so, Lottie knew. Butcher came back. "You have time for a quick shower," Lottie said. He was beginning to smell.

"Shut up." Butcher sprawled in the recliner, his feet bare.

Lottie tried not to see his thick toes, grimy with warehouse dust. She got up and went to the kitchen for a bag, and started to throw the garbage into it. The cans clattered.

"Knock it off, will ya!" Butcher yelled. He stretched to see around her.

He was watching the blonde braid her hair. Lottie threw another can into the bag.

9:00 p.m. Saturday

Butcher sat on the edge of the chair, biting a fingernail. "See that?" he breathed. "You see it?" He was shiny with perspiration.

Lottie nodded, watching the white dots move on the aerial map, watching the blue dot moving, stopping for a long time, moving again. Clyde and the bears were approaching each other minute by minute, and Clyde knew now that there was something ahead of him.

"You see that?" Butcher cried out hoarsely.

"Just be still, will you?" Lottie said through her teeth. The black man was sniffing the air.

"You can smell a goddam lousy bear a country mile!" Butcher said. "He knows."

"For God's sake, shut up!"

"Yeah, he knows all right," Butcher said softly. "Mother bear, cubs . . . she'll tear him apart."

"Shut up! Shut up!"

Clyde began to back away. He took half a dozen steps, then turned and ran. The bear stood up; behind her the cubs tumbled in play. She turned her head in a listening attitude. She growled and dropped to four feet and began to amble in the direction Clyde had taken. They were about an eighth of a mile apart. Any second she would be able to see him.

Clyde ran faster, heading for thick trees. Past the trees was a cliff he had skirted earlier.

"Saw a cave or something up there," Butcher muttered. "Betcha. Heading for a cave."

Lottie pressed her hands hard over her ears. The bear was closing the gap; the cubs followed erratically, and now and again the mother bear paused to glance at them and growl softly. Clyde began to climb the face of the cliff. The bear came into view and saw him. She ran. Clyde was out of her reach; she began to climb, and rocks were loosened by her great body. When one of the cubs bawled, she let go and half slid, half fell back to the bottom. Standing on her hind legs, she growled at the man above her. She was nine feet tall. She shook her great head from side to side another moment, then turned and waddled back toward the blueberries; trailed by her two cubs.

"Smart bastard," Butcher muttered. "Good thinking. Knew he couldn't outrun a bear. Good thinking."

Lottie went to the bathroom. She had smelled the bear, she thought. If he had only shut up a minute! She was certain she had smelled the bear. Her hands were trembling.

The phone was ringing when she returned to the living room. She answered, watching the screen. Clyde looked shaken, the first time he had been rattled since the beginning.

"Yeah," she said into the phone. "He's here." She put the receiver down. "Your sister."

"She can't come over," Butcher said ominously. "Not unless she's drowned that brat."

"Funny," Lottie said, scowling. Corinne should have enough consideration not to make an issue of it week after week.

"Yeah," Butcher was saying into the phone. "I know it's tough on a floor set, but what the hell, get the old man to buy a wall unit. What's he planning to do, take it with him?" He listened. "Like I said, you know how it is. I say okay, then Lottie gives me hell. Know what I mean? I mean, it ain't worth it. You know?" Presently he banged the receiver down.

"Frank's out of town?"

He didn't answer, settled himself down into his chair and reached for his beer.

"He's in a fancy hotel lobby where they got a unit screen the size of a barn and she's got that lousy little portable . . . "

"Just drop it, will ya? She's the one that wanted the kid, remember. She's bawling her head off but she's not coming over. So drop it!"

"Yeah, and she'll be mad at me for a week, and it takes two to make a kid."

"Jesus Christ!" Butcher got up and went into the kitchen. The refrigerator door banged. "Where's the beer?"

"Under the sink."

"Jesus! Whyn't you put it in the refrigerator?"

"There wasn't enough room for it all. If you've gone through all the cold beers, you don't need any more!"

He slammed the refrigerator door again and came back with a can of beer. When he pulled it open, warm beer spewed halfway across the room. Lottie knew he had done it to make her mad. She ignored him and watched Mildred worm her way down into her sleeping bag. Mildred had the best chance of winning, she thought. She checked her position on the aerial map. All the lights were closer to the trucks now, but there wasn't anything of real importance between Mildred and the goal. She had chosen right every time.

"Ten bucks on yellow," Butcher said suddenly.

"You gotta be kidding! He's going to break his fat neck before he gets out of there!"

"Okay, ten bucks." He slapped ten dollars down on the table, between the TV dinner trays and the coffee pot.

"Throw it away," Lottie said, matching it. "Red."

"The fat lady?"

"Anybody who smells like you better not go around insulting someone who at least takes time out to have a shower now and then!" Lottie cried and swept past him to the kitchen. She and Mildred were about the same size. "And why don't you get off your butt and clean up some of that mess! All I do every weekend is clear away garbage!"

"I don't give a shit if it reaches the ceiling!"

Lottie brought a bag and swept trash into it. When she got near Butcher, she held her nose.

6:00 a.m. Sunday

Lottie sat up. "What happened?" she cried. The red beeper was on. "How long's it been on?"

"Half an hour. Hell, I don't know."

Butcher was sitting tensely on the side of the recliner, gripping it with both hands. Eddie was in a tree, clutching the trunk. Below him, dogs were tearing apart his backpack, and another dog was leaping repeatedly at him.

"Idiot!" Lottie cried. "Why didn't he hang up his stuff like the others?"

Butcher made a noise at her, and she shook her head, watching. The dogs had smelled food, and they would search for it, tearing up everything they found. She smiled grimly. They might keep Mr. Fat Neck up there all day, and even if he got down, he'd have nothing to eat.

That's what did them in, she thought. Week after week it was the same. They forgot the little things and lost. She leaned back and ran her hand through her hair. It was standing out all over her head.

Two of the dogs began to fight over a scrap of something and the leaping dog jumped into the battle with them. Presently they all ran away, three of them chasing the fourth.

"Throw away your money," Lottie said gaily, and started around Butcher. He swept out his hand and pushed her down again and left the room without a backward look. It didn't matter who won, she thought, shaken by the push. That twenty and twenty more would have to go to the finance company to pay off the loan for the wall unit. Butcher knew that; he shouldn't get so hot about a little joke.

1:00 p.m. Sunday

"This place looks like a pigpen," Butcher growled. "You going to clear some of this junk away?" He was carrying a sandwich in one hand, beer in the other; the table was littered with breakfast remains, leftover snacks from the morning and the night before.

Lottie didn't look at him. "Clear it yourself."

"I'll clear it." He put his sandwich down on the arm of his chair and swept a spot clean, knocking over glasses and cups.

"Pick that up!" Lottie screamed. "I'm sick and tired of cleaning up after you every damn weekend! All you do is stuff and guzzle and expect me to pick up and clean up."

"Damn right."

Lottie snatched up the beer can he had put on the table and threw it at him. The beer streamed out over the table, chair, over his legs. Butcher threw down the sandwich and grabbed at her. She dodged and backed away from the table into the center of the room. Butcher followed, his hands clenched.

"You touch me again, I'll break your arm!"

"Bitch!" He dived for her and she caught his arm, twisted it savagely and threw him to one side.

He hauled himself up to a crouch and glared at her with hatred. "I'll fix you," he muttered. "I'll fix you!"

Lottie laughed. He charged again, this time knocked her backward and they crashed to the floor together and rolled, pummeling each other.

The red beeper sounded and they pulled apart, not looking at each other, and took their seats before the screen.

"It's the fat lady," Butcher said malevolently. "I hope the bitch kills herself."

Mildred had fallen into the stream and was struggling in waist-high water to regain her footing. The current was very swift, all white water here. She slipped and went under. Lottie held her breath until she appeared again, downstream, retching, clutching at a boulder. Inch by inch she drew herself to it and clung there trying to get her breath back. She looked about desperately; she was very white. Abruptly she launched herself into the current, swimming strongly, fighting to get to the shore as she was swept down the river.

Andy's voice was soft as he said, "That water is forty-eight degrees, ladies and gentlemen! Forty-eight! Dr. Lederman, how long can a person be immersed in water that cold?"

"Not long, Andy. Not long at all." The doctor looked worried too. "Ten minutes at the most, I'd say."

"That water is reducing her body heat second by second," Andy said solemnly. "When it is low enough to produce unconsciousness . . . "

Mildred was pulled under again; when she appeared this time, she was much closer to shore. She caught a rock and held on. Now she could stand up, and presently she dragged herself rock by rock, boulder by boulder, to the shore. She was shaking hard, her teeth chattering. She began to build a fire. She could hardly open her waterproof matchbox. Finally she had a blaze and she began to strip. Her backpack, Andy reminded the audience, had been lost when she fell into the water. She had only what she had on her back, and if she wanted to continue after the sun set and the cold evening began, she had to dry her things thoroughly.

"She's got nerve," Butcher said grudgingly.

Lottie nodded. She was weak. She got up, skirted Butcher, and went to the kitchen for a bag. As she cleaned the table, every now and then she glanced at the naked woman by her fire. Steam was rising off her wet clothes.

10:00 p.m. Sunday

Lottie had moved Butcher's chair to the far side of the table the last time he had left it. His beard was thick and coarse, and he still wore the clothes he had put on to go to work Friday morning. Lottie's stomach hurt. Every weekend she got constipated.

The game was between Mildred and Clyde now. He was in good shape, still had his glasses and his backpack. He was farther from his truck than Mildred was from hers, but she had eaten nothing that afternoon and was limping badly.

Her boots must have shrunk, or else she had not waited for them to get completely dry. Her face twisted with pain when she moved.

The girl was still posing in the high meadow, now against a tall tree, now among the wildflowers. Often a frown crossed her face and surreptitiously she scratched. "Ticks," Butcher said. "Probably full of them."

Eddie was wandering in a daze. He looked empty, and was walking in great aimless circles. Some of them cracked like that, Lottie knew. It had happened before, sometimes to the strongest one of all. They'd slap him right in a hospital and no one would hear anything about him again for a long time, if ever. She didn't waste pity on him.

She would win, Lottie knew. She had studied every kind of wilderness they used and she'd know what to do and how to do it. She was strong, and not afraid of noises. She found herself nodding and stopped, glanced quickly at Butcher to see if he had noticed. He was watching Clyde.

"Smart," Butcher said, his eyes narrowed. "That son-abitch's been saving himself for the home stretch. Look at him." Clyde started to lope, easily, as if aware the TV truck was dead ahead.

Now the screen was divided into three parts, the two finalists, Mildred and Clyde, side by side, and above them a large aerial view that showed their red and blue dots as they approached the trucks.

"It's fixed!" Lottie cried, outraged when Clyde pulled ahead of Mildred. "I hope he falls down and breaks his back!"

"Smart," Butcher said over and over, nodding, and Lottie knew he was imagining himself there, just as she had done. She felt a chill. He glanced at her and for a moment their eyes held—naked, scheming. They broke away simultaneously.

Mildred limped forward until it was evident each step was torture. Finally she sobbed, sank to the ground and buried her face in her hands.

Clyde ran on. It would take an act of God now to stop him. He reached the truck at twelve minutes before midnight.

For a long time neither Lottie nor Butcher moved. Neither spoke. Butcher had turned the audio off as soon as Clyde reached the truck, and now there were the usual after-game recaps, the congratulations, the helicopter liftouts of the other contestants.

Butcher sighed. "One of the better shows," he said. He was hoarse.

"Yeah. About the best yet."

"Yeah?" He sighed again and stood up. "Honey, don't bother with all this junk now. I'm going to take a shower, and then I'll help you clean up, okay?"

"It's not that bad," she said. "I'll be done by the time you're finished. Want a sandwich, doughnut?"

"I don't think so. Be right out." He left. When he came back, shaved, clean, his wet hair brushed down smoothly, the room was neat again, the dishes washed and put away.

"Let's go to bed, honey," he said, and put his arm lightly about her shoulders. "You look beat."

"I am." She slipped her arm about his waist. "We both lost."

"Yeah, I know. Next week."

She nodded. Next week. It was the best money they ever spent, she thought, undressing. Best thing they ever bought, even if it would take them fifteen years to pay it off. She yawned and slipped into bed. They held hands as they drifted off to sleep.

In order to play a sport that primarily requires hitting an object with a stick while sliding around on ice once meant you needed a climate that was sufficiently cold enough to provide, at least seasonally, reliably solid ice. Nowadays we have indoor rinks and you can play ice hockey in the desert as long as someone pays for the power and the refrigeration system works. On a planet covered with ice, hockey becomes a game of hundreds of yards rather than inches, meters become miles, and the rules can involve life and death, not just a penalty box. Václav Zajac loves the intoxicating, powerful isolation of the breakaway: no defender between him and the goal, free to skate and shoot at will, ultimately deking (originally a Canadianism for "decoying" or faking out) the goalie to score. In this particular game, both his breakaway and deke turn out to be—at the very least—dramatic.

Breakaway

George Alec Effinger

Old Number 12 stood by a port and looked down at the playing field. The port, for some reason, was shaped like the rounded rectangle of a CRT screen. It gave you the feeling that you were watching television, even while you stared out at real life. It had the effect of creating boredom and dissatisfaction, something the ship's designers never foresaw, because real life never moved so fast or so frantically as television. After thirty seconds at the port, you had a sneaking desire to change the channel. There was no way to do that, of course, and then you'd remember that you weren't watching television, that you were instead aboard an orbiting plastic and steel ball, and you were so far from home that sometimes your eyes stung with tears.

Václav Zajac, Number 12, turned away from the port. There really wasn't anything to see: a pale green-white world of ice turning in the dim light of a distant cold sun. He leaned against the bulkhead, feeling the machinery of the orbiting station thrumming in the wall at his back. He chewed his lip and stared at the deck without seeing anything in particular. He was avoiding the locker room, and he didn't want to take another glance through the port. There wasn't much else to do. That was one of the main troubles with the station: there was really nothing to do.

"Hey, Jackie," called another player. "You coming?"

"Sure," said Zajac. He didn't look up. The other man went into the locker room. Zajac studied the rippled sole of one shoe. Finally he took a long breath, exhaled slowly, and followed the other through the pastel green door.

Only the lack of personal decoration set his locker area apart from any of the others. Some of the players had adorned theirs, added bits of individuality, audio dots and holoscenes that were intended to portray something about their owners' tastes. The fact that most of these scenes were the same—running to ghostly, beckoning women apparently afflicted with respiratory difficulties—didn't diminish their value. Zajac's locker space was bare except for his uniform suit and a few toilet and training articles on the shelf. He never felt the need to express himself by decorating his person or his belongings. He believed that his personality and his essential nature were well-enough defined downstairs, on the playing field. On the ice.

Václav Zajac was right about that. There wasn't another hockey player in the Havoc Force amateur league with his reputation and statistics. He didn't need tiger stripes on his faceplate to unnerve an opposing defenseman. That defenseman was already frightened of him, and had been since before the opening face-off.

He sat on the bench in front of his locker and listened to the cheerful conversation of his teammates. They were excited and just a little artificially high-spirited. They were beginning to wind themselves tighter, to allow their controlled hysteria to get them to the competitive peak they would need to play the game down below. Zajac didn't participate in their jokes and shouts and laughter and curses. He waited quietly until he felt ready, and then he began to dress. He had always been sober, oddly silent and disturbingly distant, even as a young rookie many years before. He stood up and took a roll of broad tan adhesive bandage from the shelf. He began strapping his ankles. Around him in the locker room soap and protective cups and wet towels flew through the air. If Zajac noticed, he showed no sign. The younger men respected him, but they played around him. Their missiles defied his air space, but no one ever presumed to include him in the locker room play.

The Condors were the station's entry in the Havoc Force Hockey Association, Second Quadrant champions for the last four seasons, league champions twice in that period. Zajac was a major reason for that success. His ice time was the only real life he knew. The endless days he spent monitoring the emptiness around the frozen rock of Niflhel seemed like punishment, with the occasional reward of liberty two hundred fifty miles below, on the nightmarish surface of the little world.

The game today was against the Rome IV Stingers, a weak team from the Third Quadrant. Rome IV was an outpost halfway across the spiral from Niflhel, and the two teams had never played each other before. Zajac, as he finished taping his ankles, wasn't even curious about them. He hadn't watched any of the tapes of the Stingers' previous games. He hadn't even studied the defensemen he would be facing. It didn't make any difference who they were, he thought. When he got down there, on the familiar but deadly pale green ice, he would own the game. He would establish his dominance early, and he would skate and score at will. He told himself this over and over, in a kind of self-hypnotic way. It was as important to his readiness as his physical condition and equipment.

The ice hockey tournament had been invented by the psych maintenance division to deal with the peculiar claustrophobia that always threatened to turn into an epidemic at the isolated outposts. They couldn't prevent the panic that gripped people who felt themselves lost and permanently abandoned in space, but if the hostile environments and lonely scenes could be made more familiar, the experts said that maybe the screaming red horror would diminish and eventually all but disappear. It was a nice theory, and it even worked after a fashion. None of the hockey players, for instance, ever felt the choking terror growing in them while they glided over the ice fields of Niflhel. The game was great therapy. It was fun, there was an exciting and considerable welcome relief from the tedium of their passive military duties. Down on the ice all was well. But in the shuttle ride back to the station . . .

The temperature on the surface of Niflhel was only a little pocket change of Kelvin, just enough to register on the meters, to differentiate the dusky world from the near-absolute of the surrounding interstellar medium. The place had once been a marvelous laboratory where gases that could be liquefied under difficult circumstances on Earth were found in solid prairies of unusual ice, or pools of sluggish liquid with dreamlike properties. Niflhel would have been of immense interest to physicists and chemists except that since the expansion through the spiral, worlds of this kind had become so common they were no longer even named: silent, lifeless planets circling so far from their central sun that the stars were just a glimmer of divorced energy in the daytime darkness of the sky.

Zajac put on a thin set of long underwear, made of cotton all the way from Earth. He chose only the best when it came to his equipment. He had tried synthetic fiber underwear as a rookie and it had almost cost him his life in a game on a forgotten and nameless world in the First Quadrant. His suit's climate sensors had failed briefly. The synthetic material didn't soak up his perspiration and tended to trap body heat. Zajac had almost stifled and dehydrated within the protective armor of his game uniform.

The suits were the most sophisticated pieces of equipment the technical teams could devise. They were lightweight, made of a dynaprene material that gave almost as much freedom as everyday clothing, yet insulated and protected the wearer against the harshest environments in the spiral—or anyway against most of them. The dynaprene had a little trouble dealing with certain atmospheres of very high pressure and very low pH. But in the general realm of conditions, the suits were miracles of efficiency and comfort. Because of them, people inhabited places that were bluntly uninhabitable, a paradox the human beings resolved by ignoring it. The suits were specially modified for the athletes. They were a little larger, a little roomier, in order to fit in pads for shins, ankles, elbows, and shoulders. These fiber and foam pads were snug, comfortable, and didn't restrict movement in the least.

Clothed in the suit, Zajac sat on the bench and waited. His helmet, his gauntlets, and his skated boots still rested on the shelf. He was finished dressing and there was nothing more for him to do until it was time for the team to head for the shuttle. None of the others had even begun getting into his suit. Zajac closed his eyes and breathed slowly. He relaxed. He felt mildly happy, as though something marginally pleasant was just about to happen, like a healthy sneeze or a good yawn. He remained confident about his performance during the game, but he didn't think about it any longer.

"Jackie, the rest of you jokers, listen up." Zajac opened his eyes. The coach had come into the locker room. It must be almost time, thought

Zajac. "These guys we're playing today are basically your everyday type of clowns," said the coach. "But that doesn't mean you don't have to pay attention to what you're doing down there. They're clowns and princesses, but they've scored a few goals, too. So watch yourselves. Check them hard a few times right in the beginning, and they'll probably skate clear of you the rest of the day. All right?" There was a murmur from the younger players. Zajac had heard all of this many times before. The coach gave the same speech before every game; every other team in the association seemed to be made up of clowns and princesses.

"Any change in their lineup?" asked Moro, the Condor goalie.

"No, so just go with the game plan. Keep the puck down at their end, don't pay any attention to their crazy defense. They do that a lot, I don't know why. Maybe they think it will confuse you. It's probably why they're always losers. Almost always. So just play your own game, control the puck, move it up and put it in. Get that first goal, and they'll have to play catch-up the rest of the day. You know that you can skate rings around them, they don't have anybody who can catch even Anangi, here." There was a sharp, quick laugh from the players, and Number 44, Bashake Anangi, spat angrily. He was a Condor defenseman not famed for his winged skates.

"Anything else?" asked the coach. He didn't look like what a coach ought to look like. He didn't have a big cigar or a Condor cap on his head. He wasn't wearing an old sweatshirt or a natty suit or ancient sneakers. He wore a white lab coat with an ID badge clipped to a lapel, and a headset and microphone over his thinning blond hair. He looked more like a communications technician, and when he wasn't coaching the hockey team, that's what he was.

There was a silence. The coach looked around the room, then clapped his hands. "So let's hit the ice," he said.

Zajac stood and stretched. The others hurried to complete their dressing. He took his gauntlets and boots and helmet and walked in his stockinged feet across the carpet of the locker room to the corridor leading to the shuttlecraft. Inside the shuttle he took his place on the long padded seat. He was all alone. There was a loud humming in the shuttle; it annoyed him and he tried to block it out. He busied himself. He went to the rack of hockey sticks against the aft bulkhead and found one of his. He used a low lie Victoriaville, a number four. He carried it back to his seat and rubbed the blades of his skates against the stick, dulling them a little. You had to do this for every game; if the skates were too sharp, they tended to stick to the ice, rather than cutting and gliding. You'd have a restricted stride and a little trouble turning. On ice, on water ice back on Earth, this would be inconvenient and might cost a player and his team eventually in the final score. On Niflhel, where the ice was made of complex hydrocarbons frozen harder than steel by the fearful coldness of space, that kind of inconvenience could develop into a perilous situation. One of the secrets of the game—not much of a secret, really, because every player in the league understood it well enough—was that you had to keep moving. The weight of the person pressed the skates into the surface, the pressure melted a molecular layer of the hydrocarbon ice under the blade, just enough to allow the skate to slide along. If the skate stood there a millisecond too long, though, it froze in place and Niflhel had itself a brand new surface feature. The skates could be loosed from the boots, being held there by the same dileucithane tape that closed the uniform gauntlets and boots. But that meant the player, skateless, would have to run and slide over the ice, on the broad boot bottoms, and it was unlikely that anyone could travel that way more than three steps without falling. The layer of melted hydrocarbon ice under a human foot made virtually a frictionless surface. And a fall in that situation could prove fatal.

So the players kept moving. Even the goalies, who wouldn't see action nearby sometimes for the greater part of the game, even they skated back and forth, around and around their domains, rather than become brittle, frozen statues on the face of the little green world.

After a few minutes five other Condors filed into the shuttle. They took seats and waited. The coach didn't come with them; there wasn't a single thing he could do for the team down on the surface of Niflhel. From the station two hundred fifty miles above he could monitor the game and make decisions. The rest of the team, the substitutes, stayed behind with the coach, ready to be ferried down when they were needed. The starting six players looked at each other, just a little nervously. Zajac felt a little tension, a little tightening of his shoulders, a little tingling in his head and hands. It would have distressed a rookie, but it was vaguely pleasant to Zajac. He welcomed it. He had learned long ago to use every bit of his pregame agitation, to channel and focus it all.

"Well, Jackie, what do you think?" Zajac turned to face Gill, Number 16, the starting center. Zajac had no close friends, but he had played alongside Gill for more than five years and they had a kind of wordless communication on the ice, a coordinated effort that derived from intelligence and long experience. Conviviality counted for little on the glacial plain.

"No problem," said Zajac. His face was expressionless.

"Right," said Gill, "no problem." He seemed a little uncomfortable, as though, despite knowing Zajac's mood and manner, he wanted to make a deeper, more personal contact. "How do you feel?"

"Fine," said Zajac. "I feel good. You?"

Gill was quiet for a moment. He knew that he was being outmaneuvered. Whatever he said, Zajac would reply with just the right words to kill the conversation. Even when Zajac asked about Gill's condition, he did it in a way that demanded a meaningless answer. "Great," said Gill sadly, "really great. I got to tape." He busied himself taping his stick, winding the pearl gray dileucithane tape around the flat part of the stick's blade, just where he would want to keep the puck as he moved it down the ice toward the Stingers' goal.

The trip down took almost thirty minutes. Zajac used the time to finish checking out his suit. He put on the boots and skates, tucking the ends of the suit's legs into the high tops of the boots, then winding gray tape tightly around the ankles of the boots. Dileucithane tape had the molecules of its sticky stuff polarized on one side. When the tape was stretched tight and wrapped over itself, no man alive was strong enough to pull it apart. A weak electric current, however, applied from within the suit, released the hold and the tape became just a dull-colored length of rough cloth. There was no way to pull the boots off without first removing the tape; Zajac's foot would pull off first.

Next he checked the neoprene laces of the boots and the tape that held the skates themselves tight. In the first year of the association, players used skates brought from Earth made for use under Earthlike conditions. The rawhide thongs held moisture, froze as solid as a rope of glass, and shattered under the first application of stress. Men suffered because of that small unforeseen aspect of the eternal winter. It didn't take long, though, to find replacement materials that wouldn't be affected by the temperatures near absolute zero. Dynaprene, neoprene, and dileucithane performed perfectly. Or, at least, well enough so that no one had perished on the pale ice fields since their introduction.

Zajac nested his helmet into the locking rings around the neck of his uniform suit. He heard the buzz and click of the helmet's circuits cutting in. He saw the projection of the playing field at the top of the faceplate, a rectangular map laying on its long side with two vertical slashes for the goals and a vertical stripe for the center line. The map represented the whole field of play, which was huge, immense compared to the hockey rinks on Earth. The rectangle marked out on the surface of Niflhel measured one mile by three.

Zajac touched on the receiver and switched from one channel to another. On the first channel he heard two of his teammates talking to each other, telling grotesque stories in two languages. On the second channel there was only static; later he would be able to hear the communications of the Stingers' players, scrambled so that none of the Condors could intercept their strategy. On the third channel there was gentle music, instrumental versions of show tunes from faraway stage successes and popular entertainers. During the game on the fourth channel he would be able to hear the coach's directions; now there was only the sound of slow, regular breathing, a kind of irritating whistling, and the coach's unconscious humming. Zajac switched to the fifth channel and listened to the internal communications of the orbiting station.

A red warning light flickered on his faceplate, indicating that his suit's integrity was breached. Of course that was true, since he hadn't put on his gauntlets and closed the sleeves of the uniform. He did that, winding the dileucithane tape around his forearms. He was now sealed into the suit, and he made a quick check of the life support circuits. Every gauge showed green, healthy, fine, perfect, ready to go. Zajac clutched his stick and waited for landfall.

The shuttle set down in a great silent explosion of clouds of methane and formaldehyde liberated from the craggy face of Niflhel. The hydrocarbons sublimed instantly, invisibly, from ice to gas, leaving ringed depressions of melted frost which solidified immediately into pocked craters. Václav Zajac climbed out of the shuttle and skated away in long, lazy curves. The shuttle shook and flared and lifted back into the black sky, but he didn't watch it go. The men from the Niflhel station were delivered one by one to their starting positions on the ice. When they left the shuttle they skated around in circles, getting the feel of the hard ice again, enjoying the freedom and the peace, welcoming the change from their devastatingly dull jobs in orbit. They waited for the arrival of the Rome IV Stingers. They didn't care how long that would take.

"Here they come," said a voice over Zajac's receiver. He looked up and saw another shuttle—or maybe the same one, he couldn't tell.

"Okay, boys, line up," said Gill, who was the team's captain. "Niflhel Station, this is Gill. Plug in the position markers, please."

"Right, Maxie," said a voice from the station. Zajac's faceplate lit up with seven colored dots, laid over the rectangular map of the playing field. Five of the dots were green, and represented the positions of Zajac's teammates. One dot was orange, resting on the center stripe, and marked the puck. One dot was fiery red, and showed Zajac's own relative position. When the Stingers hit the ice, they would show up as blue dots. The system was necessary because for extended stretches of play some of the players would be out of sight of each other.

Even with the suit lamps and the photo amplifiers in the helmets, the upper limit of visibility was slightly under twelve hours. The game lasted fourteen hours by the clock on the orbiting station. A skater's endurance was figured at about eight hours; after that his judgment and precision began to suffer, to deteriorate so rapidly that very shortly he had difficulty merely keeping himself upright. It was the coach's job to keep track of his players' condition by monitoring their vital signs and analyzing their performance during the game. Substitutions were made carefully, protecting the players and preventing the other team from seizing an advantage. The coach's role was vital. The game was more than a battle to wrestle a neoprene puck into the other team's cage; it was a deft balance of strength and conditioning, of skill and shrewd guesswork and decision.

Václav Zajac skated in the twilight at his wing position. He was stationed at a point one mile from his team's goal, where Moro patrolled the six-foot-wide net, and a half mile from the center line. He was at one wing, a quarter mile from Gill at center, a half mile from Pete Soniat at the other wing. A half mile behind him were the two defensemen, Seidl and Brickman. He saw their green dots on his faceplate, wavering about as they skated around waiting for the game to begin. The orange puck still rested at center ice. There would be no face-off as such; referees were of little value on a playing field of three square miles. They couldn't hope to follow all of the action and catch all of the penalties. The game would begin when a signal bell sounded in their helmets, triggered by an association observer and impartial umpire aboard the orbiting station. As for fouls—there weren't any. The play sometimes got a little testy and just a little physical, but real fights were infrequent because the suits were so well padded and insulated that a punch did little damage.

The bell rang. Gill shot off his mark toward the stationary puck. His opposite number on the Rome IV team raced toward him. Zajac and Soniat angled toward the center, skating easily. There was no chatter on the first channel; Zajac switched to channel four, to hear the coach. "All right, boys," said the coach, "let's go, let's go." The coach didn't have anything terribly cogent to suggest yet; it was all cheerleading until somebody got hold of the puck. That wouldn't be for a few minutes, because Gill had a half mile to skate before he could begin to locate it.

"They're fanning out, Jackie," said the coach. When he had something. important to say, he could broadcast on both channels one and four.

"Right, I hear you, coach," said Zajac. He saw on his faceplate the rapid movement of the Stinger wings heading out from their starting position. They were going to flank the Condors' front line, gambling, banking that their center would come up with the puck and then they'd be past the Condors' first line of defense without a struggle. Of course, if Gill reached the puck first the Stingers would be in bad shape. "Pete," called Zajac to his other wing, "what do you want to do?"

"What's it look like, Maxie?" asked Soniat.

"Too soon," said Gill, huffing a little as he sprinted toward the center line.

"Maxie has it," said the coach calmly. "The projection is that he'll reach the puck forty-four seconds before their boy."

"We'll be through them," said Soniat.

"Sixteen strong side," said the coach, calling the play.

"Okay," said Soniat.

"Right," said Gill.

"Did you hear that?" asked Zajac. The two defensemen behind him answered that they did.

"That's assuming Maxie doesn't fall on his face getting there," said Moro from his lonely goalie post.

"Uh," snorted Gill.

The two wingers, Zajac and Soniat, were converging on center ice. When the three Condor players got sufficiently close together, they would appear as one large blue blur on the faceplates of the Stingers. The puck would be a muted glow submerged beneath them. One of the Condors would carry the puck toward the Stinger goal and the others would swing away, but it would be a moment before the dots on the faceplate maps would separate enough for the Stingers' defensemen to know who had the puck and in what direction he was going. Those seconds would mean a considerable head start. Under normal circumstances it would be almost impossible for the Stingers to chase down the puck carrier. Only superb play and a good deal of luck would save them. The Condors would converge again in the area of the goal, so the Stinger goalie would not have advance warning of where the puck was coming from. He would see three streaking Condor skaters, and have no notion which man would be the attacker. They would come at him from straight on and from oblique angles to the right and left, and he would be helpless until the final instant of the approach. Then everyone watching the game would learn what the poor man's reactions were like.

Soniat would take the puck off to the left, crossing the routes of Gill and Zajac. The three would weave their way down the ice, skating apart as far as an eighth of a mile and then returning, passing the puck to each other whenever one of the Stinger defensemen seemed to analyze the pattern too well.

The play was a good one. The trouble was that it just never got off the ground.

"Damn it to hell," muttered Gill in Zajac's ear.

"What's wrong?" asked the coach.

"The damn puck isn't here."

"Oh boy," murmured Seidl, "he missed it."

"I was off by less than a hundred yards," said Gill. "Get moving, Maxie!"

"Too late, he's got it," said Gill. "Look out, here he comes."

"We see him," said Zajac. Because he and Soniat had been closing in, they weren't far from the Stinger center's path. Gill hooked around in vain pursuit, but Zajac closed in on an angle that would intercept the puck carrier before either of the Rome IV wingers could arrive to help out.

"Take it away, take it away," called Moro. Calling out encouragement was about all he had to do at this stage of the game.

"I'll get the son of a buck," said Gill. He was still trailing Zajac, who was shortening the distance between himself and the puck carrier. After a minute he announced that he had visual contact with the Stinger center.

"Crease the bastard!" cried the coach. The game transformed him from a pleasant, amiable technician into a half-crazy commander who lusted to get out on the ice himself.

"Exactly what I'm going to do," said Zajac. Some players would have skated alongside the opposing player, trying to fish the puck away with swipes of the stick. Zajac's technique was a little more direct, and accounted for his intimidating reputation. The two men skated directly at each other; for a while it seemed that the Stinger center didn't know Zajac was coming. Then he must have been warned, because he looked up and jerked as if startled. He began skating away from Zajac, but Zajac was faster. He closed the gap between them, coming in from the Stinger's side. He let himself glide past the man a few feet, planted one skate, and swung around. Zajac took off after the puck carrier and caught up to him in five or six powerful strides. They skated silently together, matched stroke for stroke. The Stinger protected the puck by changing his stick to his other hand, keeping the puck out of range of a slashing reach by Zajac, but that wasn't Zajac's plan. He, too, transferred his stick to his outside hand. He raised his left arm to shoulder height, then brought it down and back, catching the Stinger skater in the chest with his elbow. The man leaned backward, arms flailing, off balance. Zajac gave him a slight push, and the nameless man toppled over on the ice. Zajac slapped the puck away a few feet, skated after it, then changed direction and began cutting smoothly back toward Maxie Gill, the center line, and—one-and-a-half miles beyond—the Stinger goal.

"You got it?" asked the coach.

"Sure," said Zajac, not even breathing hard, "no problem."

"No problem," said Gill.

"Way to go, Jackie," said Brickman.

"Sixteen strong side?" asked Soniat.

"As before," said the coach. "Nice playing, Jackie." Zajac aimed for his rendezvous with Gill and Soniat.

The play developed exactly as it had so many times on the coach's animated board. Zajac brought the puck up, fed it to Gill. Zajac crossed over to the left wing, Gill continued up the middle, then passed the puck to Soniat. Soniat drove toward the goal, and Gill slipped into the right wing. Soniat crossed left, abandoned the puck to Zajac, and Zajac skated toward Gill. The puck leapt from blade to blade, and the puck carrier swooped and changed. The three men wove a braided pattern in the ancient chill of Niflhel. Soon the Stingers were faced with a problem. Only two defensemen, and then the goalie, stood between the three Condors and the first score of the game. The Stingers would have to make a choice, and a speculative one at that. It would be a poor decision for both defensemen to gang up on a single charging Condor lineman, so each picked one of the three and intercepted. One of the Rome IV skaters went after Gill, and the other decided upon Soniat. At that precise moment, however, Zajac had the puck on the right wing, and undeterred he sped through the last of the Condor defense, unhindered now toward the goal.

"Nothing to it now, Jackie," said Gill, a little short of breath.

"Breakaway, breakaway!" chanted the coach. He had offered a minimum of thoughtful guidance, but so far this game hadn't needed any.

"No one to stop you now, Jackie," said Soniat. "We checked these fools hard. You're in the clear."

Alone. All alone on the pale green ice, beneath the unwavering stars of a stranger world, Zajac skated, exhilarated, cheered and warmed by his own skill and luck and daring. A little over a mile to the goal, according to the rough estimate he could make from his faceplate map. Then would come the final dramatic thrill of deking the Stinger goalie out of position, the silent man-on-man confrontation and the slamming home of the puck, the flash of the neoprene stick and the clean flight of the puck into the corner of the net. He pictured the goalie lying sprawled vainly across the ice, and Zajac celebrating all alone, all alone until Gill and Soniat joined him for the cross-country journey back into position for the next face-off. . . .

All alone. It was the time of the game that Václav Zajac loved the best. He luxuriated in the feeling of solitude, of purposeful activity, of being the focus of energy in the dynamic effort. He leaned forward and skated with long, powerful strides. He looked around him to the close horizon: there was nothing to see, no other people, no physical features of dramatic interest. The photo amps in his helmet showed him just smooth glass underfoot and velvet sky above, the gliding orange puck and the diamond chip stars. This was exaltation. Perhaps this had always been the utter joy of the sport, since the days when Indians skated on frozen lakes with the ribs of elks bound to their feet. When Zajac had been a small boy he had played shinny, battling a small rubber ball across the frozen river of his native Moravia. He had learned the game, learned the techniques, subjected himself to the necessary conditioning, accepted the demands and rewards, at an early age. Now, separated from those games by many years and uncountable miles, he was still getting the same intoxicating sensation as he ripped the puck away from the other team and set out alone toward the goal. He was inexorable. He was overpowering. He was alone.

He skated with his head up, his knees slightly bent. He kept the puck ahead of him, moving it forward with little taps, first to the left, then to the right. The feeling of pure speed was like a passionate embrace. He wanted it to go on and on, never to end, and it wouldn't end, not until he climaxed the overwhelming surge down the ice with the conquering drive into the goal. Even then the excitement would linger, fading a little of course, but the giddy arousal would remain, spoiled only by the arrival of his teammates and their chattering congratulations. That always ruined it a little for Zajac, but it never destroyed the experience completely. The race was always his, and he lived for it alone. Now, on the home ice of Niflhel, he exulted.

"Let's go!" said Brickman, who was miles behind, completely out of the action, who had nothing to do but skate about somewhat bored and watch Zajac's green dot streak toward the goal on his faceplate.

"Okay, Jackie, okay!" said the coach.

Zajac grimaced and changed the channel. He listened to the soft, lilting, excruciating music for a while.

He was thinking about the move he was going to use on the Stinger goalie. His mind wasn't on his skating, on the immediate condition of the playing field. He didn't see the frozen ripple, the small raised scar on the glacial floor. He didn't know it was there until his skate hit it with a numbing shock. There was a raw grinding feeling, and then Zajac was flying flat in space, falling. He landed heavily on his left side, his left arm pinned under him. There was a noiseless push of liberated gases; it was as jarring as a blow to the jaw in a beer-soaked brawl. Then everything was still. Everything was very quiet. Everything waited. Zajac was stunned and probably dying, but he didn't know it yet. He was caught in a billion-year-old trap, and he hadn't even heard it spring shut. He would have to learn the rules one by one, the hard way, and if he was going to survive he had no time to lose.

"Oh, hell," he said. He took a deep breath.

No one answered. No one wondered what had happened.

"I guess I'm all right," he said.

No one asked him what he meant.

"Coach?" he said.

The black coldness waited.

"I fell pretty hard out here but I'm okay. I can feel the puck. I'm lying right on top of it. Give me a minute to catch my breath." He felt warm. Actually, as he calmed down a little, he felt hot. His suit wasn't cooling him off enough. He wondered what was wrong. He tried to sit up, to take a quick inventory of his monitoring systems. He learned with an ice-cold shiver of fear that his helmet was frozen fast to the rock-solid ice. He nearly dislocated a shoulder trying to raise his head.

Zajac was afraid. He had never before felt this particular kind of fear, this awareness of the nearness of death. It was so close, the end of his life, that he could not see how he could avert it. He knew he couldn't deke death with a good feint in one direction, then go skating off free and clear in another. It would take more than that. He didn't know what it would take, and that thought terrified him. He needed help, and that thought mortified him. But his terror was greater.

"Coach?" he called. He waited in vain for a reply. He switched channels. "Maxie? Pete?" There wasn't even the sound of static. He went back and forth through the five channels: there were four channels of utter, terminal silence, but channel three was coming through clearly. The damned music, sweet strings and a binging triangle playing a sprightly march. It was a paralyzing insult added to his calamity.

"Hey, coach!" Zajac screamed. His voice sounded raw and harsh to himself, and the effect was ominous. He was in trouble, that was definite, but he was ashamed that he was losing control so quickly. He forced himself to calm down, to think. He carefully appraised his situation.

Evidently he wasn't receiving his teammates' communications. That didn't mean, though, that they weren't receiving his. "Coach, Maxie, Pete, if anybody can hear me, I had a tumble and I'm frozen onto the ground. My helmet and my shoulder. I landed on a couple of the trade-off buttons and they melted the ice, and then I got caught in it. I can't hear a thing. I can't hear you, and I can't see where you are. My faceplate map isn't functioning. I don't know what to do. You're going to have to come get me, because I can't move. I only have one arm free, and the trade-off buttons are going to be overworked, trying to compensate for the coldness of the ground. So hurry." He stopped talking. He felt a little foolish, not knowing if anyone could hear him.

What next? He didn't know. The climate control would be raising the temperature of his suit as the internal heat bled away. Eventually the heating unit would fail, and then it wouldn't be long before Zajac, suit and all, would be lifeless solid human ice. He didn't know how much longer the suit's unit could function.

As he waited, an unpleasant thought returned again and again: his only hope was that he'd be found and rescued in time. The prime concern, therefore, was that if the others weren't receiving his calls, and if neither his suit nor the puck were sending out signals, they would never stumble across him in time. And stumble across him is what they'd do—eventually. If they ever found him at all, they'd trip across his marble-stiff corpse in the dark.

There was no way of judging how quickly the time passed. The sun—the dim, distant star that barely held Niflhel in its weak grasp—cast no shadows on the enemy ice. Zajac couldn't see that sun from his sprawled position, so he wouldn't be able to observe it as it cut its way through the strange constellations. He doubted if he'd be alive long enough to notice much stellar movement in any case. There was nothing else within sight that could help him in any way. There was nothing else at all but ice, endless ice, murderous ice.

Zajac waited and studied himself closely for any sign of panic. The notion that at the end, as he began to feel the sting of death creeping along his rigid limbs, he might lose control of his mind was more repellent to him than the threat of death. He feared madness more. Though his suffering would be limited by the mercilessness of the environment, he swore that he would choose an immediate end by his own hand rather than descend muttering and weeping into insanity. It occurred to him that his promise was one he might not want to keep at that final instant, or even be able to remember.

There were many things to regret while he waited between life and death. He thought about his joyless childhood, about the unkindness he had often shown others, about the broken vows and broken dreams, about all the things of a lifetime that are without meaning and are given importance only by an ultimate realization that they can now never be corrected. Zajac felt contempt for his own remorse, because he knew how shallow he was. Even as the tears slipped from his eyes, he laughed skeptically. "You don't mean a word of it, Jackie," he whispered. "Try to die like a man." Whatever that meant. . . .

This gelid vista would be the last thing he would see: a jagged horizon, low ridges of pallid green shining in his suit's lamplight, ice of a color he had seen sometimes in a young woman's eyes, a sky as black and empty and devoid of hope as Hell—and wasn't Hell described just like this? A lake of ice, rather than pits of flame? And Lucifer frozen in the middle of it, immobile and bitter? The comparison made Zajac laugh aloud, and it was not a healthy laughter, with just the faintest tinge of hysteria. It brought his wandering thought to a sudden focus. His experiment with fancy ended abruptly.

Was there anything that he could do to release the helmet from the tenacious ice? His hockey stick lay on the rough surface not far from his outstretched right hand, within reach. Zajac didn't believe he could use it to chip the helmet free; the neoprene was tough, but not as hard as the ice. Still, he reached out and grasped the end of the blade, then drew the stick near. He would never be able to use it to pry the helmet loose, either. The stick would snap like a dry bone.

If he were to live, to free himself from the frozen tomb, he needed an audacious idea. In order to find the key, he needed all the coolness of thought on which he prided himself. And, he admitted, he might need all the crazy reasoning of desperation, as well. In the same way that he might have proceeded to fix a leaking faucet at home, he took it by the numbers.

How could he get free? By removing himself from the ice, of course. How could that be done? By getting rid of the ice, by breaking it or melting it. Could he break it? He had already decided the answer to that was no.

That left melting.

What could melt the ice? Under these circumstances, only the heat inside his suit. The warmth from the trade-off buttons was melting the ice in that immediate area, leaving a bowl-like depression under his left side, but his helmet was too far away and there was no way of delivering the heat from between his shoulders to the necessary point.

Was there another way of transferring heat from inside his suit to the place where the helmet was welded to the ground?

Zajac didn't have an immediate answer. More accurately, at first he didn't want to examine the only solution that did present itself.

"Well," he murmured after a moment, "there is a way." He had a flickering, half-formed notion.

It was unpleasant. It was very unpleasant.

The idea grew, and Zajac realized that there was every reason to believe it would work. But the more clearly he understood what had to be done, the more grotesque and awful it seemed. Yet it was a choice between sacrifice and certain death. Rational thought demanded—

Zajac pressed the button in the handle of his hockey stick. The dileucithane tape that wound around the blade immediately lost its adhesiveness. With his free hand he removed the relaxed tape from the stick. Now it was ready to be used again, and he was careful not to foul it in tangles because he would never be able to untwist it, and that would be the end of him. He transferred an end of the tape to his left hand and clumsily wrapped the length of it around and around his right arm, just above the tape that sealed his right gauntlet to his sleeve. He pulled the tape as tight as he could, so tight that he knew he was shutting off the circulation in his arm.

It occurred to Zajac that if he managed to save himself and then stay alive until he could be rescued, he might look back on this nightmare and realize that there had always been a simple and easy way to solve the crisis. If there were he couldn't see it now, and as he became more frantic he cared less about what he would think in the future. The terrible present overshadowed all that. Maybe he would curse himself for a fool. Maybe his teammates would be shocked by the means he had selected to save himself, when there was some other obvious method he had overlooked. Zajac's mouth was very dry, and there was a loud buzzing in his head that distracted his attention. He was near emotional collapse, and he put the thought of hypothetical painless answers in the back of his mind. He had not been able to find one, and so he was compelled to follow the path he had chosen.

His right hand tingled with a myriad sharp pinpricks. He closed his eyes tight and tried to calm his agonized thoughts. The pain in his hand became a throbbing that he couldn't ignore. Needles of pain stabbed up his arm from his fingertips to his shoulder. It was time to act, but the process of summoning courage and strength was more difficult than he had imagined. "Come on, Jackie," he whispered, "just do it. Do it or you'll die right here."

His left thumb found the button on his right gauntlet. He pressed it, giving as he did an odd, high-pitched cry. The tape on the gauntlet went dead. He unwrapped it quickly and flung it away. He ripped the gauntlet off with his left hand and shrieked as the unbearable cold attacked his exposed hand. He grabbed at the back of his helmet, twisting as much as he could so that he could reach the frozen bond. The remaining warmth in his freezing hand turned the ice to thin and poison gas. He rolled over, and his helmet was free. He sobbed loudly and rose to his knees. His right hand remained on the ice where he had rested.

Zajac got to his feet, staggered, stumbled, fell again to his knees. He felt dreamlike, a little dazed. He felt no pain; that meant that he was in shock. He was alive, but he didn't know for how long. The ragged end of his forearm was exposed beyond the tourniquet of tape, and the killing cold would soon crawl through his veins like serpent's venom. He was very cold. He looked back to where he had lain prisoner. His right hand, his strong hand, was blanched white as new snow in the glare of his lamp. The thumb had snapped off. The light flashed from a gold ring on the fourth finger. Zajac's eyes opened wide and he stared, sickened. He clutched his ruined arm to his chest. Suddenly, like a vast and overpowering expulsion of evil, he vomited inside his helmet.

With an effort he got to his feet again, a bit unsteady on his skates. Freeing the helmet had been only part of the problem, although he hadn't wanted to think about the rest until now. He was faced with the difficulty of staying alive until he could find the other players. Evidently they couldn't find him, or they would already have come to his aid. His uniform suit wasn't transmitting its signal. The puck, though, ought not to have been affected. He remembered, however, that he had been on top of it the entire time. It was likely that its position had just reappeared on the faceplate maps of both the Condors and the Stingers. If Zajac were lucky, they'd all be sprinting toward him that very instant, and they'd be there to call for help in a few minutes.

If he weren't lucky, of course, the puck was as lost as he, and therefore he'd have to find his own salvation. He grimaced. That was the way it had always been, the way he had always preferred. He was too lightheaded from shock and loss of blood to recall how only a short time before he had rejected that delusion.

In the single-mindedness of his condition, Zajac decided to head for the Stinger goal, the nearest place where he could be certain of finding another person. He tried to find traces of his passage across the ice before his accident, to get an idea of the direction of the goal. The ice was so hard that his tracks were almost invisible, but he caught them in the oblique beam of his lamp. He saw the small wrinkle of ice that had caused his fall, and he mouthed a vicious Slovak curse. He picked a place on the horizon, a tiny landmark of three sharp spires of ice, and skated weakly toward it. He estimated that the goal should be only a bit more than a half mile beyond it.

His right arm, from the shoulder to the torn end, felt paradoxically warm. The rest of the body was colder than before, and he shook with chills. He tried not to think about the loss of his hand, but the image of it lying abandoned on the ice kept occurring to him, and he had to fight down new sickness again and again.

After fifty yards he realized that he was carrying his hockey stick. "Stupid," he said to himself. He dropped it to the ground, and then came to a halt. "What I ought to have is the damn puck." The puck may or may not have been transmitting. If it were, it would give the others his position. It was worth taking along. He bent down and picked up his stick, then turned and went back for the puck. It took him several minutes to find it; he spent the whole time muttering angrily. When he located the puck he started off again toward the Stinger goal, holding his stick left-handed, stick-handling the puck across the ice. He was too confused to realize that he could simply have carried the puck in his left hand, that he didn't need to obey the rules of hockey: for Václav Zajac, that game ought to have been over. But his thoughts were sluggish and wrapped in a kind of muffling peace. At intervals a great, sharp, piercing pain broke through the fog, the first tentative bits of the massive anguish to come. Clumsily, holding the hockey stick in the crook of his right elbow and guiding it with his left hand, Zajac maneuvered the puck toward the indifferent horizon.

Zajac wandered in the dream delirium that accompanies serious bodily trauma. He patted the puck along, directing all of his attention to that small chore, forgetting for the moment what had happened to him and where he was going. The only thing that seemed to matter was nudging that neoprene puck forward in a straight line. At one point he assembled his senses enough to ask himself why this task was so vital. He had no ready response. It had something to do with the game. He recalled the game well enough, and the team and the station. He tried to imagine what everyone was doing back aboard the station. He wondered if they were following his progress, if they were excited or concerned or completely bored. The game must mean very little to the others aboard the station, he realized. To them it was only a pattern of glowing points of color on a two-dimensional map. How involved could they be with that? The action was rapid, as the orange dot sped toward one end of the rectangle or the other. But there was no indication that these points of light even presented living players. As far as the people on the station knew, the hockey team may never actually have been delivered to the surface of Niflhel. The games might really be played at a keyboard console in another room.

If that were true, though, Zajac mused, why did he hurt so terribly? And what the hell was he doing?

The numbing clouds in his mind dispersed to several bright, clean brass notes. It was the music again on channel three. This time, however, Zajac welcomed it; it was reassurance that he wasn't alone in the world. He had begun to feel like the last survivor of his race, or like a solitary spirit of the cosmos awaiting physical reality. He listened to an appalling trumpet improvisation based on the Horn Call from *Siegfried*. In addition to the trumpet there was a piano, a snare drum, a string bass, a vibraharp played with a heavy hand, and a guitar. The music pulled Zajac along, and he was grateful for it. Utter silence would have killed him, would have persuaded him that he was tired, that he shouldn't bother to go on, that an attempt to prolong his life was an affront to the entire entropic basis of the universe. But human beings had shouldered aside that silence and filled the space with sappy music, and that accomplishment heartened Zajac. He would not surrender until he, too, had made a mark equal to that trumpet solo.

Less than a quarter mile from his goal the agony dispelled all the soft sleepy thoughts. He saw and felt with a clarity that unnerved him. He was isolated as few people ever had been. He had been singled out, he was marked, and he had been made ready for death. His futile struggles were worse than useless—they were humiliating. How could Václav Zajac believe that he had the resources to repel all that a hostile world chose to throw at him? It was arrogance of the sort that hastened death.

Movement caught his eye. He looked up from the ice and saw a man in the green and white uniform suit of the Rome IV Stingers about a hundred yards away. It was their goalie. The man waved at him. Whether the goalie was signaling concern or boastful challenge Zajac couldn't tell. Even if the receiver in his helmet were functioning, the two men wouldn't have been able to communicate. Zajac took a better grip on his hockey stick and skated for the net. He was so dazed that his highest priority was scoring the goal. He forgot his own terrible condition. He slanted over on a path that would take him past the goal net at about a forty-five degree angle. He didn't worry about rocketing the puck past the goalie on the first pass; he wanted to get a look at the man's moves, his defensive tendencies.

Zajac's eyes tried to peer through a red haze that exploded into golden points of light. He heard his own heartbeat and the roaring of his blood, and the noise bore the hollow echoes heard usually only in dreams and drunkenness. The world seemed to pulse around him, to grow larger and then shrink so there was barely room for Zajac to breathe. In all the universe there was only Zajac's troubled brain, his bewildered senses, and the unwanted freight of ghastly pain. His terror had dissipated, replaced first by fatigue, then by mindlessness, finally by a growing resentment. His anger was directed entirely toward the Stinger goalie, whose duty it was to thwart him. Zajac desperately needed to slam the puck home, but now he doubted if he was strong enough to accomplish it.

Two familiar skaters in Condor uniforms approached him from the left wing. "Maxie, Pete," he said, sighing. He left the puck on the ice: he didn't need it any longer. They had found him.

Zajac skated in a wide loop toward the goal, then toppled forward. He sank to his knees, blinded by the throbbing pain. It was now a rhythmic beating that filled his entire consciousness. He stood again, unaware that he did, and he moved blindly over the ice. He cried softly to himself, and in a short while the pain subsided. It didn't vanish completely, but the hammering was pushed down to a manageable level, and allowed Zajac to clear his head.

He looked around and saw the goalie, who seemed unusually intent on Zajac. It had been compassion, then, that the man had been expressing. That made Zajac feel good. He expected to see the Stinger player crouched, wound tight, motionless as a stalking cat waiting for the first glimpse of the puck. Instead he was moving slowly over the ice, toward Zajac. Zajac waved his left arm wildly, ignoring the increase in pain, trying to tell the foolish goalie that everything was all right, that the worst had happened and Zajac was no longer worried, that the goalie had better tend to his own troubles because Gill and Soniat were speeding toward the open net, passing the puck between them. Zajac, not thinking clearly, tried to shout, "Get back to the net, you damn fool!" The effort cost him, and he was struck down by an angry slash of pain. He lay still for a moment, an indefinite length of time. When his awareness returned, the goalie was only fifteen feet from him. Soniat had one arm in the air, Gill had the puck on his stick, in front of the goal. He did not take the shot. He swooped by and swung around, toward Zajac.

Zajac smiled placidly to himself. He rose to his knees, and he knew then that he was exhausted, used up. He might never skate away from that spot. He leaned on his stick and watched. He tried to see the face of the Stinger goalie through the man's faceplate, but it was obscured. Zajac listened to the music; it was partially drowned out by the drumming in his head. Gill skated close by, and Zajac wanted to wave but he couldn't. Gill dropped the puck by Zajac's side. It skidded a few inches and came to a stop against his knee. The goalie was bending forward, reaching out a hand, helpless, perhaps frightened. Gill was gesturing to Soniat, evidently suddenly aware of Zajac's desperate state. Soniat skated toward them. Gill pointed first to Zajac, then into the black sky. Zajac nodded; yes, yes, he understood, they were coming for him.

Zajac was fading. He wondered idly, as if he had no personal stake in the answer, if the shuttle would arrive in time. He looked up at the stars, then at Gill, then at the puck beside him. He pushed the puck with his stick, more than slapped it, awkwardly, from his kneeling position. An angry noise began to burr in his head. Gill was waving an arm wildly but Zajac never took his gaze from the puck. It slid straight and true for the far side of the empty cage, and it seemed to take forever to cross the distance. It skimmed over the victorious ice, and as Zajac struggled to clear his vision, the puck came to rest at last, home in the corner of the goal.

Freerunning and trainjumping—high-risk urban games of a future in which Seattle has highly efficient mass transit—become popular, if illegal, sports for teens in the world of "Kip, Running." But some things never change. Whether it is street-racing hot rodders in an era when hydrocarbon-fueled vehicles are common, slam dunking in the neighborhood gym, making the game-winning goal, hitting a home run, or dashing through danger like these kids—sometimes you want more than an adrenaline high or even the thrill of winning, you want the attention and admiration of a certain special someone.

Kip, Running

Genevieve Williams

The runners are lithe and young. None are older than sixteen. Nothing about their hair or clothing dangles in excess, though they ornament themselves in other ways: hair cut in patterns like ornamental lawns, tint cascading through the patterns like advertising. Tattoos adorn them like jewelry or ripple across their bodies like silk scarves, wet and shining in the omnipresent April rain.

Kip, small and subtle, gathers with the rest of them on top of the platform shelter at Pike Station, 120 feet above the Street. There are fourteen runners besides herself, eying her and each other as though plotting how best to throw their competition off a building. Like her, they're masked and mirrored: a combination of camouflaged clothing, surveillance-reflective skins, and sensor-scrambling biosign suppressors will make watchful eyes slide right off them. Trainjumping is illegal, as are most of the other things runners do to win a race. Freerunning, bubble-riding, running along slidewalk rails—all of it.

Johnny has the starting gun. His silver, bullet-shaped dirigible—one of very few allowed in Seattle airspace, Johnny is a rich kid—is moored nearby, ready to carry him and assorted hangers-on, hollabacks, and boytoys to the finish point atop Northgate Research Center, some eight miles away. Lily is among the girlfriends, bottle-redhead, dressed in green. She's there for Narciso, but Kip pretends Lily's there for her.

"'Kay," Johnny says. "Rules, you know 'em: no driving, no fares. No throwing the competition off a maglev, skyscraper, airship, bubblevator, or taxicab. You run or you freeride. No exceptions." A high-pitched whine emanates from the tracks below, announcing the impending arrival of the northbound to Seattle Center. "First to reach the finish point wins. Wait for the flash." Johnny raises his right hand above his head. There's a black oblong shape in it, gleaming wet: not a real gun, but a flashbox that makes a hell of a bang when it goes off. Their eyes are pinned to it, and Johnny grins: he sincerely loves this shit.

The train arrives. Johnny presses the firing button. Something bright pops out the top of the gun like a muzzle-flash, and the bang cuts through the noise echoing up the city canyons: the whine of the maglevs, the hiss and patter of the rain, and all the celebratory racket of a Friday night.

Almost as one, the runners leap from the shelter roof. When the train leaves the station, they'll be on it, heading for the labyrinthine transfer station beneath the eye of the ancient, decaying Space Needle.

Kip, though, leaps extra far, vaulting the train entirely to drop fifty feet into a different, dirtier, older rail system. She knows the city's interconnected transit systems like the veins on the backs of her hands; she knows a better route than the one the others will take.

In freefall, she realizes she's not alone. Narciso has taken the plunge with her.

Lily wasn't in Kip's class, in any sense of the word. Kip knew this instinctively, if not logically, and it was not simply a matter of their never encountering one another in school, or in parties, or in games, or in any of the other locales where the ten-to-sixteens of the city or the world might find themselves. Lily sang full-throated arias with almost purely natural ability, serenading Narciso and the other runners at the afterparties; Kip's favorite singers owed their politics, songwriting, and gullet-scraping hollers to a guy from Kip's great-grandmother's generation named Jello Biafra. Lily read books with titles like *The Importance of Being Earnest* and *The Life and Adventures of Nicholas Nickleby*, seemed to understand them, and looked down her nose at the know-along adaptations they did in school. Kip read, too, but none of her friends knew it, and nothing any teacher would assign. Lily did light bloodborne intoxicants, but nothing more. Kip bought blackmarket ID masks and lived with the resulting sensory deprivation in order to take advantage of their considerable benefits. Upper city versus understory; Kip knew the distinctions as only a fifteen-year-old could. She and Lily never should have met, never should have known of one another's existence.

Lily stood out at the races. She might have anyway, but in addition to pale skin unmarked by tattoos or scars accidental or deliberate, long hair in a cascade of sculpted false red ringlets that nonetheless looked absolutely right on her, and a wardrobe more confident than her age would suggest, she moved in stark contrast to the runners' light quickness. Graceful as they, she possessed a slow languor that made Kip's skin prickle with unaccustomed heat.

There were plenty of good freerunners in Seattle, but Narciso, on whose arm Lily arrived one night like a movie queen, was the only one her own age who Kip had never beaten.

That night, Lily looked at Kip with wide brown eyes. Kip could not look away. She felt exactly as though she had leaped from a platform with no train to catch her.

Kip spreads her arms. Wings like a flying squirrel's patagium unfurl to slow her descent. To her left, Narciso's doing the same thing, except with a contraption that looks something like a giant umbrella.

The crosstown pulls in below them, slower and easier to time than a maglev. It's still a near thing. This system isn't on the maglev's schedule, which is perfectly optimized to shuttle uptown commuters, who never come below the eightieth story if they can help it, to their hilltop enclaves. Runners trying this very trick have been known to be crushed under the steel wheels. Trainrunning isn't a sport for the slight of heart.

But she lands on the train car's wet roof without incident, tucking her arms close to her chest to draw in the wings, and dropping monkeylike to the car's roof. Her bare toes cling like a gecko's as the crosstown departs with a squeal and an ancient, polluting roar.

Narciso is one car down, his slippers and gloves gripping the surface. He grins at her, slick black lenses shiny over his eyes, and peels one hand away to wave. Kip doesn't wave back.

■ ■ ■

Kip discovered trainjumping when she was eight, on a rare night out on the Street with her mother, her aunt, her grandmother, and her older sister. Her mother held her hand from the funicular station at the bottom of Queen Anne all the way to the dinner theater by the canal. The Street's cracks spread in intertwingled spiderwebs, a beautifully incomprehensible interaction of weather and upheaval and wear. Kip sought sense in them, but found only detritus: weeds pushing through the cracks with the stupendous determination of several millions of years of evolution; the last fragmented degradations of a thousand kinds of trash dropped thoughtlessly from uptown, biodegrading noiselessly in the depths of the Street.

Kip ignored the dinner and the show, her mind playing in fascinated obsession with that lattice of cracked asphalt. The lines that joined, separated, and reconnected further than she could see were the city in miniature: the train tracks, the slidewalk routes, the carefully circumscribed way to get from her family's understory apartment to the gymnasium where she went for face time with her schoolmates. The lines had no beginning and no end. They admitted deviation.

As they waited for the funicular after the show, Kip looked up. This station was the end of the line, open to the world above all the way to the sky, though it was impossible to tell whether those tiny lights were stars, or just the illuminations of uptown. Kip stared unblinking past the edge of the platform shelter, willing them to twinkle, until her eyes stung.

The train rolled in with much creaking of brakes and ancient cables. The doors opened, spilling light onto the tilted platform, though no passengers: no one came to the Street at this time of night.

The darkness above deepened in its contrast to the fluorescent light from inside the car. An even darker shadow flickered across the narrow space between the platform shelter and the car.

Kip might have imagined it; except, when they reached the stop halfway up Queen Anne, where they would take the slidewalk home to what Kip's grandmother called their lower-lower-middle-class apartment, there was another flicker. It passed from the top of the car to the platform shelter, and in the late-night silence Kip was positive she heard the light patter of running feet.

"Come along, Kip," her mother said, because even this far above the Street, it wasn't safe after dark. Shining multifaceted orbs, like the eyes of giant flies, floated in the dark, watching them and everyone else. Except that shadow that had passed and gone so quickly that Kip still was not sure she had seen it, despite seeing it twice.

Kip jumped her first train three years later, and met her first fellow runner two weeks after that, and thence entered into the secret culture that ran above and across the rails and rooftops of every major city in the world. It carried routes, schedules, secret passages, and jackable doors in its collective memory and traded in illegal masks, physical and chemical, to hide itself from the constant observers Kip had never really noticed in her life until she spotted something they hadn't seen. It had been going on for decades, as every metropolis of half a million or more became a tightly interconnected lattice of highly efficient mass transit routes, and simultaneously built up, up, up. Every city was a game of *Chutes and Ladders*—the game Kip played at the overly bright, excessively padded gymnasium—writ large.

Kip's clinging to the roof of the crosstown and feeling pretty good; from the look of things, Narciso's the only other runner to plot this route. Even if she doesn't win the race, if she outdashes him she'll be happy. He's taller and has a longer stride, but she's lighter and nimbler, which in her mind makes things about even.

Then: off schedule, and nowhere near a station, the train slows.

Kip puts her ear against the cool metal of the car's roof. The train's hum gets much louder, but she can also hear the announcement inside the car: *"Due to a mechanical failure, this train is out of service. All passengers must exit to the emergency platform on the left side of the train and take the Broadway slidewalk to Broadway & Roy Station. We apologize for the inconvenience."*

"Shit," Kip says, thrown. On the car ahead, Narciso mouths the same thing, small comfort. Even if the next train plows up the ass of this one, she's going to miss her northbound connection; slidewalks, by definition, are not fast. Stuck on top of a stopped train twelve stories above the Street doesn't suggest a hell of a lot of options.

Above her, though, is the maglev: a branch of the same system that has carried the competition to Seattle Center by now, where they navigate its tangle of imperfectly internetworked systems and, probably, piss off evening commuters.

Kip knows she's lost the race. But she still wants to beat Narciso, who disappears over the side of the train and joins the small flood on the slidewalk.

Kip's lip curls. Another option floods her mind like prophecy.

The emergency platform and the slidewalk run alongside a building dark and shiny as black glass. Beads of semi-permeable plastic skim its surface like water droplets, carrying people inside them. Some, summoned by stranded passengers with the necessary connections, converge on the platform. As one of them ascends, expanded like a pregnant belly from the small crowd inside, Kip leaps and grabs a handful of the bubble-stuff and lets it carry her aloft. No one notices, including the bubble itself: the mask she bought really is top quality.

As the bubble slides past the maglev rail, Kip clambers up the outside, slipping a little on the bubble's wet surface. Now people notice. Their exclamations sound like kittens in a bag. Kip ignores them; attempting to catch a maglev in motion is an excellent way to get killed, and her timing must be perfect. She takes a breath and thinks of Lily's deep red hair.

The instant she spots approaching lights, she launches herself from the top of the bubble. It's like jumping off a pillow. The train's still approaching as she drops; when she lands, it's on the second to last car.

She's back in motion. The maglev is an express going south, not north, at 125 miles per hour; but even an express stops on occasion. At the next station, she can switch directions.

Kip jumped her first race when she was twelve. She couldn't get enough of it. She buzzed her hair, to her mother's distress, and assembled fitted clothes of slick material that wouldn't snag. Prices jumped as people who didn't even know what trainjumping was caught onto the clothing trend. She got the Sticky Fingers mod that gave her hands and feet a grip like a gecko's. She assembled a cocktail of masks that blocked positive ID from the surveillance net, and painted her face and arms with black and dark-blue stripes before each race. She had design and motion patterns all picked out for when she got to the top of the waiting list at Firebird Design, the best tattoo house in the city. She was short, something genetic modification still couldn't do a thing about, but she was long-muscled and lean, and being small was sometimes an advantage.

She got so she could pick out other runners on her networks and in the gymnasium; they had no net of their own, initially for pragmatic reasons—freerunning and trainjumping were illegal—and later for idealistic ones. But once you did it for awhile you could spot your own kind. They moved through the world as though it existed for their purpose; every building was a jungle gym, every obstacle a toy.

Kip would stand on the roof of Tytos Tower, one of the tallest buildings in Seattle, home to two dozen high-powered law firms, and think to herself that runners were the secret masters of the city. They knew things about it that it didn't know about itself.

Her performance in the races improved. She began to win.

The problem is, the maglev doesn't stop at any of the stations. Her only mistake so far might mean she won't finish the race at all: this train has finished its service run and is heading for home. It whips south, descending from Capitol Hill and skating the edge of Old Downtown before heading south down the Duwamish Valley: penthouses above, ancient industrial wasteland of empty warehouses and illegal nightclubs and theaters below. Then it whisks underground and stops at the Terminus with a whine just on the edge of hearing.

The Terminus is in what used to be called Tukwila. It's close to twenty miles from Northgate, and it might as well be on the moon: jumpers call it the Terminus because there are no connections here. End of the line.

"Shit," Kip says, again, and hops off.

The first time she raced against Narciso, they'd followed the same route from start to finish. She'd chased him through a network of concrete walkways that opened onto a treed plaza, a city park and incidentally also the race's finish point. Johnny had laid out a red target circle that lit up when the winner landed on it.

She'd been running, eyes on Narciso's black tank top and his brown arms and his dark, dark hair, when he leaped into the air with a flash of white slippers and landed in an athletic crouch. The red circle lit up around him.

Narciso always beat her after that. And once the race was over, he'd come up to her at the afterparty, his arm slung loosely over Lily's neck, and grin. "Tough luck, kid. Next time, eh?" And Lily would smile at her in a way that made Kip think of pity, and she'd hate them both.

But later, lying in bed, waiting for sleep to come, she'd forget the look on Lily's face and think of her hair, the paleness of her skin, the sharp line of her jaw. How all that would feel, under her fingers.

If she could beat Narciso. If only.

But right now, stuck in the deserted Terminus, Kip can only imagine how he'll grin and do a backflip or some other such stupid, flashy shit into the finish point. She wants to beat him so badly that the desire tastes like blood in her mouth.

No train will come to the Terminus for another ten minutes. Kip runs along the service platform. She could go out to the Street and hail a taxicab, the luxury conveyance of the uptowner who wants to explore the theaters, bars, fleshpots, and strange temples of the Street, but not too closely. But the cabs' impressive on-board security systems, which include a surface wired to deliver a ten thousand-volt charge and automatic evasive maneuvers to foreign contact, prevent her from hopping onto their roofs as she would onto a train, and actually getting into and paying for a cab is specifically and explicitly against the rules of the race.

Kip knows how she'll feel if she wins the race on those terms.

Something tickles at the back of her head. She turns her attention to it, and it blooms into a full-scale announcement:

"There is a power outage in the Seattle Center area. Affected transit routes have been re-routed, re-scheduled, or cancelled. Please plan accordingly."

It must be one hell of an outage if they're bothering to announce it on the citywide net instead of just quietly re-routing people. Which means an effect big enough that people would actually notice. Which means a lot of dead trains.

Which means she's back in the game.

The service door will bloom alarms if she opens it, but the ceiling and the wall of the Terminus don't quite meet: ventilation. It's small, but so is she. She scales the wall, squeezes through the gap, and rolls and splashes into a gutter on the Street.

She pops to her feet and starts running. This is a quiet, deserted area: a part of the Street called the Underground, even though it isn't. Fast movement attracts attention. Her instincts, trained for the freerunning environment, are wrong here. A skinny man lurches out of a doorway like a zombie. She dodges him and runs up the middle of the street, in the dim light that filters down from the understory, then up the first staircase she sees.

There are people here, enough to remind her that it's Friday night in the world that still waits for the weekend to have a good time. The rain has stopped. And there, just to the north, is Skyway Station. Routes and timetables slam together behind Kip's eyes. She fades into the shadow of a building, scales a wall to a narrow ledge overlooking the station, waits perhaps twenty seconds, and drops onto the Street-level light rail, pressing her body against the roof to avoid notice.

It's not nearly as fast as the maglev, but ten minutes later she's back in the city core and riding a bubble up a building to the maglev, which will take her directly past Lake Union. The bubble is slow, so she has time to consider that right now, as she positions herself to jump off at the platform, a train is leaving the Terminus; right now, as the bubble rises blindly past and she leaps out to the shelter roof, it's accelerating out of the tunnel; right now, as she hops aboard a maglev northbound from Sixth and Pine Tower, that other train is rising toward the understory. She's beaten it by five minutes.

It might be enough.

And as she crouches there, the wind tearing at her scalp, fingers and toes gripping against the force of the train's acceleration, she spots another lithe, dark shape crouched against the top of the car ahead. Lights flash above them in rapid succession and she sharpens her gaze. She just knows that it's Narciso.

She crawls forward, fighting the wind of the train's speed that peels her fingers from the cold metal, seeing Lily's face and how different it will be if she reaches the finish point before Narciso.

The train slows around a curve, slinging her weight to one side as it swings east of Lake Union and then hits the northbound straightaway. Two stops until Northgate, which will be closest to the finish point. Four minutes.

The maglev decelerates with a falling hum. Some instinct makes Narciso turn. He sees her. He grins that grin, the one that's so charming, and shouts something. All she catches of it is "caught up."

She wants to throw him off the damn train. Onto the platform. He wouldn't be hurt. He'd catch the next one. And then he'd lose.

Narciso sees what she's thinking, maybe catches a bit of it in the aether of the net. The grin fades. And then, when the train's braking shoves her forward like a giant hand, sliding sideways off the car, her fingers and toes peeling from the surface like old tape, he reaches out and she thinks it's to shove her away or throw her off, but she ducks and her balance goes and she rolls sideways, off the maglev for the second time that night and into the endless glass and metal canyon of Lake City Way.

She spreads her wings, and looks down.

You never do this when jumping. Look at the ground and you'll hit it, that's the way the word goes. A red line across the city map in her mind: Roosevelt slidewalk, below and to the right. Crowded, but a damn sight nearer than the Street.

Her feet hit the slidewalk's moving rail. People stare as she runs, jumping over their hands to avoid mashing fingers, hopping over their heads from one side to the other. The maglev passes overhead with a magnetic whine and shoots away to the north. She ignores it and keeps running.

The slidewalk empties out. She jumps onto its moving surface and runs, runs, runs. She runs all the way to the damn Research Center. It glitters in the lights of the moon and the city, walled on all sides by nightclubs, galleries, restaurants, and luxury homes except where the maglev line cuts through.

She passes the maglev station. The train has been and gone. But when she glances up again, to the lip of the canyon that is the roof of the towers of the Northgate complex, there is a slim shape running. Ahead of her, where the slidewalk ends, stands a building artfully draped in vines growing from somewhere above and falling across the sheer, glossy wall like hair across a girl's bare back.

Kip catches the vines and climbs. The buildings are shorter here, slanting toward the water, a sprawled last-century office park with a disused helipad on one of the roofs. Kip reaches the top, runs across a flat roof, leaps a gap, runs through an asphalt field planted in parallel white lines, leaps another gap. To her left, along another row of buildings, Narciso is doing the same thing. Further away to the west comes the rest of the pack, delayed at Seattle Center by the power outage.

Kip grins. *Now* it's a race.

There's a crowd gathered on the helipad. The red finishing dot lies right in the middle of the old landing target. Kip's gaze locks onto it. Narciso has fallen back from her peripheral vision. She leaps another gap. Across one more roof and there's the final leap, biggest she's ever jumped, by the time it occurs to her that she might not make it she's already hurtling through the air, a war-whoop tearing from her lungs, she hits the other side rolling, she's up again and she pelts to the finish point and leaps onto the dot. It lights up. Only then does the silence recede into cheering.

They'd cheer anyone, they would. But she grins all the same, and looks for Lily's face in the crowd. See? she wants to say. See? See?

The crowd rushes. Things grow confused. The other racers arrive. Narciso grins at her and hugs her. Around them melt a hundred hearts, but Kip doesn't care. Johnny's saying something about posting their reels and the small mob begins to ooze toward an open-air Street-level place on the lakeshore for the afterparty, but Kip trails behind. She's just behind Lily, who's following the crowd with her head down.

Kip's heart stops. She trots a few steps and touches Lily's arm. Lily turns and smiles, and Kip tries to smile back, but she can't, because she's seen that smile on Lily before, and it's the way she smiles at everyone who isn't Narciso.

"Good job," Lily says, in a friendly way. Her heels click on the concrete.

Narciso comes up next to her. "Hey," he says softly. And Lily takes his hand, and they wander away from the crowd, to some other corner of the helipad, where the breeze off the lake will ruffle Lily's hair.

Kip stands very still. So still that no one notices. Oh, she could scream, cry, fling up her hands. But it's occurred to her that she has built this entire fantasy, as complex and far-reaching as the cracks in the ancient road, and neither Lily nor Narciso know a thing about it.

She feels like she's standing on the roof of a tall tower, looking down at an entire city that doesn't know she's there, imagining herself its secret master.

Then she goes home.

▪ *Knuckleballer Eri Yoshida was the first female drafted by a Japanese professional baseball team, the Kobe 9 Cruise. In 2009, she played in eleven games. In 2010, she joined the Chico (California) Outlaws in the independent Golden League. She met with little success: 0-4 with a 12.28 ERA. In 2012, she played for Na Koa Ikaika Maui of the North American Baseball League. Her W/L for 2012 was 4-6 with a 5.56 ERA.*

▪ *On 2 February 2011, Justine Siegal, age 36, became the first woman to throw in batting practice for a Major League ballclub, the Cleveland Indians. She went onto pitch BP to the Athletics, Rays, Cardinals, Astros, and Mets.*

▪ *"In 2005, Ronald Evans, a hormone expert working at the Salk Institute of Biological Studies . . . showed how genetic modification can increase the athletic power of mice. . . . Evans's mice could run for an hour longer than normal mice, were resistant to weight gain no matter what they were fed on, and remained at peak fitness even when they took no exercise."*—UK Daily Mail Online, *31 July 2012*

Diamond Girls

Louise Marley

Ricky sat alone in her private locker room, turning a baseball in her elongated fingers. The pregame had begun, and the speakers in the main locker room rattled with music and announcements and advertisements. She leaned forward, her elbows on her knees, and cradled the baseball in her palm. *Just another game,* she told herself. *It's a long season.*

But it wasn't true. Long season, sure.

Someone hammered on the door and shouted, "Arendsen! Skip says to join the guys now."

"Coming," she called back. She stood and stretched her arms over her head, her fingers ritually brushing the ceiling. She put the ball, her first major-league game ball, back into its protective cube. Lew had saved it for her, gotten it signed.

She missed Lew. No one called a better game than he did, but he had retired at the end of last year, her rookie season, his bat worn out, his knees gone. It had been tough this season without him, a different catcher every rotation, a different attitude every game. She'd lost her last three starts. The sports columns had her on her way back to the minors after two of them, and they weren't far from the truth.

Her agent tried to shield her from the worst of management's comments, but she knew her career was on the line. Three losses were a bad way for anyone to start a season. It was worse for Ricky Arendsen.

And now this. Skip had tried to warn her, in his bluff, half-articulate way. "Management took a risk on you," he had said this morning, shuffling through the scouting reports on Everett. "Not worth the grief if you aren't the best." She only nodded. She knew that already.

Now she closed her locker and tucked her mitt under her arm. She left the cramped space that was hers and walked around the corner to the other door. The official statement to the press said that Ricky Arendsen had a separate locker room for her own privacy, but Ricky—and everyone else—understood it was more complicated than just that. Maybe the guys didn't want a woman in their locker room. More likely, they didn't want *her* in their locker room.

It had been the same in high school, in college, in the minors. It didn't matter that she possessed a killer curve, a hundred-plus fastball, a splitter that made grown-up men wave their bats like beginning T-ballers. What mattered, not to everyone, but to enough of them, was what she was and how she got that way.

Ricky adjusted her cap and pulled open the door with its vivid team logo.

The Skipper looked up when she came in, pointed to the bench in front of him. Raimundo grinned at her and moved over to make room. He was catching her today, which was good. She felt a bit better when he was behind the plate. She didn't have to shake him off as often as she did Baker.

"Hey, Rick," he said as she eased herself onto the bench. He moved another couple of inches over to give her space. She nodded down at him. Raimundo was a good six inches shorter than she was, just clearing six feet four.

"Hey, Ray," she said. She quirked her lips and lifted her eyebrows, pretending a calm she didn't feel. "Place is crawling with reporters."

"Whatcha get, Newsmaker." He said it with sympathy, his forehead crinkling.

"Yeah. I know."

Newsmaker was the least offensive of the many appellations attached to Ricky Arendsen when she came up to the show. The worst had been coined by a conservative preacher in a weekly newspaper column. The fans picked it up, shouting it whenever she took the mound. *Lab Rat, Lab Rat,* a one-two rhythm, a bit of doggerel that irritated her dreams.

She fiddled with the laces on her mitt, hooking them tight with the extra-long first joint of her finger, flexing the designer muscles of her wrists. She was a hell of a specimen, just as they said. Her thighs were smoothly muscled, perfectly jointed at the hip. Her calves were long and strong, her ankles like steel. Her eyesight was off the charts.

She wondered what Grace Everett's eyesight was like.

They were calling Everett The Natural. No engineered virus, no stem-cell modifications, no Lab Rat. Just a wiry, quick second baseman, a freckled girl with a stringy red ponytail and a wicked bat. In the minors they called her Gracie, or Little Red. Now, coming up against Ricky Arendsen, Grace Everett had become The Natural.

"Okay, guys," the Skipper said. He stood in front of the chalkboard, where someone had scribbled the lineups, a few names crossed out, substitutes chalked in. Some of the players were chowing down from the buffet, but Ricky never ate right before a game.

Skip nodded to her. "You okay, Rick?"

She gave him a thumbs-up and pulled off her cap to scratch her scalp through her short scruff of brown hair.

"Good. So," the Skipper began. "Everybody. The main thing is, don't let it all get to you today, okay? Everett's just another ballplayer. Let's play it that way. Cool and calm."

Someone standing beside the row of open lockers snorted, "Yeah, Skip. That'll work."

The Skipper shot him a heated look. "I mean it," he growled. "No crap out there."

"Hey, Skip, it's not us," someone protested. "It's the fans. Worse than New York!"

Ricky hunched her shoulders. Ray murmured, "Easy, Rick."

"Yeah."

"It's a stunt," he added under his breath. "I hear they brought her up just to face you. She'll fan a few times, fall on her face, and go straight back to Triple-A."

Ricky turned her head without changing position. "Where'd you hear that?"

Ray shrugged. "Talk around the office."

"I don't know, Ray. Her stats are solid."

Ricky didn't want to think about Everett, about what this game must mean to her. She had to concentrate on her own problems. Three straight losses after her twelve-and-eight last year. If they sent her down, she'd never get called up again, not after all the stuff that happened last season. She needed a W today as much as she ever had in her life.

"Listen," the Skipper said. "Anybody's out of line, in the stands or on the field, security throws 'em out of the park, okay?"

"If it's not too late," someone said from the back of the room. Ricky didn't need to turn to know who the grumbler was. Center field. Ditch Daniels, they called him, because he wore a ditch in the grass between left and right. Ditch had been struck by something when she was pitching her second game, a cup or a ball or something thrown from the outfield bleachers. He was touchy and hot-tempered on the best of days, and that really tipped him over. He never had a good word for her, not even when she came in on one day's rest to save the last game of the season, propelling the team into the playoffs. Ditch knew about every death threat she'd received since she came up. As if Ricky didn't remember them well enough without his quoting them word for word when he knew she could hear him.

"Look at it this way," the Skipper said finally. "The park's sold out, even the bleachers. For a regular season game. Management's happy, which is good news at contract time, right? Let's just get this one. Let security worry about the nutcases."

The team grunted assent and filed out of the locker room and up the ramp to the dugout. Ricky headed for the bullpen to warm up.

A solid wall of sound greeted her, defeating the announcer as he read the rosters. When Ricky trotted to the mound, tossed a few pitches to Ray, the volume dissipated, gradually, like a spent wave, leaving an electric silence in its wake. A familiar prickle crept across Ricky's shoulders and up under her cap, as if something were pointed at the back of her neck or between her shoulder blades. Jackie Robinson had felt the same thing, she supposed. Like a great big target. Sometimes Ricky felt as if the mound was a bull's-eye, with her smack in the center.

Ray gave the ump a nod, and the first batter, a leftie, stepped into the box, bat describing semicircles above his shoulder. Ricky leaned forward, bent at the waist. She held the ball behind her back, turning it in the fingers of her left hand till she found just the right spot, the seams fitting perfectly between her fingers and her long, flexible thumb. Ray gave her the sign, curve down and in, and she nodded. She straightened. Her right leg lifted in the high kick, hands above her head. The windup. The throw. Strike one. Ragged cheers from the hometown fans, half-hearted taunts from the visitors, and the game was underway. The first two innings went hitless and scoreless on both sides, despite several long at bats that went the full count and a dozen or more foul balls. Ricky rested after the second, her warm-up jacket tugged up over her left arm, her chin on her chest.

Everett would come up in the third, batting eighth in the lineup. She'd hit over .300 in the minors, Ricky knew, but otherwise the scouts hadn't had much to say about her. No one had expected Little Red to be sent up, not now, not ever.

When the second ended, Ricky stood and pulled the jacket off her arm. The crowd began to stir, a deep murmur rather than the usual calls and cheers. Camera flashes glimmered in the stadium like stars in a multicolored sky.

The first hitter grounded to third, and the murmuring grew. Ricky turned her back on the mound, walked a little way toward second, bent to tighten a shoelace. She caught some rosin on the way back. As she walked to the top and started to dig her toes into the dirt, Everett moved into the box, swinging her bat with one hand, eyeing Ricky over her right shoulder. Her red ponytail swung between her shoulder blades. Matching red freckles dusted her nose and cheeks.

She deserved to be called The Natural, Ricky thought. There was nothing unusual about her physique, except that she looked strong, a little bigger than most women. But lots of women were big, lots of women were athletic. It took a special combination of speed and coordination and eyesight, as well as strength, to make a major-league ballplayer.

Ricky shook off Ray's first sign. He wanted to surprise the batter, try the curve instead of the fastball she expected. But Everett was a fastball hitter. Ricky wanted to see what she had.

Ray extended a forefinger. Fastball. Ricky nodded, straightened, kicked, wound, threw.

The crowd's murmur broke into shouts as the radar flashed a one-hundred and five, but it wasn't the speed of the pitch that made the difference. It was that little kick at the end, the tail. Ricky's long fingers could hold the seams right where she wanted them, and her fastball was almost impossible to hit.

Everett watched it go by with just a lift of her elbows, as if she thought it might be inside. It wasn't. Ricky stared at her opponent and wondered if Everett felt like she did. Like a target. Like an outsider. Like no matter how well she played, it would never be enough.

Ray flashed the sign for the curve, and Ricky shook him off again. He tried the changeup, and she shook her head. She couldn't quite see his shrug before he extended the forefinger, but she was sure it was there. She didn't care. She wanted to play it this way

Everett glanced at the third-base coach and then faced her again. Ricky threw. One-hundred and two. Everett's bat never left her shoulder.

She backed out of the box, shaking her head, talking to herself. She put up a hand to ask for time. The ump gave it, and Ricky stepped off the mound to shake out her arms.

The next pitch was another fastball, but Ricky missed with it, just inside, brushing Everett's thighs so close her uniform rippled. A roar of fury erupted from the stands.

Ricky caught her breath at the sound. She had learned to tune out the jeers that greeted her trips to the mound, but this surge, when the fans thought she might have hit Everett, was staggering. Lew had talked her through it all the first few times, and by the end of her first season she hardly heard the chants and catcalls. But this was different. She glanced up into the colorful mass of people, banners waving, hands in the air, hand-lettered signs dancing here and there. Were they hoping Everett would show her up, or hoping Everett would fail? Was there anyone out there just rooting for their favorite team, the way they used to?

She caught sight of a placard with her name on it, and beneath it a circle with "Jackie Robinson" inside, a black line crossing the circle. Ricky Arendsen is no Jackie Robinson. She'd seen it before.

Lew had told her to laugh it off. "They're right anyway, kid," he had said. "You're no Jackie Robinson—you're bigger, faster, and stronger than he was. You'll show 'em."

Now Ray was jogging out to the mound, and she'd lost track of time. Not like her, to let anything interfere with her concentration.

"Hey, Rick," he said. The two of them turned their backs to the plate, and Ricky dropped her head to hear. "What's the matter? You got two strikes, one ball, you're ahead in the count. Nothing to worry about."

"Yeah, yeah, I know. I just . . . " She breathed deeply, adjusted her cap, and then shook her head. "I'm okay. Sorry, Ray."

"Let's go with the splitter now, okay? Quit messing around?"

She shook her head. "No. Fastball. I can get her. Let's do it."

He frowned and tugged at his mask. "Well, Rick, you're the pitcher. Don't lose her though, or Skip will be pissed."

"I won't lose her."

Ray slapped her back with his mitt and jogged back to the plate, pulling his mask down as he went.

Grace Everett chewed on her tongue, trying to get some moisture into her mouth as she faced Ricky Arendsen once again. Arendsen didn't look like someone whose career was in trouble. She looked unbeatable, her long form perfectly proportioned, her face calm, her eyes like steel. And the fastball!

Grace wished she'd taken the bubble gum someone had offered her. Her mouth felt like a desert. She stubbed her toe into the dirt, wiggled it, set her foot. She'd hit a hundred-and-five before, she reminded herself. Just the other day, down in Triple-A. Today was no different. Just another ballgame, the beginning of a long season . . .

But still, as she faced the Newsmaker, her heart pounded in her throat. She glanced up at the coach and saw the signs. The splitter: he thought Arendsen would throw the splitter. It didn't seem right to Grace. She looked back at Arendsen, at the poker face, the forward-leaning posture, the hand hidden behind the back. Well, the coach was the coach, and this was her first game in the bigs. It was no time for independence. She lifted her bat from her shoulder, let it describe small, tight circles, watched Arendsen straighten, kick, wind, and throw.

Fastball! Again!

At least this time Grace had a swing at it, but she was looking for the splitter, and the fastball surprised her. It smacked into the catcher's mitt before her bat crossed the plate. With a grunt and a gritting of her teeth, she turned and marched back to the dugout, her cheeks burning.

She didn't look at the coach or her teammates. She didn't know them yet, didn't know what their expressions meant, what they might be thinking. Just thinking about their own at bats, probably. She took off the batting helmet and picked up her mitt. She pulled her cap out of her belt as she trotted out to second base. Arendsen was walking in the other direction, to the home side, her lanky height making Grace feel like a half-pint. She pulled on her cap and settled into her place between first and second.

So she struck out. Everybody struck out once in a while, right?

But you only get this chance, Gracie. This one chance. She sighed and smacked her fist in her mitt. She knew they'd only brought her up to face Arendsen. Her Triple-A coach told her so.

"You're playing great, Little Red. None better. But it took guts for those guys to take Arendsen on. It's cost 'em plenty. Extra security, vandalism to the stadium, bad press. Only way they got through it was they made the play-offs. Our guys don't want to risk all that."

She had protested. "I'm hitting .326!"

"Yeah, but we're not the show, Gracie."

"So what, they're giving me one game, and that's it?"

"Depends, Red. You do well, get a couple hits, they might give you another shot."

"A couple hits? Against Ricky Arendsen? That's hardly fair."

"You're right. It's a stunt, is what it is, but I couldn't talk 'em out of it. Arendsen's a fastball pitcher, and you're a hell of a fastball hitter. And the boss is an old-fashioned guy. I think he wants to prove you can't do it, that The Natural can't cut it in the bigs."

Grace had pounded the cement floor with the heel of her spikes. "I hate that name. They only call me that because Arendsen—"

"Yeah, yeah, I know, kid. Tough breaks all around."

"And so what, the boss wants me out?"

The coach shrugged. "All I know is, he's been whining to the commissioner ever since Arendsen signed. Doesn't believe in women in baseball. Not in the majors."

Grace stood up and fixed the coach with a direct stare. "Arendsen's a great ballplayer." He stood up too, and grinned. "Damn straight, Gracie. And so are you."

Neither team scored until the bottom of the sixth, when Ray manufactured a run by stealing second and then scoring on Smitty's double. Ricky gave him the thumbs-up as she shrugged out of her warm-up jacket. He grinned, pulling on his chest protector and reversing his cap. As he pulled down his mask, he said, "Hold 'em now, Rick, okay?"

"Do my best."

Ricky knew her pitch count was already at eighty-four, but that didn't concern her. Among the gifts her mother's engineered virus had bestowed on her was stamina. In her first season she'd pitched five complete games, to the astonishment of the coaches and the envy of the rest of the pitching staff. Now, in the top of the seventh, she sent down the first batter on four pitches. She was beginning to breathe easier, feeling as if her season could turn around at last. The ump was giving her the called strikes, keeping the hitters honest, unlike the earlier games of the season. She didn't let the last batter of the inning rattle her, though he got a single and advanced to second on a fielder's choice, then stole third while she was dealing with their cleanup hitter. She eyed him before her last pitch. Ray flashed the splitter, and she nodded. It was her signature pitch, fast and smooth, toppling out of its trajectory just as it reached the plate. No one could read it, not even the umpire half the time.

This time the pitch was perfect. The hitter spun on his heels as he tried to adjust, but he was about an hour too late. Ricky grinned at Ray as they headed back to the dugout, feeling a burst of confidence. It felt like last year, with Lew. "Good work, Catch," she said as they stepped down into the shade and she folded her lengthy frame onto the bench. She pulled the warm-up over her arm.

Ray said, "Yeah. Some long at bats, Rick, but you can get six more."

"Let's hope."

The Skipper glanced over at her. "How you holding up, Ricky?"

"Great, Skip."

He indicated the pitch counter with his chin. "You're at a hundred and three."

"I'm fine." She looked across the field to the bullpen. The relievers still sprawled on the bench, none of them throwing, which meant Skip was going to let her stay in.

She knew what would happen as her pitch count went up, into the eighth, into the ninth. A hundred and twenty. A hundred and thirty. The catcalls would grow louder, more frantic. *Lab Rat, Lab Rat.*

Had her mother known, when she was perfecting her virus? When she was injecting it into her own womb, targeting her unborn child's stem cells?

It could have failed, after all. Ricky Arendsen could have been some sort of monster. The others—the other experiments—had all had terrible problems. She was the only success, out of a dozen modified fetuses.

Involuntarily, Ricky glanced out at the infield, where The Natural danced between first and second. She wondered if Everett knew what it was like to be Ricky Arendsen. She might even have preferred to be like her, to have her genes modified within days after conception, her body engineered to be bigger, stronger, faster. If today was Everett's only chance at the bigs, her only shot . . . that was tough.

Ricky hunched her shoulders and slid further down on her long, pliable spine. She didn't want to feel sorry for Grace Everett. She had to work hard enough not to be sorry for herself, not to be wounded by the nasty articles, the placards, the threatening letters.

It didn't matter now. Let them yell what they wanted. She would turn it off. Tune it out. Just six batters, and the whole season would turn around.

The rancor of the fans stunned Grace when she came out for her third at bat, at the top of the ninth. She read the sports columns, of course, like everyone else, but even those criers of doom hadn't prepared her for the insults that were shouted at Ricky Arendsen, for the hysterical screams of fans waving signs that said things like "Baseball, not biology." She'd spotted one that read, "Put the balls back in baseball," but security had escorted the bearer of that one from the stadium before the first pitch. The din rose at her own appearance, rhythmic shouts of *The Natural, The Natural*, at a volume that banged inside her helmet as if someone were beating it like a drum. There had to be supporters in the stands, people shouting encouragement for Ricky Arendsen, but Grace couldn't hear them. Hate had a stronger voice.

Something unwelcome and surprising twisted in her belly, and she recognized it as a surge of sympathy. She thrust it aside. Her team was down two to zip, ninth inning, one down, one on. And Grace's gut told her, in a cold voice, that this was it. Now or never.

And yet, if Ricky Arendsen weren't out there on the mound, she, Grace Everett, would still be riding the bus with the Triple-A team. No big league team ever gave a girl a chance before Arendsen. Ricky Arendsen stood alone on the mound, awash in antagonism, when all she wanted was to play ball.

Grace wanted to play ball, too. She swung her bat as she walked to the plate, trying to push away the useless thoughts. The coach was flashing her signs, and she nodded obediently, but it was a sham. No point now in sucking up. Her opportunity was slipping away. The coach didn't know what Ricky Arendsen was going to throw. Grace thought she just might.

It was because they were facing each other, she thought. Arendsen could get her with the splitter, that evil slicing arc that made veterans look like Little Leaguers. Or she could fool her with her changeup that looped over the plate like a turtle on Valium. But Arendsen had thrown her nothing but fastballs. She wanted a test, head to head, Lab Rat against The Natural. And she would do it again.

Grace dug in her toe, lifted her bat above her shoulder, flexed her thighs in her stance. Arendsen bent at the waist, nodded to the catcher, and went into her high kick, that incredible kick that made her look like a seven-foot ballet dancer.

Fastball. Grace swung, pivoting on her heels, the bat whistling. Miss.

She stepped out of the batter's box and took a couple of swings. Arendsen circled the mound, bent to the rosin bag, stretched her shoulders. Grace saw the coach flashing signs at her, and she nodded again. He wore a glum look, and she knew he thought the game was already over. The runner took a long lead at first. Arendsen glanced at him from under her cap, but didn't bother with a throw. Her eyes came back to Grace, gleaming with determination across the sixty feet and six inches' distance. Grace paused at the edge of the batter's box. She felt the ump's questioning glance, but she was transfixed by Arendsen's gaze.

She knew all about the Newsmaker's stem-cell modifications, her incredible speed, coordination, the flexibility in her hips and knees and shoulders. She knew her height was enhanced, her musculature, her vision.

But Ricky Arendsen's mother's patent had failed. The other recipients of the engineered virus had been failures. One child was born with a beautiful body and incredible strength but with a brain that never matured. Another grew so fast in infancy that her bones deformed. One volunteer gave birth to twins who became implacable competitors—with each other. They had to be institutionalized when they were five.

Ricky Arendsen—and only Ricky Arendsen—had grown into a superb athlete, with a mind to match. But the gleam Grace saw in her eye was all hers. No virus had made her the competitor she was. She was a ballplayer. A gamer.

And so was Grace.

Grace's nerves vanished as if they never were. As if this was just another game, another ballpark, one in a long season. The din seemed to fade from her hearing as if someone had turned down the volume on a radio. She nodded to the umpire, glanced briefly at the coach, turned her face to Ricky Arendsen. She wanted—really wanted—that fastball.

The second pitch missed way outside, and Grace raised her eyebrows. Arendsen tiring? The catcher fell to his left, barely spearing the ball before it escaped to the wall. The runner dashed to second base. Scoring position.

Grace grinned and lifted her bat, painting air circles. The coach stared at her, eyes hopeless. She watched Arendsen shake off her catcher's signs, one, two, three.

She'd thrown nothing but fastballs to Grace. But now it was the ninth inning, a runner on, only one away. Would she do it again? Grace dug her feet into the dirt and eyed the pitcher.

The kick, the windup, Arendsen's impossibly long arms high over her head . . .

Time slowed, in that way it sometimes did, that way that let Grace Everett know the pitch that was coming was all hers. Great ballplayers, she knew, saw pitches differently, understood their speed and trajectory and spin in a way no ordinary mortal could. Grace didn't know if she had it in her to be a great ballplayer, but once in a while she experienced that perfect moment of perception, that pinnacle of sight and sense and instinct. This pitch, turning seam over seam on its sixty-foot-six-inch path, was no fastball. Grace couldn't have said how she knew, but she knew. It was the splitter, Arendsen's famous, nasty pitch, that fell over the plate as if it had run into a wall.

Grace's heels braced, her gut tightened, her thighs flexed as she wheeled on that ball. She knew exactly where it would be. And she connected.

She felt the impact from her shoulders to her toes, that sweet, hard jolt that sent the baseball leaping for the infield, bouncing in the base path, dodging the shortstop as if it had eyes.

Grace didn't watch it go. She knew. She tossed her bat away and dug for first base, head down to hide her grin.

As she approached first base, she looked up and saw the coach waving her on. She spun on toward second, seeing Ditch Daniels scoop up the ball—her ball—and heave it toward home plate. She could hear the fans again, the shouts of dismay, the yells of approbation. She pulled up on second, panting, grinning. A double. An RBI. Whatever happened now, she'd had her chance, and it felt great. She felt like she had wings on her heels.

She flicked a quick glance at Arendsen.

Ricky Arendsen stood, baseball in hand, watching Grace. She lifted the baseball with a flick of her wrist. A salute. Then she pulled down her cap and turned to face the next batter.

"You think I don't know what you're up to?" demanded the Skipper, glaring down at Ricky. She sat with her head back against the dugout wall, her cap tipped up, her legs stretched out to their full length.

"What, Skip?" she asked languidly.

"You wouldn't take Ray's calls, you wouldn't use the curve or the change. You just had to see if she could hit your fastball."

"I threw the splitter, Skip. She got lucky."

"Well, now the damned game is tied, and their closer's out there. We'll probably go into extra innings. You're already in trouble, Ricky! What did you think you were doing?"

She pulled her cap over her eyes. "Just playing ball, Skip. I'll get 'em next inning."

"You will not." He wheeled and stamped away to the bullpen phone.

Ricky abruptly sat up. "Skip, no! Don't take me out. I'll get 'em, I promise."

He stopped and glared back at her. "Oh, yeah? You know what your count is?"

"I'm fine. Look, I'm sorry." Ricky stood up and went to stand beside the manager. "I just—" She shrugged. "I wanted to see what she's got. This may be the only day she gets."

"It's a fuckin' game, Rick," the Skip said with disgust. "It's not tea and crumpets."

She stiffened, and her cheeks flamed. "Come on. I get enough of that from the stands."

He hesitated, and then his stiff stance relaxed. "Yeah, yeah, I know, Rick. Sorry. It's been tough on you. It's tough every time you go out."

"I don't care about that, Skip, you know I don't. But let me have another inning."

He shrugged. "What the hell. It's early in the season." He pointed a thick finger at Ray, listening from the bench. "But remember, you pay attention to Ray's calls, okay? Your losses are mine, too, and the rest of the guys'. No more grandstanding."

Ricky grinned at him and touched the bill of her cap with her forefinger.

■ ■ ■

In the bottom of the ninth, Grace watched the closer mow down the batters in order: one, two, three. She hardly had to move her feet. In the tenth, Ricky Arendsen was still pitching, unbelievably. Her shaky start seemed to have evaporated with Grace's double, and she, too, started mowing down batters.

In the dugout, the manager groaned, watching her. "She oughta be beat," he said. "There oughta be nothing left in that arm."

Somebody swore. "That's Arendsen for you."

Somebody else said, "Too bad we don't have our own Lab Rat."

Grace stiffened at that, but the player closest to her—the left fielder, a veteran who'd been one of her heroes when she was in high school—patted her shoulder. "We're doin' okay with Little Red, here," he said gruffly. "Game'd be over if it weren't for The Natural."

Two or three of the guys added their compliments. Grace blushed and ducked her head.

She didn't have another at bat until the twelfth. They were still tied at two. Arendsen had settled into a rhythm, and since the ninth, no batter had looked at more than five pitches. There had been two hits, three guys on base, but no one scored. Arendsen's count was high, but it didn't seem to matter, to her or to her manager.

The fans seemed to have fallen into a rhythm, too. When Grace appeared in her batting helmet, the chant of *Natural, Natural* washed out across the field. The stands were still full. No one, it seemed, had left the ballpark. They'd bought tickets to see The Natural go against the Lab Rat, and they were getting their money's worth.

Arendsen had stopped trying to tempt her with the fastball. This time she threw a curve, a change, a splitter that missed outside, and then another change, that also missed outside.

Grace stepped out of the box to catch her breath. Two and two. She had that feeling in her gut again. One last chance.

She heaved a deep breath and stepped back in. She lifted her bat and met Ricky Arendsen's cool gaze across the expanse of grass and dirt.

Ricky rolled her left shoulder. Her arm, at last, was starting to tire. Heat ran from her shoulder to her elbow, and she felt the warmth in her ribs and in her wrist as well. When Ray flashed the sign for the splitter, she hesitated. He looked at her for a long moment and then called time and trotted out to the mound, pushing up his mask as he went. She stepped down to meet him, and they turned their backs to the box.

"You okay?" Ray asked.

"Getting tired," she admitted.

"Wanta call in Baxter?"

Ricky glanced out to the bullpen and saw that Baxter and one of the middle relievers were both up and throwing. She scratched her neck. "No," she said finally. "No, I want this one, this inning. Get this over with."

"Yeah. But you don't want to risk letting Everett get another hit."

Ricky looked back over her left shoulder, where Everett was swinging the bat and squinting out at them. Shadows stretched across the infield now, fingers of darkness pointing away from the setting sun. "What do you think, Ray? You think the splitter?"

"Yup."

She nodded, and he jogged back to the plate. She bent at the waist, then straightened. Everett's blue eyes glittered slightly as they met hers.

She lifted her left knee, high, and brought her hands above her head. She threw the splitter, but it got away from her. Chin music, they called it. It sure wasn't anywhere it was supposed to be. It didn't drop, but spun directly at Everett's face.

The rookie spun backward, landing on her butt in the dirt, her bat dropped, her helmet gone. The screams of the fans intensified, an eruption of rage.

Ray called time again and sprinted to the mound. When he got there, Skip was there, too. Ricky turned her back, pulled off her cap to rub her fingers through her hair, and ducked her head to hear what the Skipper had to say.

They were shouting it now, *Natural, Natural,* against the screams of *Lab Rat.* But they were wrong, Grace reflected. This wasn't about modified genes, about great eyesight or elongated fingers or a designer skeleton. This was about desire.

Grace *wanted* it. She didn't want to walk; she didn't want to get on base by being struck by a pitch. She wanted a hit. She wanted to win, not because of Arendsen, not because it was her first day in the big leagues, not to prove the Natural could do it. She wanted to win because it was baseball and she was in the game.

She lifted her bat to her shoulder and met the Newsmaker's eyes once again. Ricky Arendsen straightened her shoulders, dropped her chin. She wasn't looking at her catcher now. She was looking at Grace.

Grace looked back. Her bat circled above her, and time slowed down.

It should have been something crafty, of course, another splitter, or the curve, or the change. But she knew in her bones the fastball was coming. She would have to anticipate, to be there before Arendsen was, to see it barreling toward her . . .

And she did. This time the crack of her bat made her wrists ache, drove her heels deep into the dirt around home plate. The ball exploded from her bat, a long, high arc that had nowhere to land except in the left-field bleachers, far beyond the reach of the outfielder, into the outstretched hands of the fans. A roar greeted her as she jogged around the bases. Arendsen watched her, tossing a new ball in her hand, turning on the mound as she made her circuit.

Before she reached home, the manager was on the mound and the catcher was on his way to join the conference. Grace touched the plate and turned to the dugout, the chant following her. *Natural, Natural.* The coach met her, grinning, and swatted her rear as she passed him.

Ricky said, "No, Skip. Just this inning."

"Hey, Rick, I gave you more time than I should have. You lost her."

Ricky stared down at him, her jaw clenching. "I didn't lose her. She hit the fastball. Just like she hit the splitter. There's a reason she hit over .300 in Triple-A."

Ray grunted, "True, Skip. It was a great pitch. They both were."

The Skipper glared at them both for a long moment, and Ricky saw movement over her shoulder as the umpire started out toward the mound to break it up. "Okay," the Skipper growled, half under his breath. "Okay. But this is it, Rick."

"Right. Thanks, Skip."

The last two outs were easy. One batter fanned on the curve, the other on the splitter. Ricky walked with deliberate slowness back to the dugout, letting the catcalls fall around her like warm rain. She stretched her arms, her shoulders, and reached for her batting helmet. It was the bottom of the order, and she was the bottom of the bottom. She had never hit .300, not even in high school. It didn't help that she made such a big strike zone.

Ditch Daniels singled to right. Ray came next, waging a long battle at the plate, but it ended with Ray flying out to short, not even advancing the runner. Williams, the third baseman, grounded to third. And then it was Ricky's turn.

The closer smirked at her, expecting an easy out, anticipating the W. Ditch poised just off first base. At second, Everett half-crouched, mitt at the ready for Ditch's steal attempt.

Whenever she came up to bat, Ricky thought of her father. Her mother, the doctor, the research scientist, had never forgiven him for encouraging Ricky's enthusiasm for athletics. When she decided baseball was her game, he spent hours lobbing balls to her, playing catch, and later, catching her first pitches. When the virus failed in every case except her daughter's, Ricky's mother hoped that Ricky's achievements would prove her right after all, validate her tireless, all-consuming endeavors. But Ricky's father—who had spent six years in the minor leagues in his youth—found her athletic ability his only consolation for what he regarded as betrayal by his wife. It was when the two of them divorced, and Ricky overheard their last bitter argument, that she learned her mother had injected herself with the engineered virus without telling her father. Ricky was already determined to be the first woman to play major-league baseball. She felt no resentment, but her father never willingly spoke to her mother again.

What she remembered when she came to the plate was her dad laughing that as a hitter she made a great pitcher.

The closer's first pitch was a low strike, a neat fastball just at the knees. It was in the zone. She swung, but it dropped away over the plate. She missed by two inches. The catcher threw hard to second, but Ditch was in there, standing up. Tying run in scoring position.

The next two pitches Ricky let go, seeing before they reached her that they would be outside, tumbling off to the catcher's left. The fourth pitch was a slider, the pitch Ricky hated the most. It came inside just at belt level, a nasty height for a batter with long arms. She bent back away from it, and the umpire called a second strike.

The closer tried to tempt her with the change, but Ricky knew by his stance, a slight hesitation at the release point, what he was throwing. It dropped too soon, bouncing right off the edge of the bag. Ditch was on it, tearing to third before the catcher had his mask off. Full count. Runner ninety feet away. A little spark of hope flickered in Ricky's belly, and she called time to eye the coach's signs and ponder what the next pitch might be.

As she stepped back in, she glanced out to the infield. Everett looked back, her cap pulled low, that skinny ponytail flopping over one shoulder. The infield was fully in shadow now. Game time.

Ricky lifted her bat, loosened her shoulders. Okay, she wasn't the hitter Everett was. But she could keep the game alive, get something. She eyed the closer. What would she throw, if she were on the mound and the game were on the line, the stands packed, the press box jammed? She wouldn't take a chance walking the batter and facing the top of the lineup. She'd throw her very best pitch and locate as if she were doing surgery. This guy didn't have a splitter, but he had a mean slider, if it didn't miss.

The pitch looked as if it would be outside, but she knew it wouldn't. It would turn, whip across the plate at the last moment, slide across the corner, jam her hands. She watched the pitch come, seeing it so clearly she could almost see the seams revolve. She thought of Everett, poised just beyond the infield. *Okay, Gracie. Try this.*

The din from the stands deafened Grace, and the tension in the ballpark electrified the short red hairs on her arms. *Lab Rat, Lab Rat.* Did they ever shout *for* Arendsen?

Arendsen slapped at the last pitch, and it spiked between Grace and the shortstop. The shortstop leaped to his left, but the ball bounced just beyond his reach. Grace launched herself like an arrow, arms extended, torso parallel to the ground. She hit with a mighty grunt, rolled, closed her mitt tight, and hoped for the best.

As she bounced to her feet, the roar from the crowd had changed somehow. Cheers blurred the chant as Ricky Arendsen loped to first base. Ditch Daniels charged, head down, toward home. Grace opened her mitt, found the ball in it, seized it, and threw.

The ball smacked into the catcher's mitt just one split second after Daniels crossed the plate. Ricky Arendsen, one foot on first base, grinned across the diamond. Tied again.

Chagrined, Grace ducked her head, brushing at the infield dirt on her uniform.

The next batter smacked a double into right field, and the closer, getting desperate, threw the next man four straight balls. The third man in the order hit a long, looping fly ball that dropped into left field, and Arendsen galloped easily into home to score the winning run.

It was over. Over for the night. Over for Grace.

Her feet felt like lead as she crossed the infield. She kept her eyes down, not wanting to look at the fans, to look up into the now-shadowed bleachers, at the flashing scoreboard with its garish ads and celebratory displays. It was over. Her big chance. She allowed herself one glance at Arendsen before she stepped down into the dugout.

Arendsen was surrounded by press, a microphone in her face, the lights of television cameras shining on her as she pulled off her batting helmet, pushed a hand through her hair. Someone ran out with an ice pack and wrapped it around her arm as she answered questions.

Grace paused. The Newsmaker, as if sensing her, looked up, past the clutch of reporters. Grace nodded to her and touched two fingers to her cap. She hoped Arendsen understood that it was a gesture of respect. And of farewell. Surely Ricky Arendsen understood that Grace's moment had passed.

She made her leaden feet move then, down the steps, away from Arendsen's triumph.

"So, Ricky, the season's looking a lot better now, isn't it?"

Ricky nodded to the reporter, though she couldn't see him past the glare. "Yeah."

"Nice hit you got. Did that surprise you?"

Ricky laughed. "Yeah. Yeah, kind of a surprise. Wasn't very pretty."

"Hey, Rick." She turned her head, searching for the sportswriter. He grinned up at her, gestured toward the visitors' dugout. "Did you see The Na—um, did you see Everett's dive?"

"No. Was it good?"

"Fantastic. What did you think of them bringing her up to face you? Just a cheap trick?"

Ricky turned all the way around at that, putting her back to the television camera. "Why do you say that?"

"Well, you know, Ricky. Because you're the only woman in the big leagues."

Now Ricky recognized his face from the grainy photo at the head of his newspaper column. He had been the first to predict her own trip back to the minors. She squinted at him. "I'm not the only one," she said flatly. "Not now."

"Hey," he said, with a scornful laugh. "No way Everett's gonna stick after this loss. It was all about the novelty."

Ricky stared at him for a long moment, her jaw tight. He stared back, unabashed. Slowly, she swiveled back to look directly into the television cameras. "The girl can play. Hit, field, run. Management's nuts if they don't keep her. They deserve to lose."

She spun on her heel then, ducking her head as she moved down the dugout steps, on to her locker room. At the door she paused when she spotted the Skipper. "Hey, Skip. Anybody get Everett's ball for her? The homer?"

"Nah, it's gone," he said. "It'll show up on eBay tomorrow. We got the other one, though, the grounder."

"Get it for me, will you?"

Grace leaned against the outer wall of the locker room, arms folded, waiting for the men to finish so she could use the showers. Family members and friends of the players lounged about the door, talking with each other, obviously trying not to stare at her. The other ballplayers emerged one by one, and the little crowd began to diminish. Grace slumped against the wall and closed her eyes.

" 'Scuse me."

Grace opened her eyes and shot upright.

It was Ricky Arendsen, still in her uniform, standing in front of her with a baseball in her left hand. She stuck out her right, and Grace could see those incredible fingers up close, the sculpted wrist, the powerful forearm. She said, "Ricky Arendsen."

"Oh!" Grace said, inadequately. "Oh. Wow. Ricky. Hey, it's great to meet you, really great." She put out her own hand and shook Arendsen's.

"This is yours," Arendsen said, holding out the ball. "The homer's gone, but this was your infield hit. I signed it. Hope that was okay."

Grace took the ball and turned it in her hand. In blue ink, Arendsen had scrawled, "First hit in the bigs," and signed her name and the date. Grace felt her cheeks burn. "This is—this is so nice of you."

"Nah." Arendsen shrugged. "No problem."

A camera flashed, and they both looked up. Someone had snapped a picture of the two of them together.

" 'Spose that'll be on eBay tomorrow, too," Arendsen said.

"Do you think so?"

Arendsen grinned. "Oh, yeah. First time we faced each other."

Grace made herself smile. "Probably the last, Ricky."

Arendsen shook her head. "Nah. You'll be back, Gracie." She raised an impressive forefinger. "And I'm gonna get you on the splitter next time."

Grace's heart lifted. She said, laughing, "We'll just see about that."

Ricky Arendsen clapped her on the shoulder and then turned and left, stopping once or twice to sign autographs. Grace went in for her shower, nodding to the security guys beside the door. Arendsen was right. She'd be back. She'd gotten her hits, made a good throw. If this team wouldn't have her, she'd get her agent to put her someplace else. She'd face Arendsen again, one way or another.

But she was going to watch out for that splitter.

As Cory Doctorow wrote in an introduction to this story, "The easiest way to write futuristic (or futurismic) science fiction is to predict, with rigor and absolute accuracy, the present day . . . 'Anda's Game' is a sterling example of this approach. I ripped a story from the headlines—reports on blogs about . . . 'gold farmers' in Latin America who were being paid a pittance [to] undertake boring, repetitive wealth-creating tasks in a game, with the product of their labor sold to rich northern gamers who wanted to level-up without all the hard work." Unfortunately, exploitation and oppression, just like competition, seems to be an eternal characteristic of humanity. (And, yes, the title is an intentional reference to "Ender's Game" found elsewhere in this anthology.)

Anda's Game

Cory Doctorow

Anda didn't really start to play the game until she got herself a girl-shaped avatar. She was twelve, and up until then, she'd played a boy-elf, because her parents had sternly warned her that if you played a girl you were an instant perv-magnet. None of the girls at Ada Lovelace Comprehensive would have been caught dead playing a girl character. In fact, the only girls she'd ever seen in-game were being played by boys. You could tell, cos they were shaped like a boy's idea of what a girl looked like: hooge buzwabs and long legs all barely contained in tiny, pointless leather bikini-armor. Bintware, she called it.

But when Anda was twelve, she met Liza the Organiza, whose avatar was female, but had sensible tits and sensible armor and a bloody great sword that she was clearly very good with. Liza came to school after PE, when Anda was sitting and massaging her abused podge and hating her entire life from stupid sunrise to rotten sunset. Her PE kit was at the bottom of her school-bag and her face was that stupid red color that she *hated* and now it was stinking maths which was hardly better than PE but at least she didn't have to sweat.

But instead of maths, all the girls were called to assembly, and Liza the Organiza stood on the stage in front of Miss Cruickshanks the principal and Mrs Danzig, the useless counsellor.

"Hullo chickens," Liza said. She had an Australian accent. "Well, aren't you lot just precious and bright and expectant with your pink upturned faces like a load of flowers staring up at the sky?

"Warms me fecking heart it does."

That made Anda laugh, and she wasn't the only one. Miss Cruickshanks and Mrs. Danzig didn't look amused, but they tried to hide it.

"I am Liza the Organiza, and I kick arse. Seriously." She tapped a key on her laptop and the screen behind her lit up. It was a game—not the one that Anda played, but something space-themed, a space-station with a rocketship in the background. "This is my avatar." Sensible boobs, sensible armor, and a sword the size of the world. "In-game, they call me the Lizanator, Queen of the Spacelanes, El Presidente of the Clan Fahrenheit." The Fahrenheits had chapters in every game. They were amazing and deadly and cool, and to her knowledge, Anda had never met one in the flesh. They had their own *island* in her game. Crikey.

On screen, The Lizanator was fighting an army of wookie-men, sword in one hand, laser-blaster in the other, rocket-jumping, spinning, strafing, making impossible kills and long shots, diving for power-ups and ruthlessly running her enemies to ground.

"The *whole* Clan Fahrenheit. I won that title through popular election, but they voted me in cos of my prowess in *combat.* I'm a world-champion in six different games, from first-person shooters to strategy games. I've commanded armies and I've sent armies to their respawn gates by the thousands. Thousands, chickens: my battle record is 3,522 kills in a single battle. I have taken home cash prizes from competitions totaling more than 400,000 pounds. I game for four to six hours nearly every day, and the rest of the time, I do what I like.

"One of the things I like to do is come to girls' schools like yours and let you in on a secret: girls kick arse. We're faster, smarter, and better than boys. We play harder. We spend too much time thinking that we're freaks for gaming and when we do game, we never play as girls because we catch so much shite for it. Time to turn that around. I am the best gamer in the world and I'm a girl. I started playing at ten, and there were no women in games—you couldn't even buy a game in any of the shops I went to. It's different now, but it's still not perfect. We're going to change that, chickens, you lot and me.

"How many of you game?"

Anda put her hand up. So did about half the girls in the room.

"And how many of you play girls?"

All the hands went down.

"See, that's a tragedy. Practically makes me weep. Gamespace smells like a boy's *armpit*. It's time we girled it up a little. So here's my offer to you: if you will play as a girl, you will be given probationary memberships in the Clan Fahrenheit, and if you measure up, in six months, you'll be full-fledged members."

In real life, Liza the Organiza was a little podgy, like Anda herself, but she wore it with confidence. She was solid, like a brick wall, her hair bobbed bluntly at her shoulders. She dressed in a black jumper over loose dungarees with giant, goth boots with steel toes that looked like something you'd see in an in-game shop, though Anda was pretty sure they'd come from a real-world goth shop in Camden Town.

She stomped her boots, one-two, thump-thump, like thunder on the stage. "Who's in, chickens? Who wants to be a girl out-game and in?"

Anda jumped to her feet. A Fahrenheit, with her own island! Her head was so full of it that she didn't notice that she was the only one standing. The other girls stared at her, a few giggling and whispering.

"That's all right, love," Liza called, "I like enthusiasm. Don't let those staring faces rattle yer: they're just flowers turning to look at the sky. Pink scrubbed shining expectant faces. They're looking at you because *you* had the sense to get to your feet when opportunity came—and that means that someday, girl, you are going to be a leader of women, and men, and you will kick arse. Welcome to the Clan Fahrenheit."

She began to clap, and the other girls clapped too, and even though Anda's face was the color of a lollipop-lady's sign, she felt like she might burst with pride and good feeling and she smiled until her face hurt.

>Anda

her sergeant said to her,

> how would you like to make some money?

> Money, Sarge?

Ever since she'd risen to platoon leader, she'd been getting more missions, but they paid gold—money wasn't really something you talked about in-game.

The Sarge—sensible boobs, gigantic sword, longbow, gloriously orcish ugly phiz—moved her avatar impatiently.

> Something wrong with my typing, Anda?
> No, Sarge

she typed.

> You mean gold?
> If I meant gold, I would have said gold. Can you go voice?

Anda looked around. Her door was shut and she could hear her parents in the sitting-room watching something loud on telly. She turned up her music just to be safe and then slipped on her headset. They said it could noise-cancel a Blackhawk helicopter—it had better be able to overcome the little inductive speakers suction-cupped to the underside of her desk. She switched to voice.

"Hey, Lucy," she said.

"Call me Sarge!" Lucy's accent was American, like an old TV show, and she lived somewhere in the middle of the country where it was all vowels, Iowa or Ohio. She was Anda's best friend in-game but she was so hardcore it was boring sometimes.

"Hi, Sarge," she said, trying to keep the irritation out of her voice. She'd never smart off to a superior in-game, but v2v it was harder to remember to keep to the game norms.

"I have a mission that pays real cash. Whichever paypal you're using, they'll deposit money into it. Looks fun, too."

"That's a bit weird, Sarge. Is that against Clan rules?" There were a lot of Clan rules about what kind of mission you could accept and they were always changing. There were kerb-crawlers in gamespace and the way that the Clan leadership kept all the mummies and daddies from going ape-poo about it was by enforcing a long, boring code of conduct that was meant to ensure that none of the Fahrenheit girlies ended up being virtual prozzies for hairy old men in raincoats on the other side of the world.

"What?" Anda loved how Lucy quacked What? It sounded especially American. She had to force herself from parroting it back. "No, geez. All the executives in the Clan pay the rent doing missions for money. Some of them are even rich from it, I hear! You can make a lot of money gaming, you know."

"Is it really true?" She'd heard about this but she'd assumed it was just stories, like the kids who gamed so much that they couldn't tell reality from fantasy. Or the ones who gamed so much that they stopped eating and got all anorexic. She wouldn't mind getting a little anorexic, to be honest. Bloody podge.

"Yup! And this is our chance to get in on the ground floor. Are you in?"

"It's not—you know, *pervy*, is it?"

"Gag me. No. Jeez, Anda! Are you nuts? No—they want us to go kill some guys."

"Oh, we're good at that!"

The mission took them far from Fahrenheit Island, to a cottage on the far side of the largest continent on the gameworld, which was called Dandelionwine. The travel was tedious, and twice they were ambushed on the trail, something that had hardly happened to Anda since she joined the Fahrenheits: attacking a Fahrenheit was bad for your health, because even if you won the battle, they'd bring a war to you.

But now they were far from the Fahrenheits' power-base, and two different packs of brigands waylaid them on the road. Lucy spotted the first group before they got into sword-range and killed four of the six with her bow before they closed for hand-to-hand. Anda's sword—gigantic and fast—was out then, and her fingers danced over the keyboard as she fought off the player who was attacking her, her body jerking from side to side as she hammered on the multibutton controller beside her. She won—of course! She was a Fahrenheit! Lucy had already slaughtered her attacker. They desultorily searched the bodies and came up with some gold and a couple scrolls, but nothing to write home about. Even the gold didn't seem like much, given the cash waiting at the end of the mission.

The second group of brigands was even less daunting, though there were twenty of them. They were total noobs, and fought like statues.

They'd clearly clubbed together to protect themselves from harder players, but they were no match for Anda and Lucy. One of them even begged for his life before she ran him through,

> **please sorry u cn have my gold sorry!!!!!!**

Anda laughed and sent him to the respawn gate.

> **You're a nasty person, Anda,**

Lucy typed.

> **I'm a Fahrenheit!!!!!!!!!!**

she typed back.

The brigands on the road were punters, but the cottage that was their target was guarded by an altogether more sophisticated sort. They were spotted by sentries long before they got within sight of the cottage, and they saw the warning spell travel up from the sentries' hilltop like a puff of smoke, speeding away toward the cottage. Anda raced up the hill while Lucy covered her with her bow, but that didn't stop the sentries from subjecting Anda to a hail of flaming spears from their fortified position. Anda set up her standard dodge-and-weave pattern, assuming that the sentries were non-player characters—who wanted to *pay* to sit around in gamespace watching a boring road all day?—and to her surprise, the spears followed her. She took one in the chest and only some fast work with her shield and all her healing scrolls saved her. As it was, her constitution was knocked down by half and she had to retreat back down the hillside.

"Get down," Lucy said in her headset. "I'm gonna use the BFG."

Every game had one—the Big Friendly Gun, the generic term for the baddest-arse weapon in the world. Lucy had rented this one from the Clan armory for a small fortune in gold and Anda had laughed and called her paranoid, but now Anda helped Lucy set it up and thanked the gamegods for her foresight. It was a huge, demented flaming crossbow that fired five-metre bolts that exploded on impact. It was a beast to arm and a beast to aim, but they had a nice, dug-in position of their own at the bottom of the hill and it was there that they got the BFG set up, deployed, armed, and ranged.

"Fire!" Lucy called, and the game did this amazing and cool animation that it rewarded you with whenever you loosed a bolt from the BFG, making the gamelight dim towards the sizzling bolt as though it were sucking the illumination out of the world as it arced up the hillside, trailing a comet-tail of sparks. The game played them a groan of dismay from their enemies, and then the bolt hit home with a crash that made her point-of-view vibrate like an earthquake. The roar in her headphones was deafening, and behind it she could hear Lucy on the voice-chat, cheering it on.

"Nuke 'em till they glow and shoot 'em in the dark! Yee-haw!" Lucy called, and Anda laughed and pounded her fist on the desk. Gobbets of former enemy sailed over the treeline dramatically, dripping hyper-red blood and ichor.

In her bedroom, Anda caressed the controller-pad and her avatar punched the air and did a little rugby victory dance that the All-Blacks had released as a limited edition promo after they won the World Cup.

Now they had to move fast, for their enemies at the cottage would be alerted to their presence and waiting for them. They spread out into a wide flanking manoeuver around the cottage's sides, staying just outside of bow-range, using scrying scrolls to magnify the cottage and make the foliage around them fade to translucency.

There were four guards around the cottage, two with nocked arrows and two with whirling slings. One had a scroll out and was surrounded by the concentration marks that indicated spellcasting.

"GO GO GO!" Lucy called.

Anda went! She had two scrolls left in her inventory, and one was a shield spell. They cost a fortune and burned out fast, but whatever that guard was cooking up, it had to be bad news. She cast the spell as she charged for the cottage, and lucky thing, because there was a fifth guard up a tree who dumped a pot of boiling oil on her that would have cooked her down to her bones in ten seconds if not for the spell.

She power-climbed the tree and nearly lost her grip when whatever the nasty spell was bounced off her shield. She reached the fifth man as he was trying to draw his dirk and dagger and lopped his bloody head off in one motion, then backflipped off the high branch, trusting to her shield to stay intact for her impact on the cottage roof.

The strategy worked—now she had the drop (literally!) on the remaining guards, having successfully taken the high ground. In her headphones, the sound of Lucy making mayhem, the grunts as she pounded her keyboard mingling with the in-game shrieks as her arrows found homes in the chests of two more of the guards.

Shrieking a berserker wail, Anda jumped down off of the roof and landed on one of the two remaining guards, plunging her sword into his chest and pinning him in the dirt. Her sword stuck in the ground, and she hammered on her keys, trying to free it, while the remaining guard ran for her on-screen. Anda pounded her keyboard, but it was useless: the sword was good and stuck. Poo. She'd blown a small fortune on spells and rations for this project with the expectation of getting some real cash out of it, and now it was all lost.

She moved her hands to the part of the keypad that controlled motion and began to run, waiting for the guard's sword to find her avatar's back and knock her into the dirt.

"Got 'im!" It was Lucy, in her headphones. She wheeled her avatar about so quickly it was nauseating and saw that Lucy was on her erstwhile attacker, grunting as she engaged him close-in. Something was wrong, though: despite Lucy's avatar's awesome stats and despite Lucy's own skill at the keyboard, she was being taken to the cleaners. The guard was kicking her ass. Anda went back to her stuck sword and recommenced whanging on it, watching helplessly as Lucy lost her left arm, then took a cut on her belly, then another to her knee.

"Shit!" Lucy said in her headphones as her avatar began to keel over. Anda yanked her sword free—finally—and charged at the guard, screaming a ululating war cry. He managed to get his avatar swung around and his sword up before she reached him, but it didn't matter: she got in a lucky swing that took off one leg, then danced back before he could counterstrike. Now she closed carefully, nicking at his sword-hand until he dropped his weapon, then moving in for a fast kill.

"Lucy?"

"Call me Sarge!"

"Sorry, Sarge. Where'd you respawn?"

"I'm all the way over at Body Electric—it'll take me hours to get there. Do you think you can complete the mission on your own?"

"Uh, sure." Thinking, *Crikey, if that's what the guards* outside *were like, how'm I gonna get past the* inside *guards?*

"You're the best, girl. Okay, enter the cottage and kill everyone there."

"Uh, sure."

She wished she had another scrying scroll in inventory so she could get a look inside the cottage before she beat its door in, but she was fresh out of scrolls and just about everything else.

She kicked the door in and her fingers danced. She'd killed four of her adversaries before she even noticed that they weren't fighting back.

In fact, they were generic avatars, maybe even non-player characters. They moved like total noobs, milling around in the little cottage. Around them were heaps of shirts, thousands and thousands of them. A couple of the noobs were sitting in the back, incredibly, still crafting more shirts, ignoring the swordswoman who'd just butchered four of their companions.

She took a careful look at all the avatars in the room. None of them were armed. Tentatively, she walked up to one of the players and cut his head off. The player next to him moved clumsily to one side and she followed him.

>Are you a player or a bot?

she typed.

The avatar did nothing. She killed it.

"Lucy, they're not fighting back."

"Good, kill them all."

"Really?"

"Yeah—that's the orders. Kill them all and then I'll make a phone call and some guys will come by and verify it and then you haul ass back to the island. I'm coming out there to meet you, but it's a long haul from the respawn gate. Keep an eye on my stuff, okay?"

"Sure," Anda said, and killed two more. That left ten. *One two one two and through and through,* she thought, lopping their heads off. Her vorpal blade went snicker-snack. One left. He stood off in the back.

> no porfa necesito mi plata

Italian? No, Spanish. She'd had a term of it in Third Form, though she couldn't understand what this twit was saying. She could always paste the text into a translation bot on one of the chat channels, but who cared? She cut his head off.

"They're all dead," she said into her headset.

"Good job!" Lucy said. "OKAY, I'm gonna make a call. Sit tight."

Bo-ring. The cottage was filled with corpses and shirts. She picked some of them up. They were totally generic: the shirts you crafted when you were down at Level 0 and trying to get enough skillz to actually make something of yourself. Each one would fetch just a few coppers. Add it all together and you barely had two thousand gold.

Just to pass the time, she pasted the Spanish into the chatbot.

> no [colloquial] please, I need my [colloquial] [money|silver]

Pathetic. A few thousand golds—he could make that much by playing a couple of the beginner missions. More fun. More rewarding. Crafting shirts!

She left the cottage and patrolled around it. Twenty minutes later, two more avatars showed up. More generics.

> are you players or bots?

she typed, though she had an idea they were players. Bots moved better.

> any trouble?

Well, all right then.

> no trouble
> good

One player entered the cottage and came back out again. The other player spoke.

> you can go now

"Lucy?"

"What's up?"

"Two blokes just showed up and told me to piss off. They're noobs, though. Should I kill them?"

"No! Jeez, Anda, those are the contacts. They're just making sure the job was done. Get my stuff and meet me at Marionettes Tavern, okay?"

Anda went over to Lucy's corpse and looted it, then set out down the road, dragging the BFG behind her. She stopped at the bend in the road and snuck a peek back at the cottage. It was in flames, the two noobs standing amid them, burning slowly along with the cottage and a few thousand golds' worth of badly crafted shirts.

That was the first of Anda and Lucy's missions, but it wasn't the last. That month, she fought her way through six more, and the paypal she used filled with real, honest-to-goodness cash, Pounds Sterling that she could withdraw from the cashpoint situated exactly 501 meters away from the schoolgate, next to the candy shop that was likewise 501 meters away.

"Anda, I don't think it's healthy for you to spend so much time with your game," her da said, prodding her bulging podge with a finger. "It's not healthy."

"Daaaa!" she said, pushing his finger aside. "I go to PE every stinking day. It's good enough for the Ministry of Education."

"I don't like it," he said. He was no movie star himself, with a little potbelly that he wore his belted trousers high upon, a wobbly extra chin and two bat wings of flab hanging off his upper arms. She pinched his chin and wiggled it.

"I get loads more exercise than you, Mr. Kettle."

"But I pay the bills around here, little Miss Pot."

"You're not seriously complaining about the cost of the game?" she said, infusing her voice with as much incredulity and disgust as she could muster. "Ten quid a week and I get unlimited calls, texts, and messages! Plus play of course, and the in-game encyclopedia and spellchecker and translator bots!" (this was all from rote—every member of the Fahrenheits memorized this or something very like it for dealing with recalcitrant, ignorant parental units) "Fine then. If the game is too dear for you, Da, let's set it aside and I'll just start using a normal phone, is that what you want?"

Her da held up his hands. "I surrender, Miss Pot. But *do* try to get a little more exercise, please? Fresh air? Sport? Games?"

"Getting my head trodden on in the hockey pitch, more like," she said, darkly.

"Zackly!" he said, prodding her podge anew. "That's the stuff! Getting my head trodden on was what made me the man I are today!"

Da could bluster all he liked about paying the bills, but she had pocket-money for the first time in her life: not book-tokens and fruit-tokens and milk-tokens that could be exchanged for "healthy" snacks and literature. She had real money, cash money that she could spend outside of the 500 meter sugar-free zone that surrounded her school.

She wasn't just kicking arse in the game, now—she was the richest kid she knew, and suddenly she was everybody's best pal, with handfuls of Curly Wurlies and Dairy Milks and Mars Bars that she could selectively distribute to her schoolmates.

"Go get a BFG," Lucy said. "We're going on a mission."

Lucy's voice in her ear was a constant companion in her life now. When she wasn't on Fahrenheit Island, she and Lucy were running missions into the wee hours of the night. The Fahrenheit armorers, non-player-characters, had learned to recognize her and they had the Clan's BFGs oiled and ready for her when she showed up.

Today's mission was close to home, which was good: the road-trips were getting tedious. Sometimes, non-player-characters or Game Masters would try to get them involved in an official in-game mission, impressed by their stats and weapons, and it sometimes broke her heart to pass them up, but cash always beat gold and experience beat experience points: *Money talks and bullshit walks,* as Lucy liked to say.

They caught the first round of sniper/lookouts before they had a chance to attack or send off a message. Anda used the scrying spell to spot them. Lucy had kept both BFGs armed and she loosed rounds at the hilltops flanking the roadway as soon as Anda gave her the signal, long before they got into bow range.

As they picked their way through the ruined chunks of the dead player-character snipers, Anda still on the lookout, she broke the silence over their voicelink.

"Hey, Lucy?"

"Anda, if you're not going to call me Sarge, at least don't call me 'Hey, Lucy!' My dad loved that old TV show and he makes that joke every visitation day."

"Sorry, Sarge. Sarge?"

"Yes, Anda?"

"I just can't understand why anyone would pay us cash for these missions."

"You complaining?"

"No, but—"

"Anyone asking you to cyber some old pervert?"

"No!"

"Okay then. I don't know either. But the money's good. I don't care. Hell, probably it's two rich gamers who pay their butlers to craft for them all day. One's fucking with the other one and paying us."

"You really think that?"

Lucy sighed a put-upon, sophisticated, American sigh. "Look at it this way. Most of the world is living on like a dollar a day. I spend five dollars every day on a Frappuccino. Some days, I get two! Dad sends Mom three thousand a month in child-support—that's a hundred bucks a day. So if a day's money here is a hundred dollars, then to a African or whatever my Frappuccino is worth like *five hundred dollars.* And I buy two or three every day.

"And we're not rich! There's craploads of rich people who wouldn't think twice about spending five hundred bucks on a coffee—how much do you think a hotdog and a Coke go for on the space station? A thousand bucks!

"So that's what I think is going on. There's someone out there, some Saudi or Japanese guy or Russian mafia kid who's so rich that this is just chump change for him, and he's paying us to mess around with some other rich person. To them, we're like the Africans making a dollar a day to craft—I mean, sew—T-shirts. What's a couple hundred bucks to them? A cup of coffee."

Anda thought about it. It made a kind of sense. She'd been on hols in Bratislava where they got a posh hotel room for ten quid—less than she was spending every day on sweeties and fizzy drinks.

"Three o'clock," she said, and aimed the BFG again. More snipers pat-patted in bits around the forest floor.

"Nice one, Anda."

"Thanks, Sarge."

They smashed half a dozen more sniper outposts and fought their way through a couple packs of suspiciously bad-ass brigands before coming upon the cottage.

"Bloody hell," Anda breathed. The cottage was ringed with guards, forty or fifty of them, with bows and spells and spears, in entrenched positions.

"This is nuts," Lucy agreed. "I'm calling them. This is nuts."

There was a muting click as Lucy rang off and Anda used up a scrying scroll to examine the inventories of the guards around the corner. The more she looked, the more scared she got. They were loaded down with spells, a couple of them were guarding BFGs and what looked like an even *bigger* BFG, maybe the fabled BFG10K, something that was removed from the game economy not long after gameday one, as too disruptive to the balance of power. Supposedly, one or two existed, but that was just a rumor. Wasn't it?

"Okay," Lucy said. "Okay, this is how this goes. We've got to do this. I just called in three squads of Fahrenheit veterans and their noob prentices for backup." Anda summed that up in her head to a hundred player characters and maybe three hundred nonplayer characters: familiars, servants, demons . . .

"That's a lot of shares to split the pay into," Anda said.

"Oh ye of little tits," Lucy said. "I've negotiated a bonus for us if we make it—a million gold and three missions' worth of cash. The Fahrenheits are taking payment in gold—they'll be here in an hour."

This wasn't a mission anymore, Anda realized. It was war. Gamewar. Hundreds of players converging on this shard, squaring off against the ranked mercenaries guarding the huge cottage over the hill.

Lucy wasn't the ranking Fahrenheit on the scene, but she was the designated general. One of the gamers up from Fahrenheit Island brought a team flag for her to carry, a long spear with the magical standard snapping proudly from it as the troops formed up behind her.

"On my signal," Lucy said. The voice chat was like a wind-tunnel from all the unmuted breathing voices, hundreds of girls in hundreds of bedrooms like Anda's, all over the world, some sitting down before breakfast, some just coming home from school, some roused from sleep by their ringing game-sponsored mobiles. "GO GO GO!"

They went, roaring, and Anda roared too, heedless of her parents downstairs in front of the blaring telly, heedless of her throat-lining, a Fahrenheit in berzerker rage, sword swinging. She made straight for the BFG10K—a siege engine that could level a town wall, and it would be hers, captured by her for the Fahrenheits if she could do it. She spelled the merc who was cranking it into insensibility, rolled and rolled again to dodge arrows and spells, healed herself when an arrow found her leg and sent her tumbling, springing to her feet before another arrow could strike home, watching her hit points and experience points move in opposite directions.

HERS! She vaulted the BFG10K and snicker-snacked her sword through two mercs' heads. Two more appeared—they had the thing primed and aimed at the main body of Fahrenheit fighters, and they could turn the battle's tide just by firing it—and she killed them, slamming her keypad, howling, barely conscious of the answering howls in her headset.

Now *she* had the BFG10K, though more mercs were closing on her. She disarmed it quickly and spelled at the nearest bunch of mercs, then had to take evasive action against the hail of incoming arrows and spells. It was all she could do to cast healing spells fast enough to avoid losing consciousness.

"LUCY!" she called into her headset. "LUCY, OVER BY THE BFG10K!"

Lucy snapped out orders and the opposition before Anda began to thin as Fahrenheits fell on them from behind. The flood was stemmed, and now the Fahrenheits' greater numbers and discipline showed. In short order, every merc was butchered or run off.

Anda waited by the BFG10K while Lucy paid off the Fahrenheits and saw them on their way. "Now we take the cottage," Lucy said.

"Right," Anda said. She set her character off for the doorway. Lucy brushed past her.

"I'll be glad when we're done with this—that was bugfuck nutso." She opened the door and her character disappeared in a fireball that erupted from directly overhead. A door-curse, a serious one, one that cooked her in her armor in seconds.

"SHIT!" Lucy said in her headset.

Anda giggled. "Teach you to go rushing into things," she said. She used up a couple scrying scrolls making sure that there was nothing else in the cottage save for millions of shirts and thousands of unarmed noob avatars that she'd have to mow down like grass to finish out the mission.

She descended upon them like a reaper, swinging her sword heedlessly, taking five or six out with each swing. When she'd been a noob in the game, she'd had to endure endless fighting practice, "grappling" with piles of leaves and other nonlethal targets, just to get enough experience points to have a chance of hitting anything. This was every bit as dull.

Her wrists were getting tired, and her chest heaved and her hated podge wobbled as she worked the keypad.

> Wait, please, don't—I'd like to speak with you

It was a noob avatar, just like the others, but not just like it after all, for it moved with purpose, backing away from her sword. And it spoke English.

> nothing personal

she typed

> just a job

> There are many here to kill—take me last at least. I need to talk to you.

> talk, then

she typed. Meeting players who moved well and spoke English was hardly unusual in gamespace, but here in the cleanup phase, it felt out of place. It felt wrong.

> My name is Raymond, and I live in Tijuana. I am a labor organizer in the factories here. What is your name?

> i don't give out my name in-game

> What can I call you?

> kali

It was a name she liked to use in-game: Kali, Destroyer of Worlds, like the Hindu goddess.

> Are you in India?

> london

> You are Indian?

> naw im a whitey

She was halfway through the room, mowing down the noobs in twos and threes. She was hungry and bored and this Raymond was weirding her out.

> Do you know who these people are that you're killing?

She didn't answer, but she had an idea. She killed four more and shook out her wrists.

> They're working for less than a dollar a day. The shirts they make are traded for gold and the gold is sold on eBay. Once their avatars have leveled up, they too are sold off on eBay. They're mostly young girls supporting their families. They're the lucky ones: the unlucky ones work as prostitutes.

Her wrists *really* ached. She slaughtered half a dozen more.

> The bosses used to use bots, but the game has countermeasures against them. Hiring children to click the mouse is cheaper than hiring programmers to circumvent the rules. I've been trying to unionize them because they've got a very high rate of injury. They have to play for 18-hour shifts with only one short toilet break. Some of them can't hold it in and they soil themselves where they sit.
> look

she typed, exasperated.

> it's none of my lookout, is it. the world's like that. lots of people with no money. im just a kid, theres nothing i can do about it.
> When you kill them, they don't get paid.

no porfa necesito mi plata

> When you kill them, they lose their day's wages. Do you know who is paying you to do these killings?

She thought of Saudis, rich Japanese, Russian mobsters.

> not a clue
> I've been trying to find that out myself, Kali.

They were all dead now. Raymond stood alone amongst the piled corpses.

> Go ahead

he typed

> I will see you again, I'm sure.

She cut his head off. Her wrists hurt. She was hungry. She was alone there in the enormous woodland cottage, and she still had to haul the BFG10K back to Fahrenheit Island.

"Lucy?"

"Yeah, yeah, I'm almost back there, hang on. I respawned in the ass end of nowhere."

"Lucy, do you know who's in the cottage? Those noobs that we kill?"

"What? Hell no. Noobs. Someone's butler. I dunno. Jesus, that spawn gate—"

"Girls. Little girls in Mexico. Getting paid a dollar a day to craft shirts. Except they don't get their dollar when we kill them. They don't get anything."

"Oh, for chrissakes, is that what one of them told you? Do you believe everything someone tells you in-game? Christ. English girls are so naive."

"You don't think it's true?"

"Naw, I don't."

"Why not?"

"I just don't, okay? I'm almost there, keep your panties on."

"I've got to go, Lucy," she said. Her wrists hurt, and her podge overlapped the waistband of her trousers, making her feel a bit like she was drowning.

"What, now? Shit, just hang on."

"My mom's calling me to supper. You're almost here, right?"

"Yeah, but—"

She reached down and shut off her PC.

Anda's da and mum were watching the telly again with a bowl of crisps between them. She walked past them like she was dreaming and stepped out the door onto the terrace. It was nighttime, eleven o'clock, and the chavs in front of the council flats across the square were kicking a football around and swilling lager and making rude noises. They were skinny and rawboned, wearing shorts and string vests with strong, muscular limbs flashing in the streetlights.

"Anda?"

"Yes, Mum?"

"Are you all right?" Her mum's fat fingers caressed the back of her neck.

"Yes, Mum. Just needed some air is all."

"You're very clammy," her mum said. She licked a finger and scrubbed it across Anda's neck. "Gosh, you're dirty—how did you get to be such a mucky puppy?"

"Owww!" she said. Her mum was scrubbing so hard it felt like she'd take her skin off.

"No whingeing," her mum said sternly. "Behind your ears, too! You are *filthy.*"

"Mum, *owwww!*"

Her mum dragged her up to the bathroom and went at her with a flannel and a bar of soap and hot water until she felt boiled and raw.

"What *is* this mess?" her mum said.

"Lilian, leave off," her dad said, quietly. "Come out into the hall for a moment, please."

The conversation was too quiet to hear and Anda didn't want to, anyway: she was concentrating too hard on not crying—her ears *hurt.*

Her mum enfolded her shoulders in her soft hands again. "Oh, darling, I'm sorry. It's a skin condition, your father tells me, *Acanthosis Nigricans*—he saw it in a TV special. We'll see the doctor about it tomorrow after school. Are you all right?"

"I'm fine," she said, twisting to see if she could see the "dirt" on the back of her neck in the mirror. It was hard because it was an awkward placement—but also because she didn't like to look at her face and her soft extra chin, and she kept catching sight of it.

She went back to her room to google *Acanthosis Nigricans.*

> A condition involving darkened, thickened skin. Found in the folds of skin at the base of the back of the neck, under the arms, inside the elbow and at the waistline. Often precedes a diagnosis of type-2 diabetes, especially in children. If found in children, immediate steps must be taken to prevent diabetes, including exercise and nutrition as a means of lowering insulin levels and increasing insulin-sensitivity.

Obesity-related diabetes. They had lectures on this every term in health class—the fastest-growing ailment among British teens, accompanied by photos of orca-fat sacks of lard sat up in bed surrounded by an ocean of rubbery, flowing podge. Anda prodded her belly and watched it jiggle.

It jiggled. Her thighs jiggled. Her chins wobbled. Her arms sagged.

She grabbed a handful of her belly and squeezed it, pinched it hard as she could, until she had to let go or cry out. She'd left livid red fingerprints in the rolls of fat and she was crying now, from the pain and the shame and oh, God, she was a fat girl with diabetes—

"Jesus, Anda, where the hell have you been?"

"Sorry, Sarge," she said. "My PC's been broken—" Well, out of service, anyway. Under lock-and-key in her dad's study. Almost a month now of medications and no telly and no gaming and double PE periods at school with the other whales. She was miserable all day, every day now, with nothing to look forward to except the trips after school to the newsagents at the 501-meter mark and the fistsful of sweeties and bottles of fizzy drink she ate in the park while she watched the chavs play footy.

"Well, you should have found a way to let me know. I was getting worried about you, girl."

"Sorry, Sarge," she said again. The PC Baang was filled with stinky spotty boys—literally stinky, it smelt like goats, like a train-station toilet—being loud and obnoxious. The dinky headphones provided were greasy as a slice of pizza, and the mouthpiece was sticky with excited boy-saliva from games gone past.

But it didn't matter. Anda was back in the game, and just in time, too: her money was running short.

"Well, I've got a backlog of missions here. I tried going out with a couple other of the girls—" A pang of regret shot through Anda at the thought that her position might have been usurped while she was locked off the game "—but you're too good to replace, OKAY? I've got four missions we can do today if you're game."

"Four missions! How on earth will we do four missions? That'll take days!"

"We'll take the BFG10K." Anda could hear the savage grin in her voice.

The BFG10K simplified things quite a lot. Find the cottage, aim the BFG10K, fire it, whim-wham, no more cottage. They started with five bolts for it—one BFG10K bolt was made up of twenty regular BFG bolts, each costing a small fortune in gold—and used them all up on the first three targets. After returning it to the armory and grabbing a couple of BFGs (amazing how puny the BFG seemed after just a couple hours' campaigning with a really *big* gun!) they set out for number four.

"I met a guy after the last campaign," Anda said. "One of the noobs in the cottage. He said he was a union organizer."

"Oh, you met Raymond, huh?"

"You knew about him?"

"I met him too. He's been turning up everywhere. What a creep."

"So you knew about the noobs in the cottages?"

"Um. Well, yeah, I figured it out mostly on my own and then Raymond told me a little more."

"And you're fine with depriving little kids of their wages?"

"Anda," Lucy said, her voice brittle. "You like gaming, right, it's important to you?"

"Yeah, 'course it is."

"How important? Is it something you do for fun, just a hobby you waste a little time on? Are you just into it casually, or are you committed to it?"

"I'm committed to it, Lucy, you know that." God, without the game, what was there? PE class? Stupid *Acanthosis Nigricans* and, someday, insulin jabs every morning? "I love the game, Lucy. It's where my friends are."

"I know that. That's why you're my right-hand woman, why I want you at my side when I go on a mission. We're bad-ass, you and me, as bad-ass as they come, and we got that way through discipline and hard work and really *caring* about the game, right?"

"Yes, right, but—"

"You've met Liza the Organiza, right?"

"Yes, she came by my school."

"Mine too. She asked me to look out for you because of what she saw in you that day."

"Liza the Organiza goes to Ohio?"

"Idaho. Yes—all across the U.S. They put her on the tube and everything. She's amazing, and she cares about the game, too—that's what makes us all Fahrenheits: we're committed to each other, to teamwork, and to fair play."

Anda had heard these words—lifted from the Fahrenheit mission statement—many times, but now they made her swell a little with pride.

"So these people in Mexico or wherever, what are they doing? They're earning their living by exploiting the game. You and me, we would never trade cash for gold, or buy a character or a weapon on eBay—it's cheating. You get gold and weapons through hard work and hard play. But those Mexicans spend all day, every day, crafting stuff to turn into gold to sell off on the exchange. *That's where it comes from*—that's where the crappy players get their gold from! That's how rich noobs can buy their way into the game that we had to play hard to get into.

"So we burn them out. If we keep burning the factories down, they'll shut them down and those kids'll find something else to do for a living and the game will be better. If no one does that, our work will just get cheaper and cheaper: the game will get less and less fun, too.

"These people *don't* care about the game. To them, it's just a place to suck a buck out of. They're not players, they're leeches, here to suck all the fun out."

They had come upon the cottage now, the fourth one, having exterminated four different sniper-nests on the way.

"Are you in, Anda? Are you here to play, or are you so worried about these leeches on the other side of the world that you want out?"

"I'm in, Sarge," Anda said. She armed the BFGs and pointed them at the cottage.

"Boo-yah!" Lucy said. Her character notched an arrow.

> Hello, Kali

"Oh, Christ, he's back," Lucy said. Raymond's avatar had snuck up behind them.

> Look at these

he said, and his character set something down on the ground and backed away. Anda edged up on them.

"Come on, it's probably a booby-trap, we've got work to do," Lucy said.

They were photo-objects. She picked them up and then examined them. The first showed ranked little girls, fifty or more, in clean and simple T-shirts, skinny as anything, sitting at generic white-box PCs, hands on the keyboards. They were hollow-eyed and grim, and none of them older than she.

The next showed a shantytown, shacks made of corrugated aluminum and trash, muddy trails between them, spray-painted graffiti, rude boys loitering, rubbish and carrier bags blowing.

The next showed the inside of a shanty, three little girls and a little boy sitting together on a battered sofa, their mother serving them something white and indistinct on plastic plates. Their smiles were heartbreaking and brave.

> That's who you're about to deprive of a day's wages

"Oh, hell, *no,*" Lucy said. "Not again. I killed him last time and I said I'd do it again if he ever tried to show me photos. That's it, he's dead." Her character turned towards him, putting away her bow and drawing a short sword. Raymond's character backed away quickly.

"Lucy, don't," Anda said. She interposed her avatar between Lucy's and Raymond. "Don't do it. He deserves to have a say." She thought of old American TV shows, the kinds you saw between the Bollywood movies on telly. "It's a free country, right?"

"God *damn* it, Anda, what is *wrong* with you? Did you come here to play the game, or to screw around with this pervert dork?"

> what do you want from me raymond?

> Don't kill them—let them have their wages. Go play somewhere else

> They're leeches

Lucy typed

> they're wrecking the game economy and they're providing a gold-for-cash supply that lets rich assholes buy their way in. They don't care about the game and neither do you

> If they don't play the game, they don't eat. I think that means that they care about the game as much as you do. You're being paid cash to kill them, yes? So you need to play for your money, too. I think that makes you and them the same, a little the same.

> go screw yourself

Lucy typed. Anda edged her character away from Lucy's. Raymond's character was so far away now that his texting came out in tiny type, almost too small to read. Lucy drew her bow again and nocked an arrow.

"Lucy, *don't*!" Anda cried. Her hands moved of their own volition and her character followed, clobbering Lucy barehanded so that her avatar reeled and dropped its bow.

"You *bitch*!" Lucy said. She drew her sword.

"I'm sorry, Lucy," Anda said, stepping back out of range. "But I don't want you to hurt him. I want to hear him out."

Lucy's avatar came on fast, and there was a click as the voicelink dropped. Anda typed one-handed while she drew her own sword.

> dont lucy come on talk2me

Lucy slashed at her twice and she needed both hands to defend herself or she would have been beheaded. Anda blew out through her nose and counterattacked, fingers pounding the keyboard. Lucy had more experience points than she did, but she was a better player, and she knew it. She hacked away at Lucy driving her back and back, back down the road they'd marched together.

Abruptly, Lucy broke and ran, and Anda thought she was going away and decided to let her go, no harm no foul, but then she saw that Lucy wasn't running away, she was running *towards* the BFGs, armed and primed.

"Bloody hell," she breathed, as a BFG swung around to point at her. Her fingers flew. She cast the fireball at Lucy in the same instant that she cast her shield spell. Lucy loosed the bolt at her a moment before the fireball engulfed her, cooking her down to ash, and the bolt collided with the shield and drove Anda back, high into the air, and the shield spell wore off before she hit ground, costing her half her health and inventory, which scattered around her. She tested her voicelink.

"Lucy?"

There was no reply.

> I'm very sorry you and your friend quarreled.

She felt numb and unreal. There were rules for Fahrenheits, lots of rules, and the penalties for breaking them varied, but the penalty for attacking a fellow Fahrenheit was—she couldn't think the word, she closed her eyes, but there it was in big glowing letters: EXPULSION.

But Lucy had started it, right? It wasn't her fault.

But who would believe her?

She opened her eyes. Her vision swam through incipient tears. Her heart was thudding in her ears.

> The enemy isn't your fellow player. It's not the players guarding the fabrica, it's not the girls working there. The people who are working to destroy the game are the people who pay you and the people who pay the girls in the fabrica, who are the same people. You're being paid by rival factory owners, you know that? THEY are the ones who care nothing for the game. My girls care about the game. You care about the game. Your common enemy is the people who want to destroy the game and who destroy the lives of these girls.

"Whassamatter, you fat little cow? Is your game making you cwy?" She jerked as if slapped. The chav who was speaking to her hadn't been in the Baang when she arrived, and he had mean, close-set eyes and a football jersey and though he wasn't any older than she, he looked mean, and angry, and his smile was sadistic and crazy.

"Piss off," she said, mustering her braveness.

"You wobbling tub of guts, don't you *dare* speak to me that way," he said, shouting right in her ear. The Baang fell silent and everyone looked at her. The Pakistani who ran the Baang was on his phone, no doubt calling the coppers, and that meant that her parents would discover where she'd been and then—

"I'm talking to you, girl," he said. "You disgusting lump of suet—Christ, it makes me wanta puke to look at you. You ever had a boyfriend? How'd he shag you—did he roll yer in flour and look for the wet spot?"

She reeled back, then stood. She drew her arm back and slapped him, as hard as she could. The boys in the Baang laughed and went *whoooooo!* He purpled and balled his fists and she backed away from him. The imprint of her fingers stood out on his cheek.

He bridged the distance between them with a quick step and punched her, in the belly, and the air whooshed out of her and she fell into another player, who pushed her away, so she ended up slumped against the wall, crying.

The mean boy was there, right in front of her, and she could smell the chili crisps on his breath. "You disgusting whore—" he began and she kneed him square in the nadgers, hard as she could, and he screamed like a little girl and fell backwards. She picked up her schoolbag and ran for the door, her chest heaving, her face streaked with tears.

"Anda, dear, there's a phone call for you."

Her eyes stung. She'd been lying in her darkened bedroom for hours now, snuffling and trying not to cry, trying not to look at the empty desk where her PC used to live.

Her da's voice was soft and caring, but after the silence of her room, it sounded like a rusting hinge.

"Anda?"

She opened her eyes. He was holding a cordless phone, silhouetted against the open doorway.

"Who is it?"

"Someone from your game, I think," he said. He handed her the phone.

"Hullo?"

"Hullo, chicken." It had been a year since she'd heard that voice, but she recognized it instantly.

"Liza?"

"Yes."

Anda's skin seemed to shrink over her bones. This was it: expelled. Her heart felt like it was beating once per second, time slowed to a crawl.

"Hullo, Liza."

"Can you tell me what happened today?"

She did, stumbling over the details, back-tracking and stuttering. She couldn't remember, exactly—did Lucy move on Raymond and Anda asked her to stop and then Lucy attacked her? Had Anda attacked Lucy first? It was all a jumble. She should have saved a screenmovie and taken it with her, but she couldn't have taken anything with her, she'd run out—

"I see. Well it sounds like you've gotten yourself into quite a pile of poo, haven't you, my girl?"

"I guess so," Anda said. Then, because she knew that she was as good as expelled, she said, "I don't think it's right to kill them, those girls. All right?"

"Ah," Liza said. "Well, funny you should mention that. I happen to agree. Those girls need our help more than any of the girls anywhere in the game. The Fahrenheits' strength is that we are cooperative—it's another way that we're better than the boys. We care. I'm proud that you took a stand when you did—glad I found out about this business."

"You're not going to expel me?"

"No, chicken, I'm not going to expel you. I think you did the right thing—"

That meant that Lucy would be expelled. Fahrenheit had killed Fahrenheit—something had to be done. The rules had to be enforced. Anda swallowed hard.

"If you expel Lucy, I'll quit," she said, quickly, before she lost her nerve.

Liza laughed. "Oh, chicken, you're a brave thing, aren't you? No one's being expelled, fear not. But I wanta talk to this Raymond of yours."

Anda came home from remedial hockey sweaty and exhausted, but not as exhausted as the last time, nor the time before that. She could run the whole length of the pitch twice now without collapsing—when she'd started out, she could barely make it halfway without having to stop and hold her side, kneading her loathsome podge to make it stop aching. Now there was noticeably less podge, and she found that with the ability to run the pitch came the freedom to actually pay attention to the game, to aim her shots, to build up a degree of accuracy that was nearly as satisfying as being really good in-game.

Her da knocked at the door of her bedroom after she'd showered and changed. "How's my girl?"

"Revising," she said, and hefted her maths book at him.

"Did you have a fun afternoon on the pitch?"

"You mean 'did my head get trod on?' "

"Did it?"

"Yes," she said. "But I did more treading than getting trodden on." The other girls were *really* fat, and they didn't have a lot of team skills. Anda had been to war: she knew how to depend on someone and how to be depended upon.

"That's my girl." He pretended to inspect the paint-work around the light switch. "Been on the scales this week?"

She had, of course: the school nutritionist saw to that, a morning humiliation undertaken in full sight of all the other fatties.

"Yes, Da."

"And—?"

"I've lost a stone," she said. A little more than a stone, actually. She had been able to fit into last year's jeans the other day.

She hadn't been in the sweets-shop in a month. When she thought about sweets, it made her think of the little girls in the sweatshop. Sweatshop, sweetshop. The sweets shop man sold his wares close to the school because little girls who didn't know better would be tempted by them. No one forced them, but they were *kids* and grownups were supposed to look out for kids.

Her da beamed at her. "I've lost three pounds myself," he said, holding his tum. "I've been trying to follow your diet, you know."

"I know, Da," she said. It embarrassed her to discuss it with him.

The kids in the sweatshops were being exploited by grownups, too. It was why their situation was so impossible: the adults who were supposed to be taking care of them were exploiting them.

"Well, I just wanted to say that I'm proud of you. We both are, your mum and me. And I wanted to let you know that I'll be moving your PC back into your room tomorrow. You've earned it."

Anda blushed pink. She hadn't really expected this. Her fingers twitched over a phantom game-controller.

"Oh, Da," she said. He held up his hand.

"It's all right, girl. We're just proud of you."

She didn't touch the PC the first day, nor the second. The kids in the game—she didn't know what to do about them. On the third day, after hockey, she showered and changed and sat down and slipped the headset on.

"Hello, Anda."

"Hi, Sarge."

Lucy had known the minute she entered the game, which meant that she was still on Lucy's buddy-list. Well, that was a hopeful sign.

"You don't have to call me that. We're the same rank now, after all."

Anda pulled down a menu and confirmed it: she'd been promoted to Sergeant during her absence. She smiled.

"Gosh," she said.

"Yes, well, you earned it," Lucy said. "I've been talking to Raymond a lot about the working conditions in the factory, and, well—" She broke off.

"I'm sorry, Anda."

"Me too, Lucy."

"You don't have anything to be sorry about," she said.

They went adventuring, running some of the game's standard missions together. It was fun, but after the kind of campaigning they'd done before, it was also kind of pale and flat.

"It's horrible, I know," Anda said. "But I miss it."

"Oh thank God," Lucy said. "I thought I was the only one. It was fun, wasn't it? Big fights, big stakes."

"Well, poo," Anda said. "I don't wanna be bored for the rest of my life. What're we gonna do?"

"I was hoping you knew."

She thought about it. The part she'd loved had been going up against grownups who were not playing the game, but gaming it, breaking it for money. They'd been worthy adversaries, and there was no guilt in beating them, either.

"We'll ask Raymond how we can help," she said.

"I want them to walk out—to go on strike," he said. "It's the only way to get results: band together and withdraw your labor." Raymond's voice had a thick Mexican accent that took some getting used to, but his English was very good—better, in fact, than Lucy's.

"Walk out in-game?" Lucy said.

"No," Raymond said. "That wouldn't be very effective. I want them to walk out in Ciudad Juarez and Tijuana. I'll call the press in, we'll make a big deal out of it. We can win—I know we can."

"So what's the problem?" Anda said.

"The same problem as always. Getting them organized. I thought that the game would make it easier: we've been trying to get these girls organized for years: in the sewing shops, and the toy factories, but they lock the doors and keep us out and the girls go home and their parents won't let us talk to them. But in the game, I thought I'd be able to reach them—"

"But the bosses keep you away?"

"I keep getting killed. I've been practicing my swordfighting, but it's so hard—"

"This will be *fun*," Anda said. "Let's go."

"Where?" Lucy said.

"To an in-game factory. We're your new bodyguards." The bosses hired some pretty mean mercs, Anda knew. She'd been one. They'd be fun to wipe out.

Raymond's character spun around on the screen, then planted a kiss on Anda's cheek. Anda made her character give him a playful shove that sent him sprawling.

"Hey, Lucy, go get us a couple BFGs, OKAY?"

In martial arts, the importance of Zen (primarily for practitioners of the Japanese school) and Taoism (Chinese) have often been noted. They affect both the mind and the body. As the author commented on this tale: "Judo and Zen are a discipline and a philosophy grounded in the human experience. I was interested in exploring how they might interact, translate, and transcend with a nonhuman race that knows illusion and is in fact its master." All the editor can add is this: Once she was—by far—the least trained, least athletic person visiting a karate dojo. *The* sensei *asked her to break a board with the side of her hand. Of course, she was not successful. The* sensei *said, "I know you. This is only a matter of the mind. You can do this. Now. Break the board." She did. Without injuring her hand. No trick. In her world of the time—mostly that of easily impressionable elementary-school-age boys—she became, briefly, a legend: the mom who could break boards with her mind.*

Listen

Joel Richards

Kata.

Cameron moved slowly and fluidly on an unseen path. Each movement flowed from the one before, yet there was no clear line of demarcation between where one left off and the next began. But there was precision.

One step. Two. Turn and pivot.

But no one to throw. Or to throw him.

Cameron switched his mindset from judo to karate, and wished that he had trained more in that art. He had only a white belt's skill and complexity to work from. Still, a *karateka* could punch and kick at chimeras and feel fulfilled. Judo required an *uke* to offer resistance and a *tori* to counter throw. There were no other *judokas* on this world.

But somehow, improbably, there was a *karateka*. The air shimmered before Cameron, a heat refraction, perhaps. Cameron smelled the straw of Earthside *tatami* beneath him.

He looked up to see the serene features of Hideo Nakajima, his old *sensei*, advancing toward him, his faded black belt and its embroidery before him in perfect detail to the smallest thread.

The *sensei* advanced deliberately, with none of the speed that he could produce against a high ranked opponent in free combat. He launched a series of blows. Cameron blocked, pivoted and delivered a roundhouse kick. In a movement of grace and economy, the black belt evaded the blow and landed a sidekick of his own. Cameron saw his *sensei*'s foot meet his *gi*, but he felt nothing. His mind raced back to that first series of blows that he had blocked, his mind registering what he had ignored in the instinctive transition to counter kick. No impact. He had blocked nothing.

He turned to face his partner and found himself alone.

Off to the side stood the head of the diplomatic mission, the consul. Beside him was a visiting Alcaidan, one Cameron had not seen before. Or had he?

The Alcaidan smiled and turned away.

The consul folded his hands neatly on the desk before him and looked at them with near respect. How many forms they had shuffled, how many memos they had signed!

"Peter," he said with something of a sigh, "It relieves and gratifies me that our hosts have finally extended a social invitation to us. It pains me that it has been extended to you. But so be it."

Cameron waited, but the consul's gaze had once more retreated to his manicured and immobile hands.

"An invitation," Cameron stated, with no interrogatory inflection.

"They invite you to an interview. If you comport yourself satisfactorily—whatever that may mean—then you will be invited to a Hunt."

"I see."

"Do you?" The consul raised his eyebrows. "There's a lot I don't see. What these Alcaidans are really like. They're shapeshifters, but what do they really look like when they're not trying to make some sort of impression on us? How do they think? Why do they invent and have us process endless forms and have us carry on to little purpose? My job has been all idle paper pushing, even—I'll be frank—by my standards.

And I've pushed a lot of meaningless paper in my fight to the top of the tree."

"Very Savoyard," Cameron observed.

"Yes, Peter, I *do* understand my own allusion, even if I need help with yours. We're not all the fools you think us. Just frustrated and worn out. We've got to oversee the scientists researching this planet's botanicals. Pharmaceuticals of great value, I understand. What we can give back to the Alcaidans I don't know, but I'm supposed to find something in case they ask for compensation. Perhaps this Hunt will give you some insight." The consul looked at Cameron's expectant face. "Or do you have one already?"

Cameron regarded the consul soberly. "Straw mats and judo *gis*."

The consul opened his mouth, then closed it. He silently waved Cameron out.

Ansari Farhal was this year's Master of the Hunt and therefore inheritor of the Alcaidan title of *kir*. Kir—an Earthside drink of cassis and wine. Very cool and refreshing, as Cameron remembered it. Ansari *kir* looked cool. Refreshing, however, was not the word. Noble was more it. Noble in purpose, not in effete decay.

Ansari's eyes glittered. His clothes glittered. He shimmered as he moved. His motions were economical, smooth, purposeful. Nothing wasted. He used his hands, did not study them. He motioned Cameron to a chair.

"Would you like to join our Hunt?" he asked.

"Yes."

"Do you know what it is, what is its quarry, what it is about?"

"No."

Ansari *kir* turned from his desk to the window and looked out on the forest that began beyond his walls. No tended greensward, no formal gardens to the estate of this nobleman. A local Schwarzwald seemed his estate.

Cameron studied his profile and thought of Roman coins.

Ansari *kir* turned back to look at Cameron full face. "We come to a gorge with an untried bridge over turbulent rapids. Someone must try the bridge—or the quarry escapes. You or a companion of the Hunt. How do you choose?"

Cameron turned and looked about him in studied scrutiny.

"I see no bridge, no rapids, no companions."

Ansari kir nodded. "You'll do."

■ ■ ■

"That answer did it?" the consul asked.

"Seems so."

The consul shook his head. "I don't see that this tells us much. I don't understand the mode of thinking, the allusion. Perhaps that's why I wasn't chosen. But, Peter—would you explain?"

"Explaining spoils it," Cameron said, then relented at the sight of the consul's visage. Nothing noble there. This was no longer the bureaucratic superior who had formerly plagued him, his officiousness to be combated with irreverent flippancy. "It's self-referential. The answer is part of the question. The question is rhetorical. All their questions are. And this was an interior joke, acknowledging our own idiom. A bridge that shouldn't be crossed till we get to it. Perhaps we never will."

Silence from the consul.

"They're telling us to stop making elaborate contingency plans," Cameron added gently. "Stay in the moment."

The Hunt was gathering in the courtyard when Cameron arrived, but Ansari *kir* disengaged himself from the preparations to meet his offworld guest. Glass in hand and with a lazy camaraderie that transcended *noblesse oblige*, he placed his arms about Cameron's shoulder and escorted him up the broad steps and into his hall. A great punch bowl of crystal rested on a roughhewn trestle table covered by a damask cloth. A pleasing set of contrasts. Heaped on silver trays was an array of rolls and loaves, some with warmth rising from them. Several sportsmen busied themselves with cutting the breads and layering them with spreads from nearby bowls. All turned toward the master of the hall and the Hunt as he neared with Cameron in tow, and all raised their glasses in salutation.

"Mr. Peter Cameron," Ansari *kir* announced. He stepped back and raised his glass. "Our new companion of the Hunt!"

All the company swung glasses to lip in graceful parabolic arcs. The nearest took a crystal goblet chased in silver, filled it from the bowl and extended it to Cameron.

"The Hunt!" Cameron toasted. "And the Field!"

To an approving murmur all drank again. Cameron as well.

"Drink up and eat, gentlemen," Ansari *kir* said. "We mount up in ten *tecors*."

In that time, about fifteen minutes by his reckoning, Cameron learned the names to a dozen faces and had eaten a hunt breakfast that would have done for dinner at many an Earthside inn.

The company turned out again to the courtyard, where it met up with an assemblage of mounts and trackers. Ansari *kir* again detached himself from the general preparations to see Cameron firmly in the saddle of a handsomely turned out *gaffa*, its trappings and harness gay and colorful in the early sun.

"Here," Ansari *kir* handed up a helmet of local design, its utilitarian plastsheen leathered and painted in the amber and green colors of the Hunt. "Wear it and be at one with your mount."

And with the world, he might have said. Cameron pulled the helmet on and found the colors about him jumping at him in augmented brilliance. He heard sounds of forest wildlife beyond the courtyard walls: timid ground rodents; arboreal creatures; raptors soaring. His *gaffa*'s mind was strongest and closest to hand. It awaited not his commands but his impulses, and to foray with him as a companion, not as a mere beast of burden. The minds of the trackers, a feeling of all-consuming quest, impinged impatiently. And those of his companions—their swirl and energies flowed about him without words.

Cameron looked about him. If the company felt him, his alienness, they showed no sign. They wore no helmets.

"No need," said/thought Ansari *kir*. "And, yes, they see/feel your presence. With welcome and anticipation."

He waved and the gates folded open. The eager parade flowed out, not into the forest but across a meadow of spring grass and wild flowers. Not at all as Cameron remembered it. He recalled the impinging forest just outside of every wall. *Every* wall? Were there more outlooks here, more points to the compass than the usual thirty-two?

Another question that held its own answer. It was the best kind. It went unasked.

"Ride!" Ansari *kir* commanded.

Cameron rode.

When Cameron looked back on it later, it seemed a timeless idyll. Perhaps it had been. Perhaps it had all been a nanosecond synaptic flash, a compression beyond words. Words. Words were seldom used. The helmet obviated the need for words, save those that held their own intrinsic and autonomous body and were to be held up and admired as they sparkled.

Or words as shorthand for an abstract shard of thought. There were more of these than a morning of coursing through wood and field might be expected to produce.

The Hunt ranged across meadows wet with morning dew, then hot under a noonday sun. Early hour cricket sounds ceased as they rode through the grass, but the small internal hummings carried unabated through the helmet. The insect hummings of midday never stopped.

There were also dark copses of bay and laurel to be traversed, and forest trails that had to be taken at a slower pace and in single file. No matter that the quarry might not choose to hold to wooded paths.

As the day reached its hottest they emerged from the forest coolness to a grassy swale by the river. The sun was at its zenith, but an array of tents, striped with brightness, drew the eye and promised shade. The party dismounted and turned the *gaffas* loose to graze, drink, and dream. The tents were airy, the fabric ending several feet off the ground with only the guylines to tie them down. Within were trays of cheeses and breads, drinks in beds of ice, refreshing sorbets. All as if just laid out, though there were no retainers to be seen.

The company looked as if refreshment was in order. Though Cameron was warm, it seemed as nothing compared to Ansari *kir* and the others of the field. Perspiration flowed on their faces, seeming to melt the promontories of their features, flattening them visibly. Ansari *kir*'s aquiline nose seemed to have broadened and spread, appearing almost squashy. Cameron looked closer at his companions. Their clothes, too, though they must have been designed for the Hunt, appeared to be too flimsy for the task. They seemed to be bursting at the seams and rent where twigs and branches had torn and snagged. Beneath appeared patches of mottled skin.

None paid any mind; all addressed themselves to the refreshments. Cameron did as well, till Ansari *kir* called a halt and led them to the largest tent of all. Before his eyes had adjusted to the shadowed light within, Cameron's feet and nose told him that he was in a *dojo*. He felt the firm springiness of *tatami* underfoot. The smell of fresh straw hung in the sunwarmed air. Cameron sat down on the edge of the mat and removed his shoes. When he looked up he saw his companions in a new guise. They were humaniform again, of varying statures and weights, all attired in judo *gi*s. He recognized the faces of old friends and opponents, smelled their body odors around him, felt the rough softness of his often-washed *gi* on his shoulders. A faint breeze stirred the hairs on his naked chest.

"Your *dojo*, your art, Cameron," Ansari *kir* said. He alone kept his features as Cameron remembered them. "Lead us through the stretches and *ukemi*."

The crisp sounds of rollups and arm slaps permeated the air, rebounding off the tent walls. *Uchikomi* followed, as the *judokas* paired off and practiced repetitions of step-ins, taking their lead from Cameron. Cameron's partner was Ansari *kir*, the player on the defensive. Cameron played *tori*, attacking with *ogoshi* in a reverse pivot, spiraling in and down to slam his hips in below his partner's belt. He slid his arm around Ansari *kir*'s waist to pull him onto Cameron's back, and realized something was wrong. He was coming in too high, not breaking his partner's balance. And Cameron's arms were not succeeding in encircling a girth that seemed broader than met the eye.

Instinctively, Cameron pivoted out to stand face to face with his partner. Ansari *kir* bowed. "My apologies," he said.

Cameron looked again and saw the squatter and heavier form that Ansari *kir* had presented at the refreshment tent. Only the face remained as before. Cameron nodded in understanding. He took Ansari *kir* through a series of shorter players' moves—hip throws, mainly. The other *judokas* took their cue from the main pair and followed along in the repetitions. In-out; in-out. The air became heavier and moister, overlaid with an exudation subtly different from human sweat.

They were fast learners.

Expectation also hung in the air, as palpable as these other aromas. At last Ansari *ki*r voiced the collective desire. "*Randori*?"

Cameron nodded. He stepped to the center of the mat together with Ansari *kir*. They bowed, then grasped each other's lapels and sleeves and began.

Cameron took them in a wheel counter clockwise. He tried an ankle block. Ansari *kir* hopped over it. Cameron closed for a right side *osoto gari* and found his opponent pivoting away. They resumed their circling movement. Cameron tried using his tall man's leg reach into a *tai otoshi*, a good throw to use on a short, stocky opponent. He spun on his left foot, shot his right leg out to block Ansari *kir*'s ankle, and tried to wheel him over his extended leg. Again, his opponent hopped over the block, then pivoted into a *kubi nage*, his hips coming in swiftly to break Cameron's balance, his arm going for a headlock. Cameron dropped his hips just in time to get his weight low enough to avoid being doubled over and to slip the encircling arm. Ansari *kir* was fast. Too fast.

They circled again and Cameron thought it over.

And then he had it. He stopped thinking, adopted a state of *no mind*. He let his body think, allowing no premeditation that could be read. When his body found the opening and moved in, it was with a hip throw of his own, unlooked for from a taller man. It was Ansari *kir*'s turn to plant his legs and drop low to block Cameron's *seoi nage*. But as Cameron swung in he reversed his pivot, hooking his opponent's left leg with his right, catching it just below the knee. Cameron slammed his left shoulder into Ansari *kir*'s, driving him back to his left corner. His opponent's right leg was off the ground, and Cameron kept driving, hopping on his left leg and hooking Ansari *kir*'s remaining leg out from under till his opponent fell backwards on his back and slapped the mat hard.

Cameron helped him up. They disengaged to straighten their *gi*s and bowed.

"The technique?" Ansari *kir* asked with raised eyebrow.

"*Ouchi gari*. Inside leg hook."

They made way for others to spar. They changed partners and reengaged again.

Time passed. The sun lowered till its rays pierced the tent opening, illumining dust motes that danced about them as they sparred.

They were back at the refreshment tent. Cameron regarded his companions over the ices and the fruits. They were back in their clothing of the Hunt, and their transmogrification continued. To what end? How much of their reality could he and humankind accept?

What was reality and what was illusion? Could they be the same thing, different forms?

Cameron felt a wetness on his bare arm and looked up. A transfigured and no longer handsome Ansari *kir* stood over him, in his hand several pellets of ice. Between his hairy fingers and trickling onto Cameron's arm were droplets of cold water.

Same thing. Different forms.

The ride back was more leisured. The forest itself seemed less sylvan, more brushy and dotted with down wood and dead snags. Cameron watched with interest but no apprehension as the clothes seemed to tear off the huntsmen, leaving only rags to cover mottled skin blotched by almost random tufts of fur. But still the exhilarating mental byplay went on, a stimulating canopy to whatever was the corporeal underneath.

There continued a certain nobility of thought. Another had said it before: an ordinary man *is* a Buddha; illusion is salvation. A foolish thought—and we are ordinary, vulgar, stupid. The next enlightened thought—and we are the Buddha.

Ansari *kir* pulled abreast of Cameron, his face a hairy and feral mask. But the mental clarity and fineness was there.

I would have put it differently: a foolish thought—and we are enlightened. An enlightened thought—and we are again ordinary creatures.

Ansari *kir* squeezed his mount with his thighs and pulled ahead. *Enough talk. Enlightenment is an activity, not a state. Let us ride.*

The consul's office was cluttered. Desk drawers open; containers on the floor. Wall hangings were down, leaning against boxes at floor level. The consul's desk was untypically empty, dotted only by a holocube of his family, and a single pad of scratch paper.

"The Alcaidans want you to stay," the consul said flatly. "They want me to go."

Cameron nodded.

"I don't understand much of this," the consul went on. "They ask that future teams include Zen practitioners. Also martial artists. Karate, judo, the business with the staffs—what's the word?"

"Kendo." Cameron did not bother to explain that the "staffs" were practice swords made of bamboo slats—*shinai*—or wood—*bokutō*.

"Yes. I gather they're getting all this from you."

"From you, too," Cameron said. "From all of us. Don't plan on keeping many secrets. They keep us happy by talking to us, but they don't have to. They're telepathic."

The consul didn't seem as perturbed by this as Cameron had expected. Perhaps he was more focused on the damage of this assignment to his career.

"What do they want with martial artists?"

"The mindset mostly," Cameron said. "A way of looking at things. That and the engagement, the sparring—physical and mental. That's what they value in every new culture they encounter, and that's how we earn what we want of them."

The consul was back to the habit of folding and steepling his hands. "I suppose they can adapt to the physicality of our martial arts, being shapeshifters."

"They're not shapeshifters," Cameron said.

The consul looked up.

"That's an assumption our contact party made when observing their artwork and contrasting it with the appearance they presented us," Cameron said. "But it's wrong. They can influence our minds, overlay them with their illusions. They give us a reassuring image, what makes us comfortable."

Including an inventively useless amount of busy work for you. Cameron thought it, didn't say it.

"Do you know what they really look like, then?"

Cameron shook his head. *Hopeless.* "Perhaps. It doesn't matter, sir. To them that's all illusion."

"Well," the consul said, "I doubt I'll ever understand. But I do try."

"Perhaps you're trying in the wrong way."

"Is there a right way?"

Cameron looked surprised, then nodded his approval. "That's better."

"Do I want to go around asking your kind of questions?" The consul turned to Cameron with the first trace of self-directed humor that Cameron could recall. "And with you not there, whom do I ask?"

Cameron looked at the lacquered desktop for a moment, then reached across it for the scratch pad. Cameron eyed its thickness, then turned it on edge and rapped the desk sharply with it, producing a crisp wooden sound.

The consul started, then settled back in his chair.

Cameron reached out to return the pad. The consul regarded him with a raised eyebrow, then held out his hand to take it. Cameron turned the pad on edge and rapped the consul's hand smartly. The consul cried out, more in surprise than in pain.

"Why didn't the desk cry out?" Cameron asked.

The consul held his hand and looked at Cameron in bewilderment.

Cameron spoke into the silence.

"Learn to listen, and you can hear it."

Game shows have waxed and waned through several cycles of popularity since their introduction on radio in the 1930s. That they might garner intergalactic audiences some day is as valid a speculation as any other in fiction. True, these are games, and not sports, but the Olympic hendiatris Citius, Altius, Fortius *(Latin for "Faster, Higher, Stronger") can certainly apply to intellectual ability as well as physical prowess. Elizabeth Ann Scarborough also presents us with a secret mission and a life-threatening mystery, as well as asking the eternal question: Will dinette sets exist in the far future? Oh . . .* hendiatris*? Let's Name That Noun! Is it: (a) three words used to express one idea; (b) a Roman motto coined by Julius Caesar; (c) the same thing as a tricolon? No fair googling! Have you made your final decision? You'll find the answer at the end of the story. If you answer correctly, you'll win . . . our sincere thanks for reading this introduction!*

Name That Planet!

Elizabeth Ann Scarborough

"Welcome to *Naaaame That Planet!* The game that tests your powers of observation and knowledge as you try to guess where in the cosmos you are!

"The game is simple. A three-member panel of intergalactic citizens chosen randomly from our studio audience provides sensory clues they feel are typical or symbolic of each of their home worlds. Each panel member must provide up to five clues to our intrepid space explorer contestant, sealed into a sensory input globe. Though we can see them, the contestants won't be able to see us. Successful contestants win fabulous prizes donated by our sponsors, naturally. But additionally, panel members who successfully stump the contestants also win great prizes. So let's begin this week's round.

"Our first contestant is the communications officer of a class A starship. Her duties include deciphering alien hieroglyphs and petroglyphs, as well as establishing and maintaining contact between her ship and other cosmic entities. Her hobbies include playing 3-D chess, reading old Terran classics in their original languages, belly dancing, and cake decorating. Let's have a round of applause for Lt. Shalula Makira!"

Shalula understood the game show conventions as easily as she understood classical Venusian. She jogged out onto the platform situated high above the heads of the audience members in the stadium below. She bounced. Her white-gold hair and breasts augmented for the occasion lifted up and down—but not too far down since the *Name That Planet!* studio was on the low gravity moon of a wholly owned planetary subsidiary of the FLOG Corporation. The moon was also wholly owned by the FLOG Corporation of course. FLOG stood for Furthering Logistical Organization Galaxy-wide, one of those meaningless acronyms that took in hundreds of thousands of otherwise unrelated enterprises.

Shalula wore a perky red dress uniform with gold piping that matched her Galaxy Corps rank insignia. A miniscule skirt showed off a slice of her thighs between the hem and the tops of the scarlet form-fitting over-the-knee boots. It actually was not a current issue uniform, being from earlier days when the grizzled male upper echelon of the Corps considered part of the duty of younger female personnel included raising the morale of male personnel. The outfit wasn't hers and she felt a little uncomfortable in it. The coverall uniform she and all other crewmembers wore on shipboard was far more practical. Actually, her idea had been to wear civvies, something floaty and ethnic, possibly one of her colorful gilt-edged thwabs from the flower ships of Griba-Prime, but the producers of the show said seeing a woman in Galaxy Corps uniform made viewers feel safe and gave them a sense of pan-galactic pride. So they provided this one. It definitely made her feel feminine and sexy. From communications nerd to communications bimbo with a simple change of clothing. That was show business.

The producers also insisted that contestants enthuse and bubble and preferably jump up and down with excitement when they won something, though they were not allowed to curse if they lost. Shalula agreed to respond appropriately. Accomplishing her mission required that she be on the show so she could hardly disagree, even if she were inclined to do so. Besides, it was interesting to study the intergalactic messaging modes in the theatrical subculture represented by the show's cast, crew, other contestants, panelists, and the studio audience.

When she bounced toward the host and the array of cameras—whether because of the bounce, the uniform, or the vid prompts—the crowd cheered and applauded wildly. She laughed in a manner that did not show her teeth. There were some present whose culture viewed revealing one's dentition as an act of hostility. She waved both hands in the flop-wristed universal gesture of greeting. Among beings possessing wrists to flop, that was.

"Welcome, Lieutenant!" the host cried out a full three meters before she reached him. He had no compunctions about displaying his dentition to her or the crowd and let interpretations of his expression fall where they may. Large even teeth on full parade were an age-old badge of the game show host, even on Nilurian Amphibats such as *Name That Planet!*'s own Jiminy Jimson (a stage name, Shalula felt certain). "It's an honor to have you on our show. Are you ready to *Naaame That Planet?*"

It didn't matter that Jiminy's species spoke by sequencing air bubbles emitted from their nostrils, game show protocol and host behavior was well established in the annals of popular history and custom. A multi-faceted universal communication device translated Jiminy's remarks and witticisms into every conceivable method of transmission and disseminated it by appropriate means to the wide and varied audience. Shalula heard the host's words in a smooth, sexy computer-simulated masculine voice as well oiled as Jiminy's leathery wings.

"Indubitably, Jiminy! I mean, I certainly *am*. I've been looking forward to this and studying assiduously to be equal to whatever challenges the panel may present."

"Well, Shalula—I hope I may call you Shalula?"

She remembered to giggle enthusiastically, "Of course."

"Shalula, as you know, it will not be possible for you to meet your fellow contestants or our panel beforehand so you will have no prior clues to their identities, species, race, and most important of all, planetary affiliation. You must determine that by correctly identifying their clues and answering their questions. You will be allowed to ask one question per panelist in return. With each planet that you name correctly, you will win a fabulous prize and the opportunity to try for another. If you choose to continue after your first success, and answer incorrectly, your game is forfeit and you lose your previous prizes. The clues will be given to our audience as well so they can guess right along with you. Now then, let me just ask, why did you wish to appear on our show?"

She had her answer all prepared. She and the captain and the Galaxy Corps agents had gone over it several times, and crew members of the more exotic species from the her starship, the Havago, were in the audience to provide verisimilitude to her story. "Well, Jiminy, as I'm sure you've heard, when Sol 169582 went supernova, the inhabitants of that solar system became refugees, homeless. The GCS *Havago*, aboard which I serve, helped evacuate many of these fine folks. I plan to use any prizes I win to help find them a swell new solar with life-compatible gaseous exchanges, temperatures, humidities, and other life-supporting factors where they can live in peace and harmony."

"Well, say, Lt. Shalula, that's a tall order even for a plucky little starship officer such as yourself. I'm sure everyone in our audience wishes you luck." It was perfectly acceptable for Jiminy to patronize her since presumably he knew all the answers to the questions and she did not.

"Thanks, Jiminy. Actually, some of the refugees are in the studio audience today. May I wave to them?"

"Certainly!" Jiminy said, waggling his forelegs as well. "Hellllooo there, all you displaced entities! I know you're all keeping your appendages crossed that your friend wins big for you. See there, you folks at home, our cameras are picking up the encouraging waves, wiggles, color changes, and odor emissions of Shalula's refugees. Everyone give them a big round of applause!"

Shalula blushed. The color change peculiar to her species was by now understood throughout the galaxy as signifying either humility or embarrassment, possibly of a sexual nature. The translator interpreted it as "maidenly modesty" for the benefit of those in doubt of its precise significance. Actually, she was embarrassed at having to lie, even though the lies were crucial to her mission.

"And now, Shalula, it's time for you to step into our sphere and receive the first clue to your first planet! We wish you all the luck in the worlds!"

Shalula laughed, feigning appreciation, though she wasn't sure that the pun translated universally even with the best efforts of the studio's equipment. Humor as humans understood it was totally unknown in some alien societies. Come to think of it, humor was not understood in all human societies either. Or, for that matter, by all humans in any particular society.

She stepped into the transparent globe, which was transparent only from the outside. Once inside, Shalula could see nothing except the matte silver lining of the sphere and the clear plascine chair with the pull-down goggles and keypads at her fingertips. Nasal tubes projected from the bottom of the goggles for olfactory clues.

Shalula settled herself in, aware that although she could not see another living being, the multiverse was watching her every move and listening to her every utterance.

There was a long silence in her earphones as she had been warned there would be while Jiminy introduced the first panelist to the audience.

She sat breathlessly silent and alert, waiting. Suddenly the light inside the sphere dimmed and turned an odd shade of pale periwinkle, while the temperature plummeted. She shivered. The chair extruded a fleece wrap that wound around her like the tendrils of a plant climbing a trellis. Ice began to frost the inner skin of the globe.

"Have you figured it out yet, Shalula?" Jiminy's computer generated voice asked.

"It's a g-good clue, J-Jiminy," she said earnestly. "I c-can tell that this world is not close to its star. But I need to know a t-teensy bit more."

"Okay, Shalula, here it comes. This beautiful item is found on the mystery planet."

She started to tell him to wait, that her goggles were frosting over, and then the frost inside them began thickening in some places, spreading in others, until it formed a perfect three-dimensional blossom shape. Her nose tingled sharply, as if little icicles were forming on the hairs of her nostrils. Could it really be this easy? "That is one of the floral frost folk of Feldstar, Jiminy. So the planet must be Feldstar."

"Must it?" Jiminy asked. "Is that your answer or do you need another clue?"

"That's my answer," Shalula said. "Ah, can the audience see how the frost tendrils are lengthening and shortening at the points of the leaves? This frost fella is congratulating me on my perspicacity." She lifted her hand and, tucking the top knuckles of her middle fingers in, then straightening them, politely thanked the frost person for his felicitations.

The tendrils lengthened and shortened once more, but this time the sequence surprised Shalula. The frost being was telling her to "beware."

She mimicked the sequence and added the knuckle tip flip signaling interrogatory request for information but the floral frost fellow's image faded from her screen.

Jiminy's laughter, or the facsimile thereof, burbled out of her headphones. "Looks as though you have had frequent associations with the floral portion of the Feldstar population, Shalula. It seemed quite chatty just now. Don't tell me they are on your ship's regular route? We try to make our little game challenging for everyone."

"Oh, it is, Jiminy. The floral frost folk have interested me in particular since I first learned of them. They remind me of a children's book my paternal aunt used to play for me."

"And a lucky thing that was for you too. Because—well, come on out here and just look at what your correct answer won for you."

The sphere floated down to the stage and she alighted from it. Jiminy appeared in front of her and waved at a revolving platform containing what looked like some sort of movable furniture. "This *lovely* Etin Island Dinette Set with two pullout sections and seating for sixteen. And that's not all! You will be able to serve your guests from the finest porceplast dinnerware in the classic Rings of Saturn pattern. And in case you don't want to serve them finger food, you will also receive this stunning set of titanium alloy flatware complete with attachments to accommodate the appendages of three different alien species and all serving pieces! In addition you receive this elegant synlin lace tablecloth and serviette set aaaand . . . " The revolving stand revolved to reveal another piece of furniture. "Your dinette set includes this finely crafted buffet and hutch!" His voice dropped to a totally serious tone as he said, "Now, I know it's a hard decision to make, whether to take all of these wonderful prizes or risk it all to continue the game but our clock is ticking and will give you five seconds to decide."

She didn't need five seconds, or any seconds at all. What in the world would she do with all that stuff on shipboard? Her quarters were barely big enough for her bed, lamp, desk, and chair. Nevertheless, the producers wanted her to appear to be very tempted. She chewed her lip and twirled her hair around her index finger and just as the buzzer sounded, sighed and said, "Gee, it's really tempting to take that marvelous prize and run. I know it would come in handy for the refugees once they get settled, Jiminy, but I guess I'd better keep playing and hope I can win them a home to keep it in!"

"Spoken like the intrepid officer and explorer you are, my dear! Very well, back into the sphere with you to identify your second planet."

While she awaited the first clue, Shalula pondered how the floral frost fella had been able to communicate with her. Surely it wasn't an actual entity present in the studio? It was far more likely to be a holo chip. So why had it signaled her to "beware"? Had it been in danger at the time it was recorded? Was it therefore sending an all-purpose message? Common sense said it could know nothing about her, much less her mission or any danger she might be courting.

Before she came to a conclusion, music filled the sphere.

Music was, of course, a valid form of communication based on mathematics and therefore far more universal than language per se, but like many alien art forms, it could seem incredibly unattractive to a human. However, Shalula was highly trained and had taken courses 1-6 in Galactic Musical Appreciation at the academy. Although the piece was played on instruments with which she was so unfamiliar she could not rightly say if they were string, wind, or percussion, its melodic structure was not unappealing.

Judging from its time signature, it would be from one of the peripheral moons of the fourth planet in the Scathach Galaxy.

But which one?

She shook her head.

"Stumped you, did we?" Jiminy crowed. "Well, never mind, little lady, here comes clue number two."

Another holo appeared, this one of some sort of rectangular mauve-colored fruit. The goggles extruded a flat wafer, which pushed at her lips.

"Have a taste of this, Shalula! It is considered quite a delicacy by the people of the mystery world."

She bit down. It was slimy and bitter but with a surprisingly pleasant aftertaste. She had never tasted anything like it, which was saying something. The Havago had an extremely adventurous chef. "I'd like to ask my first question if I may, Jiminy," she said.

"Certainly! But remember, only one per panelist."

"If I were actually biting into the foodstuff depicted in the holo, would it be toxic to my species?"

There was a long pause for consultation. During this time Shalula felt her tongue growing numb and her throat beginning to close. Finally Jiminy said, laughing heartily, "Oh dear, our panelist says that is entirely possible. Bite down on the antidote now, won't you, before the next clue?"

Another flat object extruded itself from her goggles and she bit, then, when she was able, drew a long breath. Jiminy's levity was highly inappropriate. When her tongue moved freely again she said, "I'm ready for the next clue, Jiminy. I hope it won't be as hard to take as that last one."

Was the clue a simple mistake or an attempt to murder her? Had the producers somehow learned about her mission? Was this one of the ways in which the previous six Galaxy Corps personnel who had appeared on this show had disappeared from their lives after it?

"Well, as we on the program say, considering the many and varied species with which we deal, one contestant's meat is another one's poison."

How did an ancient Terran aphorism find its way to this alien moon? Shalula wondered. She had been briefed on FLOG's ownership and supposed corporate structure, but it was as vague and difficult to pinpoint exactly what the corporation did or who was in charge of which section as any other intergalactic enterprise. *Name That Planet!* was a fairly new show. It had been airing for only part of a single season but it was already tremendously popular. Dinette sets were definitely at the low end of the prize spectrum. The top prize, for contestants who met the ultimate challenge, was an enormous amount of credits. So far, only two contestants had come close to winning that prize, but both had given an incorrect answer just one step away from their goal. Both were also starship personnel. Four other Galaxy Corpsmen, from lesser ships, made it through several rungs of the game before failing. All were given very nice consolation prizes, which were duly delivered to their units. The crewmen never returned to their units to claim the prizes, however. All were now considered AWOL. The common theory was that the contestants were too humiliated by their public failures to show their faces among their fellows again. Shalula didn't believe it, and neither did Corps headquarters.

As one of the brightest officers with the most versatile knowledge of alien peoples and places in the Corps, Shalula was recruited to investigate, posing as a contestant. She had never done undercover work before. So far she found it stimulating, though a bit confusing since her usual goal was to clearly communicate a message rather than to dissimulate. Perhaps this would be useful training for a diplomatic post later in her career?

"Ready for your next clue, Shalula?" Jiminy asked in a challenging tone—or rather, his translation device made it sound challenging. Perhaps it was programmed that way.

"You bet, Jiminy! Bring it on!"

And with a quick shift of color and space she found herself inside cascade of swirling turquoise and blue rock. Light shot through translucent sections turning them to orchid glass. Mint green lichen-like growths clung to some of the surfaces.

"Where are you now, Shalula?"

"Lost in wonder, Jiminy! My stars, but this is beautiful! Who would think that the dung heaps of the ancient Zanticoran Pzitsaaurus would be so lovely that their interior, once dried to a hollow shell, would make ideal housing for vacationing monarchs from surrounding star systems? I am on Zanticora, Jiminy. Therefore, that toxic fruit you offered me before must be no fruit at all but the solidified resin from the sap of the Tatatata tree. It's now widely believed that once great groves of the Tatatatas covered Zanticora and their bark and sap provided food as the trees themselves provided habitat for the Pzitsaaurus. The Pzitsaaurus is thought to have consumed sixteen acres of trees every lunar cycle. It then shat so copiously that . . . "

"Yes, yes, right you are, Shalula! Come on out now and see what you've won."

She stepped down, but the surroundings of her last clue didn't change, except to become larger and more spacious. She gasped appreciatively as a group of muscular blue-tinged avian Zanticoran males danced onto the platform, their antics engineered to showcase the pieces of sleek and serviceable luggage each carried. "Yes, Shalula, it's a good thing you are so intrigued by Zanticora's colorful history and culture. In addition to your lovely dinette set you have won a lunar cycle leave from your duty station aboard the *Havago* to vacation on Zanticora. You will bask in the blue light of Zanticora's sun! At night you will dine, dance, and rest in a luxury suite within one of the deluxe structures you so aptly described. To properly equip you for the journey, you will have this full set of fabulous Saturite luggage—it dehydrates with the push of a button so the entire set will fit into this convenient pocket-sized packet. To fill the luggage, we are also equipping you with a fashionable wardrobe of Zanticoran resort wear courtesy of Tzany Design Studio, Designers for the Stars. You will attend shows, gamble at the casinos, and may either take a companion of your choice or choose from among a bevy of Zanticoran escorts such as these here with us today. So what do you say, will you claim this prize and your dinette set or go on for the big jackpot?"

Shalula had carefully punctuated each of Jiminy's revelations with a little hop, a squeal and a clapping of her hands. Sometimes a gasp was in order. But now she took her clasped hands away from her mouth and said seriously, "I think we should let your audience know, Jiminy, that as swell as all these prizes are, none of them are actually what I will win."

"That's right, Shalula. Ladies and gentlemen and beings of all species, this generous little lady will not actually receive any of these things, though she could have them if she wished. Instead, by special arrangement with our sponsors, Shalula has asked that credit prizes of equal value be substituted for the prizes you see here, to go toward the resettlement of her refugee friends. Isn't that special? Isn't she an exceptional contestant and an exceptionally fine example of her species? Let's have a round of applause for this little lady!"

The crowd went wild, in a controlled way that ended the applause and cheering when the prompter went blank.

"What we haven't told her is that our sponsor values altruism such as hers and wishes to reward her unselfishness. If she chooses to take these prizes now, the money will go to her friends as agreed. However, if she wins our jackpot, she will receive not only the cash value of all the prizes but the prizes themselves for herself!"

Shalula gasped, squealed, and jumped up and down. The down part was difficult, given the light gravity. "Oh, Jiminy, that is so wonderful! And I know just who I'll bring with me if I win this prize. There is a little orphaned Beltarian boy who could really use cheering up. I think Zanticoran beaches are just the ticket!"

"I am filled with admiration," Jiminy said, fluttering his wings and baring his large teeth again. "Always thinking of others. So I gather you're going for the jackpot then?"

"You betcha!"

"You do realize that so far on our show, no one has managed to go *aaaallll* the way and score the grand prize?"

"There's always a first time, Jiminy, and I am after all a professional pioneer of previously unexplored places and experiences! Not to mention my own personal potential."

"Well spoken! Okay then, Shalula, pop back up inside the sphere and prepare yourself for a *reeaaaallly* tough round."

"Ready and willing, Jiminy!" she said, regaining her seat. Even though she knew the game was rigged against her, she couldn't help feeling a sense of elation. She had watched vids of all of the previous show episodes prior to embarking on the assignment. She was far better prepared than previous contestants, she felt sure. Her hunger for and grasp of esoteric knowledge of the people, places, and languages of the multiverse was vast and comprehensive. She also had a photographic memory courtesy of the implant her parents had given her for her third birthday.

"For your first clue to this world, the panelist will ask you to answer a question, Shalula. Are you ready?"

She nodded enthusiastically.

A voice did not so much speak as rearrange its secretions. Its supposed language sounded like phlegm being hacked up, rearranged, swallowed, and hacked up again. The very sound of it gave Shalula goosebumps she thought the studio audience probably could see clear to the back row. She was at a loss as to what tongue contained such fearsome noises. It had none of the common features that distinguished a tongue from a mere set of subvocalizations.

Watching the vids of the shows on which her fellow Corp members were contestants, Shalula had noticed that among the last set of questions, the clues were usually a bit indistinct in sound or image. Audience members were meant to think that the puzzle was simply extremely difficult but now Shalula wondered. Perhaps the clues were hard because they were not actually legitimate clues at all?

To test her theory, she scoured her throat to make similar sounds, as if she were about to vomit.

It took several moments, probably while Jiminy decided how to respond. She waited for him to say, "What was that you said?" or something of the sort but instead he said, "Our panelist says that was the correct answer. For the benefit of our audience, the panelist asked Shalula if she spoke the native language of Emeticus Trine and she replied that she did, a little. However, Shalula, that was a trick question as the planet in question here is *not* Emeticus Trine, though the panelist speaks the language. You must tell us which planet is the panelist's home world. Do you need another clue?"

"Yes," she said, and then added, "or should I say, 'Hrrracccchacch?' "

"Heh heh. Very good. Here it is then, for the grand jackpot, tell us where you will find our next clue."

A lacey tracery of interlocking outwardly expanding ripples of multicolored lights filled the interior of the sphere. At the center of each set of ripples a strong clear light pulsed. There was something familiar about the sequencing of the pulses—three short bursts, three long, then three short. Versed in ancient messaging modes as she was, Shalula, to her amazement, recognized that the light beams were signaling SOS, the once well known distress signal in a system of dots and dashes used by obsolete antique communications equipment. Who could be sending such a message except another communications expert? Like, for instance, the one who had preceded her on this show, and who was presently listed as AWOL from the GCS *William Gates*.

"Well, Shalula, do we have your answer?"

"Help," she murmured, still considering the message.

"Does that mean you wish to ask the panelist a question?"

"Er—yes. Yes, it does Jiminy. Except my Emeticus Trine isn't quite up to it, so I'd like to ask my question in Standard."

"And your question is . . . ?"

"It is . . . it is . . . what does the dominant species on your planet look like?"

"I'm not sure that is the sort of question that is authorized, Shalula," Jiminy told her cautiously.

"Oh, gee, Jiminy, nobody told me there were restrictions on what I could ask."

Jiminy's teeth looked bigger than ever as he smiled. "Gee, I'm sorry too, Shalula but that question is just too broad. We might as well let you ask what planet are you from?"

"Yes, well then, let me rephrase my question. We know your language is from Emeticus Trine but the planet we are speaking of is not Emeticus Trine. Are you yourself or your species dominating *another* planet?"

There were more gurgling hawking choking sounds. Shalula had identified them now that she read the feeling behind the noises rather than trying to make words of them. For the sounds represented to her as language were merely the pre-digestive utterances of a hungry slavering bestial being in search of a meal.

Jiminy looked extremely skittish. "I don't think that question is quite authorized either."

"Oh, but it should be, Jiminy. Because the answer to it holds the key to many of the riddles posed on and by this very show! I *did* recognize the light show from the last clue. It's the transmission waves from this station bouncing off FLOG's world below us and back out into space. And the rulers of this planet, FLOG's Board of Directors, are dominated by the beings who make those horrible noises. I wonder if the audience can see the Emeticus Trinian as it really is. Because it is my contention that if they saw the true nature of this being, they would see it as one of the data-devouring demons of the Damaclesian Delta. No wonder no one guessed before. The demons are shapeshifters and can assume any form. In fact, Jiminy, I wonder if you yourself are what you seem to be?"

"Ladies and gentlemen of all species, we are going to cut to our commercial now. It seems our contestant is suffering from space sickness that is making her delusional."

Shalula, still suspended inside the sphere, could see nothing outside except what Jiminy projected into her sphere. She could only hope her co-crew members were advancing on the stage.

"What better cover than a game show for a race that devours the data transmission and reception waves of living beings?" she continued. "Your so-called sponsors are these beings and *you*, Jiminy, are their leader! Not being content to manipulate from behind the scenes, you assumed the guise of a Nilurian amphibat and sought center stage yourself!"

Jiminy said nothing but through her earphones Shalula heard the scuffle of feet, the futile flap of wings, and the voices of her comrades barking orders.

A moment later her captain's voice reached her. "We're bringing you down now, Shalula."

Her sphere was lowered to the stage and she stepped out. Jiminy was blurring around the edges.

"Aha!" she said. "I was right. For a data-devouring demon, being the host of a show such as this would allow you to satisfy your appetite before any of your fellows. If you had left it at that, Jiminy, or whatever your real name is, you would not have sparked a Galaxy Corps investigation. But six Galaxy Corps troops disappeared after playing your game. We want to know their fate and we want them or their remains returned at once."

Havago's special task force waved weapons at the blurry but still grinning host.

"Calm yourselves," Jiminy said with a flutter of rapidly fading wings. They were morphing into a huge warty hump behind his head, which was also changing shape. The teeth now looked vaguely green and instead of being broad and square, were pointed. "We eat intellectual energy, not the beings that possess it. Your colleagues are all unharmed. We have simply given them the vacation we promised them, though we extended it somewhat. They are safe on one of our farms, hooked up to computers feeding them data indigestible to us in electronic form. They are more like cooks than meals to us. It takes very high-level intellects to absorb some of this material and some of what we are given even so is indigestible. This we recycle as questions for contestants."

"Aha!" Shalula said. "That is how two of our people were able to get their mayday messages to me—one implanted a message within a frost flower holo and one in the pulsing of those lights."

"But that's cheating!" Jiminy said indignantly. "I'm afraid we can't award you any prizes after all, Shalula."

"No need," she said grimly. "Breaking up your operation will be prize enough."

Later, when the contestants, civilian and Galaxy Corpsmen alike, had been rescued, the off-duty members of the *Havago*'s crew sat around the recreation lounge feeling at loose ends. Usually, this was the time when they could tune in for another game of *Name That Planet!* But now, of course, that was no longer possible. To her dismay, Shalula, who had been hailed as a heroine, now found herself the target of resentful glances. But as a second-voyage replicator technician was flipping frequencies, the ship's intercom crackled to life.

"Lt. Makira, please report to the bridge. We have an incoming communication for you from Corps headquarters."

Shalula arrived on the bridge to see the captain and other personnel standing at attention before the com screen. General Azimblii herself stood beside an amphibat much like the one Jiminy Jimson appeared to be. The amphibat also had large teeth and carried a briefcase. Shalula also snapped to attention in front of the general.

"At ease, Lt. Makira. This is Consul Flaabaat of Flaabaat, Flaabaat, and Smith Attorneys of Intergalactic Law, Incorporated. He is representing the being known to most of us as Jiminy Jimson and the FLOG corporation, who have brought a lawsuit against the corps."

"I thought they would be incarcerated by now, General!" Shalula said indignantly. "Why are they suing us?"

"It's complicated," the general said, "But they have a great deal of power and money and the Galactic Congress has recently cut our own legal budget. Therefore, I hope you will consider FLOG's proposition, which they wished Consul Flaabaat to present to you personally."

"With respect, ma'am, I will not, even for the Corps, become one of FLOG's data-feeding drones."

Consul Flaabaat fluttered his wings in a soothing sort of way that indicated her assumption of his purpose was unwarranted. "Once your dramatic rescue of your colleagues (which, by the way, caused extreme public humiliation, harm, mental suffering, and constituted an invasion of privacy) was broadcast, beings throughout the cosmos realized what our sponsors required. All positions for data processors vacated by former contestants have been filled. We have quite a waiting list of applicants, in fact."

"Then what?" Shalula asked.

"Well, our clients wish to invite you to appear as a hostess on another show they have in production. You see, the show on which you appeared garnered the highest ratings *Name That Planet!* ever enjoyed in its brief history. Viewers simply ate up—if you'll pardon the expression—the drama of a game involving a live rescue. Our clients quickly realized that reality game shows are the wave of the future and you, you intrepid pioneer you, showed them the way. Therefore, they have agreed to drop their suit against Galaxy Corps if you will sign a contract to host the first six episodes of *Save That Alien!* So what will it be, Lt. Makira? Will you risk losing your commission in Galaxy Corps or go for the big rewards of hosting another popular FLOG TV production?"

Shalula said, in the appropriate communications mode for the situation, "I choose option number two, Consul Flaabaat."

[Editor's Note: A hendiatris is (a) three words used to express one idea. Other examples are "wine, women, and song" and William Shakespeare's "Friends, Romans, countrymen . . . "]

Be a bit patient with this story, sports fans. It's clever scientific mystery will hold your attention, but the sports connection may be, at first, obscure. Once a certain gentleman from British Colombia enters the picture, some readers will, at least, have a good clue about what sport is involved . . . but even once you figure that out, there's still mystery involved. And if it takes a little longer for the rest of you to figure it all out, just remember: In any sport, it may not all *be in the numbers, but a great deal of the game is. And since numerals are the closest thing we have to a universal language, then how might others first try to communicate to us . . . ?*

Distance

Maya Kaathryn Bohnhoff

In the movies, you were slumped at your computer console, fast asleep, surrounded by empty Pepsi cans and candy wrappers, when the system pinged. You woke on a tide of adrenaline, flinging candy wrappers and crumpled cans to the lab floor and, after a moment of disorientation, realized WHAT THAT SOUND MEANT.

In reality, Dr. Santiago Rodriguez was standing in the middle of the lab stuffing his face with nachos when the Signal Detection System spoke—figuratively speaking. What the interface actually did was fire an alarm that played the five-note sequence from *Close Encounters of the Third Kind*, at Dr. Mukerjee's whimsy.

When he'd first come to Project Quetzalcoatl, Santiago had jumped out of his skin every time the system pinged. Now, three years and many false alarms later, he didn't even twitch. Now, he stood chewing like a contented cow, contemplating a response to the summons. Most likely it meant another bogey or that Kev and Roz would have to run diagnostics, which would mean pulling the Spectrum Analyzer and Signal Detection Subsystem offline for a day or two.

He was strolling over to the SDS console when Gita Mukerjee poked her head in the door. "Snag a tire, Sandy?" she asked, but her eyes were hopeful.

Santiago laughed, set aside the nachos, and dusted his hands off on his jeans. "Heck, no, Gita. I got me a live one this time." He dropped into his chair and swiveled to the display.

"Any of those nachos left?"

"Uh, yeah . . . Kitchen." His mind was already occupied with the data. He got a raw read on the left, a waterfall plot of the data on the right. He was still studying the waterfall plot of the side band when Gita returned from the kitchen with a small plate of nachos.

"What have we got?" she asked.

"Not sure. Come look at this." He felt a peculiar wriggling in his stomach. Nachos were no longer of any interest. He was seeing pulses in the microwave window—pulses that were clearly patterned. They played in series, paused, then picked up again. There was very little drift. *But* the carrier wave was in the 1500 MHz range and looked familiar. In fact, Santiago could put his hands on any number of archived log entries that had recorded the same signal.

It didn't look like a glitch. Those were generally more capricious. And the few hackers who'd tried to get bogeys into the system had been unable to get past the first Follow-Up Detection Device or couldn't resist tapping out "ET phone home" in Morse code or something equally precious.

Santiago looked up at Gita. "What do you think, Dr. Mukerjee?"

"Well, Dr. Rodriguez, I think we need to call a powwow. This looks like a job for the FUDDs."

The small conference room was dim and hushed. The handful of scientists sat, expectant, their eyes on the screen at the front of the room where Santiago Rodriguez stood next to the podium that held his laptop.

"The data signal is in the 2 GHz range," Santiago told the gathering. "It's regular and it repeats in cycles. It *seems* to be coming from the direction of the constellation Taurus." He hesitated, allowing himself a bit of wonder at the words he would say next. "At a distance of 100 AU."

He watched the others' faces as they digested the information; saw that Gita Mukerjee, seated at the edge of the group, was doing the same.

Their Program Director, Dr. Kurt Costigyan, studied the screen intently, eyes roving over and over the figures there.

"That's outside the heliosphere," said one of the Techs, a lanky redhead named Kevin.

Santiago tapped the touch pad on the laptop and the projection on the screen beside him changed to a graphic representation of the signal's source. He tapped a second time and a waterfall plot from the spectrum analysis opened on the right side of the screen.

"Oh, wow," said Kevin.

"Here's the carrier signal . . . " Santiago switched the display again to show a second waterfall plot.

"I'll be damned." Kurt Costigyan sat back in the plastic conference chair. He was a big man; the chair squeaked loudly in protest. "That's Pioneer 10."

Santiago didn't realize he'd leaned so heavily against the podium until it scraped away from him across the floor. He straightened. "That's what we thought, but . . . " He glanced over at Gita Mukerjee. "We don't see how. She's so far out."

"And she's so dead," said Kevin. "Those old power cells couldn't possibly send from that distance. Even if she was turned in the right direction."

"Couldn't possibly?" asked Gita, gesturing at the screen.

"Okay, *shouldn't* be able to."

Kurt looked up at Santiago. "I didn't know you were scheduled to ping Pioneer."

"We weren't."

"Then why—?"

Santiago licked his lips. "We didn't ping her—if this really *is* her—she pinged us."

"With this . . . pattern?"

Santiago nodded, then clicked up another screen. This one came with a shower of noise that sounded like a Flamenco dance played at warp-speed. The graphical display showed the pulses as dashes and dots of white on black. The sequence was composed of multiple series of long and short pulses divided by mere seconds of silence.

"Oh, please tell me that's not Morse code," said Kurt.

"Not Morse code," Santiago assured him. "If you listen real carefully, you might be able to catch the pattern, but I'm glad we're not relying on our ears to decipher this. The spectrum analyzer pulled it apart pretty efficiently, and came up with this." A key press brought up a window atop the display of dashes and dots. This one showed a series of eight numbers:

18.9, 27.44, 27.44, 27.44, 27.44, 103.6, 121.9, 99.1

Kurt's eyes flickered between the exposed portion of the graphic and the numbers. "Okay, so it's eighteen long pulses and nine short?"

" 'Long' being purely arbitrary," said Gita. "Those pulses can't be more than . . . "

"A quarter-second," said Santiago. "Then there's a half-second pause before the next set starts: twenty-seven long; forty-four short, and so on. Then, there's a three second pause after the last repeat of 27.44. Then there's about a nine second pause after the last number and the whole sequence starts up again with 18.9. It repeats twice per minute, roughly. It's sending steadily—hasn't stopped since we picked it up."

"Without variation?"

"Without variation."

"God Almighty," said Roz Klein. A software technician, she sat beside Kevin, elbows on her knees, eyes glued to the screen.

"Probably not," said Kevin.

Roz reached out and punched his arm without taking her eyes from the screen.

"Ow! Look, that's a complex signal. Do you think it could possibly be latent? Some piece of programming that's just started regurgitating old messages?"

Gita Mukerjee smiled. "You mean Pioneer is dreaming?"

Kevin chuckled. "You're not going to get all mystical are you, Dr. Mukerjee?"

Gita ignored him. "I'd say our next step would be to set this contact up for follow up and check Pioneer's logs to see if a similar pattern occurred during a previous transmission."

Kurt nodded. "What FUDDs do you want to use?"

"Lick and Parkes," said Gita. "Jodrell Bank is the middle of an equipment upgrade."

"Consider it done." Santiago shut off his laptop, sending the screen into darkness. The roomful of scientists gave up and audible sigh.

"In the meantime," said Kurt, "let's design and prep a return signal." He paused, took a deep breath. "And call NASA."

"Been awhile." Santiago's Aussie counterpart at Parkes Observatory sounded preternaturally perky. "ET not biting much these days?"

"ET's not biting at all," said Santiago.

"Then what's up?"

"We think we've gotten a message from an old friend; we need you to verify. We've got a carrier wave in the 1500 MHz range and pulses that fall inside the microwave window. Distance approximately 100 AU in the direction of Taurus."

"Pioneer? You're kidding."

Santiago chuckled. "Well, if I am, you'll be the first to know."

He called Lick Observatory in Santa Cruz, California next, receiving a similar reception. As he downloaded the contact information, he was amused to find that his palms were sweating. And why not? Pioneer 10 was supposed to be dead, her batteries and fuel cells long exhausted, her antenna eternally locked in whatever direction she happened to have tumbled.

She might have been struck by something that coincidentally aimed her in the right direction, but no amount of coincidence could energize her defunct fuel cells or grant them the power to transmit a coherent sequence of numbers back to Earth.

And they were still transmitting, he discovered upon returning to the lab. He was surprised, too, not by the fact that the sequence of numbers was still repeating, but that Gita had held the huge main radio array trained on that target all afternoon.

"Dr. Mukerjee, this is highly irregular," he teased. "You're neglecting a goodly portion of the heavens."

Gita glanced up from the notepad she was scribbling on and said, "Yeah, well, this is the only portion of the heavens that's interested in conversing at the moment."

Santiago crossed the room and slid into a chair at the console next to her, noticing that the pad was covered with tight clumps of numbers. "Composing a reply?"

"No, actually, I was trying to make something out of these numbers." She grinned ruefully, tucking a strand of ebony hair behind one ear. "For all the good it's doing. There's *clearly* a pattern, I just don't get it."

Santiago looked at the top row of figures. "Divisible by anything constant?"

"This figure that repeats is divisible by 13.72. Ring any bells?"

Santiago smiled. "No."

Gita dropped her pen onto the pad. "I like your idea better. What should we send?"

"Uh, well . . . I'd say we should probably send one of her old command sequences. See if we can't get her to wiggle her ears at us."

"Makes sense. Or we could send a one to ten count, then count down from ten to one."

He stared at her for a moment. "Why would we send that? It wouldn't mean anything to Pioneer."

She dropped her eyes to the note pad. "I suppose not."

"But you're just a cock-eyed optimist."

She didn't answer, but picked up her pen, once more, tapped at the sequence of numbers she'd written across the top of the page. "Spatial coordinates? A location?"

"It's not longitude and latitude. At least not by any system I know."

She shook her head. "I guess we should just send a command sequence. Let's ask her to ping us."

They did just that, and roughly twenty-seven hours later, there was a pause in her broadcast. But then, instead of giving the programmed response to the command sequence, she simply began sending her original sequence of numbers again. Shortly thereafter, both follow-up detection locations called to verify the "hit," and confirmed location and range. The contact could only be Pioneer 10.

Kurt Costigyan sat in silence for a moment after Santiago delivered the news, then grinned and said, "Cool. I'm going to call a press conference. Contact NASA and let them know it's official—the prodigal has phoned home."

NASA was delighted; the press, full of questions, mostly unanswerable: Why was Pioneer signaling now, after such a long silence? What had prompted it? What did the signals mean? Why didn't she respond to their command sequences?

That at least, Kurt thought, was fairly easy to explain. "Chances are," he told the flock of science reporters, "the receiver is damaged."

"Does that mean you won't try contacting her any more?"

"Not at all. We'll certainly keep trying. It's also possible that her signal processor is malfunctioning. The sequence we sent may not raise her, but another one might."

While bits of their press conference played in living rooms across the US and Canada, Team Quetzalcoatl pondered their next message to Pioneer 10. It was Kurt Costigyan who came up with the winning entry.

"Why don't we echo the sequence she's sending back at her?"

"Doesn't it make more sense to send a standard message?" Santiago argued.

The project liaison, Dr. Peter Grace, who had arrived that morning from NASA, was quick to agree. "It makes a lot more sense. Sending a message she won't even recognize is just a waste of project time and money."

"We've already sent a standard command sequence and were roundly ignored," said Kurt. "I'd like to try something different."

"Why not compromise?" suggested Gita. She sat so far forward in her chair, Santiago was afraid she was going to fall out of it. "Send a standard sequence followed by the echo. Or *vice versa*."

"Look," said Grace, "Pioneer is still a NASA spacecraft. You guys drew the job of monitoring her, but I think in this department, NASA should call the shots. Send a command to run a diagnostic and report status."

"It's *our* processor time, dammit! If we want to send a recipe for Masoor Dal we should be able to send it."

Kurt let out a crack of laughter. "Good Lord, Gita! Save some energy for the House Budget Committee."

"Yeah," said Kev, eavesdropping from where he huddled in a tangle of wires behind one of the equipment racks, replacing a bad cable. "Besides, if you sent Masoor Dal to ET, you'd start an interstellar war. They'd think it was a biological weapon."

"Just because you can't handle Indian food—" Gita began, but Kevin popped out from under the console waving the faulty cable.

"You're ready to rock, boss," he told Santiago.

Santiago glanced at Kurt. "What are we sending?"

Kurt shrugged. "Standard command sequence requesting a diagnostic and status. If that doesn't work, we'll take it from there."

"Meaning we'll send the echo?" asked Gita.

"Meaning we'll cross that bridge when we come to it."

They sent the request for status exactly as stipulated. During the wait for Pioneer's response, they fielded several emails from their loyal Quetzalcoatl devotees offering all manner of explanations for the message Pioneer had sent. The most interesting ones encouraged them to work the numbers out as dimensions. But while it was true the repeated figure could form a square 27.44 inches, feet, meters or whatever on a side, the other figures seemed to bear no relation to each other.

The window of probability exhausted itself on a Sunday afternoon. Pioneer stopped transmitting for a period of five minutes, suggesting that she had received the command sequence and was processing it. Then she began transmitting again—the same eight numbers in the same order.

At that point, Drs. Rodriguez and Mukerjee, finding themselves alone with a titanic radio telescope and 75 gigaflops of computational horsepower, decided to queue a message of their own to Pioneer 10 so that if, by some chance it were approved, they'd be ready to send it.

Santiago was keying in the message when their Program Director strolled into the lab. Gita jumped guiltily and straightened from where she had been peering over her colleague's shoulder.

"My, but you two look like a couple of cats caught sizing up the canary," observed Kurt. "What's up?"

The two exchanged glances, then Santiago said, "We just wanted to be ready in case Dr. Grace let us send another sequence."

"Dr. Grace will not be back until Tuesday. He had a pressing matter to attend to at Kennedy Space Center."

Gita's face fell. "You mean we have to wait until Tuesday to try again? Kurt, that's a waste of time! We should send *now.*"

Kurt's eyebrows rose in an exaggerated arc. "Who said we had to wait? As I recall, the transmission schedule is the Program Director's purview. I assume you've queued the echo?"

Santiago nodded.

"Well, then why don't you just ask the Program Director if you can send it?"

Drs. Rodriguez and Mukerjee exchanged glances, and Dr. Rodriguez asked. "Dr. Costigyan, is it your opinion that we should echo the Pioneer's last message?"

"Make it so."

Santiago hit SEND, confirmed, then sat back in his chair. "Well, there it goes. Now we wait."

"You did *what*?" Dr. Grace was incredulous.

Kurt looked up at him from behind his desk. "I said: We sent the echo."

"It's a waste of time, Kurt."

"I happen to disagree. We're still scanning other areas. The only time it took was Sandy's time queuing the sequence."

"Sandy?"

"Dr. Rodriguez. Of course, Dr. Mukerjee was in attendance, so I suppose you'd want to argue that she wasted her time, too."

Grace shrugged and dropped into the chair across the desk. "It's your staff, doctor. If you don't mind them pursuing wild geese—"

"Excuse me—Dr. Costigyan?" Roz Klein stood in the door of his office, her face flushed. "Pioneer is responding."

The lab was as quiet and tense as a hospital waiting room. Quetzalcoatl staffers—techs, engineers, software experts, and the science crew—had come out of the woodwork to attend, every one of them trying to peer over Santiago Rodriguez's shoulder at his screen.

"What do we have?" Kurt asked, pushing through a cluster of techs.

Santiago glanced up and Gita vacated her chair to allow Kurt to take her place.

"She paused, as usual. This time for exactly three minutes, fifteen seconds. Then she resent the original sequence. We thought, okay, that's it, she's just . . . " He glanced at Gita. " . . . just dreaming."

"Dreaming?" repeated Dr. Grace.

Gita flushed. "Spinning off old data. Reliving old broadcasts."

"But then the sequence changed," said Santiago.

"Show me." Kurt rolled his chair closer.

"The pattern is the same," Santiago told him as he shifted the display to show the decoded output of the Multi-Channel Spectrum Analyzer. "And the first part of the sequence is the same: 18.9 and 27.44 repeated four times. Then it changes: 103.6, 134.1, 99.1. One digit off from the first sequence. Now, the third sequence—"

"The *third* sequence?" repeated Kurt.

Santiago nodded. "The third sequence starts out just like the other two—an identical sequence of five numbers. But this time the last three numbers are: 108.2, 121.9, 107.6."

"Completely different," observed Grace.

"But the seventh number is the same as in the first sequence," said Kurt. "That could be significant."

Grace shrugged. "And it could be mere chance."

"But look at the first set of five numbers," said Santiago. "It's the same for all each set. That's hardly random."

Grace shrugged again. "Why should it be? Pioneer may not possess any intelligence of her own, but she was created by an intelligence. She's spitting out available data—data we've given her—she's just not doing it in a form we understand."

"Whoa! There's a fourth sequence!" Santiago Rodriguez's voice, quiet as it was, cut through the discussion taking place over his head. The silence was immediate and thick.

"First five figures, the same . . . then 96.9, 124.4, 95.7."

Kurt leaned in to look at the series of numbers now lining up across the screen. "Okay, now the end of the sequence is completely different. The only thing obviously common is that the seventh figure is always larger than the others."

"You think we'll see that same pattern in the next sequence?" asked Grace.

"If there is a next sequence," said Santiago.

There was. It began as they all began, but the last three digits were 96, 122.5, 96. Not one of them matched a previously sent number. New sequences of numbers continued to come in—thirty unique sequences in all. Then there was a pause and they began to repeat, beginning with the initial sequence, and replaying in exactly the same order as they were originally received. Occasionally, there was a repeated digit, but there seemed to be no pattern. When it became clear that no new sequences were going to appear, Kurt called an analysis session.

While machine intelligences compared numbers, biological intelligences mulled patterns in their own way. They considered spatial coordinates, global coordinates, geometric figures.

"The second, third, and fourth numbers form a square," said Santiago, doodling on the white board in the conference room. He used a scale of one-half inch per unit, so the figure would fit on the board. "And the last three numbers could be the sides of a triangle."

"What about the first figure?" asked Gita. "What do you make of that? A line?"

Santiago drew a line 30.3 inches in length. "Yeah. Maybe . . . maybe that's it—a line between two points, then a figure with three points, then a four sided figure."

"Except," said Grace, "that they didn't arrive in that order. They came one, four, three."

"Maybe 18.9 is the diameter of a circle," suggested Gita. "Or the circumference. They could be showing us that they understand geometric constructs."

"They?" repeated Grace.

Gita flushed. "Did I really say that?" She shook her head. "Too many episodes of *X-Files*. Sorry."

"Hey," Kurt said, "it's why we're here—right, Dr. Grace? But why would the triangle—and only the triangle—vary in size?"

The question was met with silence.

They resorted to computer assistance at that point, generating two different sizes of circles, a square, and a series of thirty triangles—thirty lopsided, irregular triangles. They put the circles inside the squares, and the squares inside the triangles, oriented them in numerous ways. Nothing rang a bell, for either human or machine. In the end they sat back, mentally exhausted, and stared at the pages taped to the walls of the conference room—circles, squares, and/or triangles on every one.

"All right," said Kurt. "It's geometry. But why the subtle differences? Why such regularity in the first set of numbers and such irregularity in the second? And why the oddball matches? They've got to be significant."

"Do they?" asked Santiago. "If this is Pioneer spinning dreams or having the machine equivalent of a near death experience, then maybe the variations are merely extrapolations on a program they created for a First Contact scenario."

Gita shook her head. "They didn't program a geometry set like that into Pioneer. Roz and I went over every one of the First Contact protocols. There's nothing like this anywhere in her routines. Besides, Pioneer can't extrapolate. She's a machine. An *old* machine. A dying machine."

"Look," said Kurt, rubbing his forehead, "let's assume for a moment that Pioneer is merely expiring much later than expected and that for whatever reason she went off on her own, scrambled a bunch of old messages and sent them home. Let's assume that she refused to respond to familiar command sequences because they no longer seemed familiar. That she responded to an echo of her own unprovoked transmission because it *did* seem familiar. And let's further assume that receiving that echo caused her to randomly change the second set of numbers in what is now her default data set. Let's also assume that these numbers are dimensions for geometric shapes. What should our response be?"

"Why respond at all?" asked Gita. "That's what our friend from NASA would say. If this is Pioneer, the only significance is that she seems to have resurrected herself."

"Like Quetzalcoatl?" murmured Santiago.

Gita's dark brows arced gracefully. "Exactly. Score one for old rocket scientists. But if that's the case, there is no intrinsic significance to her message, above the incredible fact that she was able to send it at all. Any return messages we send should be targeted to keeping her online as long as possible, maybe getting her to return to an old routine, send some real data."

"I hear a definite 'but,'" said Kurt.

"But . . . if this *isn't* Pioneer, then this message is more significant than we can possibly imagine and our response should be targeted to letting whoever programmed that message know we got it and understand what we got."

"They already know we got it," said Santiago. "If there is a 'they.' And we *don't* understand it completely."

Gita ground the heel of her hand into her forehead. "But isn't that enough? Can't we send some geometry of our own?"

"Let's work on it," Kurt said. "Tomorrow, when I don't feel so much like a zombie. Let's sleep on it. Maybe one of us will have an epiphany."

If there were no epiphanies to be had in Puerto Rico that night, there was at least a piece of one in British Columbia. It came during the ten o'clock news in a living room in the town of Chilliwack.

The man had half risen from the sofa, mentally already in bed when the story about messages from space caught his attention and the numbers being scrolled out across the screen, his curiosity.

He sat back down.

Four orderly rows of figures later, he reached for a steno pad, flipped to a page devoid of Scrabble scores and wrote the numbers down. In the end, his pad contained thirty rows of eight figures each.

18.9, 27.44, 27.44, 27.44, 27.44, 103.6, 121.9, 99.1
18.9, 27.44, 27.44, 27.44, 27.44, 103.6, 134.1, 99.1
18.9, 27.44, 27.44, 27.44, 27.44, 108.2, 121.9, 107.6
18.9, 27.44, 27.44, 27.44, 27.44, 96.9, 124.4, 95.7
18.9, 27.44, 27.44, 27.44, 27.44, 96, 122.5, 96
18.9, 27.44, 27.44, 27.44, 27.44, 102.2, 111.3, 96.9
18.9, 27.44, 27.44, 27.44, 27.44, 100.6, 120.4, 100.6
18.9, 27.44, 27.44, 27.44, 27.44, 103, 125, 103
18.9, 27.44, 27.44, 27.44, 27.44, 99.1, 121.9, 99.1
18.9, 27.44, 27.44, 27.44, 27.44, 100.6, 123.7, 100.6
18.9, 27.44, 27.44, 27.44, 27.44, 100.6, 122.5, 100.6

18.9, 27.44, 27.44, 27.44, 27.44, 99.7, 123.4, 100.6
18.9, 27.44, 27.44, 27.44, 27.44, 100.6, 121.9, 100.6
18.9, 27.44, 27.44, 27.44, 27.44, 100.6, 123.1, 100.6
18.9, 27.44, 27.44, 27.44, 27.44, 102.1, 121.9, 102.1
18.9, 27.44, 27.44, 27.44, 27.44, 100.6, 124.4, 100.6
18.9, 27.44, 27.44, 27.44, 27.44, 100.6, 124.9, 100.6
18.9, 27.44, 27.44, 27.44, 27.44, 99.1, 123.1, 99.1
18.9, 27.44, 27.44, 27.44, 27.44, 104.9, 124.4, 99.7
18.9, 27.44, 27.44, 27.44, 27.44, 100, 121.9, 100
18.9, 27.44, 27.44, 27.44, 27.44, 105.8, 121.9, 105.8
18.9, 27.44, 27.44, 27.44, 27.44, 101.5, 121.9, 96.9
18.9, 27.44, 27.44, 27.44, 27.44, 102.2, 123.1, 105.2
18.9, 27.44, 27.44, 27.44, 27.44, 101.8, 121.9, 99.1
18.9, 27.44, 27.44, 27.44, 27.44, 99.1, 123.4, 99.1
18.9, 27.44, 27.44, 27.44, 27.44, 205.8, 135.6, 106.7
18.9, 27.44, 27.44, 27.44, 27.44, 102.1, 122.2, 100.6
18.9, 27.44, 27.44, 27.44, 27.44, 100.6, 124.1, 101.8
18.9, 27.44, 27.44, 27.44, 27.44, 96, 123.1, 98.1
18.9, 27.44, 27.44, 27.44, 27.44, 100.9, 123.4, 99.4

The pattern seemed familiar. Damn familiar. But elusively so.

"Bill? You coming to bed?" Barbara had apparently finished her crossword puzzle.

"In a minute, babe."

"You're not writing are you? You know you're more likely to write crap than cream at this hour of the night."

She was right, of course. "I'm not writing. I'm watching the news."

"All right then." Barbara subsided.

Bill leaned his head toward the TV to catch what the SETI guy was saying about geometrical figures. They thought the old Pioneer 10 spacecraft was speaking to them in geometry. When asked why this was happening, a pretty East Indian woman—a Dr. Mukerjee—said that they thought her deteriorating condition had caused the old space craft to start running some mangled first contact programming.

She smiled (it was a dynamite smile) and said, "I like to think she's dreaming."

Bill sat back on the sofa. Now that was one for the books—a dreaming spacecraft. He waited for them to show the geometrical shapes they thought lived in the neat rows and columns of numbers. They didn't.

Miffed, he hunkered down to do the math himself.

"Bill? Are you sure you're not writing?"

He flipped the steno pad shut, slid the pencil back into the spiral binding, clicked off the TV, and went to bed.

Peter Grace rubbed the back of his neck absently. "Okay, next time you guys come up with a hare-brained idea I'll just chalk it up to thinking 'outside the box' and go with it."

Kurt grinned. "Hey, that hare-brained idea got us 240 data points."

"Don't rub it in." Grace shook his head. "You're an unorthodox son of a bitch, Kurt, but I guess that's why you're out here, in the first place."

"And not at NASA with the real scientists?"

"Didn't say that; didn't mean to imply it." He pushed his glasses back up his nose. "So, what's our next move?"

Kurt laughed. "What makes you think we've got one?"

The steno pad lay on the coffee table in the living room. Bill picked it up on the way to the kitchen, where he pecked his wife on the cheek, poured himself a cup of fresh, hot coffee and sat at the kitchen table to think about geometric figures. By the time Barbara put a plate full of scrambled eggs in front of him and sat down caddy corner, he was doodling lines, circles, squares, and triangles. He studied what he'd done as he shuttled eggs to his mouth.

"What's that?" Barbara asked.

His mouth full, he rotated the pad so she could see what he was doodling.

She frowned, shrugged, shook her head. "I still don't know what it is."

"Well, neither do I, exactly," Bill said. "These rows of numbers are being sent to Earth by the old Pioneer 10 spacecraft. Problem is, the scientists weren't expecting her to send anything and they can't figure out why she's sending this all of a sudden. They don't know what it is, either."

Barbara smiled, puckering the little crow's-feet at the corners of her eyes and firing up her dimples. They were turning to creases now, but he still loved them. "And you think an old writer can figure out what a bunch of NASA brainiacs can't?"

Bill shook his fork at her, flipping eggs across the table. "Don't disparage old writers. There is a compendium of knowledge about a great many things in this noodle. Scientists on the other hand, tend to specialize. I just need to figure out which of my many veins of generalized knowledge this pertains to."

He reached for the pad, glancing as he did at the page full of circle-square-triangles. They were tip-tilted now, standing on end.

He set down his fork. "Son of a bitch."

"What?" Barbara asked, but he didn't hear her.

He snagged the pad back and stared at it, caddy-wumpus, then turned to a clean sheet. "We got a ruler, babe?"

"Uh-huh." She got up, pulled it out of the junk drawer beneath the telephone, and flipped it to him. He caught it without looking up.

After watching him for a moment, Barbara cleared her dishes and left him to his doodles.

"This number appears eight times in the sixth place and nine times in the eighth place—that's seventeen times altogether."

Santiago brought his laser pointer to the number 100.6 in the chart projected onto the screen in the conference room. Kurt Costigyan and Gita Mukerjee followed the red beam in the semi-darkness.

"It *never* occurs in the seventh place," continued Santiago. "*This* figure—121.9—occurs nine times in the seventh place, but *never* occurs in the sixth or eighth. All in all, there seems to be no actual pattern, although in fourteen cases, the number from place six is repeated in place eight. In seven instances, the repeated number is 100.6."

Kurt rubbed his hands over his face in a gesture of weariness. "I don't even know what to suggest we send next."

"So far," said Gita, "the geometric figures seem to be nested. Circle in square in triangle. What if we add a larger circle that contains all the previous figures?"

"Bring it full circle?" punned Kurt wryly.

"Har-har-har," said Gita.

"Okay." Santiago scrolled through the thirty rows of data. "Which data set do you want to work with?"

"The first one," Gita suggested. "I'm thinking we calculate the circle so that its diameter is a multiple of the first circle's diameter. If this is some kind of progressive loop, then we should see another square that is built on a multiple of the first one in some way."

"Sounds like a plan," said Santiago. "Let me just rack 'em up. What multiple of 18.9 would you like, ma'am?"

"Oh, how about seven? That ought to clear the points of the triangle."

Kurt Costigyan had just gotten up to stretch when the phone rang. He picked it up, expecting it to be his wife demanding to know when he intended to come home. It was their admin, Rosa, sounding a bit flustered.

"Doctor, there's a man calling long distance from *British Columbia*. He wants to talk to . . . um . . . one of our experts about the messages from Pioneer."

"Does he say why, in particular?"

"He saw the story on the news the other night and he *says* he thinks he knows what the message is about."

"Oh? And what does he think it's about?"

"He won't say. He wants to talk to an expert."

"I guess that would be one of us. Okay, put him on," Kurt said, reasoning that if he talked to the guy and made him think they took him seriously, he'd be much more likely to go away and stay gone.

"Hello?" The voice sounded dubious, as though the guy suspected he'd been put on hold indefinitely.

"Hello, this is Dr. Costigyan. I'm Director of the Project Quetzalcoatl Signal Detection Group. You . . . you have some information relating to Pioneer 10?"

There was a moment of profound silence, then the caller said, "Look, I know you figure me for a crackpot, and in some ways you'd be right, but I really do have an idea about this message."

It was Kurt's turn for thoughtful silence. "All right. What do you think it's about?"

"If I told you flat out, you'd be sure I was a crackpot. Let me ask you this: what's it doing now?"

"It's . . . still sending the same sets of data."

"Thirty of 'em?"

"Yes."

"And no more?"

"No more."

"In the same order every single time?"

Now Kurt was intrigued. *Order.* "Yes, as a matter of fact. Is that significant?"

"Could be. Have you sent anything back yet—since it started sending the thirty sets, I mean?"

"Not yet. We were just now preparing a response."

"What were you planning to send?"

"A number that would describe the diameter of a circle that will encompass the entire set of geometric figures."

"Wrong. That's not it."

"No?"

"No. What you need to do is this: take the first set of numbers. The ones you got first, I mean." He repeated them for good measure. "But either at the beginning of the sequence or at the end, add this: 4, 20, 19, 12."

"May I ask why?"

"Just testing a theory. What've you got to lose, right? The ship's on her way out—hell, you thought she was gone already, didn't you? If I'm wrong, you lose a little chatting time. If I'm right . . . "

"If you're right—what?"

The caller laughed. "Hell, I don't know. Damn! I really don't know."

"May I ask who this is?"

"My name's Bill. Bill Kinsella."

"Well, thank you, Mr. Kinsella. If we can't raise a response with our current approach, maybe we'll try yours."

"When?" Kinsella insisted.

"Well, we'll try our response tonight. And then it will take about twenty-seven hours to see if there's a response."

"Twenty-seven hours?"

"She's one hundred astronomical units out from Earth, Mr. Kinsella. That's a long—"

"I know how far it is. I read."

"Sorry, I didn't mean to—"

"That's all right. But if you do try my . . . my idea, you let me know what happens. I left my number with your secretary. If I don't hear in a week, I'll call back."

Of course you will, Kurt thought wryly, and rang off.

"Four-twenty-nineteen-twelve? Isn't that one of those low cost call gimmick numbers?" Gita leaned back in her chair and put her feet up on the conference table.

"Did he say why he thought that would work?" asked Santiago.

"Nope. He was pretty tight-lipped."

"You're not really thinking of sending that, are you?"

Kurt shook his head. "We want to keep Pioneer chatting with us. I think our best chance of that is to follow the geometric progression as Gita suggested."

It made perfect sense to do that, Kurt thought twenty-seven hours later when they received Pioneer's response. As usual, she paused to receive the data and process it, before sending a return message. This time the pause was longer, as if their response puzzled her, then she continued sending her thirty sets of data as if they'd sent nothing at all. She seemed only to take a very deep breath before taking it, once again, from the top.

Like a teacher dealing with a particularly slow student, Kurt thought, staring across the lab where a screen saver wove multi-colored twists.

"Apparently, that wasn't what Pioneer was expecting," said Gita.

"Expecting?" Peter Grace took a sip of his coffee, made a face and added more sugar. "Dr. Mukerjee, Pioneer wasn't expecting anything. She's just firing back broken bits of data."

"What was it you said about us thinking outside the box?" Kurt asked mildly.

"Oh, all right. But be honest, Kurt—isn't it just as likely that Pioneer changing her message earlier was just coincidence?"

"No."

"True believer."

"Jade. Maybe you should get out of space science and into something that requires less imagination—accounting maybe."

"I hate to interrupt this mutual admiration society," said Gita, "but what's our next move? Are we going to send that guy's message?"

Grace frowned through the steam that lingered above his coffee cup. "What guy? What message?"

"A gentleman from Chilliwack, B.C. saw a news broadcast of our last press conference and called to say he knew what we should send next."

"Oh really. And that would be?"

"'4, 20, 19, 12,'" Kurt said.

"Why?"

"Didn't give a reason why. Just testing a theory, he said."

Grace's brow puckered again. "Is that a date?"

"A date?" Santiago returned blankly.

"I don't know," said Kurt. "I hadn't thought of it that way, but I suppose it could be. He asked about the order the numbers came in. Wanted to know if the sequences were always in the same order. Maybe this date—if it is a date—has something to do with the order the data is delivered in. Though I can't imagine what."

"Hm. And maybe it's the date his mommy and daddy were abducted by aliens."

Santiago looked over at Kurt from the Signal Detection console. "You did tell him you'd use his sequence if ours failed. And I'm fresh out of ideas. We might as well send it while we're trying to come up with something else."

Grace snorted. "You're kidding. You're not going to authorize—"

Kurt smiled, tapped his forehead, and said, "Outside the box, Peter."

"Do you have any reason to think this might work?"

"None. But Sandy's right—we might as well send something."

They sent: 18.9, 27.44, 27.44, 27.44, 27.44, 103.6, 121.9, 99.1, 4, 20, 19, 12.

Just over twenty-seven hours later, Pioneer's return message began with the characteristic pause. Then she started into a sequence: 18.9, 27.44, 27.44, 27.44, 27.44, 108.2, 121.9, 107.6, she said. The *second* sequence. And she added: 4, 20, 19, 12.

"Whoa," said Santiago, taking in the complete sequence. He glanced up over his shoulder at Kurt Costigyan, colors from the MCSA display patterning the side of his face. "Now what do we do?"

"Now, we give Mr. Kinsella a call back."

"Well, this *is* a surprise. I didn't expect to hear from you. I kind of figured I'd have to nag." Bill Kinsella raised eyebrows at his wife and mouthed, "It's *them,*" across the kitchen table.

"No, Mr. Kinsella," said the caller, "we tried your sequence of numbers right after . . . well, right after our sequence failed to get Pioneer's attention."

When the man from SETI—Dr. Kurt Costigyan, he called himself—hesitated, Bill prompted, "Well, don't keep me in suspense, Kurt. Did it work?"

After a moment more of hesitation, Costigyan said, "Pioneer returned a second set of numbers, and added the same sequence you gave us to the end of it."

"Damn. Which set was it?"

"The second set."

Bill looked at the list of names and numbers he'd scribbled in his steno pad. "*Damn*," he said again.

The scientist cleared his throat. "Does that number mean something to you, Mr. Kinsella?"

"Yes sir, it does."

"May I ask *what* it means? Some of us thought it might be a date."

"It is a date. At least, to me, it's a date. I don't know what it is to your little robot friend."

"If you were to . . . What would you send next?"

"Well, the logical thing would be to send the third sequence again and add 4, 23, 19, 14 to the end of it."

There was a pause before Costigyan asked, "May I ask why that would be logical?"

Bill sighed. This man was going to think he was a lunatic. "Trust me: that date goes with the third sequence of numbers."

"Mr. Kinsella—"

"I know I'm being cantankerous and mysterious, but if I tell you what I'm thinking, you'll hang up on me."

"I won't, I promise, Mr. Kinsella. I won't hang up."

"Call me 'Bill.'"

"I promise I won't hang up, Bill."

"Look, try this—send this batch of numbers, and if it comes back with . . . well, with the next logical sequence, I'll tell you what I think it's all about."

"Wait, you're telling me . . . you can predict what Pioneer is going to say *next*?"

"In a nutshell, yeah. If I'm right, Pioneer's response to this message will be to add 4, 18, 19, 23 to the fourth set of numbers."

"But you won't tell me why," said Costigyan, frustration creeping into his voice. "Will you at least tell me what you think the numbers are—generally speaking?"

"Well, sir, I think they're dimensions. But not geometrical shapes, exactly."

"Dimensions." There was another pause, then the scientist asked, "Are you a mathematician, Mr. Kinsella—Bill?"

"No sir. I'm a writer. Of fiction. Not science fiction, though, in case you were wondering."

■ ■ ■

"He's a *writer*?" repeated Peter Grace. "A *fiction* writer is driving your game plan?"

"He's getting results," argued Gita. "Which is more than our well-considered responses are doing."

"Let me guess—he writes science fiction, right?"

"He says not," said Kurt. "Besides, as Gita said, he's getting results. You can't argue with that. I think we're pushing the envelope of coincidence. So here's our test case—he's given me a new sequence and told me what response he expects. We might as well send it and see what happens."

Grace muttered something under his breath about looking silly, then said, "I'll tell you what you're going to get. She's going to repeat what you send, just like she did this last time."

"But she added it to a different sequence of numbers."

"Of course she did, Kurt. She's locked into that program of thirty data sets. She ran what's now her normal sequence and tacked exactly what you sent to the end of it. No mystery, there."

Kurt shrugged. "Maybe you're right. But we've got nothing to lose, right?"

"Hell, no," said Grace. "Just our professional dignity."

They sent the data. They waited. Within ten minutes of Pioneer's answer, Kurt Costigyan called Chilliwack, B.C.

"Well, Bill," he said, "she gave the answer you were expecting. I think we need to talk face to face. Are you willing to meet with me?"

"In Puerto Rico?"

Kurt chuckled. "I was thinking of someplace in between. There's an observatory in Santa Cruz, California . . . "

"William Patrick Kinsella," the man said, holding out his hand.

Kurt Costigyan took it, thinking that he surely must have meant to say "Mark Twain." Tall, lanky, and spare, he had a wavy fringe of collar-length hair that was going from gray to white. Mustache and beard to match. Hazel eyes sparkled behind wire-rim glasses. There, the resemblance to the Twain archetype ended; he wore a cowboy hat and a blue chambray shirt. Kurt guessed him to be in his seventies.

"Dr. Kurt Costigyan," Kurt said. "This is my colleague, Dr. Peter Grace, from NASA."

"Kinsella," repeated Grace, shaking the older man's hand. "Didn't you write that movie—"

"I wrote a book that got made into a movie," Kinsella said, warily, Kurt thought.

"A fantasy movie," said Grace, passing him a look.

"Fantasy," said the writer, "is in the mind of the reader. You're talking across millions of miles of space to a glorified Tinkertoy. How fantastic is that?"

Grace raised his eyebrows but didn't offer a comeback.

"Can you send messages to Pioneer from here?" Kinsella gestured around the observatory's main lab.

"No, but we can have Arecibo send them."

"And what messages will we be sending?" asked Grace, his voice patronizing.

In answer, Kinsella pulled a steno pad out from under his arm, flipped it open and handed to him. On the exposed page was a table. Looking over Grace's shoulder, Kurt saw the sequences of numbers he'd come to know so well, each sequence in a neat row that ended with a date and a name.

"What . . . what are these?" Grace asked brushing the names with a fingertip.

Kinsella cleared his throat and gave Kurt an almost apologetic glance. "They're . . . um . . . ballparks."

Kurt could feel Grace's eyes on him. "*Ballparks*?"

Kinsella scratched around in his longish white hair. "Your numbers there are the internal dimensions of a baseball diamond, in meters. The first number is the distance from home plate to the mound—18.9 meters, or 60 feet, 6 inches. The second, third, fourth and fifth numbers are the distance between the bases—27.44 meters or 90 feet. Those numbers are constant for every major league ballpark ever built. The last three numbers are outfield dimensions, which are different in every park."

"And the dates?" Grace asked.

"Opening days."

Grace's mouth, which had been open, snapped shut. "Come sit down, won't you, Mr. Kinsella?"

The old guy smiled. "Call me 'Bill.' "

"Why would Pioneer 10 be talking to us in baseball?" asked Gita, the bemusement in her voice clear even through the speakerphone. "Was there some sort of database on board that might be spilling first contact information? I mean, maybe one of the scientists on the project was a baseball buff or something."

"A database?" Kurt repeated. "Gita, Pioneer was launched in 1972."

"But there's got to be some reason she's spitting ballpark dimensions at us." There was a moment of puzzled silence, then she said, "Okay. So we've got an aging spacecraft that wants to talk baseball. What do we do about it?"

Kurt looked at Bill Kinsella. "I'd like to try sending all thirty sets of dimensions and dates. Cut to the chase."

Peter Grace looked dubious. "What do you expect to happen?"

"I don't know. Bill, you have any ideas?"

"She might start on player stats next," said Kinsella, then shrugged. "Maybe she'll start giving us box scores. Beats me."

They scanned the handwritten list of dimensions and dates and emailed it to Arecibo where Santiago and Gita fed it to the transmitter.

"Now what?" Kinsella asked.

"Now we wait," said Grace.

Kinsella shook his head. "You scientists do a lot of waiting, don't you?"

Pioneer's response, when it came was anti-climactic. She simply stopped sending. The absence of any signal stretched into minutes, then hours. When three days had passed without her commentary, Peter Grace went back to NASA and Bill Kinsella, after taking in two Giants games, prepared to fly back to B.C.

He was, in fact, standing in the main concourse at SFO with Kurt Costigyan when a bleary sounding but excited Dr. Rodriguez called from Puerto Rico.

"She's sending again."

"*What* is she sending?" Kurt clutched his cell phone as if it might fly out of his hand, and met Bill Kinsella's eyes.

"It's not so much what as where from. I've checked this through the FUDDs at three separate observatories. Pioneer—if this is Pioneer—is transmitting from *inside* the solar system."

"That's impossible."

"Tell me about it. Can you get back to Lick, ASAP?"

"With bells on. I'll call when I'm there." He hung up, pocketed the phone and blinked at Kinsella. "Well, Bill, I've got to go back to Lick."

"Our girl get talkative again, did she?"

"Yes, she's sending again. And she's apparently headed back toward Earth."

"I didn't think that could happen."

"It can't. You can still catch your plane—"

"You kidding? I wouldn't miss this for the world."

The two men picked up their bags and began to wend their way toward the Ground Transport area.

"By the way, what's she sending?"

Kurt laughed. "I forgot to ask."

She was sending new coordinates—longitude and latitude, Santiago thought. And by the time Kurt Costigyan and the "psychic writer" had checked back in at Lick Observatory, he had been able to generate a map. It displayed on Kurt Costigyan's borrowed computer monitor in Lick's main lab as a U.S.-shaped outline populated with about two-dozen points of light.

"I've got to say," Santiago told them as they sat down to study the map, "when we put this together and saw what it looked like, it made us a bit . . . uh, nervous out here. Those coordinates correspond to major American cities."

"No need to be nervous," said Bill, raising salt and pepper eyebrows. "I don't think."

"Then they're not cities?" Gita sounded relieved.

"Oh, I'm pretty sure they're cities," said Kinsella. "Can I ask what order you got the coordinates in?"

"Is that significant?" Santiago asked.

"Could be. Let me guess—the first four were Boston, Detroit, Chicago, and New York."

"Uh . . . yeah. Oh, wait. You're thinking they should line up with the—the list of dimensions. But they don't. There aren't thirty of them."

"Some cities have more than one professional ballpark," said Kinsella patiently.

Kurt closed his eyes. "Okay, okay. Let's think things through. Pioneer 10 suddenly, and without provocation, starts sending us the dimensions of major league baseball parks."

"Except that the list isn't up to date," said Kinsella. "Some of these parks have been replaced."

"Yeah, but how would Pioneer know that?" asked Santiago.

Into the pregnant silence that followed, Kurt Costigyan said, "Sandy, Pioneer 10 doesn't *know* anything. And she doesn't—she *couldn't*—have any information her programmers didn't have back in 1972. Unless . . . "

"Unless," repeated Gita, "someone's been able to hack that archaic code and-and what—send her the dimensions of *baseball parks*?"

"Pre-2000 baseball parks," said Kinsella.

Kurt cleared his throat, making way for words that sounded unreal even in his head. "Let's assume someone could hack her code. How could they reach her *outside* the solar system, when an array as powerful as Arecibo's couldn't raise her? And how could any hacker, no matter what his or her technology, turn her around and bring her back to Earth?" He paused to let it sink in. "The answer is, they couldn't."

"Maybe they're only making it *seem* as if she's coming back to Earth," said Santiago. "Maybe they've hacked *our* system and the diagnostics just didn't pick it up."

"Then they would have had to hack all the Follow-Up Detection Systems we used too. That's four separate installations all together." Kurt closed his eyes and sat back in his chair.

"We're talking ETs, now, aren't we?" said Kinsella.

Kurt turned to stare at him; the Arecibo side of the connection was silent.

Kinsella's eyes blinked behind their oval lenses. "Well, good Lord, Kurt. When you eliminate all the other possibilities what are you left with? Isn't this what you SETI guys have been working for all these years?"

"He's right, Kurt," said Gita and laughed, nervously. "This could be it."

"It," repeated Kurt.

"But *why*?" asked Santiago. "Why would—well, *aliens*—talk *baseball*?"

"Maybe because *we* do," said Kinsella softly.

"But we *don't*," said Santiago. "We speak mathematics—"

"Baseball *is* mathematics. And it's geometry, and music, and poetry, and art. Art made of time and space and motion. Sunlight and grass and earth. Maybe they even *play* baseball back where they come from. Or maybe they've been picking up broadcasts from Earth and the beauty and perfection of it just . . . enchanted them so much they had to come here to see."

Gita said, "You wrote that baseball was too perfect to have been created by human beings—that God must've had a hand in it."

Bill blinked at the speakerphone, wishing the lady scientist were there so he could see her smile. "You've read my stories."

"All right," said Kurt. "Let's assume that an extraterrestrial intelligence is using Pioneer to talk to us. What are they trying to say?"

"If you send it, we will come?" suggested Kinsella wryly.

Gita stifled another giggle. "I think Mr. Kinsella's right. I think maybe they've just adopted a language they think we'll understand."

"Or maybe they think baseball diamonds have some sort of religious or political significance," said Santiago.

"Don't they?" asked Kinsella.

"Let's have that discussion later," interrupted Kurt and Gita said: "Maybe they think they're grounded spacecraft. Some of them *look* like spacecraft."

"Whoa!" Santiago's voice rose half an octave. "Kurt, she's sending again. A whole different set of numbers. Oh, man, she's—Wow. Double-check this with the Signal Detector at Lick, would you? Gita, get on line with, um, with Parkes, okay? This is wild. Kurt, this signal's coming from inside the orbit of Jupiter."

Kurt swung around, catching the eye of one of the tensely hovering observatory staff. "Can you check that telemetry?"

The woman nodded, wide-eyed, moved to a terminal, and brought up Lick Observatory's Signal Processor. "Have him send coordinates."

"I heard that," Santiago said. His fingers, tapping across his keyboard, sounded like the clatter of dice in a cup.

Roll the bones, Kurt thought.

"Okay, listen," said Santiago. "I'm going to send you the first sequence of numbers. See what Mr. Kinsella makes of them. They don't mean a damn thing to me."

The numbers rolled down the screen, pulling scientist and writer close enough to bathe their faces in its light.

1/2.40

2/.302

3/.311

4/.250

5/.330

6/.279

7/.289

8/.350

9/.306

"There's a full second pause between the first number in each group—the ascending numbers—and the rest. That's what I've indicated with the slash. There's a three second pause between each set. I notice the first number seems . . . out of keeping with the others."

"They look like batting averages," said Kinsella. "Except for the first one, which looks like a pitcher's ERA. That'd be my guess."

"I think you've had more than enough guesses, Mr. Kinsella."

Kurt turned to see Peter Grace standing in the middle of the lab, looking windblown and harried.

"I think," Grace continued, smoothing his hair, "that it's time you gave science back to the scientists."

"What were you thinking?" Grace asked when he'd closed the door on the borrowed conference room. "Letting a *civilian* take control of the situation? That's nuts."

"It was working."

"Oh, come on. For all you know, this could be a monumental hoax."

"Hoax? Perpetrated by whom, Peter? A Canadian fiction writer? You can't hoax a FUDD. Parkes and Lick both confirm—Pioneer 10's signal is now coming from local space."

"Right. Meaning that your friend may have precipitated an attack on us by . . . "

"By what? A bunch of geeks with a fleet of daisy-chained Pentiums? You can't have this both ways. Either it's incredibly sophisticated hoaxers, or it's . . . it's what we've been waiting for, working for, *praying* for all these years. First contact with an alien race." Kurt had to force himself to breathe.

"Who are interested in old baseball diamonds."

Kurt shook his head. "Life's strange, isn't it?"

"It's time to stop playing games and call in the people who know how to handle this sort of thing."

"And who would that be? The CIA? The FBI? Interpol? The Marines? The cast of the latest Star Trek movie stands a better chance of handling this right than any of them. At least they've dealt with this situation in theory."

Grace's face reddened. "Regardless, I . . . I've taken the precaution of alerting the State Department."

"And told them what?"

"That an unidentified spacecraft is heading for Earth with unknown intentions and that it has expressed some interest in a number of major American cities."

"It expressed interest in major league ballparks."

Grace snorted. "If I'd told them that they'd have laughed me off the line. Look, Kurt, you and I both know that Pioneer 10 can't possibly be hurtling toward Earth under her own power, nor is there any natural phenomenon that could account for it. Whatever the interest is, we are soon going to face an unknown . . . intelligence."

"All right. So the military is involved. What's next? What do we do?"

"We keep Pioneer—whatever it is—talking. Now, I think we have to lock this project down. No press conferences, no more media coverage, no one talks to anyone outside of this lab. In fact, no one *leaves* this lab. We don't want to cause a panic."

Panic. That was something Kurt hadn't considered. He had gone from curiosity to intellectual challenge to giddy anticipation without considering the reaction of the non-geek majority of human beings.

"No one leaves," he agreed.

Left to his own devices, Bill continued his conversation with the scientists in Puerto Rico, mulling over the sequences of data, trying to figure out what they meant.

"So," Santiago asked, "how do you figure it's batting averages and a—what did you call it—an ERA?"

"Earned Run Average," said Bill. "An ERA is the number of runs a pitcher allows per nine innings. So this pitcher allows 2.40 runs every nine innings."

"Okay, but why are you so sure that's what this is?"

"Context, first of all. In baseball, each position has a number. Pitcher is one, catcher is two, first baseman is three, and so on all the way out to right field, which is position number nine."

"Oh, okay. I think I—"

Gita's voice cut across him with "Oh, *wow*."

"What?" Bill asked. "What?"

"She's changed again. She's sending . . . "

"Damn!" Santiago's expletive coincided with the sudden appearance on the computer screen at Bill's elbow of a perfect outline of the United States. Within the map's glowing tracery, a pattern of bright dots lit up the dark interior.

Bill shuffled through the papers littering the desktop, finally coming up with a printout of the map Santiago had created earlier from the transmitted coordinates. A glance confirmed the match. This was the same map, only brighter, clearer.

He looked back at the computer screen. The dots had begun to flash. One by one, they winked off, then on again: Boston, Detroit, Chicago, New York, Milwaukee . . .

Hair stood up on the back of Bill's neck. "You flashing those lights, son?"

"No sir. She—it, whatever it is, it's got direct control of the receiver. It's in the driver's seat, now."

"Is Kurt there?" Santiago asked, his voice tight and anxious.

"Nope. Still closeted with that NASA guy. Look, Sandy—may I call you Sandy? Kurt isn't here and Pioneer needs an answer. And I think I got one. Will you send it?"

"If Dr. Costigyan okays it—"

"It's a repeat of an earlier message, so he's already approved it."

"A repeat?" said Gita.

"Yeah."

"Kurt's not available; I'm his second; I'll approve it," she said.

There was a moment of silence, then Santiago said, "Okay, Bill. What am I sending?"

"He *what*?" Peter Grace sat heavily in the swivel chair, rolling backwards several feet before coming to a stop against a workbench.

"He had us repeat a sequence," said Santiago, "from an earlier transmission. Then he excused himself and took off."

"Why?"

"Why'd he take off?"

"Why repeat the sequence?"

"Oh. Because of the map."

"The map?"

"They . . . she . . . Pioneer sent a map of her own. Should still be on screen over there."

"They sent this?" asked Kurt, leaning over Grace to see the screen better. "It's not our construct?"

"What you see is what we got. They're apparently quick studies tech-wise. They drove this right through our MCSA."

"Oh, God," murmured Grace.

"Anyway, Bill had me send the sequence and—"

"Whoa, that was quick," said Gita.

"Oh, God," said Grace a second time. He pressed a finger to the map where a lone spot of brilliance now blinked steadily. All the others had dimmed.

"Which sequence did you send?" Kurt asked.

"The third sequence."

"The signal, Sandy. Where's the signal coming from now?"

"Approaching Saturn's orbital plane. At that rate—"

"Sometime tomorrow," Kurt finished.

The National Guard arrived first, elite units sealing off streets and rerouting traffic. It was an above-average spring day for Chicago, less blustery than usual. Clouds chased each other across a cerulean sky—they'd have no trouble seeing whatever was descending upon them—be it the remains of Pioneer 10 or an alien ship.

An alien ship. Kurt tried on the thought for size—wasn't sure how it fit, after all. He was almost ready to believe this was an elaborate hoax. Something they'd simply not anticipated when they built all their security protocols and firewalls. Something loosed on them by a particularly clever hacker who'd been able to hijack their Signal Detection System and completely flummox two FUDDs . . . and the NASA tracking computers, and the sophisticated radar arrays of any number of nations whose every attention was on the object—much larger than the hapless Pioneer—currently on an obviously controlled descent to Earth.

Kurt shook himself. No, he wasn't ready to believe that, after all. Occam's Razor cut this particular pie such that the big half went to ET. And yet, he irrationally half-hoped it was a hoax. He had to wonder why, after all these years of daydreaming, anticipating, even praying for contact with THEM.

He looked up now into the cloud-draped expanse of heaven and prayed none of the fighter jets assigned to fly escort for anything that entered Earth's atmosphere contained trigger-happy pilots.

He thought it was a bird soaring high overhead when he first saw it, but a second later, he decided it was a helicopter. Then realized it was neither. He straightened from the hood of the Army Jeep he'd been leaning against, catching peripheral movement as the soldiers around him stirred. Peter Grace, who'd been sitting in the Jeep monitoring radio traffic, slid out of the cab and stared skyward with everyone else.

It descended swiftly, wavering not at all, bracketed by fighter jets. A deep thrumming filled the air, audible even beneath the scouring roar of jet engines. The fighters had to pull up when the alien vessel—the ALIEN VESSEL—continued to descend toward the corner of Addison and Wheatland.

Kurt devoured it with his eyes, his heart galloping wildly beneath his Kevlar vest. It wasn't saucer-shaped, or cigar-shaped, or ice-cream-cone-shaped, or bristling with instrumentation. It was a perfect sphere of light-sucking black and had no distinguishing marks on the exterior except for . . . Kurt squinted at the image that sat at about the equator on the side the ship presented to him. It looked like a *face*. But before he could catch more than a glimpse, the huge black ball had dropped into Wrigley Field like a pop fly into a fielder's outstretched glove.

Kurt found himself being swept along in a group that included Peter Grace, a four-star general named Garner, a tactical expert named Quinn, and a couple of sharpshooters. Walkways, staircases, and corridors unfolded in a blur as they made their way into the park through an access that brought them out behind the home dugout.

They came up short along the railing, staring at the alien vessel. It hovered above center field, a ramp extending down to the grass. A man stood at the bottom of the ramp, looking up. He wore an unfamiliar baseball uniform with a royal blue cap. A collar length mane of white hair stuck out from underneath.

"Who—" General Garner began.

"Kinsella," Grace growled. "We need to get him out of there, the damned idiot."

"No, wait." Kurt put up a hand. "It may be all right. I . . . think he may speak their language."

Peter Grace gasped, pointed. "The ship!"

Around them, the sharpshooters tensed. A figure had appeared at the top of the ramp, and now proceeded down it, out into the sun. It was shorter than Kinsella, but had two arms, two bandy legs, and a slightly too-large head with a pointed face. It was followed by a small squad of similarly built beings, all of which differed slightly in size and shape. Like most of the people currently in the confines of the ballpark, they were wearing uniforms—baseball uniforms.

Even as Kurt took that in, Kinsella reached out to shake hands with the alien leader and waved expansively at the field. They seemed, incredibly, to be exchanging words. Then the alien repeated Kinsella's gesture and, without hesitation, the crew of the alien ship trotted across the outfield to the visitor's dugout. From the home dugout, just below where Kurt stood, exploded a squad of human players, racing to take positions on the diamond.

"What the hell is going on here?" asked General Garner, his voice barely above a whisper. "Are they—are they going to *play*?"

"It certainly looks that way." Kurt found himself tipping toward giddiness again. He could just see the headlines: *Aliens Visitors On Field of Dreams!* Or *ET Goes the Distance to Play Ball!*

"We got a small problem."

Kurt looked down over the railing. Bill Kinsella stood just this side of the on-deck circle, grinning up at him. The blue cap sported a gray, heart-shaped alien face, the top of its head stitched like a baseball. Across the front of his uniform the words *Las Vegas* were embroidered in blue and silver.

"What uniform is that?"

"Huh? Oh—Las Vegas Area 51s—Dodger Triple-A affiliate. They were out here for an interleague against the Iowa Cubs. I tried to get the Major League Cubs, but they were down in Florida against the Marlins. (Stupid name for a ball club, if you ask me.) But this—" He flicked the bill of the ET-bedecked cap with a fingertip. "This was a real serendip, finding the Area 51s right next door."

"But how did you—?" Peter Grace gestured at the field, from which he seemed unable to take his eyes.

"I've got friends in baseball," Kinsella said. "I made some calls from the taxi." He shrugged.

General Garner spoke now, his eyes on the alien players. "These . . . people . . . came all the way from . . . wherever they came from—"

"Oh, um, out Taurus way, manager said."

"Out *Taurus* way?" repeated Grace. "He *said* that? In *English*?"

"Well, he started out in Japanese, I think, then switched to Spanish. I don't speak Japanese, and my Spanish is pretty shaky, so he went to English when he saw I wasn't getting him. Spoke it pretty well, too. Hardly any accent. A little trouble with the letter 'p,' maybe. Seemed as if his Japanese and Spanish were pretty good too, though not speaking any, I couldn't say. Anyway, I'm pretty sure he said their star was out Taurus way. They've had their eye on us for while, he said. Or maybe 'ear' is a better choice of words. They've been listening in to space chatter, TV and radio broadcasts—that sort of thing—trying to figure out how to communicate with us."

Grace moved his head slowly from side to side like a man trying to shake off a decrepit gnat. "Did he explain why they chose baseball?"

Kinsella tugged at the bill of his cap. "Not as such. They've been picking up our baseball games, of course—trying to figure out our rules, he said. But when I asked how they came to be playing baseball in the first place, he just blinked at me and repeated the question. Didn't figure we were going to get anywhere after that, so I suggested we play ball."

Kurt looked up at the sharp sound of a ball smacking a catcher's glove. An odd tingle of memory took him. A memory of sultry summer afternoons that passed in a timeless haze of cheers and chants, popcorn, peanuts, and hot dogs, all punctuated with the cries of hawkers and the crack of the bat meeting a little lump of horsehide.

Kurt dragged his eyes away from the gray-skinned batter who had taken his place in the on-deck circle to take his practice swings. "You had a problem, you said."

"Well, seems they didn't bring any umps with 'em and ours didn't believe me when I told them where we were going and why. So, we were hoping maybe among the troops here, there might be some folks who'd be willing and able to umpire the game."

"I've umped at my daughter's little league games," Kurt said. "Usually behind the plate."

Bill Kinsella's grin deepened. "Great! I'll bet we can scramble some gear up from the clubhouse."

"Actually, all I need is a mask. This helmet and Kevlar ought to do fine for gear." Giddiness washed over him again.

Kinsella was looking up at Garner now. "General, care to spare a couple of your soldiers?"

The General finally managed to look away from the spectacle on the field. "You're serious?"

"Well, we've got home field advantage, which means we play by home field rules. Rules say: in order for this game to be official, we need umpires."

"You want U.S. Army troops to umpire an alien ballgame?"

"Well, not troops—we only need four—and an official scorekeeper, of course. The rest can watch."

"Watch?" He swung his eyes to Grace. "Dr. Grace, you're the space program expert. Your opinion of these proceedings?"

Grace seemed dazed. "These . . . people don't seem dangerous, General.

But the situation is . . . well, it's unprecedented, and probably does bear watching."

The General's brows rose.

"What would *you* do?" Grace asked. "Capture them? Ignore them? This is First Contact, General Garner. That means it's never happened before. There are no rules of engagement. There are no precedents. I guess we'll have to set those as we go along."

"Well," said Garner, eyes going back to the sunny diamond. "They seem to pose no immediate threat. Under the circumstances, I suppose participating in a ritual of the visitors' choice might be appropriate." He swung around to the tactical officer beside him. "You ever do any umping, Tommy?"

Kurt didn't wait to hear the answer. He was already over the railing and into the dugout. Bill Kinsella met him there, handed him a catcher's mask, and walked him to the plate. He nodded to the Area 51s catcher, who flashed a brilliantly white smile from the depths of his mask then turned to receive the last of the pitcher's warm-up throws.

A little painted alien face stared up at Kurt from the back of the catcher's helmet. He glanced up at Kinsella, already on his way back to the home dugout. "What do the visitors have on their caps?"

Bill touched his own headgear above the bill. "Same as ours. Alien faces."

The visiting leadoff hitter had stepped into the left-hand batters box. Kurt looked at the logo on his helmet. The face was human.

Kurt couldn't be sure, but he thought it might be the same face that was etched into the anodized aluminum plate that had been aboard Pioneer 10. Along with the two human figures, the plaque had carried an etching of the solar system and various mathematical figures that had apparently successfully conveyed the pertinent information about base-ten arithmetic. He made a mental note to recommend a few modifications to the plaque before they sent up their next deep space probe.

The alien ship had withdrawn from the field of play now, moving to hover over the park at a respectful distance, and looking for all the world like game-day blimp. Kurt wondered if the aliens had the technology to transmit the game all the way home. An interleague game, indeed.

He looked out over the brilliant diamond, seeing the home team in their positions, the other umpires taking the field, and a crowd of spectators—mostly in khakis and camouflage—filling the stands. He felt the spring sun warm on his shoulders, smelled the perfume of grass and earth, and perhaps popcorn, though that might have been his imagination.

He did not imagine that unique, expectant hush that had preceded the first pitch of every baseball game since the beginning. He filled his lungs with air and officially opened the first encounter between humanity and beings from another world.

"Play ball!"

[Editorial note: The Area 51s are now the Triple-A team of the New York Mets.]

Is chess just a game or is it a sport? At least at the championship level, modern-day chess demands physical fitness, mental stamina, regular training, and constant study. It's also been known to have political implications, and not just internationally. As Garry Kasparov said, "I learned that fighting on the chessboard could also have an impact on the political climate in the country." The future version of chess depicted by Timons Esaias is truly a deadly competition and involves both internal and external politics. But in this game, luck and skill make two pawns more powerful pieces than one might expect.

Pawn

Timons Esaias

What Winstead knew about Squire Yvor was this: the Squire was a pawnbroker. Years ago he had brokered the more important pieces as well—your knights, your rooks—but for several years now it was pawns only. Reliable pawns, but not the most expensive or the most stylish.

What Winstead knew about chess was nothing, but his boss had sent him down here to get some decent material, and suggested that his, Winstead's, job might be on the line. Winstead knew that meant the boss's head was probably pretty close to the block itself. O the times. O the business climate.

The real bitch of it was that he actually had to physically go to the place, with nothing but a monocle to keep him connected to the datastream. Brokers positively refused to deal material over the publink. Tradition or something. Customer had to get out of their workpit or pentsuite and march down to the shop to take responsibility for the choice themselves. And responsibility was another bitch in this bitchy business. Who took responsibility these days?

Taking responsibility stinks of bad form.

So anyway, there was this going out thing. Pitters like Winstead wore their agoraphobia as a medal of distinction, an effing *croix de* salary. Took him an hour to bring himself to ask his monocle for routing instructions.

And another hour to get started.

Taxi had four-inch armor. "Yeah," the drivebot complained, "had to have this slab a junk plated with another two inches. All these buildings running a mile high, and they never think of the effect on the driving public. It's no biggie for the trucks, cause they're all down in the substreets. But stuff falls off those monsters all the time, and smacks the ground pretty hard. City don't care, insurance companies don't care. Guess they both make money off filling in the impact craters. And you can't just armor the top, neither, 'cause there's no telling what funny ricochets stuff'll take when it comes down."

Winstead toggled the viewcamera up to vertical so he could see the subject being discussed. The sky was a narrow line, interrupted by causeways. If that was the sky, and not some balcony lighting. Winstead hoped, suddenly, that it wasn't the sky, so that he'd feel more enclosed. This cab was twice the size of his workpit, though the thought of the armor made it more comfortable. Cozy.

"Say, since I'm taking you to the renowned Yvor's, I should ask you. Are you a player yourself, or just running an errand? I used to play chess myself, with some of my spare processing time, the old chess that is. Not what you folks play today."

Winstead flipped off the viewer. Instantly he felt better. "I'm just rounding up a pawn for a game tomorrow. Our corporation's sponsoring a player in the summer tournament."

"Ah," said the taxi. "So what's at stake in this tournament?"

He didn't respond at first because he didn't know, and then didn't respond because he had never realized that he didn't know.

"Yeah, I know, 'Don't Ask, Don't Think,' right?" The taxi swerved, and then seemed to be on an elevator. "Forget I enquired. There are just two serious games in the world, and at your level, chess is it, I bet. Don't worry, just hope it stays that way. Life only gets tougher if you outgrow chess."

When the cab let him out, the door's tunnel didn't mate tightly with the shop entrance, and some street air got in and bothered him. Car stink, and moss stink and what was that stuff plants sometimes grew in? Dirt? Dirt.

That's what he hated about the outside. Things don't fit together outside a building. Corners aren't square and clear, joints don't fit tightly, color schemes go straight to netherland. It nauseated him, and his head was swimming as he entered the shop. Very odd place, very odd.

"Are you the gentleman from NixFax? Mr. Oglestairs, isn't it?"

The voice came from above, and his monocle put the source crosshairs on a very tall gentleman several dozen yards up. The man was standing on a clear floor, so Winstead was looking at his feet, mostly, and foreshortened body. Even so, he could see the man was very tall.

His monocle also diagrammed the room, which he now understood to be sixty meters high, ten meters long, and three wide. The entire space was solidly walled with display cases containing shelf after shelf of chess sets, old-style chess sets with inanimate pieces. The boards were mounted vertically, behind the set each belonged to. His monocle started counting the sets, but Winstead lost interest before the result came in.

"If you will step onto the hexagram, you can join me in my office," said the man, who took a step into the glass wall beside him and disappeared.

I wish I could do that, thought Winstead. Take one step and just disappear. Instead he took two, and rose on the elepad. Thousands of little kings and queens watched him, their armies seeming ready to move at command.

Squire Yvor proved to be about twelve feet tall, and stood in a depression in his office nook, so that his standup desk seemed normal from the other side. Normal if you were used to seeing a desk, which Winstead wasn't. Only the rich and powerful, or the anachronistic, bothered with work surfaces. This made the swimming sensation in his head even worse, trying to guess which category this broker belonged to.

The next two questions deepened the mystery, because his monocle indicated that the answers were already known to the broker. This old-fashioned wordiness could also be an affectation of power, of pretending not to consult a monocle.

"What piece would you be in the market for?"

"A pawn. A queen's knight pawn, whatever that is."

"And what would you be authorized to spend on this pawn?"

Winstead hesitated, because this was the first point where he could make a huge mistake.

The broker nodded his head slightly, and a tiny but elaborately woven carpet rolled out onto a bench against the side wall. "Please recline, my friend. I understand your hesitation. *I have been given a budget*, you are thinking, *but how much of it am I really intended to spend. Should I hold back a portion for myself? Should I economize and return a percentage to my employer?"*

Winstead sat on the bench and drew up one leg.

"Let me advise you, then, from my considerable experience," the man said, laying his hands palm up on the desk. Winstead noticed that undisguised scars crossed the palm on the left. "There are two factors I would emphasize. One is that this is obviously your first commission. Another is that tomorrow's game involves a major business agreement. Your corporation is merging with the Moloch-Thanat chikarabatsu. The winners of tomorrow's matches will be the dominant partners in each sector of the new entity."

Why do I learn this now? wondered Winstead. Why am I sent in ignorance on so important a mission?

"In regards to the first point," Squire Yvor continued, closing his left hand, "let me tell you why you are here. Usually when a new person comes in to buy a piece, with a smallish fee, it means that whoever sent this new person is unsure of themselves. If a client has a big budget and a sound position in the company, they come themselves. When the client fears failure, or has not budgeted well, then they send a potential scapegoat."

Winstead could only nod, shakily.

The man gently closed his right hand. "On the second point, I would suggest that this game is too important to skimp on, and that your supervisors would not be happy with the diversion of any funds from the object at hand, even the return of a percentage into their accounts. In the future, very likely, you will be expected to benefit from handling such tasks, but today I suggest that you spend the full fifty thousand lucrechits."

Winstead wondered whether the broker made more profit that way, than in helping a buyer skim a bit off the top. He supposed so. But the argument had force.

"As you say. The full amount."

The dealer activated a bit of the desk top, displaying a chessboard with various notations in some of the squares. "I took the liberty of finding out the previous choices that have been made. Yours will be the seventh pawn. I see that four of the others are to be Tungpins, which is sadly typical. Everybody goes for the big sword, the dragonslayer cachet. But it gives the set no balance. The other two are a Hanny and a Chang. Did you have a sense of the type of pawn you would prefer?"

Winstead admitted that he did not follow chess at all. "I am afraid I don't really know the different kinds."

The broker stifled a brief moue of disappointment, and studied the diagram. "There would be good value in Litis, or Chungs. Neither is very popular. But your side is deficient in ambiguity. Might I suggest a Lanny? Let me see who is available."

He consulted a list, and muttered about casualties. Winstead vaguely recalled some pop-eds complaining that too many chess games used real weapons these days, but the company pished all over that. Can't play for keeps in the business world with ritual restrictions on the most important encounters. That would encourage insincerity, and insincerity is the death of dividend. A broker, however, would probably not enjoy the combat turnover.

"Yes. I have a proper candidate." The area upon which he stood and Winstead's bench both became elepads and began to recede into the floor, so he tucked in his other leg. "Follow me."

They emerged in a lobby from which six hallways radiated, and actually walked down one of them past a number of closed doors. Winstead couldn't remember the last time he'd seen an interior doorway sealed.

"The doors are for our protection," observed his host. "Can't have missiles wandering around the hallways."

They entered a room, at last, the broker's robes swinging so wide they brushed the edge of the door, which sent a shudder through Winstead. Perhaps this was graciousness, the walking, the loose robes, the long hallways and closed doors, but it made him nervous. It had been a mistake to leave his workpit, he felt certain now.

The floor was soft, and the broker made a deep bow when stepping onto it. The room seemed far too large, though a shelftite had lowered into it cutting the space nearly in half. A woman stood in front of it, inspecting the amazing array of gunpowder weapons it held. There must have been two hundred machine guns, and she had already selected several that were draped from her cloak of body armor.

Her neck guard bore the emblem of a basket of red and white roses with one central black chrysanthemum, which his monocle informed him was the Lanny sigil.

She turned as they approached, and rested the long-barreled drum-feed gun she had been inspecting on her hip. All the equipment she carried, guns, grenades, ammoclips, and mags rattled quietly on their various hooks as her armor cloak swirled, lost its momentum, and became still.

Something about the way her outfit moved seemed odd. "Is that real fabric?" he blurted.

She gave the broker a look that made Winstead blush, and said, still not looking at him, "Visuwear isn't much good at killing a laser pulse or stopping a bullet."

The broker interjected smoothly. "Our client is not aware of the gritty realities associated with the game of chess. He is, however, prepared to pay full price for your services as a Queen's Knight Pawn in a game between NixFax and Moloch-Thanat tomorrow in the Cassian Fields. I hope that this might be an opportunity you would find acceptable, a challenge worthy of your gifts and training."

Her eyes changed six times during the few moments of the pawnbroker's speech. The changes were more subtle than those Winstead knew from holvid women, but he thought she was both eager and fearful, pleased and calculating. As the pawnbroker bowed slowly after his little speech, she settled into a swordfighter's stance. Only then did Winstead think: this person is trained to kill, and I am hiring her to possibly do so, to kill and to risk death.

His senses sharpened. The guns reeked of light machine oil and linseed oil and leather and neat's foot oil and primer and gunpowder and cordite and semtex and copper and the distinct solid odor of blued steel and the subtle cool smell of stainless.

The three people had their smells as well; hers were physicality and sandalwoody spirituality; the broker—electronic business scent and lemongrass leisure; and Winstead, he now realized, stank of the pit and the cab and uncertainty.

The pawn turned to him and asked a direct question, directly. "Unbated weapons?"

Winstead apologized, "I'm afraid . . . "

"There is no honor in modern chess, O warrior," Squire Yvor observed, in slow clear syllables. "The client class only understands defeat if they can see the blood." The broker shook his head in the manner of a thespian expressing grief. "But there is still duty."

"And self-knowledge," she replied. "Era?"

The broker spread his hands. "Bronze."

She sighed, slightly, and looked down at the gun still braced on her hip. Lovingly, and achingly, she cradled it in her arms. A pietà. She turned away from the two men, placed the gun back on the rack, and shouted

"Mycenae!" which caused three things to happen: the gun rack shelftite began sinking into the ceiling, a garment of some kind fell from an overhead trap, and a second rack of shiny—almost golden—swords and knives and spears rose up from the floor.

And in the midst of the rising and dropping and sinking, which was making Winstead briefly dizzy, the pawn whipped off her cloak, all the guns and grenades included, in a single gesture with her left hand and tossed it into the sinking gun rack, and with her other hand caught the falling garment and whipped it around her so that only for a moment, if he had been paying attention, was she naked before them. Or had she been tattooed or in all-over lace, or merely shadow? The picture was burned into his mind, though he could not be sure of what he had seen.

The new garment looked like nothing more than a silk burnoose. Her attention was not with them anymore, however. Her eyes were on the gleaming gold, ivory-hafted weapons.

"I accept," she said, but gave them no heed.

All the way home his mind replayed and replayed and replayed that instant when she might have been naked. And he wondered at how decisively she had shocked him, how deeply shaken him. And how casually.

He was glad to be back in his workpit the next morning, effing glad to be interacting over the publink and not looking anybody for thorsake in the face. Winstead didn't even show faces on the commlink, waste of bandwidth, invasion of privacy, and used the simplest cartoon rep. Not much more than a talking kanji, that's how he liked to see folks.

Yesterday had thrown him right out of stride with faces. He kept seeing the pawn's reluctant face when she had to give up that Tommy gun, and the broker's look that said your-job-is-on-the-line-and-you-don't-have-a-clue-do-you. Which he hadn't.

And that pawn. The women he knew, and that mostly meant holactors, smiled at a guy no matter how tough they were. Gave a guy a feeling of importance. But she had looked at him the way a programmer looks at client code. And here he sat thinking about chess again.

Task at hand: supervise the adaptation of a CRP-series robot to the task of collecting and reprocessing the droppings of wild giant sloths in an urban environment. Somebody else's job to get the robot to distinguish a megatherium from a mastodon; and some other department's brief to cleave to sloth droppings while forsaking all others; and not his job either to give it wall-climbing skills so that it could follow the sloths that pulled themselves from balcony to setback in search of munchy vegetation above street level. His task, which chess should never have interrupted for a minute, to keep the CRP from getting clobbered by the nine- or ten-foot megafaunal arm swipe, with the nasty hooked claw attached. Scores upon scores of the competitor's street cleaners had come to crunching grief because they annoyed the giant sloths, and then couldn't clear out fast enough.

Winstead loved this assignment, because he knew it could be done, and any problem had to be with the team integrating the software. No risks. No responsibility. Not a chance of a face-to-face meeting anywhere.

So it annoyed, annoyed terribly, annoyed beyond anything when a flash came down from his supervisor. "Your Presence Required Our Box Cassian Fields 1400 Hours Today."

This chess game is ruining my life, he thought. And he thought of the pawn, his pawn, and how she hadn't cared if he saw her naked. Hadn't cared at all.

"This is the moment of foreboding," said the executive seated just behind him. The NixFax box, high above the chess field, was steeply pitched and entirely glass in front. Winstead felt horribly exposed. Scores of thousands of spectators could see him, his whole body, not just above the neck. "Especially for the pawns, because they abide in the forefront of the battle line."

"Most wise," Winstead managed to say, nearly strangling on the words. He distracted himself from the huge stadium on the other side of the glass by bringing up a hol of the NixFax side of the board, and looking for his queen knight pawn. He had done a primer on the rules of chess on the way over, but couldn't follow much about it.

About all that he had grasped was that the king was the CEO of the pieces, and the queen the COO. The pawns were the foot soldiers, the pitters and dataclerks of the game. And each side moved in turn. And when pieces tried to take a square that was already occupied by an opposing piece, they fought, winner take all.

He felt wetness on his knee, cold wetness. His boss leaned over, her arm reaching awkwardly for the seat back directly below Winstead. Her drink had slopped, and dripped disgustingly over her fingers. It startled him so much he looked into her eyes. The pupils seemed very small.

She caught herself, slurring out, "Interesting choice, a Lanny. Girl, too!"

She made an attempt to sit down, but couldn't manage it. "Guess that's all I could expect for fifty. Hardware guys spent two hundred thousand for their pawns." She swore bitterly, then leaned in to whisper spittily in his ear. "Budget! We'd have sword guys, if we had that kinda coin."

Winstead had had just about all the personal contact he could manage without screaming, but it got worse. Some senior manager slid into the place beside him, his tunic embroidered with the badges of four ancient family orders. "Your pawn is moving first, from the sound of it. Larsen's Opening." The man arranged his clothing fussily. "I see she carries a short billhook. Very adaptable weapon."

Out in the stadium a trumpet fanfare was playing, which his monocle explained was signaling NixFax's first move. Which meant that somewhere above him the company's hired chessmaster, with the help of the Board, had declared a move. And, indeed, Winstead's pawn was preparing to move, and he zoomed in on her.

As the hol grew in front of him, he learned his pawn's name for the first time. Hadn't thought to ask it, before. Hadn't thought she'd have one, somehow.

Artemisia.

The name broke his heart.

A lump stuck in his throat, and the pressure of tears throbbed behind his eyes, all in an instant. He'd put a girl named Artemisia in danger of death because his drunken boss couldn't scrape enough funds out of the budget to get a decent pawn.

How noble she looked. How composed. She was stepping forward, an oval shield with a shining boss held above her head. A tight leather cap with metal cheek pieces covered that head, and a long silken sheath reached nearly to the ground. She wore a thick, quilted jacket covered with something white and bumpy. An inquiry put diagramicons around her image, explaining that her armor consisted of small clam shells sewn to her jacket, in the style of Bronze Age Scythians; and her underdress was silk, which would not be torn by an arrow or spear, and thus allow them to be extracted easily, by pulling on the silk. A sheathed sword was strapped to her back from left shoulder to right hip. A pair of short spears from right shoulder to left hip. In her hand she held a short stick, almost a wand, with a hook at the end.

She strode forward one square, and then lowered her shield into the rest position. Only then did he realize that she had one foot bare.

The Moloch-Thanat side moved the queen's bishop pawn forward one square, and then the NixFax bishop stepped into Artemisia's first square. Moloch-Thanat responded with the queen moving, very ceremoniously, one square diagonally.

The manager gasped the moment the next fanfare rang out, the NixFax bishop marching boldly down across the field, a bulky leaden mace in his hand, and disdaining to unhook the shield from his back. This should be no contest, he knew, for bishops are far better trained than pawns, but the dagger the pawn drew looked more deadly than the mace. "If I might ask, good sir," Winstead forced himself to say, "is this move dangerous?"

But even as he put the question, the bishop flung the mace with a single sharp gesture. The unfortunate pawn, half-hidden under raised shield, was hit squarely on the knee, and not the knee forward, but the one he was bracing on behind, and therefore couldn't move. A sickening crack, heard even through the glass, and the pawn wobbled for a moment on his leading leg, both shield and dagger reaching forward briefly to steady him.

The moment was enough. The bishop's second stroke, upstroke with a blade sheathed in his boot, sent the pawn unconscious or dead to the ground.

There was a scurry of spoils boys as the bishop leaned over the fallen pawn, stripping off his opponent's armor and picking through his weapons for anything useful. The bishop cast aside his own blade, now dulled perhaps, and took the pawn's. He recovered his own mace, and then let the boys put the victim on a stretcher and the prizes on another and haul them away.

"Winstead, isn't it?" the manager finally replied as the boys worked. "What is dangerous is the next move. Their bishop will now attack our bishop, while he is still fresh from a fight. Fortunately our piece didn't have a hard struggle."

And so it happened, and the bishops exchanged hideously crashing blows, until the Moloch-Thanat piece threw a mace at his opponent's face, and missed. In four quick blows the NixFax bishop won again, but two moves later he was knocked unconscious by the trunk of the rook's elephant. Play continued for several moves, when the enemy queen rook pawn stepped into the square diagonal to Artemisia. In reply Artemisia advanced diagonally into the rook pawn's square.

"I'm afraid your investment is about to be squandered to wear down a rook, my friend. Well, let's see how she does."

The opposing pawn threw a spear at Artemisia, missing. She did not throw back, but calmly advanced, holding her small wand at her side. He drew a long dagger, and thrust it at her, and then moved with great suddenness, in an attack Winstead would only see in the repeats. Leaping forward while whipping the blade behind him he brought it down as a chopping weapon, straight for her head. But Artemisia responded by stepping very slightly to one side, hopping onto her bare foot to change her center of gravity and motion. Her wand rose and hooked above the descending blade, bringing it down even faster than her enemy intended. Yanking backward as his sword hit the ground she made him fall to his knees with the force of his own blow.

As her right hand hooked his sword down, her shield had risen high in the air. Now she turned toward him and brought the edge of it down viciously into his exposed neck.

The blow bent her shield badly, and his seemed too bulky for her, so she let the boys carry them both off. Winstead realized he had been holding his breath, and gasped.

"Not bad." The manager offered Winstead a nibble tray. "But the rook will finish her."

But the rook did not finish her, though as he advanced atop his elephant, it would have been impossible to believe it.

Winstead met his pawn again at the victory reception, his mind still reeling from the few moments with the CEO. The Great Dame herself had bowed to him, had congratulated him on his choice of pawn, had handed him a ferule of honor, had made him understand that he would rise in the new, merged, NixFax-driven chikarabatsu.

But CEOs are one thing, Artemisia another. After the surviving winning pieces, both shoulders bare to emphasize their strength and one leg exposed to the hip to reveal fitness, had been introduced to the bigwigs; after he had watched her for half an hour; she strode across the room directly to him.

"I wish to thank you, sir," she said, and smiled most sweetly. It took him several seconds to take in what she had said, and that she had said it to him.

"Well, I mean . . . "

"This chance you gave me means much to my career. I will now be trained as a knight, without having to spend years seeking recognition as a pawn in minor games."

"Well. That is," he stumbled, "you've made my career as well."

"Then it was a well-omened day that we met," she replied, with more poetry in her voice than he expected from so attractive a killer. Sensing that he must say something to keep her there, he stammered the first thing he could think to ask.

"Well . . . but . . . that is, how did you do it? With the elephant, I mean?"

She smiled and leaned forward, her head conspiratorially next to his, the second woman to do this today. "I watch the elephants train. I knew if I touched them with my little hook they'd think it was a mahout goad, and be confused. So, I just gave the elephant the signal to lie down on its side, figuring to catch the rook off guard. His getting pinned under his own mount just made it more dramatic."

Winstead laughed. He had never laughed with a woman before, and certainly never laughed about a real death before, and most certainly never about a death he had paid for, and would be promoted for; but he couldn't think of another thing to say.

I wonder if chess pieces ever marry the managerial class, he was just thinking, just getting ready to ask his monocle, when his boss grabbed his arm. Artemisia had bowed and slipped away in an instant, seeing that business was at hand; before he could say anything. Before he could even think anything.

"Don't waste your time getting to know her," the boss said, honey dripping from every word. "Nobody will be sending you to chess games anymore. You and I are going to be strictly big leagues from now on. We'll be playing chikarabatsu against the world! We're going to play Go!!"

"Are there pawns, in Go?" Winstead asked, hesitantly. "Or knights?"

"Nothing of the sort," the boss assured him. "Go pieces are a different type altogether, much more austere. No overlap at all."

He turned his head furtively, quickly searching the room for Artemisia, but seeing only company employees, their spouses, the servants. All the chess pieces had been cleared away.

Hunger Games-author Suzanne Collins was not quite three years old when this story was first published in 1965. Both Collins' trilogy and Walter Moudy's story have a basis in Roman gladiatorial combat and both explore what type of person it takes to win in deadly combat. Survivors of both become heroes and their own people benefit from the "spoils"—money, food, energy—of their victory. Where the Hunger Games are fought to remind the citizens of Panem of the futility of rebellion, the Olympic War Games are staged to remind nations of the pointlessness of war. Both games are staged in specialized arenas and universally televised with color commentary and up-close-and-personal replays of death. A few of the Cold War-era details of Moudy's story are a bit dated, but it remains a chilling tale that is even more interesting in light of the current popularity of Collins' trilogy and the subsequent film versions of the books.

The Survivor

Walter F. Moudy

There was a harmony in the design of the arena which an artist might find pleasing. The curved granite walls which extended upward three hundred feet from its base were polished and smooth like the sides of a bowl. A fly, perhaps a lizard, could crawl up those glistening walls—but surely not a man.

The walls encircled an egg-shaped area which was precisely three thousand meters long and two thousand one hundred meters wide at its widest point. There were two large hills located on either side of the arena exactly midway from its center to its end. If you were to slice the arena crosswise, your knife would dissect a third, tree-studded hill and a small, clear lake; and the two divided halves would each be the exact mirror image of the other down to the smallest detail. If you were a farmer you would notice the rich, flat soil which ran obliquely from the two larger hills toward the lake. If you were an artist you might find pleasure in contemplating the rich shades of green and brown presented by the forested lowlands at the lake's edge. A sportsman seeing the crystalline lake in the morning's first light would find his fingers itching for light tackle and wading boots. Boys, particularly city boys, would yearn to climb the two larger hills because they looked easy to climb, but not too easy. A general viewing the topography would immediately recognize that possession of the central hill would permit dominance of the lake and the surrounding lowlands.

There was something peaceful about the arena that first morning. The early-morning sun broke through a light mist and spilled over the central hill to the low dew-drenched ground beyond. There were trees with young, green leaves, and the leaves rustled softly in rhythm with the wind. There were birds in those trees, and the birds still sang, for it was spring, and they were filled with the joy of life and the beauty of the morning. A night owl, its appetite satiated now by a recent kill, perched on a dead limb of a large sycamore tree and, tucking its beak in its feathers, prepared to sleep the day away. A sleek copperhead snake, sensing the sun's approach and anticipating its soothing warmth, crawled from beneath the flat rock where it had spent the night and sought the comfort of its favorite rock ledge. A red squirrel chattered nervously as it watched the men enter the arena from the north and then, having decided that there was danger there, darted swiftly to an adjacent tree and disappeared into the security of its nest.

There were exactly one hundred of them. They stood tall and proud in their uniforms, a barely perceptible swaying motion rippling through their lines like wheat stirred by a gentle breeze. If they anticipated what was to come, they did not show it. Their every movement showed their absolute discipline. Once they had been only men—now they were killers. The hunger for blood was like a taste in their mouths; their zest for destruction like a flood which raged inside them. They were finely honed and razor keen to kill. Their general made his last inspection. As he passed down the lines, the squad captains barked a sharp order and the men froze into absolute immobility. Private Richard Starbuck heard the rasp of the general's boots against the stones as he approached. There was no other sound, not even of men breathing. From long discipline he forced his eyes to maintain their focus on the distant point he had selected, and his eyes did not waver as the general paused in front of him. They were still fixed on that same imaginary point. He did not even see the general.

Private Richard Starbuck was not thinking of death, although he knew he must surely die. He was thinking of the rifle he felt securely on his shoulder and of the driving need he had to discharge its deadly pellets into human flesh. His urge to kill was dominant, but even so he was vaguely relieved that he had not been selected for the assassination squad (*the suicide squad* the men called it); for he still had a chance, a slim chance, to live; while the assassination squad was consigned to inevitable death.

A command was given and Private Starbuck permitted his tense body to relax. He glanced at his watch. Five-twenty-five. He still had an hour and thirty-five minutes to wait. There was a tenseness inside him which his relaxed body did not disclose. They taught you how to do that in training. They taught you lots of things in training.

The TV screen was bigger than life and just as real. The color was true and the images three-dimensional. For a moment the zoom cameras scanned the silent deserted portions of the arena. The sound system was sensitive and sharp and caught the sound made by a squirrel's feet against the bark of a black oak tree. Over one hundred cameras were fixed on the arena; yet so smooth was the transition from one camera to the next that it was as though the viewer was floating over the arena. There was the sound of marching feet, and the pace of the moving cameras quickened and then shifted to the north where one hundred men were entering the arena in perfect unison, one hundred steel-toed boots striking the earth as one. For a moment the cameras fixed on the flashing boots and the sensitive sound system recorded the thunder of men marching to war. Then the cameras flashed to the proud face of their general; then to the hard, determined faces of the men; then back again to the thundering boots. The cameras backed off to watch the column execute an abrupt halt, moved forward to focus for a moment on the general's hawklike face, and then, with the general, inspected the troops one by one, moving down the rigid lines of men and peering intently at each frozen face.

When the "at ease" order was given, the camera backed up to show an aerial view of the arena and then fixed upon one of the control towers which lined the arena's upper periphery before sweeping slowly downward and seeming to pass into the control tower. Inside the tower a distinguished gray-haired man in his mid-forties sat beside a jovial, fat-jawed man who was probably in his early fifties. There was an expectant look on their faces.

Finally the gray-haired man said: “Good morning, ladies and gentlemen, I’m John Ardanyon—”

“And I’m Bill Carr,” the fat-jawed man said.

“And this is it—yes, this is the big one, ladies and gentlemen. The 2050 edition of the Olympic War Games. This is the day we’ve all been waiting for, ladies and gentlemen, and in precisely one hour and thirty-two minutes the games will be under way. Here to help describe the action is Bill Carr, who is known to all of you sports fans all over the world. And with us for this special broadcast are some of the finest technicians in the business. Bill?”

“That’s right, John. This year NSB has spared no expense to insure our viewing public that its 2050 game coverage will be second to none. So stay tuned to this station for the most complete, the most immediate coverage of any station. John?”

“That’s right, Bill. This year NSB has installed over one hundred specially designed zoom cameras to insure complete coverage of the games. We are using the latest sonic sound equipment—so sensitive that it can detect the sound of a man’s heart beating at a thousand yards. Our camera crew is highly trained in the recently developed transitional-zone technique which you just saw so effectively demonstrated during the fade-in. I think we can promise you that this time no station will be able to match the immediacy of NSB.”

“Right, John. And now, less than an hour and a half before the action begins, NSB is proud to bring you this prerecorded announcement from the President of the United States. Ladies and gentlemen, the President of the United States.”

There was a brief flash of the White House lawn, a fade-out, and then:

“My fellow countrymen. When you hear these words, the beginning of the fifth meeting between the United States and Russia in the Olympic War Games will be just minutes away.

“I hope and I pray that we will be victorious. With the help of God, we shall be.

“But in our longing for victory, we must not lose sight of the primary purpose of these games. In the long run it is not whether we win or lose but that the games were played. For, my fellow citizens, we must never forget that these games are played in order that the frightening specter of war may never again stalk our land. It is better that a few should decide the nation’s fate, than all the resources of our two nations should be mobilized to destroy the other.

"My friends, many of you do not remember the horror of the Final War of 1998. I can recall that war. I lost my father and two sisters in that war. I spent two months in a class-two fallout shelter—as many of you know. There must never be another such war. We cannot—we shall not —permit that to happen.

"The Olympic War Games are the answer—the only answer. Thanks to the Olympic War Games we are at peace. Today one hundred of our finest fighting men will meet one hundred Russian soldiers to decide whether we shall be victorious or shall go down to defeat. The loser must pay the victor reparations of ten billion dollars. The stakes are high.

"The stakes are high, but, my fellow citizens, the cost of total war is a hundred times higher. This miniature war is a thousand times less costly than total war. Thanks to the Olympic War Games, we have a kind of peace.

"And now, in keeping with the tradition established by the late President Goldstein, I hereby declare a national holiday for all persons not engaged in essential services from now until the conclusion of the games.

"To those brave men who made the team I say: the hope and the prayers of the nation go with you. May you emerge victorious."

There was a fade-out and then the pleasant features of John Ardanyon appeared. After a short, respectful silence, he said:

"I'm sure we can all agree with the President on that. And now, here is Professor Carl Overmann to explain the computer system developed especially for NSB's coverage of the 2050 war games."

"Thank you, Mr. Ardanyon. This year, with the help of the Englewood system of evaluating intangible factors, we hope to start bringing you reliable predictions at the ten-percent casualty level. Now, very briefly, here is how the Englewood system works . . . "

Private Richard Starbuck looked at his watch. Still forty more minutes to wait. He pulled back the bolt on his rifle and checked once more to make sure that the first shell was properly positioned in the chamber. For the third time in the past twenty minutes he walked to one side and urinated on the ground. His throat seemed abnormally dry, and he removed his canteen to moisten his lips with water. He took only a small swallow because the rules permitted only one canteen of water per man, and their battle plan did not call for early possession of the lake.

A passing lizard caught his attention. He put his foot on it and squashed it slowly with the toe of his right boot. He noticed with mild satisfaction that the thing had left a small blood smear at the end of his boot. Oddly, however, seeing the blood triggered something in his mind, and for the first time he vaguely recognized the possibility that he could be hurt. In training he had not thought much about that. Mostly you thought of how it would feel to kill a man. After a while you got so that you wanted to kill. You came to love your rifle, like it was an extension of your own body. And if you could not feel its comforting presence, you felt like a part of you was missing. Still a person could be hurt. You might not die immediately. He wondered what it would be like to feel a misshapen chunk of lead tearing through his belly. The Russians would x their bullets too, probably. They do more damage that way.

It might not be so bad. He remembered a time four years ago when he had thought he was dying, and that had not been so bad. He remembered that at the time he had been more concerned about bleeding on the Martins' new couch. The Martins had always been good to him. Once they had thought they could never have a child of their own, and they had about half adopted him because his own mother worked and was too busy to bake cookies for him and his father was not interested in fishing or basketball or things like that. Even after the Martins had Cassandra, they continued to treat him like a favorite nephew. Mr. Martin took him fishing and attended all the basketball games when he was playing. And that was why when he wrecked the motor scooter and cut his head he had been more concerned about bleeding on the Martins' new couch than about dying, although he had felt that he was surely dying. He remembered that his first thought upon regaining consciousness was one of self-importance. The Martins had looked worried and their nine-year-old daughter, Cassandra, was looking at the blood running down his face and was crying. That was when he felt he might be dying. Dying had seemed a strangely appropriate thing to do, and he had felt an urge to do it well and had begun to assure them that he was all right. And, to his slight disappointment, he was.

Private Richard Starbuck, formerly a star forward on the Center High basketball team, looked at his watch and wondered, as he waited, if being shot in the gut would be anything like cutting your head on the pavement. It was funny he should have thought of that now. He hadn't thought of the Martins for months. He wondered if they would be watching. He wondered, if they did, if they would recognize the sixteen-year-old boy who had bled on their living room couch four years ago. He wondered if he recognized that sixteen-year-old boy himself.

■ ■ ■

Professor Carl Overmann had finished explaining the marvels of the NSB computer system; a mousy little man from the sociology department of a second-rate university had spent ten minutes assuring the TV audience that one of the important psychological effects of the TV coverage of the games was that it allowed the people to satisfy the innate blood lust vicariously and strongly urged the viewers to encourage the youngsters to watch; a minister had spent three minutes explaining that the miniature war could serve to educate mankind to the horrors of war; an economics professor was just finishing a short lecture on the economic effects of victory or defeat.

"Well, there you have it, ladies and gentlemen," Bill Carr said when the economics professor had finished. "You all know there's a lot at stake for both sides. And now— What's that? You what? Just a minute, folks. I think we may have another NSB first." He looked off camera to his right. "Is he there? Yes, indeed, ladies and gentlemen, NSB has done it again. For the first time we are going to have—well, here he is, ladies and gentlemen, General George W. Caldwell, chief of the Olympic War Games training section. General, it's nice to have you with us."

"Thank you, Bill. It's good to be here."

"General, I'm sure our audience already knows this, but just so there will be no misunderstanding, it's not possible for either side to communicate to their people in the arena now. Is that right?"

"That's right, Bill, or I could not be here. An electronic curtain, as it were, protects the field from any attempt to communicate. From here on out the boys are strictly on their own."

"General, do you care to make any predictions on the outcome of the games?"

"Yes, Bill, I may be going out on a limb here, but I think our boys are ready. I can't say that I agree with the neutral-money boys who have the United States a six-to-five underdog. I say we'll win."

"General, there is some thought that our defeat in the games four years ago was caused by an inferior battle plan. Do you care to comment on that?"

"No comment."

"Do you have any explanation for why the United States team has lost the last two games after winning the first two?"

"Well, let me say this. Our defeat in '42 could well have been caused by overconfidence. After all, we had won the first two games rather handily. As I recall we won the game in '38 by four survivors. But as for our defeat in '46—well, your estimate on that one is as good as mine. I will say this: General Hanley was much criticized for an unimaginative battle plan by a lot of so-called experts. Those so-called experts—those armchair generals—were definitely wrong. General Hanley's battle strategy was sound in every detail. I've studied his plans at considerable length, I can assure you."

"Perhaps the training program—?"

"Nonsense. My own exec was on General Hanley's training staff. With only slight modifications it's the same program we used for this year's games."

"Do you care to comment on your own battle plans, General?"

"Well, Bill, I wouldn't want to kill the suspense for your TV audience. But I can say this: we'll have a few surprises this year. No one can accuse us of conservative tactics, I can tell you that."

"How do you think our boys will stack up against the Russians, General?"

"Bill, on a man-to-man basis, I think our boys will stack up very well indeed. In fact, we had men in the drop-out squads who could have made our last team with no trouble at all. I'd say this year's crop is probably twenty percent improved."

"General, what do you look for in selecting your final squads?"

"Bill, I'd say that more than anything else we look for desire. Of course, a man has to be a good athlete, but if he doesn't have that killer instinct, as we say, he won't make the team. I'd say it's desire."

"Can you tell us how you pick the men for the games?"

"Yes, Bill, I think I can, up to a point. We know the Russians use the same system, and, of course, there has been quite a bit written on the subject in the popular press in recent months.

"Naturally, we get thousands of applicants. We give each of them a tough screening test—physical, mental, and psychological. Most applicants are eliminated in the first test. You'd be surprised at some of the boys who apply. The ones who are left—just under two thousand for this year's games—are put through an intensive six-month training course. During this training period we begin to get our first drop-outs, the men who somehow got past our screening system and who will crack up under pressure.

"Next comes a year of training in which the emphasis is on conditioning."

"Let me interrupt here for just a moment, General, if I may. This conditioning—is this a type of physical training?"

The general smiled tolerantly. "No, Bill, this is a special type of conditioning—both mental and physical. The men are conditioned to war. They are taught to recognize and to hate the enemy. They are taught to react instantly to every possible hostile stimuli. They learn to love their weapons and to distrust all else."

"I take it that an average training day must leave the men very little free time."

"Free time!" The general now seemed more shocked than amused. "Free time indeed. Our training program leaves no time free. We don't coddle our boys. After all, Bill, these men are training for war. No man is permitted more than two hours' consecutive sleep. We have an average of four alerts every night.

"Actually the night alerts are an important element in our selection as well as our training program. We have the men under constant observation, of course. You can tell a lot about how a man responds to an alert. Of course, all of the men are conditioned to come instantly awake with their rifles in their hands. But some would execute a simultaneous roll-away movement while at the same time cocking and aiming their weapons in the direction of the hostile sound which signaled the alert."

"How about the final six months, General?"

"Well, Bill, of course, I can't give away all our little tricks during those last six months. I can tell you in a general sort of way that this involved putting battle plans on a duplicate of the arena itself."

"And these hundred men who made this year's team—I presume they were picked during the last six months training?"

"No, Bill, actually we only made our final selection last night. You see, for the first time in two years these men have had some free time. We give them two days off before the games begin. How the men react to this enforced inactivity can tell us a lot about their level of readiness. I can tell you we have an impatient bunch of boys out there."

"General, it's ten minutes to game time. Do you suppose our team may be getting a little nervous down there?"

"Nervous? I suppose the boys may be a little tensed up. But they'll be all right just as soon as the action starts."

"General, I want to thank you for coming by. I'm sure our TV audience has found this brief discussion most enlightening."

"It was my pleasure, Bill."

"Well, there you have it, ladies and gentlemen. You heard it from the man who should know—Lieutenant General George W. Caldwell himself. He picks the United States team to go all the way. John?"

"Thank you, Bill. And let me say that there has been considerable sentiment for the United States team in recent weeks among the neutrals. These are the men who set the odds—the men who bet their heads but never their hearts. In fact at least one oddsmaker in Stockholm told me last night that he had stopped taking anything but six-to-five bets, and you pick 'em. In other words, this fight is rated just about even here just a few minutes before game time."

"Right, John, it promises to be an exciting day, so stay tuned to this station for full coverage."

"I see the troops are beginning to stir. It won't be long now. Bill, while we wait I think it might be well, for the benefit of you younger people, to tell the folks just what it means to be a survivor in one of these games. Bill?"

"Right, John. Folks, the survivor, or survivors as the case may be, will truly become a Survivor. A Survivor, as most of you know, is exempt from all laws; he has unlimited credit; in short, he can literally do no wrong. And that's what those men are shooting for today. John."

"Okay, Bill. And now as our cameras scan the Russian team, let us review very briefly the rules of the game. Each side has one hundred men divided into ten squads each consisting of nine men and one squad captain. Each man has a standard automatic rifle, four hand grenades, a canteen of water, and enough food to last three days. All officers are armed with side arms in addition to their automatic rifles. Two of the squads are armed with air-cooled light machine-guns, and one squad is armed with a mortar with one thousand rounds of ammunition. And those, ladies and gentlemen, are the rules of the game. Once the games begin the men are on their own. There are no more rules—except, of course, that the game is not over until one side or the other has no more survivors. Bill?"

"Okay, John. Well, folks, here we are just seconds away from game time. NSB will bring you live each exciting moment—so stand by. We're waiting for the start of the 2050 Olympic War Games. Ten seconds now. Six. Four, three, two, one—the games are underway, and look at 'em go!"

The cameras spanned back from the arena to give a distant view of the action. Squad one peeled off from the main body and headed toward the enemy rear at a fast trot. They were armed with rifles and grenades. Squads two, three, and four went directly toward the high hill in the American sector where they broke out entrenching tools and began to dig in. Squads five and six took one of the light machine guns and marched at double time to the east of the central hill where they concealed themselves in the brush and waited. Squads seven through ten were held in reserve where they occupied themselves by burying the ammunition and other supplies at predetermined points and in beginning the preparation of their own defense perimeters.

The cameras swung briefly to the Russian sector. Four Russian squads had already occupied the high hill in the Russian sector, and a rifle squad was being rushed to the central hill located on the north-south dividing line. A Russian machine gun squad was digging in to the south of the lake to establish a base of fire on the north side of the central hill.

The cameras returned to the American squads five and six, which were now deployed along the east side of the central hill. The cameras moved in from above the entrenched machine gunner, paused momentarily on his right hand, which was curved lovingly around the trigger guard while his middle finger stroked the trigger itself in a manner almost obscene, and then followed the gunner's unblinking eyes to the mist-enshrouded base of the central hill where the point man of the Russian advance squad was cautiously testing his fate in a squirming, crawling advance on the lower slopes of the hill.

"This could be it!" Bill Carr's booming voice exploded from the screen like a shot. "This could be the first skirmish, ladies and gentlemen. John, how does it look to you?"

"Yes, Bill, it looks like we will probably get our first action in the east-central sector. Quite a surprise, too, Bill. A lot of experts felt that the American team would concentrate its initial push on control of the central hill. Instead, the strategy appears to be—at least as it appears from here—to concede the central hill to the Russian team but to make them pay for it. You can't see it on your screens just now, ladies and gentlemen, but the American mortar squad is now positioned on the north slope of the north hill and is ready to fire."

"All right, John. Folks, here in our booth operating as spotter for the American team is Colonel Bullock of the United States Army. Our Russian spotter is Brigadier General Vorsilov, who will from time to time give us his views on Russian strategy. Colonel Bullock, do you care to comment?"

"Well, I think it's fairly obvious, Bill, that—"

His words were interrupted by the first chilling chatter of the American light machine gun. Tracer bullets etched their brilliant way through the morning air to seek and find human flesh. Four mortar rounds, fired in rapid succession, arched over the low hill and came screaming a tale of death and destruction. The rifle squad opened fire with compelling accuracy. The Russian line halted, faltered, reformed, and charged up the central hill. Three men made it to the sheltering rocks on the hill's upper slope. The squad captain and six enlisted men lay dead or dying on the lower slopes. As quickly as it had begun the firing ended.

"How about that!" Bill Carr exclaimed. "First blood for the American team. What a fantastic beginning to these 2050 war games, ladies and gentlemen. John, how about that?"

"Right, Bill. Beautifully done. Brilliantly conceived and executed with marvelous precision. An almost unbelievable maneuver by the American team that obviously caught the Russians completely off guard. Did you get the casualty figures on that first skirmish, Bill?"

"I make it five dead and two seriously wounded, John. Now keep in mind, folks, these figures are unofficial. Ed, can you give us a closeup on that south slope?"

The cameras scanned the hill first from a distance and then zoomed in to give a closeup of each man who lay on the bleak southern slope. The Russian captain was obviously dead with a neat rifle bullet through his forehead. The next man appeared to be sleeping peacefully. There was not a mark visible on his body; yet he too was dead as was demonstrated when the delicate sonic sound system was focused on his corpse without disclosing the whisper of a heart beat. The third man was still living, although death was just minutes away. For him it would be a peaceful death, for he was unconscious and was quietly leaking his life away from a torn artery in his neck. The camera rested next upon the shredded corpse of the Russian point man who had been the initial target for so many rifles. He lay on his stomach, and there were nine visible wounds in his back. The camera showed next a closeup view of a young man's face frozen in the moment of death, blue eyes, luster-less now and pale in death, framed by a face registering the shock of war's ultimate reality, his lips half opened still as if to protest his fate or to ask for another chance. The camera moved next to a body lying fetal-like near the top of the hill hardly two steps from the covering rocks where the three surviving squad members had found shelter. The camera then moved slowly down the slope seeking the last casualty. It found him on a pleasant, grassy spot beneath a small oak tree. A mortar fragment had caught him in the lower belly and his guts were spewed out on the grass like an overturned bucket of sand. He was whimpering softly, and with his free left hand was trying with almost comic desperation to place his entrails back inside his belly.

"Well, there you have it, folks," Bill Carr said. "It's official now. You saw it for yourselves thanks to our fine camera technicians. Seven casualties confirmed. John, I don't believe the American team has had its first casualty yet, is that right?"

"That's right, Bill. The Russian team apparently was caught completely off guard."

"Colonel Bullock, would you care to comment on what you've seen so far?"

"Yes, Bill, I think it's fair to say that this first skirmish gives the American team a decided advantage. I would like to see the computer's probability reports before going too far out on a limb, but I'd say the odds are definitely in favor of the American team at this stage. General Caldwell's election not to take the central hill has paid a handsome dividend here early in the games."

"General Vorsilov, would you care to give us the Russian point of view?"

"I do not agree with my American friend, Colonel Bullock," the general said with a crisp British accent. "The fourth Russian squad was given the mission to take the central hill. The central hill has been taken and is now controlled by the Russian team. Possession of the central hill provides almost absolute dominance of the lake and surrounding lowland. Those of you who have studied military history know how important that can be, particularly in the later stages of the games. I emphatically do not agree that the first skirmish was a defeat. Possession of the hill is worth a dozen men."

"Comments, Colonel Bullock?"

"Well, Bill, first of all, I don't agree that the Russian team has possession of the hill. True, they have three men up there, but those men are armed with nothing but rifles and hand grenades—and they are not dug in. Right now the central hill is up for grabs. I—"

"Just a minute, Colonel. Pardon this interruption, but our computer has the first probability report. And here it is! The prediction is for an

American victory with a probability rating of 57.2. How about that, folks? Here early in the first day the American team, which was a decided underdog in this year's games, has jumped to a substantial lead."

Colonel Bullock spoke: "Bill, I want you to notice that man there—over there on the right-hand side of your screen. Can we have a closeup on that? That's a runner, Bill. A lot of the folks don't notice little things like that. They want to watch the machine gunners or the point man, but that man there could have a decided effect on the outcome of these games, Bill."

"I presume he's carrying a message back to headquarters, eh Colonel?"

"That's right, Bill, and a very important message, I'll warrant. You see an attack on the central hill from the east or south sides would be disastrous. The Russians, of course, hold the south hill. From their positions there they could subject our boys to a blistering fire from the rear on any attack made from the south. That runner was sent back with word that there are only three Russians on the hill. I think we can expect an immediate counterattack from the north as soon as the message has been delivered. In the meantime, squads five and six will maintain their positions in the eastern sector and try to prevent any reinforcements of the Russian position."

"Thank you, Colonel, for that enlightening analysis, and now, folks—" He broke off when the runner to whom the Colonel referred stumbled and fell.

"Wait a minute, folks. He's been hit! He's down! The runner has been shot. You saw it here, folks. Brilliant camera work. Simply great. John, how about that?"

"Simply tremendous, Bill. A really great shot. Ed, can we back the cameras up and show the folks that action again? Here it is in slow motion, folks. Now you see him (who is that, Colonel? Ted Krogan? Thank you, Colonel) here he is, folks, Private Ted Krogan from Milwaukee, Wisconsin. Here he is coming around the last clump of bushes—now watch this, folks—he gets about half way across the clearing—and there it is, folks, you can actually see the bullet strike his throat—a direct hit. Watch this camera close-up of his face, you'll see him die in front of your eyes. And there he goes—he rolls over and not a move. He was dead before he hit the ground. Bill, did any of our cameras catch where that shot came from?"

"Yes, John, the Russians have slipped a two man sniper team in on our left flank. This could be serious, John. I don't think our boys know the runner was hit."

"Only time will tell, Bill. Only time will tell. Right now, I believe we have our first lull. Let's take thirty seconds for our stations to identify themselves."

Private Richard Starbuck's first day was not at all what he had expected. He was with the second squad, one of the three squads which were dug in on the north hill. After digging his foxhole he had spent the day staring at the south and central hills. He had heard the brief skirmish near the central hill, but he had yet to see his first Russian. He strained so hard to see something that sometimes his eyes played tricks on him. Twice his mind gave movement to a distant shadow. Once he nearly fired at the sudden sound of a rabbit in the brush. His desire to see the enemy was almost overpowering. It reminded him of the first time Mr. Martin had taken him fishing on the lake. He had been thirteen at the time. He had stared at that still, white cork for what had seemed like hours. He remembered he had even prayed to God to send a fish along that would make the cork go under. His mind had played tricks on him that day too, and several times he had fancied the cork was moving when it was not. He was not praying today, of course—except the intensity of his desire was something like a prayer.

He spent the entire first day in a foxhole without seeing anything or hearing anything except an occasional distant sniper's bullet. When the sun went down, he brought out his rations and consumed eighteen hundred calories. As soon as it was dark, his squad was to move to the south slope and prepare their defensive positions. He knew the Russians would be similarly occupied. It was maddening to know that for a time the enemy would be exposed and yet be relatively safe because of the covering darkness.

When it was completely dark, his squad captain gave the signal, and the squad moved out to their predetermined positions and began to dig in. So far they were still following the battle plan to the letter. He dug his foxhole with care, building a small ledge half way down on which to sit and placing some foliage on the bottom to keep it from becoming muddy, and then he settled down to wait. Somehow it was better at night. He even found himself wishing that they would not come tonight. He discovered that he could wait.

Later he slept. How long, he did not know. He only knew that when he awoke he heard a sound of air parting followed by a hard, thundering impact that shook the ground. His first instinct was to action, and then he remembered that there was nothing he could do, so he hunched down as far as possible in his foxhole and waited. He knew real fear now—the kind of fear that no amount of training or conditioning can eliminate. He was a living thing whose dominant instinct was to continue living. He did not want to die hunched down in a hole in the ground. The flesh along his spine quivered involuntarily with each fractional warning whoosh which preceded the mortar's fall. Now he knew that he could die, knew it with his body as well as with his mind. A shell landed nearby, and he heard a shrill, womanlike scream. Bill Smith had been hit. His first reaction was one of relief. It had been Bill Smith and not he. But why did he have to scream? Bill Smith had been one of the toughest men in the squad. There ought to be more dignity than that. There ought to be a better way of dying than lying helpless in a hole and waiting for chance or fate in the form of some unseen, impersonal gunner, who probably was firing an assigned pattern anyhow, to bring you life or death.

In training, under conditions of simulated danger, he had grown to rely upon the solidarity of the squad. They faced danger together; together they could whip the world. But now he knew that in the end war was a lonely thing. He could not reach out into the darkness and draw courage from the huddled forms of his comrades from the second squad. He took no comfort from the fact that the other members of the squad were just as exposed as he. The fear which he discovered in himself was a thing which had to be endured alone, and he sensed now that when he died, that too would have to be endured alone.

"Well, folks, this is Bill Carr still bringing you our continuous coverage of the 2050 Olympic War Games. John Ardanyon is getting a few hours' sleep right now, but he'll be back at four o'clock.

"For the benefit of those viewers who may have tuned in late, let me say again that NSB will bring continuous coverage. Yes sir, folks, this year, thanks to our special owl-eye cameras, we can give you shots of the night action with remarkable clarity.

"Well, folks, the games are almost eighteen hours old, and here to bring you the latest casualty report is my old friend Max Sanders. Max?"

"Thank you, Bill, and good evening, ladies and gentlemen. The latest casualty reports—and these are confirmed figures. Let me repeat—these are confirmed figures. For the Russian team: twenty-two dead, and eight incapacitated wounded. For the American team: seventeen dead, and only six incapacitated wounded."

"Thank you, Max. Folks, our computer has just recomputed the odds, and the results are—what's this? Folks, here is a surprise. A rather unpleasant surprise. Just forty-five minutes ago the odds on an American victory were 62.1. Those odds, ladies and gentlemen, have just fallen to 53.0. I'm afraid I don't understand this at all. Professor Overmann, what do you make of this?"

"I'm afraid the computer has picked up a little trouble in the southwestern sector, Bill. As I explained earlier, the computer's estimates are made up of many factors—and the casualty reports are just one of them. Can you give us a long shot of the central hill, Ed? There. There you see one of the factors which undoubtedly has influenced the new odds. The Russian team has succeeded in reinforcing their position on the central hill with a light machine gun squad. This goes back to the first American casualty earlier today when the messenger failed to get word through for the counterattack.

"Now give me a medium shot of the American assassination squad. Back it up a little more, will you, Ed? There, that's it. I was afraid of that. What has happened, Bill, is that, unknowingly, the American squad has been spotted by a Russian reserve guard. That could mean trouble."

"I see. Well, that explains the sudden drop in the odds, folks. Now the question is, can the American assassination squad pull it off under this handicap? We'll keep the cameras over here, folks, until we have an answer. The other sectors are relatively quiet now except for sporadic mortar fire."

For the first time since the skirmish which had begun the battle, the cameras were able to concentrate their sustained attention on one small area of the arena. The assassination squad moved slowly, torturously slow, through the brush and the deep grass which dotted the southwest sector. They had successfully infiltrated the Russian rear. For a moment the camera switched to the Russian sentry who had discovered the enemy's presence and who was now reporting to his captain. Orders were given and in a very few minutes the light machine gun had been brought back from the lake and was in position to fire on the advancing American squad. Two Russian reserve squads were positioned to deliver a deadly crossfire on the patrol. To the men in the arena it must have been pitch dark. Even on camera there was an eerie, uneasy quality to the light that lent a ghostlike effect to the faces of the men whose fates had been determined by an unsuspected meeting with a Russian sentry. Death would have been exceedingly quick and profitless for the ten-man squad had not a Russian rifleman fired his rifle prematurely. As it was, the squad captain and six men were killed in the first furious burst of fire. The three survivors reacted instantly and disappeared into the brush. One died there noiselessly from a chest wound inflicted in the ambush. Another managed to kill two Russian infantrymen with hand grenades before he died. In the darkness the Russian captain became confused and sent word to his general that the entire squad had been destroyed. The general came to inspect the site and was instantly killed at short range by the lone surviving member of the assassination squad. By a series of fortuitous events the squad had accomplished its primary purpose. The Russian general was dead, and in less than two seconds so was the last man in the assassination squad.

"Well, there you have it, ladies and gentlemen. High drama here in the early hours of the morning as an American infantry squad cuts down the Russian general. Those of you who have watched these games before will know that some of the most exciting action takes place at night. In a few minutes we should have the latest probability report, but until then, how do you see it, Colonel Bullock?"

"Bill, I think the raiding squad came out of that very well indeed. They were discovered and boxed in by the enemy, yet they still fulfilled their primary mission—they killed the Russian general. It's bound to have an effect."

"General Vorsilov, do you care to comment, sir?"

"I think your computer will confirm that three for ten is a good exchange, even if one of those three happens to be a general. Of course, we had an unlucky break when one of our soldiers accidentally discharged his weapon. Otherwise we would have suffered no casualties. As for the loss of General Sarlov, no general has ever survived the games, and I venture to say no general ever will. The leadership of the Russian team will now descend by predetermined selection to the senior Russian captain."

"Thank you, General. Well, folks, here is the latest computer report. This is going to disappoint a lotta people. For an American victory, the odds now stand at 49.1. Of course, let me emphasize, folks, that such a small difference at this stage is virtually meaningless.

"Well, we seem to have another lag, folks. While our cameras scan the arena, let me remind you that each morning of the games NSB will be bringing you a special capsule re-run of the highlights of the preceding night's action.

"Well, folks, things seem to be a little quiet right now, but don't go away. In the games, anything can happen and usually does. We lost ten good men in that last action, so maybe this is a good time to remind you, ladies and gentlemen, that this year NSB is giving to the parents of each one of these boys a special tape recording of the action in the arena complete with sound effects and a brand-new uniflex projector. Thus each parent will be able to see their son's participation in the games. This is a gift that I'm sure will be treasured throughout the years.

"NSB would like to take this opportunity to thank the following sponsors for relinquishing their time so we could bring you this special broadcast . . . "

Private Richard Starbuck watched the dawn edge its way over the arena. He had slept perhaps a total of two hours last night, and already a feeling of unreality was invading his senses. When the roll was called, he answered with a voice which surprised him by its impersonalness: "Private Richard Starbuck, uninjured, ammunition expended: zero." Three men did not answer the roll. One of the three was the squad captain. That meant that Sergeant Collins was the new squad captain. Through discipline and habit he broke out his breakfast ration and forced himself to eat. Then he waited again.

Later that morning he fired his first shot. He caught a movement on the central hill, and this time it was not a shadow. He fired quickly, but he missed, and his target quickly disappeared. There was heavy firing in the mid-eastern sector, but he was no longer even curious as to what was going on unless it affected his own position. All day long he fired whenever he saw something that could have been a man on either of the Russian-held hills. Sometimes he fired when he saw nothing because it made him feel better. The Russians returned the fire, but neither side appeared to be doing any real damage against a distant, well-entrenched enemy.

Toward evening Captain Collins gave orders for him to take possession of Private Bill Smith's foxhole. It seemed like a ridiculous thing to do in broad daylight when in a couple more hours he could accomplish the same thing in almost perfect safety. They obviously intended for him to draw fire to expose the Russian positions. For a moment he hesitated, feeling the hate for Collins wash over him like a flood. Then he grasped his rifle, leaped from his hole, and ran twenty yards diagonally down the hill to Smith's foxhole. It seemed to him as if the opposing hills had suddenly come alive. He flung himself face first to the ground and landed grotesquely on top of the once tough body of Private Bill Smith. He felt blood trickling down his arm, and for a moment he thought he had been hit, but it was only a scratch from a projecting rock. His own squad had been firing heavily, and he heard someone say: "I got one. B'god I got one." He twisted around in the foxhole trying to keep his head safely below the surface, and then he saw what it was that had made Bill Smith scream. The mortar had wrenched his left arm loose at the elbow. It dangled there now, hung in place only by a torn shirt and a small piece of skin. He braced himself and began to edge the body up past him in the foxhole. He managed to get below it and heave it over the side. He heard the excited volley of shots which followed the body's tumbling course down the hill. Somehow in his exertions he had finished wrenching the arm loose from the body. He reached down and threw that too over the side of the foxhole. And now this particular bit of earth belonged to him. He liked it better than his last one. He felt he had earned it.

The night brought a return of the mortar fire. This time he didn't care. This time he could sleep, although there was a slight twitching motion on the left side of his face and he woke up every two hours for no reason at all.

"Good morning, ladies and gentlemen, this is John Ardanyon bringing you the start of the third day of the 2050 Olympic War Games.

"And what a night it's been, ladies and gentlemen. In a moment we'll bring you the highlights of last night's action, but first here is Bill Carr to bring you up to date on the vital statistics."

"Thank you, John. Folks, we're happy to say that in the last few hours the early trend of the night's action has been reversed and the American team once again has a substantial lead. Squads five and six were wiped out in an early-evening engagement in the mid-eastern sector, but they gave a good account of themselves. The Russians lost eleven men and a light machine gun in their efforts to get this thorn out of their side. And I'm happy to say the American light machine gun carried by squad six was successfully destroyed before the squad was overrun. But the big news this morning is the success of the American mortar and sniper squads. Our mortars accounted for six dead and two seriously wounded as opposed to only two killed and one wounded by the Russian mortars. Our sniper squad, working in two-man teams, was successful in killing five men; whereas we only lost one man to enemy sniper action last night. We'll have a great shot coming up, folks, showing Private Cecil Harding from Plainview, New Jersey, killing a Russian captain in his sleep with nothing more than a sharp rock."

"Right, Bill, but before we show last night's highlights, I'm sure the folks would like to know that the score now stands forty-two fighting men for the American team as opposed to only thirty-seven for the Russians. Computer-wise that figures out to a 52.5 probability for the American team. I'm sure that probability figure would be higher if the Russians were not positioned on that central hill."

"And here now are the high spots of the night's action . . . "

On the morning of the third day, word was spread that the American general had been killed. Private Richard Starbuck did not care. He realized now that good generalship was not going to preserve his life. So far chance seemed the only decisive factor. The mortar fire grew heavier, and the word was given to prepare for an attack on the hill. He gripped his rifle, and as he waited, he hoped they would come. He wanted to see, to face his enemy. He wanted to feel again that man had the power to control his own destiny.

A few minutes after noon it began to rain, a chilling spring rain that drizzled slowly and soaked in next to the skin. The enemy mortar ceased firing. The man in the foxhole next to his was laughing somewhat hysterically and claiming he had counted the Russian mortar fire and that they had now exploded eight hundred of their thousand rounds. It seemed improbable; nevertheless Private Starbuck heard the story spread from foxhole to foxhole and presently he even began to believe it himself.

Toward evening, the sun came out briefly, and the mortars commenced firing again. This time, however, the shells landed on the far side of the hill. There was an answering fire from the American mortar, although it seemed a senseless duel when neither gunner could get a fix on the other. The duel continued after nightfall, and then, suddenly, there was silence from the American sector. In a few minutes, his worst fears were confirmed when a runner brought orders to fall back to new positions. An unhappy chance round had knocked out the American mortar.

There were five men left in his squad. They managed to withdraw from the south slope of the hill without further losses. Their new general, Captain Paulson, had a meeting of his surviving officers in Private Starbuck's hearing. The situation was not good, but before going into purely defensive positions, two things must be accomplished. The enemy machine gun and mortar must be destroyed. Squads seven and eight, who had been in reserve for a time and who had suffered the fewest casualties, were assigned the task. It must be done tonight. If the enemy's heavy weapons could be destroyed while the Americans still maintained possession of their remaining light machine gun, their position would be favorable. Otherwise their chances were fading. The mortar shells for the now useless American mortar were to be destroyed immediately to prevent their possible use by the enemy. And, the general added almost as an afterthought, at sunrise the second squad will attack and take the central hill. They would be supported by the light machine gun if, by then, the enemy mortar had been put out of action. Questions? There were many, but none were asked.

"Colonel Bullock, this is an unusual development. Would you tell us what General Paulson has in mind?"

"Well, Bill, I think it must be pretty obvious even to the men in the field that the loss of the American mortar has drastically changed the situation. An unfortunate occurrence, unfortunate indeed. The probability report is now only 37.6 in favor of the American team. Of course, General Paulson doesn't have a computer, but I imagine he's arrived at pretty much the same conclusion.

"The two squads—seven and eight, I believe—which you see on your screens are undoubtedly being sent out in a desperation attempt—no, not desperation—in a courageous attempt to destroy the enemy mortar and light machine gun. It's a good move. I approve. Of course, you won't find this one in the books, but the fact is that at this stage of the game, the pre-determined battle plans are of ever-decreasing importance."

"General Vorsilov?"

"The Americans are doing the only thing they can do, Mr. Carr, but it's only a question of time now. You can rest assured that the Russian team will be alert to this very maneuver."

"Well, stand by, folks. This is still anybody's game. The games are not over yet—not by a long shot. Don't go away. This could be the key maneuver of the games. John?"

"While we're waiting, Bill, I'm sure the folks would like to hear a list of the new records which have already been set in this fifth meeting between the United States and Russia in the Olympic War Games. Our first record came early in the games when the American fifth and sixth squads startled the world with a brilliant demonstration of firepower and shattering the old mark set back in 2042 by killing seven men in just . . . "

On the morning of the fifth day Private Starbuck moved out as the point man for the assault on the central hill. He had trained on a replica of the hill hundreds of times, and he knew it as well as he knew the back of his own hand. Squad seven had knocked out the enemy mortar last night, so they had the support of their own light machine gun for at least part of the way. Squad eight had failed in their mission and had been killed to the last man. Private Starbuck only hoped the Russian machine gun was not in position to fire on the assault team.

At first it was like maneuvers. Their own machine gun delivered a blistering fire twenty yards ahead of them and the five squad members themselves fired from the hip as they advanced. There was only occasional and weak counter-fire. They were eight yards from the top, and he was beginning to hope that, by some miracle spawned by a grotesque god, they were going to make it. Then it came. Grenades came rolling down from above, and a sustained volley of rifle-fire came red hot from the depths of hell. He was hit twice in the first volley. Once in the hip, again in the shoulder. He would have gotten up, would have tried to go forward, but Captain Collins fell dead on top of him and he could not. A grenade exploded three feet away. He felt something jar his cheek and knew he had been hit again. Somehow it was enough. Now he could die. He had done enough. Blood ran down his face and into his left eye, but he made no attempt to wipe it away. He would surely die now. He hoped it would be soon.

"It doesn't look too good, folks. Not good at all. Colonel Bullock?"

"I'm afraid I have to agree, Bill. The American probability factor is down to 16.9, and right now I couldn't quarrel with the computer at all. The Russians still have sixteen fighting men, while the Americans are down to nine. The American team will undoubtedly establish a defense position around the light machine gun on the north hill, but with the Russians still in control of the central hill and still in possession of their own machine gun, it appears pretty hopeless. Pretty hopeless indeed."

He owed his life during the next few minutes to the fact that he was able to maintain consciousness. The firing had ceased all about him, and for a time he heard nothing, not even the sound of distant gun fire. This is death, he thought. Death is when you can't hear the guns any longer. Then he heard the sound of boots. He picked out a spot in the sky and forced his eyes to remain on that spot. He wished to die in peace, and they might not let him die in peace. After a while the boots moved on.

He lost consciousness shortly after that. When he awoke, it was dark. He was not dead yet, for he could hear the sounds of guns again. Let them kill each other. He was out of it. It really was not such a bad way to die, if only it wouldn't take so long. He could tolerate the pain, but he hated the waiting.

While he waited, a strange thing happened. It was as though his spirit passed from his body and he could see himself lying there on the hill. Poor forlorn body to lie so long upon a hill. Would they write poems and sing songs about Private Richard Starbuck like they did four years ago for Sergeant Ernie Stevens? No, no poems for this lonely body lying on a hill waiting to die. Sergeant Stevens had killed six men before he died. So far as he knew he had killed none.

In the recruiting pamphlet they told you that your heirs would receive one hundred thousand dollars if you died in the games. Was that why he signed up? No, no, he was willing to die now, but not for that. Surely he had had a better reason than that. Why had he done such a crazy thing? Was it the chance to be a survivor? No, not that either. Suddenly he realized something the selection committee had known long ago: he had volunteered for no other reason than the fact there was a war to be fought, and he had not wanted to be left out.

He thought of the cameras next. Had they seen him on TV? Had all the girls, all the people in his hometown been watching? Had his dad watched? Had Mr. and Mrs. Martin and their daughter watched? Had they seen him when he had drawn fire by changing foxholes? Were they watching now to see if he died well?

Toward morning, he began to wonder if he could hold out. There was only one thing left for him to do and that was to die as quietly and peacefully as possible. Yet it was not an easy thing to do, and now his wounds were beginning to hurt again. Twice he heard the boots pass nearby, and each time he had to fight back an impulse to call out to them so they could come hurry death. He did not do it. Someone might be watching, and he wanted them to be proud of him.

At daybreak there was a wild flurry of rifle and machine gun fire, and then, suddenly, there was no sound, no movement, nothing but silence. Perhaps now he could die.

The sad, dejected voice of Bill Carr was saying " . . . all over. It's all over, folks. We're waiting now for the lights to come on in the arena—the official signal that the games are over. It was close—but close only counts in horseshoes, as the saying goes. The American team made a fine last stand. They almost pulled it off. I make out only three Russian survivors, John. Is that right?"

"Just three, Bill, and one of those is wounded in the arm. Well, ladies and gentlemen, we had a very exciting finish. We're waiting now for the arena lights to come on. Wait a minute! Something's wrong! The lights are not coming on! I thought for a moment the official scorer was asleep at the switch. Bill, can you find out what the situation is? This damned computer still gives the American team a 1.4 probability factor."

"We've located it, John. Our sonic sound system has located a lone American survivor. Can you get the cameras on the central hill over there? There he is, folks. Our spotters in the booth have just identified him as Private Richard Starbuck from Centerville, Iowa. He seems badly wounded, but he's still alive. The question is: can he fight? He's not moving, but his heart is definitely beating and we know where there's life, there's hope."

"Right, Bill. And you can bet the three Russian survivors are a pretty puzzled group right now. They don't know what's happened. They can't figure out why the lights have not come on. Two minutes ago they were shouting and yelling a victory chant that now seems to have been premature. Ed, give us a camera on that north hill. Look at this, ladies and gentlemen. The three Russian survivors have gone berserk. Literally berserk—they are shooting and clubbing the bodies of the American dead. Don't go away, folks . . . "

He began to fear he might not die. His wounds had lost their numbness and had begun to throb. He heard the sounds of guns and then of boots. Why wouldn't they leave him alone? Surely the war was over. He had nothing to do with them. One side or another had won—so why couldn't they leave him alone? The boots were coming closer, and he sensed that they would not leave him alone this time. A sudden rage mingled with his pain, and he knew he could lie there no longer. For the next few seconds he was completely and utterly insane. He pulled the pin on the grenade which had been pressing against his side and threw it blindly in the direction of the sound of the boots. With an instinct gained in two years of intense training, he rolled to his belly and began to fire at the blurred forms below him. He did not stop firing even when the blurred shapes ceased to move. He did not stop firing until his rifle clicked on an empty chamber. Only then did he learn that the blurred shapes were Russian soldiers.

They healed his wounds. His shoulder would always be a little stiff, but his leg healed nicely, leaving him without a trace of a limp. There was a jagged scar on his jaw, but they did wonders with plastic surgery these days and unless you knew it was there, you would hardly notice it. They put him through a two-month reconditioning school, but it didn't take, of course. They gave him ticker tape parades, medals, and the keys to all the major cities. They warned him about the psychological dangers of being a survivor. They gave him case histories of other survivors—grim little anecdotes involving suicide, insanity, and various mental aberrations.

And then they turned him loose.

For a while he enjoyed the fruits of victory. Whatever he wanted he could have for the asking. Girls flocked around him, men respected him, governments honored him, and a group of flunkies and hangers-on were willing enough to serve his every whim. He grew bored and returned to his hometown.

It was not the same. He was not the same. When he walked down the streets, mothers would draw close to their daughters and hurry on past. If he shot pool, his old friends seemed aloof and played as if they were afraid to win. Only the shopkeepers were glad to see him come in, for whatever he took, the government paid for. If he were to shoot the mayor's son, the government would pay for that too. At home his own mother would look at him with that guarded look in her eyes, and his dad was careful not to look him in the eyes at all.

He spent a lot of time in his room. He was not lonely. He had learned to live alone. He was sitting in his room one evening when he saw Cassandra, the Martin's fifteen-year-old daughter, coming home with some neighborhood kid from the early movie. He watched idly as the boy tried to kiss her good-night. There was an awkwardness between them that was vaguely exciting. At last the boy succeeded in kissing her on the cheek, and then, apparently satisfied, went on home.

He sat there for a long time lighting one cigarette from the last one. There was a conflict inside his mind that once would have been resolved differently and probably with no conscious thought. Making up his mind, he stubbed his cigarette and went downstairs. His mother and father were watching TV. They did not look up as he walked out the front door. They never did any more.

The Martins were still up. Mr. Martin was tying brightly colored flies for his new fly rod and Mrs. Martin was reading. They both stiffened when he entered without knocking—alarm playing over their faces like flickering firelight. He didn't pause, but walked on upstairs without looking at them.

Mrs. Martin got to her feet and stood looking up the stairway without moving. In her eyes there was the look of a jungle tiger who watches its mate pinned to a stake at the bottom of the pit. Mr. Martin sat staring at the brightly colored flies on his lap. For a moment there was silence. Then a girl's shrill screams announced to the Martins that war's reality was also for the very young.

About the Authors

Maya Kaathryn Bohnhoff is addicted to speculative fiction. For this, she blames her dad and Ray Bradbury. She's authored a dozen novels of speculative fiction, and short fiction that's appeared in *Analog*, *Amazing Stories*, *Interzone*, and others. She has been a finalist for the Campbell, Nebula, Sidewise, and British SF awards. Her most recent novel is *Star Wars: Shadow Games*—a new addition to the Star Wars expanded universe—co-authored with Michael Reaves. In an alternate existence, Maya writes, performs, and records music with husband, Jeff. She is a founding member of Book View Café (www.bookviewcafe,com) where you can read some of her short fiction.

Orson Scott Card is the author of the novels *Ender's Game*, *Ender's Shadow*, and *Speaker for the Dead*, which are widely read by adults and younger readers, and are increasingly included in educational curricula. Besides these and other science fiction novels, Card writes contemporary fantasy (*Magic Street, Enchantment, Lost Boys*), biblical novels (*Stone Tables*, *Rachel and Leah*), the American frontier fantasy series The Tales of Alvin Maker (beginning with *Seventh Son*), poetry (*An Open Book*), and many plays and scripts. Card was born in Washington and grew up in California, Arizona, and Utah. Card currently lives in Greensboro, North Carolina with his wife and youngest child. *Ender's Game* is in the process of becoming a motion picture.

Cory Doctorow (craphound.com) is a science fiction author, activist, journalist and blogger—the co-editor of Boing Boing (boingboing.net) and the author of young adult novels like *Pirate Cinema* and *Little Brother* and novels for adults like *Rapture of the Nerds* and *Makers*. He is the former European director of the Electronic Frontier Foundation and co-founded the UK Open Rights Group. Born in Toronto, Canada, he now lives in London.

George Alec Effinger (1947-2002) attended Yale University, where an organic chemistry course disabused him of the notion of becoming a doctor. A graduate of Clarion, he was the author of at least twenty novels and six collections of short fiction including the popular cyberpunk series beginning with *When Gravity Fails* (1987), Hugo, Nebula, and Sturgeon Award-winning novelette "Schrödinger's Kitten" (1988), and many satirical works including a series of stories about Maureen Birnbaum, Barbarian Swordsperson. Born and raised in Cleveland, Effinger was a lifelong fan of the Cleveland Indians and one of science fiction's most avid sports fans. Many of his science-fiction sports stories were collected in *Idle Pleasures*.

Timons Esaias is a satirist, poet, and writer of short fiction, living in Pittsburgh. His work has appeared in fifteen languages. He won an *Asimov's* Readers Award; and was a finalist for the British Science Fiction Award. He has had over a hundred poems in print, including Spanish, Swedish, and Chinese translations, in markets ranging from *Asimov's Science Fiction* to *5AM* and *Elysian Fields Quarterly: The Literary Journal of Baseball.* He is Adjunct Faculty at Seton Hill University, in the Writing Popular Fiction M.F.A. Program.

John Shirley (john-shirley.com) is the author of more than thirty novels. His numerous short stories have been compiled into eight collections including *Black Butterflies: A Flock on the Darkside*, winner of the Bram Stoker Award, International Horror Guild Award, and named as one of the best one hundred books of the year by *Publishers Weekly.* He has written scripts for television and film, and is best known as co-writer of *The Crow.* As a musician, Shirley has fronted several bands over the years and written lyrics for Blue Öyster Cult and others. The only game he is any good at is hold 'em poker, but his wife is teaching him how to comprehend football. (So far he knows it is not that sport where you throw a round ball into a basket.)

Louise Marley is a novelist working in the genres of science fiction, fantasy, and historical fiction. Her novels have been shortlisted for the Nebula, the Tiptree, and the Campbell awards, and she is a two-time winner of the Endeavour Award. Her most recent novels—*Mozart's Blood, The Brahms Deception*, and *The Glass Butterfly*—combine elements of history and speculative fiction. Louise is a former opera singer, and has been an avid baseball fan since her girlhood.

Now a #1 *New York Times* best-selling author, **George R. R. Martin** sold his first story in 1971 and has been writing professionally ever since. He spent ten years in Hollywood as a writer-producer, working on *The Twilight Zone*, *Beauty and the Beast*, and various feature films and television pilots that were never made. Martin also edited the Wild Cards series, fifteen novels written by teams of authors. In the mid-1990s he returned to prose, and began work on his epic fantasy series, A Song of Ice and Fire. In April 2011, HBO premiered its adaptation of the first of that series, *A Game of Thrones,* and he was named as one of *Time*'s most influential people of the year. A sports enthusiast, at least as a spectator, Martin is a fan of the New York Jets and Giants. He is the only author in this anthology to have ever been interviewed by *Sports Illustrated*.

James Morrow has been writing fiction ever since, at age seven, he dictated "The Story of the Dog Family" to his mother, who dutifully typed it up and bound the pages with yarn. Upon reaching adulthood, Morrow wrote such satiric novels as *Towing Jehovah* (World Fantasy Award), *Blameless in Abaddon* (a *New York Times* Notable Book of the Year), *The Last Witchfinder* (called "an inventive feat" by critic Janet Maslin), and *The Philosopher's Apprentice* ("an ingenious riff on Frankenstein" according to NPR). His short fiction has won the Nebula Award (twice), the Rickie Award, and the Theodore Sturgeon Memorial Award.

Missourian **Walter F. Moudy** (1929-1973) was an attorney, but he also authored a handful of science fiction stories after publication of his sole novel, *No Man on Earth* (1964), which tells the story of a man born of a human mother and an alien father.

Joel Richards lives in Northern California where he has attempted to do every sport known to man. However, new sports have emerged over the years faster than he's grown older, and he's given up on that goal. His favorites have been running, judo, dog sled racing, and scuba diving. Though he's written one novel, *Pindharee*, Joel is mainly a short fiction writer. His stories have appeared in a range of magazines, most frequently and recently *Asimov's*, as well as a number of original anthologies, including Terry Carr's *Universe 14* and *Universe 17*, Roger Zelazny's *Warriors of Blood and Dream*, and Harry Turtledove's *Alternate Generals II*.

Elizabeth Ann Scarborough is the author of twenty-three solo fantasy and science fiction novels, including the 1989 Nebula Award-winning *Healer's War*, as well as sixteen novels with Anne McCaffrey, most recently, the Tales of the Barque Cat series, *Catalyst* and *Catacombs* (from Del Rey). She is also the author of a numerous short stories. Her most recent works are *Spam Vs. the Vampire* (2011), *9 Tales O' Cats* (a collection) and *Father Christmas*, a novelette. In progress: *The Tour Bus of Doom: Spam and the Zombie Apocalypso* and *Shifty*, stories of shape shifting and transformation.

As Eileen Gunn once wrote, **Howard Waldrop** is "a *legendary* unknown writer." He lives in Austin, Texas, and is a devoted fisherman. He does not have a cellphone, a computer, or an email account. He's written a couple of novels and a bunch of short stories, most of which can be found in his eight collections. The winner of both a Nebula and a World Fantasy Award. *Locus* quotes him as saying: "When I wrote 'Man-Mountain Gentian' . . . most people had maybe seen one picture of a sumo wrestler and that was it. I got fascinated by the ritual . . . and if somebody comes along and messes with it, it's like the world has ended."

Scott Westerfeld was born in Texas, lived in California and Connecticut, and now—with his wife, Justine Larbalestier—divides his time between Sydney, Australia and New York City, USA. He is the author of eighteen novels: five for adults and the thirteen for young adults, including the Leviathan series (the first book of which was the winner of the 2010 Locus Award for Best Young Adult Fiction), and the *New York Times* bestselling Uglies series, *The Last Days*, *Peeps*, *So Yesterday*, and the Midnighters trilogy. He plays tennis semi-competently, but not often enough, and enjoys watching basketball—he has season tickets to the WNBA's Liberty, second row—and cricket, recently discovered in Australia. His website is ScottWesterfeld.com.

Over the span of her fifty-year career, **Kate Wilhelm** has delved into many genres. Her works have been adapted for television and movies in the United States, England, and Germany. Wilhelm's novels and stories have been translated to more than a dozen languages and she has contributed to *Quark*, *Orbit*, *The Magazine of Fantasy & Science Fiction*, *Locus*, *Amazing Stories*, *Asimov's Science Fiction*, *Ellery Queen's Mystery Magazine*,

Fantastic, *Omni*, *Alfred Hitchcock's Mystery Magazine*, *Redbook*, and *Cosmopolitan*. Wilhelm and her husband, Damon Knight (1922-2002), also provided invaluable assistance to numerous other writers over the years as teachers and lecturers. Kate Wilhelm currently lives in Eugene, Oregon. In her spare time she likes to garden.

Genevieve Williams is a Clarion West graduate and currently working toward her MFA in Popular Fiction at the University of Southern Maine Stonecoast program. Her critical essay on Geoff Ryman appeared in the Summer 2008 issue of the journal *Extrapolation*. Her current projects include a podcast, titled *Sacred Road*, to be released in 2013.

About the Editor

Paula Guran is the Senior Editor of Prime Books. Although not in a sport or a game, she thinks she may have set some sort of world record in 2012 with one original and seven reprint anthologies she edited all published within a single calendar year. This is the first to be published in 2013. She expects *Weird Detectives: Recent Investigations*, *After the End: Recent Apocalypses*, and the annual *The Year's Best Dark Fantasy and Horror* all to be published by Prime Books in 2013, as well as two all-original anthologies: *Halloween: Magic, Mystery, and the Macabre* and *Once Upon a Time: New Fairy Tales*. Constable & Robinson (UK) and Running Press (US) will be publishing her *The Mammoth Book of Angels and Demons* in spring/summer 2013.

We won't get into games, but as for sports, Guran is mostly an avid spectator. (But yes, if you read the story introductions, she really did break that board in the *dojo*.) She lives in Akron, Ohio and is a fan of the Cleveland Indians (and the Akron Aeros); learned to love basketball thanks to Akron's own LeBron James (who is *not* hated by *all* of Northeast Ohio). Thrilled he finally got his ring, she still follows King James, but supports the Cleveland Cavaliers. Guran is nominally interested in the Browns, but tends to watch more college football than pro. She is somewhat addicted to watching the Olympics.

As a mother, Guran was exposed to many sports including karate, soccer, football, skiing, tennis, informal wrestling, and orthopedic surgery thanks to her three sons' participation. Her daughter is a great "cheerleader," but of the *sincere* variety, not the type with pom-poms. One daughter-in-law has taught her something about soccer and the other about running. Now golf seems to be entering the picture again for some of her offspring.

Guran's house has a long history of participatory sports. The croquet set finally fell apart, the trampoline is gone, but the horseshoe pitch is used. There is still a punching bag in the basement not far from the weight bench, and a shotput in the sports bin along with a lot of other interesting things. She might still be a contender.

Acknowledgements

Special thanks to Ellen Datlow and Marty Halpern for suggestions.

"Distance" by Maya Kaathryn Bohnhoff © Dell Magazines, Inc. First publication: *Analog Science Fiction and Fact,* February 2003.

"Ender's Game" by Orson Scott Card © 1977 Orson Scott Card. First publication: *Analog Science Fiction/Science Fact,* August 1977.

"Anda's Game" by Cory Doctorow © 2004 Cory Doctorow. First publication: *Salon,* November 15, 2004.

"Breakaway" by George Alec Effinger © 1981 Mercury Press, Inc. First publication: *The Magazine of Fantasy & Science Fiction,* January 1981. Published with the permission of Barbara Hambly for the estate of the author.

"Pawn" by Timons Esaias © 2002 Timons Esaias. First publication: *Interzone* Number 180, June-July 2002.

"Diamond Girls" by Louise Marley © 2005 Louise Marley. First publication: *Sci Fiction,* June 8, 2005.

"Run to Starlight" by George R. R. Martin © 1974 George R. R. Martin. First publication: *Amazing Science Fiction,* December 1974.

"The Fate of Nations" by James Morrow © 1983 James Morrow. First publication: *Sci Fiction,* May 14, 2003.

"The Survivor" by Walter F. Moudy © 1965 Ziff-Davis Publishing Company. First publication: *Amazing Stories,* May 1965. Reprinted by permission of the Virginia Kidd Literary Agency on behalf of the author's estate.

Also from Prime Books

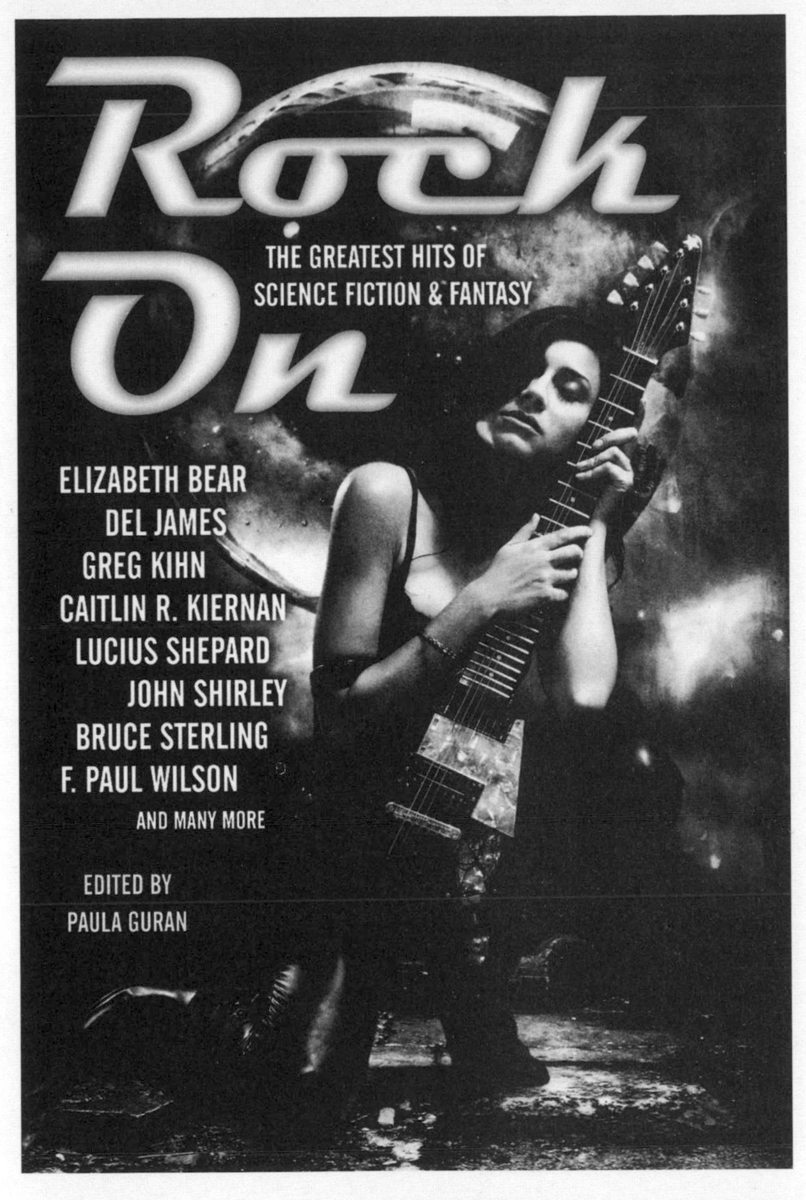